MASTERS of HORROR

compiled

by

MATT SHAW

Edited by Julie Shaw and Beth Thurlow

Additional Formatting by J.R Park

Table of Contents

INTRODUCTION
Written **by Matt Shaw**

I get disheartened looking at the horror charts when I am in bookstores or shopping online and that's not because I don't enjoy horror. I make a living in the genre so clearly I enjoy it. No, I get disheartened because I see more and more books filling shelves (both real and cyber) which claim to be horror but are nothing more than stories of vampires, witches and werewolves all falling in love and having exciting adventures together as they battle darker forces. That's not horror. Well, it is, but it's not *horror*. Horror should not make you wish to be bitten by a vampire so you too can sparkle like a little bitch, it shouldn't make you want your monthly period to see you sprout fur and howl longingly at the moon forever out of reach, and it shouldn't make you dream of creating fancy love potions to win the man who won't look at you twice. Horror should make you shit your pants. It should creep you out and make you want to leave the light on, it should make you check under the bed for monsters or intruders, it should make you feel *uncomfortable*. The point of this book is to bring that sense of dread back to you when you're reading. It's to remind you that *this* is horror. There are no vampires prancing around, struggling with high-school life, there are no wacky witches trying to put right spells that have gone wrong. There are just pages of terror and horror exploring the different aspects of the horror genre (psychological, survival, splatter, ghost stories… the list goes on and on) by some of the biggest names currently working in the market. Oh, and just a quick mention before I forget, there were more authors asked to be a part of this but, sadly, they were too

1

busy. What I am trying to say is, whilst I think I have lined up some *great* names for this anthology - I am aware there are other Masters of Horror out there too! And, who knows, maybe the ones who were too busy will be free for a follow-up if I ever choose to more forward with one...? Ooh, teasing...

THE CYPRUS SHELL
Written by **Brian Lumley**

The Oaks, Innsway
Redcar, Yorks
5 June 1962

Col. (Retd) George L. Glee MBE, DSO
11 Tunstall Court
West H. Pool, Co. Durham

My dear George,

I must extend to you my sincerest apologies for the inexcusable way I took myself and Alice out of your excellent company on Saturday evening last. Alice had remarked upon my facial *expressions*, my absolute lack of manners and the uncouth way in which, it must have appeared, I dragged her from your marvellous table; and all, alas, under the gaze of so many of our former military associates. I can only hope that our long friendship – and the fact that you know me as well as you do – has given you some insight that it was only a matter of extreme urgency which could have driven me from your house in such an extraordinary manner.

I imagine all of you were astonished at my exit. Alice was flabbergasted and would not speak to me until I gave her a solid reason for what she took to be lunatic behaviour.

Well, to cut things short, I told her the tale which I am about to tell you. She was satisfied as to the validity of the reasons for my seemingly unreasonable actions and I am sure that you will feel the same.

It was the oysters, of course. I have no doubt that their preparation was immaculate and that they were delicious – for everyone, that is, except myself. The truth is I *cannot* abide seafood, especially shellfish. Surely you remember the way I used to be over crabs and lobsters? That time in Goole when I ate two whole plates of fresh mussels all to myself? I loved the things. Ugh! The thought of it...

Two years ago in Cyprus something happened which put an end to my appetite for that sort of thing. But before I go on let me ask you to do something. Get out your Bible and look up Leviticus 11:10, 11. No, I have not become a religious maniac. It's just that since that occurrence two years ago I have taken a deep interest, a morbid interest I hasten to add, in this subject and all connected with it.

If, after reading my story, you should find your curiosity tickled, there are numerous books on the subject which you might like to look up – though I doubt whether you'll find many of them at your local library. Anyway, here is a list of four such books: Gantley's *Hydrophinnae*, Gaston Le Fe's *Dwellers in the Depths*, the German *Unter-See Kulten* and the monstrous *Cthaat Aquadingen* by an unknown author. All contain tidbits of an almost equally nauseating nature to the tale which I must relate in order to excuse myself.

I have said it was in Cyprus. At the time I was the officer in command of a small unit in Kyrea, between Cephos and Kryenia on the coast, overlooking the Mediterranean, that most beautiful of all seas. In my Company was a young corporal, Jobling by name, who fancied himself something of a conchologist and spent all his off-duty hours with flippers and mask snorkelling off the rocks to the south of Kyrea. I say he fancied himself, yet in fact his collection *was* quite wonderful for he had served in most parts of the world and had looted many oceans.

Beneath glass in his billet – in beautifully made 'natural' settings, all produced by his own hands – he had such varied and fascinating shells as the African *Pecten irradian*, the unicorn-horn *Murex monodon* and *Ianthina violacea* from Australia, the weird *Melongena corona* from the Gulf of Mexico, the fan-shaped

Ranella perca of Japan and many hundreds of others too numerous to mention here. Inevitably my weekly tour of inspection ended in Jobling's billet where I would move among his showcases marvelling at the intricacies of Nature's art.

While Jobling's hobby occupied all his off-duty hours it in no way interfered with his work within the unit; he was a conscientious, hard-working NCO. I first noticed the *change* in him when his work began to fall off and had had it in mind for over a week to reprimand him for his slackness when he had the first of those attacks which eventually culminated so horribly.

He was found one morning, after first parade, curled on his bed in the most curious manner, with his legs drawn up and arms curled about him – almost in a foetal position. The MO was called but, despite treatment, Jobling remained in this inexplicable condition for over an hour; at the end of which time he suddenly 'came to' and began acting quite normally, seemingly unable to remember anything that had happened. I was obliged to relieve the man of all duties for a period of one week and he was obviously amazed at this, swearing he was fit as a fiddle and blaming his lapse on an overdose of Cyprus sun. I checked this with the MO who assured me that Jobling's condition had in no way corresponded to a stroke but had been, in fact, closely related to a trauma, as though the result of some deep, psychological shock...

The day after he returned to duties Jobling suffered the second of his withdrawals.

This second attack took exactly the same form as the first except that it lasted somewhat longer. Also, on this occasion, he was found to be clutching in his hand a book of notes relating to his shell collection. I asked to see these notes and while Jobling, still dazed, was taken off to the hospital for an examination, I read them through in the hope of finding something which might give me some insight into the reason for his strange affliction. I had a hunch that his hobby had much to do with his condition; though just why collecting and studying shells should have such a drastic effect on anyone was beyond even guessing.

The first two dozen pages or so were filled with observations on locations where certain species of sea-snail could be found. For instance; *'Pecten irradian* – small – in rock-basins ten to fifteen feet deep. Etc., etc....' This section was followed by a dozen pages or so of small drawings, immaculately done, and descriptions of rarer specimens. Two more pages were devoted to a map of the Kyrea coastline with shaded areas showing the locations which the collector had already explored and arrowed sections showing places still to be visited. Then, on the next page, I found a beautifully executed drawing of a shell the like of which I had never seen before despite my frequent studies of Jobling's showcases, and which I have seen only once since.

How to describe it? Beneath it was a scale, in inches, drawn in to show its size. It appeared to be about six inches long and its basic shape was a slender spiral: but all the way round that spiral, along the complete track from mouth to tail, were sharp spikes about two inches long at their longest and about one inch at the narrow end. They were obviously a means of defense against oceanic predators. The mouth of the thing, as Jobling had coloured the drawing, showed a shiny black operculum with a row of tiny eyes at the edges, like those of the scallop, and was a bright shade of pink. The main body of the shell and the spikes were sand-coloured. If my powers of description were better I might be able to convey something of just how repulsive the thing looked. Instead it must suffice to say that it was not a shell which I would be happy to pick up off a beach, and not just because of those spikes! There was something nastily fascinating about the *shape* and the *eyes* of the thing which, taking into consideration the accuracy of the other drawings, was not merely a quirk of the artist...

The next page was a set of notes which, as best as I can remember, went like this:

Murex hypnotica?
Rare? Unknown???

2nd August ... Found shell, with snail intact, off point of rocks (marked on sketch of map) in about twenty feet of water. The shell was on sand in natural rock-basin. Pretty sure thing is very rare, probably new species. Snail has eyes on edge of mantle. Did not take shell. Anchored it to rock with nylon line from spear gun. Want to study creature in natural surroundings before taking it.

3rd August ... Shell still anchored. Saw most peculiar thing. Small fish, inch long, swam up to shell, probably attracted by bright pink of mouth. Eyes of snail waved rhythmically for a few seconds. Operculum opened. *Fish swam into shell and operculum snapped shut.* Have named shell well! First funny fascination I felt when I found shell is obviously felt to greater extent by fish. Thing seems to use hypnosis on fish in same way octopus uses it to trap crabs.

4th August ... Cannot visit shell today – duty. Had funny dream last night. I was in a shell on bottom of sea. Saw *myself* swimming down. Hated the swimmer and saw him as being to blame for restricting my movements. *I was the snail*! When the swimmer, myself, was gone I sawed at nylon line with my operculum but could not break it. Woke up. Unpleasant.

5th August ... Duty.

6th August ... Visited shell again. Line near shell slightly frayed. Eyes waved at me. Felt dizzy. Stayed down too long. Came back to camp. Dizzy all day.

7th August ... Dreamed of being snail again. Hated swimmer, myself, and tried to get *into* his mind – like I do with fish. Woke up. Awful.

There was a large gap in the dates here and, looking back I realized that this was the period which Jobling had spent in hospital. In fact he had gone into hospital the day after that last entry had been made, on the eighth of the month. The next entry went something like this:

7

15th August … Did not expect shell to be there after all this time but it was. Line much frayed but not broken. Went down five or six times but started to get horribly dizzy. Snail writhed its eyes at me frantically! *Felt that awful dream coming on in water*! Had to get out of sea. Believe the damn thing tried to hypnotize me like it does with fish.

16th August … Horrible dream. Have just woken up and must write it down now. *I was the snail again*! I've had enough. Will collect shell today. This dizzy feeling…

That was all. The last entry had obviously been made that very day, just before Jobling's new attack. I had just finished reading the notes and was sitting there bewildered when my telephone rang. It was the MO. All hell was on at the hospital. Jobling had tried to break loose, tried to get out of the hospital. I took my car straight round there and that was where the horror really started.

I was met by an orderly at the main entrance and escorted up to one of the wards. The MO and three male nurses were in a wardroom waiting for me.

Jobling was curled up on a bed in that weird foetal position – *or was it a foetal position*? What did he remind me of? Suddenly I noticed something which broke my train of thought, causing me to gasp and look closer. Froth was drying on the man's mouth, his teeth were bared and his eyes bulged horribly. But there was no movement in him at all! *He was stone dead*!

'How on earth …?' I gasped. 'What happened?' The MO gripped my arm. His eyes were wide and unbelieving. For the first time I noticed that one of the male nurses appeared to be in a state of shock. In a dry, cracked voice the MO started to speak.

'It was horrible. I've never know anything like it. He just seemed to go wild. Began frothing at the mouth and tried to get out of the place. He made it down to the main doors before we caught up to him. We had to *carry* him up the stairs and he kept straining towards the windows in the direction of the sea. When we got him back up here he suddenly coiled up – just like that!' He pointed to the still figure on the bed. 'And then he squirmed – that's the only way I can describe how he moved – he *squirmed* off the bed and quick as a flash he was in the steel locker there and had pulled the door shut behind him. God only knows why he went in there?' In one corner of the room stood the locker. One of its two doors was hanging by a wrenched hinge – torn almost completely off. 'When we tried to get him out he fought like hell. But not like a *man* would fight! He *butted* with his head, with a funny *sawing* motion, and bit and spat – and all the time he stayed in that awful position, even when he was fighting. By the time we got him to the bed again he was dead. I … I think he died of fright.'

By now that hideous train of thought, broken before by the horror of Jobling's condition, had started up once more in my mind and I began to trace an impossible chain of events. But no! It was too monstrous to even think of – too *fantastic* … And then, on top of my terrible thoughts, came those words from the mouth of one of the nurses which caused me to pitch over suddenly into the darkness of a swoon.

I know you will find it difficult to believe, George, when I tell you what those words were. It seems ridiculous that such a simple statement could have so deep an effect upon anyone. None the less I *did* faint, for I saw the sudden connection, the piece in the puzzle which brought the whole picture into clear, horrific perspective … The nurse said: 'Getting him out of the locker was the worst, sir. *It was like trying to get a winkle out of its shell without a pin…*'

*

When I came to, despite the MO's warning, I went to the mess – I had not met Alice at that time and so was 'living in' – and got my own swimming kit out of my room. I took Jobling's notebook with me and drove to the point of rock marked in red on his map. It was not difficult to find the place; Jobling would have made an excellent cartographer.

I parked my car and donned my mask and flippers. In no time at all I was swimming straight out in the shallows over a few jagged outcrops of rock and patches of sand. I stopped in about ten feet of water for a few seconds to watch a heap, literally a *heap*, of crabs fighting over a dead fish. The carcass was completely covered by the vicious things – it's amazing how they are attracted by carrion – but occasionally, as the fight raged, I caught a glimpse of silver scales and red, torn flesh. But I was not there to study the feeding habits of crabs. I pressed on.

I found the rock-basin almost immediately and the shell was not difficult to locate. It was lying about twenty feet deep. I could see that the nylon line was still attached. But for some reason the water down there was not as clear as it should have been. I felt a sudden, icy foreboding – a nameless premonition. Still, I had come out to look at that shell, to prove to myself that what I had conjured up in my over-imaginative mind was pure fancy and nothing more.

I turned on end, pointing my feet at the blue sky and my head towards the bottom, and slid soundlessly beneath the surface. I spiralled down to the shell, noting that it was exactly as Jobling had drawn it, and carefully, shudderingly, took it by one of those spikes and turned it over so I could see the pink mouth.

The shell was *empty*!

But this, if my crazy theory was correct, was just what I should have expected; none the less I jerked away from the thing as though it had suddenly become a conger eel. Then out of the corner of my eye, I saw the *reason* for the murkiness of the water. A second heap of crabs was sending up small clouds of sand and sepia from some dead fish or mollusc which they were tearing at in that dreadful, frantic lust of theirs.

Sepia! In abrupt horror I recoiled from my own thoughts. Great God in heaven! *Sepia*!

I wrenched off a flipper and batted the horrid, scrabbling things away from their prey – *and wished immediately that I had not done so.* For sepia is the blood, or juice, of cuttlefish *and certain species of mollusc and sea-snail.*

The thing was still alive. Its mantle waved feebly and those eyes which remained saw me. Even as the ultimate horror occurred I remember I suddenly knew for certain that my guess had been correct. For the thing was not *coiled* like a sea-snail should be – *and what sea-snail would ever leave its shell?*

I have said it saw me! George, I swear on the Holy Bible that the creature *recognized* me and, as the crabs surged forward again to the unholy feast, it tried to *walk* towards me.

Snails should not walk, George, and men should not squirm.

Hypnotism is a funny thing. We barely understand the *human* form of the force let alone the strange strains used by lesser life-forms.

What more can I say? Let me just repeat that I hope you can accept my apologies for my behaviour the other night. It was the oysters, of course. Not that I have any doubt that their preparation was immaculate or that they were delicious – to any *untainted* palate, that is. But I? Why! I could no more eat an oyster than I could a corporal.

Sincerely,
Maj. Harry Winslow

AGAIN
Written by **Ramsey Campbell**

Before long Bryant tired of the Wirral Way. He'd exhausted the Liverpool parks, only to find that nature was too relentless for him. No doubt the trail would mean more to a botanist, but to Bryant it looked exactly like what it was: an overgrown railway divested of its line. Sometimes it led beneath bridges hollow as whistles, and then it seemed to trap him between the banks for miles. When it rose to ground level it was only to show him fields too lush for comfort, hedges, trees, green so unrelieved that its shades blurred into a single oppressive mass.

He wasn't sure what eventually made the miniature valley intolerable. Children went hooting like derailed trains across his path. Huge dogs came snuffling out of the undergrowth to leap on him and smear his face, but the worst annoyances were the flies, brought out all at once by the late June day, the first hot day of the year. They blotched his vision like eyestrain, their incessant buzzing seemed to muffle all his senses. When he heard lorries somewhere above him, he scrambled up the first break he could find in the brambles, without waiting for the next official exit from the trail.

By the time he realised that the path led nowhere in particular, he had already crossed three fields. It seemed best to go on, even though the sound he'd taken for lorries proved, now that he was in the open, to be distant tractors. He didn't think he could find his way back even if he wanted to. Surely he would reach a road eventually.

Once he'd trudged around several more fields he wasn't so sure. He felt sticky, hemmed in by buzzing and green – a fly in a flytrap.

There was nothing else beneath the unrelenting cloudless sky except a bungalow, three fields and a copse away to his left. Perhaps he could get a drink there while asking the way to the road.

The bungalow was difficult to reach. Once he had to retrace his journey around three sides of a field, when he'd approached close enough to see that the garden that surrounded the house looked at least as overgrown as the railway had been.

Nevertheless someone was standing in front of the bungalow, knee-deep in grass – a woman with white shoulders, standing quite still. He hurried around the maze of fences and hedges, looking for his way to her. He'd come quite close before he saw how old and pale she was. She was supporting herself with one hand on a disused bird-table, and for a moment he thought the shoulders of her ankle-length caftan were white with droppings, as the table was. He shook his head vigorously, to clear it of the heat, and saw at once that it was long white hair that trailed raggedly over her shoulders, for it stirred a little as she beckoned to him.

At least, he assumed she was beckoning. When he reached her, after he'd lifted the gate clear of the weedy path, she was still flapping her hands, but now to brush away flies, which seemed even fonder of her than they had been of him. Her eyes looked glazed and empty; for a moment he was tempted to sneak away. Then they gazed at him, and they were so pleading that he had to go to her, to see what was wrong.

She must have been pretty when she was younger. Now her long arms and heart-shaped face were bony, the skin withered tight on them, but she might still be attractive if her complexion wasn't so grey. Perhaps the heat was affecting her – she was clutching the bird-table as though she would fall if she relaxed her grip – but then why didn't she go into the house? Then he realised that must be why she needed him, for she was pointing shakily with her free hand at the bungalow. Her nails were very long. 'Can you get in?' she said.

Her voice was disconcerting: little more than a breath, hardly there at all. No doubt that was also the fault of the heat. 'I'll try,' he said, and she made for the house at once, past a tangle of roses and a rockery so overgrown it looked like a distant mountain in a jungle.

She had to stop breathlessly before she reached the bungalow. He carried on, since she was pointing feebly at the open kitchen window. As he passed her he found she was doused in perfume, so heavily that even in the open it was cloying. Surely she was in her seventies? He felt shocked, though he knew that was narrow-minded. Perhaps it was the perfume that attracted the flies to her.

The kitchen window was too high for him to reach unaided. Presumably she felt it was safe to leave open while she was away from the house. He went round the far side of the bungalow to the open garage, where a dusty car was baking amid the stink of hot metal and oil. There he found a toolbox, which he dragged round to the window.

When he stood the rectangular box on end and levered himself up, he wasn't sure he could squeeze through. He unhooked the transom and managed to wriggle his shoulders through the opening. He thrust himself forward, the unhooked bar bumping along his spine, until his hips wedged in the frame. He was stuck in midair, above a greyish kitchen that smelled stale, dangling like the string of plastic onions on the far wall. He was unable to drag himself forward or back.

All at once her hands grabbed his thighs, thrusting up towards his buttocks. She must have clambered onto the toolbox. No doubt she was anxious to get him into the house, but her sudden desperate strength made him uneasy, not least because he felt almost assaulted. Nevertheless she'd given him the chance to squirm his hips, and he was through. He lowered himself awkwardly, head first, clinging to the edge of the sink while he swung his feet down before letting himself drop.

He made for the door at once. Though the kitchen was almost

bare, it smelled worse than stale. In the sink a couple of plates protruded from water the color of lard, where several dead flies were floating. Flies crawled over smeary milk bottles on the windowsill or bumbled at the window, as eager to find the way out as he was. He thought he'd found it, but the door was mortise-locked, with a broken key that was jammed in the hole.

He tried to turn the key, until he was sure it was no use. Not only was its stem snapped close to the lock, the key was wedged in the mechanism. He hurried out of the kitchen to the front door, which was in the wall at right angles to the jammed door. The front door was mortise-locked as well.

As he returned to the kitchen window he bumped into the refrigerator. It mustn't have been quite shut, for it swung wide open – not that it mattered, since the fridge was empty save for a torpid fly. She must have gone out to buy provisions – presumably her shopping was somewhere in the undergrowth. 'Can you tell me where the key is?' he said patiently.

She was clinging to the outer sill, and seemed to be trying to save her breath. From the movements of her lips he gathered she was saying 'Look around.'

There was nothing in the kitchen cupboards except a few cans of baked beans and meat, their labels peeling. He went back to the front hall, which was cramped, hot, almost airless. Even here he wasn't free of the buzzing of flies, though he couldn't see them. Opposite the front door was a cupboard hiding mops and brushes senile with dust. He opened the fourth door off the hall into the living-room.

The long room smelled as if it hadn't been opened for months, and looked like a parody of middle-class taste. Silver-plated cannon challenged each other across the length of the pebble-dashed mantelpiece, on either side of which were portraits of the royal family. Here was a cabinet full of dolls of all nations, here was a bookcase of *Reader's Digest* Condensed Books. A personalised bullfight poster was pinned to one wall, a ten-gallon hat to another. With so much in it, it seemed odd that the room felt disused.

He began to search, trying to ignore the noise of flies – it was somewhere further into the house, and sounded disconcertingly like someone groaning. The key wasn't on the obese purple suite or down the sides of the cushions; it wasn't on the small table piled with copies of *Contact*, which for a moment, giggling, he took to be a sexual contact magazine. The key wasn't under the bright green rug, nor on any of the shelves. The dolls gazed unhelpfully at him.

He was holding his breath, both because the unpleasant smell he'd associated with the kitchen seemed even stronger in here and because every one of his movements stirred up dust. The entire room was pale with it; no wonder the dolls' eyelashes were so thick. She must no longer have the energy to clean the house. Now he had finished searching, and it looked as if he would have to venture deeper into the house, where the flies seemed to be so abundant. He was at the far door when he glanced back. Was that the key beneath the pile of magazines?

He had only begun to tug the metal object free when he saw it was a pen, but the magazines were already toppling. As they spilled over the floor, some of them opened at photographs: people tied up tortuously, a plump woman wearing a suspender belt and flourishing a whip.

He suppressed his outrage before it could take hold of him. So much for first impressions! After all, the old lady must have been young once. Really, that thought was rather patronising too - and then he saw it was more than that. One issue of the magazine was no more than a few months old.

He was shrugging to himself, trying to pretend that it didn't matter to him, when a movement made him glance up at the window. The old lady was staring in at him. He leapt away from the table as if she'd caught him stealing, and hurried to the window, displaying his empty hands. Perhaps she hadn't had time to see him at the magazines – it must have taken her a while to struggle through the undergrowth around the house – for she only pointed at the far door and said 'Look in there.'

Just now he felt uneasy about visiting the bedrooms, however absurd that was. Perhaps he could open the window outside which she was standing, and lift her up – but the window was locked, and no doubt the key was with the one he was searching for. Suppose he didn't find them? Suppose he couldn't get out of the kitchen window? Then she would have to pass the tools up to him, and he would open the house that way. He made himself go to the far door while he was feeling confident. At least he would be away from her gaze, wouldn't have to wonder what she was thinking about him.

Unlike the rooms he had already seen in the bungalow, the hall beyond the door was dark. He could see the glimmer of three doors and several framed photographs lined up along the walls. The sound of flies was louder, though they didn't seem to be in the hall itself. Now that he was closer they sounded even more like someone groaning feebly, and the rotten smell was stronger too. He held his breath and hoped that he would have to search only the nearest room.

When he shoved its door open, he was relieved to find it was the bathroom – but the state of it was less of a relief. Bath and washbowl were bleached with dust; spiders had caught flies between the taps. Did she wash herself in the kitchen? But then how long had the stagnant water been there? He was searching among the jars of ointments and lotions on the window ledge, all of which were swollen with a fur of talcum powder; he shuddered when it squeaked beneath his fingers. There was no sign of a key.

He hurried out, but halted in the doorway. Opening the door had lightened the hall, so that he could see the photographs. They were wedding photographs, all seven of them. Though the bridegrooms were different – here an airman with a thin moustache, there a portly man who could have been a tycoon or a chef – the bride was the same in every one. It was the woman who owned the house, growing older as the photographs progressed, until in the most recent, where she was holding onto a man with a large nose and a fierce beard, she looked almost as old as she was now.

Bryant found himself smirking uneasily, as if at a joke he didn't quite see but which he felt he should. He glanced quickly at the two remaining doors. One was heavily bolted on the outside – the one beyond which he could hear the intermittent sound like groaning. He chose the other door at once.

It led to the old lady's bedroom. He felt acutely embarrassed even before he saw the brief transparent nightdress on the double bed. Nevertheless he had to brave the room, for the dressing-table was a tangle of bracelets and necklaces, the perfect place to lose keys; the mirror doubled the confusion. Yet as soon as he saw the photographs that were leaning against the mirror, some instinct made him look elsewhere first.

There wasn't much to delay him. He peered under the bed, lifting both sides of the counterpane to be sure. It wasn't until he saw how grey his fingers had become that he realised the bed was thick with dust. Despite the indentation in the middle of the bed, he could only assume that she slept in the bolted room.

He hurried to the dressing-table and began to sort through the jewellery, but as soon as he saw the photographs his fingers grew shaky and awkward. It wasn't simply that the photographs were so sexually explicit – it was that in all of them she was very little younger, if at all, than she was now. Apparently she and her bearded husband both liked to be tied up, and that was only the mildest of their practices. Where was her husband now? Had his predecessors found her too much for them? Bryant had finished searching through the jewellery by now, but he couldn't look away from the photographs, though he found them appalling. He was still staring morbidly when she peered in at him, through the window that was reflected in the mirror.

This time he was sure she knew what he was looking at. More, he was sure he'd been meant to find the photographs. That must be why she'd hurried round the outside of the house to watch. Was she regaining her strength? Certainly she must have had to struggle through a good deal of undergrowth to reach the window in time.

He made for the door without looking at her, and prayed that the key would be in the one remaining room, so that he could get out of the house. He strode across the hallway and tugged at the rusty bolt, trying to open the door before his fears grew worse. His struggle with the bolt set off the sound like groaning within the room, but that was no reason for him to expect a torture chamber. Nevertheless, when the bolt slammed all at once out of the socket and the door swung inward, he staggered back into the hall.

The room didn't contain much: just a bed and the worst of the smell. It was the only room where the curtains were drawn, so that he had to strain his eyes to see that someone was lying on the bed, covered from head to foot with a blanket. A spoon protruded from an open can of meat beside the bed. Apart from a chair and a fitted wardrobe, there was nothing else to see – except that, as far Bryant could make out in the dusty dimness, the shape on the bed was moving feebly.

All at once he was no longer sure that the groaning had been the sound of flies. Even so, if the old lady had been watching him he might never have been able to step forward. But she couldn't see him, and he had to know. Though he couldn't help tiptoeing, he forced himself to go to the head of the bed.

He wasn't sure if he could lift the blanket, until he looked in the can of meat. At least it seemed to explain the smell, for the can must have been opened months ago. Rather than think about that – indeed, to give himself no time to think – he snatched the blanket away from the head of the figure at once.

Perhaps the groaning had been the sound of flies after all, for they came swarming out, off the body of the bearded man. He had clearly been dead for at least as long as the meat had been opened. Bryant thought sickly that if the sheet had really been moving, it must have been the flies. But there was something worse than that: the scratches on the shoulders of the corpse, the teeth-marks on its neck – for although there was no way of being sure, he had an appalled suspicion that the marks were quite new.

He was stumbling away from the bed – he felt he was drowning in the air that was thick with dust and flies – when the sound recommenced. For a moment he had the thought, so grotesque he was afraid he might both laugh wildly and be sick, that flies were swarming in the corpse's beard. But the sound was groaning after all, for the bearded head was lolling feebly back and forth on the pillow, the tongue was twitching about the greyish lips, the blind eyes were rolling. As the lower half of the body began to jerk weakly but rhythmically, the long-nailed hands tried to reach for whoever was in the room.

Somehow Bryant was outside the door and shoving the bolt home with both hands. His teeth were grinding from the effort to keep his mouth closed, for he didn't know if he was going to vomit or scream. He reeled along the hall, so dizzy he was almost incapable, into the living-room. He was terrified of seeing her at the window, on her way to cut off his escape. He felt so weak he wasn't sure of reaching the kitchen window before she did.

Although he couldn't focus on the living-room, as if it wasn't really there, it seemed to take him minutes to cross. He'd stumbled at last into the front hall when he realised that he needed something on which to stand to reach the transom. He seized the small table, hurling the last of the contact magazines to the floor, and staggered toward the kitchen with it, almost wedging it in the doorway. As he struggled with it, he was almost paralysed by the fear that she would be waiting at the kitchen window.

She wasn't there. She must still be on her way around the outside of the house. As he dropped the table beneath the window, Bryant saw the broken key in the mortise lock. Had someone else – perhaps the bearded man – broken it while trying to escape? It didn't matter, he mustn't start thinking of escapes that had failed.

But it looked as if he would have to, for he could see at once that he couldn't reach the transom.

He tried once, desperately, to be sure. The table was too low, the narrow sill was too high. Though he could wedge one foot on the sill, the angle was wrong for him to squeeze his shoulders through the window. He would certainly be stuck when she came to find him. Perhaps if he dragged a chair through from the living-room – but he had only just stepped down, almost falling to his knees, when he heard her opening the front door with the key she had had all the time.

His fury at being trapped was so intense that it nearly blotted out his panic. She had only wanted to trick him into the house. By God, he'd fight her for the key if he had to, especially now that she was re-locking the front door. All at once he was stumbling wildly toward the hall, for he was terrified that she would unbolt the bedroom and let out the thing in the bed. But when he threw open the kitchen door, what confronted him was far worse.

She stood in the living-room doorway, waiting for him. Her caftan lay crumpled on the hall floor. She was naked, and at last he could see how grey and shrivelled she was – just like the bearded man. She was no longer troubling to brush off the flies, a couple of which were crawling in and out of her mouth. At last, too late, he realised that her perfume had not been attracting the flies at all. It had been meant to conceal the smell that was attracting them – the smell of death.

She flung the key behind her, a new move in her game. He would have died rather than try to retrieve it, for then he would have had to touch her. He backed into the kitchen, looking frantically for something he could use to smash the window. Perhaps he was incapable of seeing it, for his mind seemed paralysed by the sight of her. Now she was moving as fast as he was, coming after him with her long arms outstretched, her grey breasts flapping. She was licking her lips as best she could, relishing his terror. Of course, that was why she'd made him go through the entire house. He knew that her energy came from her hunger for him.

It was a fly – the only one in the kitchen that hadn't alighted on her – that drew his gaze to the empty bottles on the windowsill. He'd known all the time they were there, but panic was dulling his mind. He grabbed the nearest bottle, though his sweat and the slime of milk made it almost too slippery to hold. At least it felt reassuringly solid, if anything could be reassuring now. He swung it with all his force at the centre of the window. But it was the bottle which broke.

He could hear himself screaming – he didn't know if it was with rage or terror – as he rushed toward her, brandishing the remains of the bottle to keep her away until he reached the door. Her smile, distorted but gleeful, had robbed him of the last traces of restraint, and there was only the instinct to survive. But her smile widened as she saw the jagged glass – indeed, her smile looked quite capable of collapsing her face. She lurched straight into his path, her arms wide.

He closed his eyes and stabbed. Though her skin was tougher than he'd expected, he felt it puncture drily, again and again. She was thrusting herself onto the glass, panting and squealing like a pig. He was slashing desperately now, for the smell was growing worse.

All at once she fell, rattling on the linoleum. For a moment he was terrified that she would seize his legs and drag him down on her. He fled, kicking out blindly, before he dared open his eyes. The key – where was the key? He hadn't seen where she had thrown it. He was almost weeping as he dodged about the living-room, for he could hear her moving feebly in the kitchen. But there was the key, almost concealed down the side of a chair.

As he reached the front door he had a last terrible thought. Suppose this key broke too? Suppose that was part of her game? He forced himself to insert it carefully, though his fingers were shaking so badly he could hardly keep hold of it at all. It wouldn't turn. It would – he had been trying to turn it the wrong way. One easy turn, and the door swung open. He was so insanely grateful that he almost neglected to lock it behind him.

He flung the key as far as he could and stood in the overgrown garden, retching for breath. He'd forgotten that there were such things as trees, flowers, fields, the open sky. Yet just now the scent of flowers was sickening, and he couldn't bear the sound of flies. He had to get away from the bungalow and then from the countryside – but there wasn't a road in sight, and the only path he knew led back toward the Wirral Way. He wasn't concerned about returning to the nature trail, but the route back would lead him past the kitchen window. It took him a long time to move, and then it was because he was more afraid to linger near the house.

When he reached the window, he tried to run while tiptoeing. If only he dared turn his face away! He was almost past before he heard a scrabbling beyond the window. The remains of her hands appeared on the sill, and then her head lolled into view. Her eyes gleamed brightly as the shards of glass that protruded from her face. She gazed up at him, smiling raggedly and pleading. As he backed away, floundering through the undergrowth, he saw that she was mouthing jerkily. 'Again,' she said.

SURVIVAL
Written by **Sam West**

The rhythmic blinking of the cursor on the computer screen cruelly mocked him.

For three hours and twenty-eight minutes, Jon Oxley had been sitting at his desk but the words would not come. During those three hours and twenty-eight minutes, he had written precisely twenty-one words. And each of those twenty-one words had been taken from an online dictionary.

Just write, and the muse will eventually follow.

Except it wasn't. Not today.

Maybe not ever again.

A bead of sweat dripped off his forehead, splashing onto the keyboard. He stared at the wet-spot on the spacebar in silent desperation, eventually wrenching his gaze back up to read what had taken him so long to copy and paste from the net:

Survival. Especially under adverse or unusual circumstances.

Survival. A person or thing that survives or endures, especially an ancient custom, belief, etc.

Angrily, he typed, bashing the keyboard with all the vigor born of desperation and anxiety, letting the streams of consciousness flow through his fingers – the utter, steaming fucking dog-turd that amounted to his thoughts:

Survival.

Survival of the fittest.

Who is surviving? Who is my protagonist? The abuser or the abused? Whose POV?? The victim? If so, what does the

victim go through? How did he/she get there? WHO THE FUCK IS THE VICTIM?

He groaned aloud, clawing at his short hair.

'I have nothing to offer, but blood, toil, tears and sweat,' he murmured.

Why can't I write this damn piece? What the fuck is wrong with me?

His deadline was looming; just three days left.

Three miserable fucking days.

All the other authors had submitted their work; he was the last. He was writing a short story for an anthology, headed by one of the biggest names in horror. The only brief he had been given was one word: *Survival*.

That was it. Just one measly, solitary, motherfucking word.

Survival. Survival, survival, survival.

The word repeated on a loop in his head until it became meaningless.

'Fuck this,' he muttered, slamming down the lid of the computer.

Maybe a pint would make him feel better. Yes, that was a good idea.

Maybe, if I go now, Alice will be starting her shift at The Fox and Hound…

His cock stirred as he thought about the luscious barmaid in his local. With her long, blonde hair, angelic face and the type of skinny curves one usually only saw in the airbrushed photos of glamour-models, she was a fucking knockout.

But the sad thing was, she was never anything more than just polite to him; polite but distant. Jon was thirty-eight to her twenty-one, and he wasn't exactly beating women off with a stick, even if his debut, self-published novel, 'The Dark Inside' had been kicking some serious arse on Amazon.

Such success wasn't without its perks, but every woman he

flirted with on social media was a pale imitation of Alice Logan. And Alice wasn't even *on* social media. Or if she was, she kept herself completely private. Either that, or she had blocked him.

No. Why would she do that? I know she likes me.

The age gap between them wasn't that much, surely? What was seventeen years? Age was but a number...

I have to see her.

It was a three mile hike, but he didn't care. She was worth it. With that one thought in his head, he headed out to the pub.

*

'No Alice tonight?'

Jon took a big gulp of his beer, eyeing Brian, the old guy who owned this craphole boozer. God only knew why a babe like Alice saw fit to work in a dump like this. But she was the landlord's niece, and trying to pay her way through Uni, so he guessed it mainly made sense.

'No, it's her night off.'

Guess I'll be on my merry way after this beer, then.

'Right,' he said, dismally looking around himself.

Today, he was the only one sitting at the bar. Usually, he was joined by a couple of other barflies, but at four o'clock on a Monday afternoon, even those sad pricks were nowhere to be seen.

'And I gotta say, Jon, I don't think you should be sniffing around Alice the way you do. It ain't right, she's young enough to be your daughter. Just back off.'

'I was just being friendly. And it's her job to be nice to the punters, isn't it?'

His words were light, but inside he seethed. How dare this piece of shit imply that he was some kind of sleaze? There were only seventeen years between them, it wasn't *that* much.

The old man turned away to empty the dishwasher at the other end of the bar, and Jon caught his reflection in the mirror that ran the length of the bar behind the optics. A wave of self-disgust crashed through him.

The old git is right. Look at the state of me.

Sitting there slouched on his barstool, he looked a lot older than his thirty-eight years. His hair was beginning to thin on top, and his eyes were red, his eyelids puffy. His jawline was looking a tad sorry and sagging, the width of his shoulders seeming to decrease and his girth increase with every passing year.

No wonder she doesn't fancy me…

Searing pain stabbed behind his eyes; he was getting one of his headaches again, and he squeezed the bridge of his nose between thumb and forefinger. The headaches were a complete cunt. Sometimes, if they were really bad, he would retreat to his bed and sleep for two days straight and when he woke up he would have no recollection of the previous forty-eight hours.

Still with a third of his pint remaining, he slipped off the barstool and headed for the door.

'You haven't finished your drink,' Brian called after him, but he didn't so much as turn around.

Jon staggered outside, blinking at the brightness of the late afternoon.

*

Somehow, Jon found himself wandering through the woods. His head was throbbing now and he knew he should go home, take a couple of painkillers and lie down in a darkened room. Above him, the birds chirped in the tree canopy, but somehow, they didn't sound right, like they were coming from very far away. The low, early Autumnal sun that streamed through the green and gold leaves in thin beams distorted around him as if the trees were closing in on him. He stopped walking for a second, the wet earth with the thin layer of brown leaves unsteady beneath his feet.

Was that *toast* he could smell? Who the hell would make toast out in the middle of the woods?

No one, that's who. He hadn't passed a single soul out on his walk.

I must have a brain-tumor.

Just as he thought that, stabbing pain seared him between the eyes and he sucked in a sharp intake of breath at the intensity of it.

What if I'm just a one-hit wonder? What if I never write another word again?

The thought was terrifying and all-consuming, making his stomach twist up into a tight, anxious knot. Unbeknown to his fans, *The Dark Inside* had been loosely based on his own experiences growing up. His Uncle – who had visited once or twice a year for a few days at a time – had sexually abused him between the ages of six and twelve. He was long-dead now, having died in prison, but Jon still had nightmares about the perverted bastard-cunt.

Because the book was semi-autobiographical, in his darker moments he worried that *The Dark Inside* was all he had in him, that it was all he had to give. That he was a talentless wanker with all the imagination of a dead slug.

Survival. Yeah, I know all about survival.

He leaned against the broad trunk of a tree, his head swimming, closing his eyes for a second to compose himself. His entire body stiffened.

What the hell was that?

For a second there, he was sure he had heard the sound of a muffled cry.

First the smell of burnt toast, now the sound of whimpering.. I definitely have a brain tumor.

Just as he decided that he had imagined it, the noise came again, louder this time. And the cry sounded *feminine*. He stood still and pressed his back against the tree, his heart pounding and the blood rushing in his ears. The muffled crying grew louder, accompanied by the sound of leaves rustling underfoot.

Frantically, he scanned the woods. He had wandered off the

path, and there was not another soul in sight. Where was a fucking dog-walker when you wanted one?

Hugging the tree-trunk, he peered around it in the direction that the noise was coming from. A figure was emerging from the trees, hunched over and walking backwards, like it was dragging something heavy. Stop, start. Stop, start.. He – for Jon just assumed it was a *he* from the width of the person's shoulders and the straight-cut jeans and trainers – was wearing a black hoody with the hood pulled over his head. As Jon was viewing him in profile, his features were completely obscured.

For a second, his heart stopped beating then slammed so hard in his chest that his legs threatened to buckle beneath him, all thoughts of his headache forgotten.

Just relax, he told himself. It's probably completely innocent. Just someone fly-tipping, or something. No one's going to do anything too deviant in a public place, surely?

But if he truly believed this, then why was he so intent on remaining hidden behind the tree?

And since when did rubbish *scream* when you dumped it? Because those sounds were *not* coming from the man grunting with the effort of dragging something heavy...

That was a *person* he was dragging through the woods.

The man drew closer to Jon with those same, small bursts of movement.

Stop, start. Stop start...

Jon squeezed his eyes tightly shut, pressing his back hard against the tree. Panic washed through him, making his vision swim and his breath come in ragged gasps. He clamped his hand over his mouth, lest the man should hear him.

Don't come any closer, don't come any closer.

The dragging stopped, just a few feet away from where he stood trembling. The girl's muffled protests were like fingernails down a blackboard, making him shudder in horror.

What the hell was he supposed to do now? If he made a run for it, he would be spotted for sure. *My phone*, he suddenly thought, patting himself down with trembling hands. Shit, he didn't have the damn thing on him. Clutching his head in his hands, he pushed back the fresh wave of despair and hopelessness.

At some point during his panic, he had turned around so that he was facing the tree with his cheek pressed against the rough trunk. His fingers clawed at the bark which dug in under his nails, the sharp pain of this taking the edge of his terror and going some way to clarifying his thoughts.

You have to look.

Steeling himself, he inched his head sideways so that he was able to peek around the tree-trunk. As soon as he saw, he snapped back behind the tree again like a pinging elastic band.

Jesus.

His heart continued to slam so hard in his chest that he thought he might drop dead of a heart-attack there and then. Thankfully, the hooded figure had not seen him; he'd had his back to him, and had been leaning over the body.

But this time Jon had gotten a good look at the person he'd been dragging… The image of the girl lying on her back in the leaves and dirt blared bright in his mind. To his shame, the first thing he noticed about the girl was her lush body. Her breasts were full and high, her stomach flat and her waist narrow. The curve of her hips was pronounced and her legs were long and slim. There was silver tape over her mouth and her wrists were lashed together with rope, her bound hands nestled between her full tits.

There was also something excruciatingly familiar about her. The long, blonde hair was a tangled, matted mess of blood and dirt, her face streaked with the same. Her left eyes was completely closed over, the puffy skin a nasty shade of purple.

But still her unmistakable beauty shone through.

Alice.

That one word was an icepick in his mind, shattering his thoughts.

'On your feet, bitch,' the stranger said.

Except maybe the voice wasn't so strange after all – a shuddering glimmer of recognition coursed through him, swaying him on his feet.

He broke out in an instant sweat, his body suddenly racked by hot and cold shivers as the disgusting memories slammed into his terrified brain.

No, Uncle Jeff. Please don't do that, it hurts so much...

Uncle Jeff had been dead for years, dying in prison as so many other child abusers had done before him. Squeezing his eyes tightly shut, he tried to reign in his crazed, tumbling thoughts.

His horrendous situation was making him imagine things, the man *couldn't* be Uncle Jeff, it was impossible.

More rustling sounds assaulted his ears, accompanied by the girl's muffled sobbing.

'That's it, just stand the fuck up,' the man said.

This time, when he spoke, he didn't sound so much like Uncle Jeff, and for that he was inordinately grateful.

*I am not losing my mind, I am not losing my mind, h*e repeated over and over on a loop in his head, his eyes still tightly closed.

A fresh word popped into his mind, causing his eyes to snap open:

Survival.

He didn't understand why that word would break the cycle of the others, or why he would even think it in the first place.

Of course, he thought. A weapon. I need a weapon to survive.

Why hadn't he thought of that sooner? He cast his eyes to the ground, searching for a sizable rock that he could bash the bastard over the head with.

Am I going to attack him?

He *should* do; it was the right thing to do, after all. But in his heart he knew that he wouldn't – not unless the man came for him first.

Yeah, fuck that. Jon was going to stay hidden.

I am a coward.

Luckily, a rock right in front of his feet looked potentially big enough to cause damage to a skull and he bent down to pick it up. He dropped it from one hand to the other, testing the weight of it. Yes, that would do the job, if need be.

Tears blurred his vision at his own cowardice as he listened to the traumatized, muffled wails of the woman.

'Arms above your head,' the man said. He was panting, like he was exerting himself.

Jon strained his ears, listening. There was a lot of rustling, a lot of grunting from the man and those wet, muffled sobs coming from the woman.

'Fuck, you're gorgeous,' the man said. 'Do not move a fucking muscle, you hear me? And keep the noise down or I'll make it so much worse for you. I'll be half an hour, tops.'

Jon listened in confusion. Was the man actually *leaving*? It made no fucking sense whatsoever – who would leave a bound, beaten woman out here alone in a public area? Who the fuck could possibly think that they could get away with such a thing?

A psychopath, that's who.

The sound of footsteps made him wince in terror, as they were coming right *for him*.

Movement to the left of him caused him to scuttle round the tree like a crab to remain hidden. He was forced all the way round the tree until he was in plain sight of the woman. In utter terror of the man suddenly deciding to retrace his steps, he pressed his forefinger to his lips, silently pleading with her to shut up.

Peering round the tree, he watched the man's retreating figure until he disappeared from view. Where the fuck was he going?

He turned around to face the woman, leaning against the tree for support, his heart slamming in his chest.

'Hold on, I'm going to get you out of here.'

But in that moment, he couldn't move. His feet were welded to the spot as he drank in the sight of her. Her arms were raised high above her head, the rope that was lashed around her bound wrists looped over a low-hanging branch of a tree.

She was fucking beautiful, and his cock leapt in his underpants.

The girl renewed her struggles, pulling at the rope, but all that achieved was to make her tits wobble in the most pleasing manner. He had to physically wrench his gaze off them to meet her eyes. Or eye. The left one remained resolutely closed-over.

'You have to be quiet, or he might hear you and come back,' he said in a frantic whisper.

She wasn't quiet. If anything, she thrashed even harder, and Jon frowned at her in confusion. Why was she being like this? Did she not realize that he was trying to help her?

Her thighs parted with her twisting and wiggling, and his gaze was helplessly drawn to her cunt. He glimpsed the shadowy, fleshy folds of her labia, and his cock stiffened some more.

She's a natural blonde, came the entirely inappropriate thought as his gaze openly took in the scant, neatly-trimmed, blonde pubic hair.

In fascination, he approached her until he was standing right before her. Gently, he reached out to stroke the filthy blonde strands off her face.

'Alice, for God's sake, it's me, Jon. I'm trying to *help* you. You really do have to be quiet.'

Tentatively, he reached out to touch the rope at her wrists, his gaze following the rope all the way up to the branch it was lashed around. From the branch – which was way too high for him to reach – the rope extended down to the trunk of the tree in an elaborate pully system. In theory, all he had to do was untie the rope around the tree and she would be free.

'I'm going to the tree now, and I'm going to untie you and you'll be free, okay?'

But he didn't move. He was so close to her, he could smell her. It was a pungent mix of blood, earth and sweat. It was *primal* and his cock responded, leaping into full hardness.

He sighed heavily. This really wouldn't do; he was supposed to be *helping* her.

You could just have a bit of fun with her, before he comes back.

The wicked thought slammed into his mind, shaming him. No. He wasn't like that...

He became aware of the dull throb in his head, signaling that his headache was just around the corner.

When he looked down at his hands, he saw that he was holding a knife in one, and the rock he had picked up in the other.

His vision swam. Where had the knife come from?

He asked the question, but deep down, he already knew the answer.

Why, from my pocket, of course.

The truth came and went in waves for him, much like his headaches. In his 'sane' moments, when the idea of his true nature, of him being a psychopath, didn't sit easy with him, he liked to think that he was in his bedroom, sleeping off a migraine instead of out killing women. Or sometimes, like just now, he could slip out of the moment and imagine it was someone else doing the killing and he was just watching..

But right now he was happy to revel in his true nature. And this kill was extra special, seeing as it was being done for research for his short story.

Letting the rock fall to the ground, he reached out to rip off the tape that covered her mouth. Her mouth sprang open like a released bear-trap as she drew breath to scream.

Jon slapped her across the face, hard enough to make her head snap to the side.

'Shut up. The neighbors might hear.'

This wasn't strictly true, but the constant noise these bitches made always gave him a headache. After he killed them, he quite often had to go and have a lie down to recover. Which worked out quite well, he supposed, because then, in his mind, he had been in bed the entire time with a migraine and the whole, sorry, sordid thing had never happened.

No matter, neither did he want to risk the neighbors hearing. Jon lived in a big house in the country, and the nearest – and only – house next to his was almost a quarter of a mile away. His parents had died ten years ago, and, as he was an only child, they had left the house to him. His back-garden was over a mile long, and down the bottom of it, where he was now, it was completely private.

But even so, there was no escaping the fact that the stink of the neighbor's burnt toast had drifted all the way to the end of his garden from over a mile away, so who was to say for sure that the sound of a woman screaming wouldn't meet their ears as they sat in their kitchen all that way away?

In his head, he had concocted a fantasy that he was out for a late afternoon stroll in the village woods when he had stumbled across a psychopath torturing the object of his lust. He would be the big hero, swoop in and rescue her, and she would be so grateful that she would fall in love with him and have sex with him amongst the leaves and the dirt. But then the psycho would come back, tie him up, and torture her to death right in front of him....

'You're fucking crazy,' Alice said, shattering his fantasy into a thousand pieces.

Jon regarded her thoughtfully. 'I'm writing a short story for this anthology, and it's like, a really big deal. But I'm having a bit of trouble with it, to be honest, so I thought I'd do some research. And if you're a good girl, and you agree to help me, I might just let you live.'

She glared at him with her one good eye. 'Fuck you.'

'No, no, no, you really don't want to be talking to me like that. So here are your choices. Either I'll skin you alive, cut you a new hole right here and then fuck it,' he said, gently stabbing her with the tip of his knife right about where he guessed her ovaries to be. 'Or, if you prefer, I'll let you go, and you'll be so fucking grateful, you'll have sex with me. You'll tell me that you love me and you want to have my babies and spend the rest of your life with me.'

'Why are you doing this to me?' she sobbed.

A sudden rush of memories slammed into his mind. Now that he was 'in the moment', he vividly remembered what he had done last night; how he had kidnapped her on her way home from work at one in the morning. A pretty girl like Alice most definitely shouldn't be walking home alone at night. There were a lot of nutters out there.

It was small wonder that he had writer's block today, his subconscious mind knowing full well that there was a fucking goddess lashed to a tree at the bottom of his garden.

'Are you going to play along, or not?' he asked, keen to get back to the game.

To emphasize his words, he trailed the sharp kitchen knife over one nipple, enjoying the way the small, pink bud puckered and hardened beneath the cool kiss of the steel. For a moment there, he didn't think that she was going to reply and he was going to have to cut her a new cunt.

'Okay, okay,' she said. 'Just untie me.'

Jon narrowed his eyes at her. 'If you're lying to me, it'll get really bad for you.'

'I'm not lying,' she half-sobbed, half-hiccupped.

It was quite possible that she was telling the truth, he reasoned. She had been sleeping out in the open all night, trussed up with rope to another tree a few meters away. She probably was fed up with it all and willing to play along.

'Okay, fine, then let's do this,' he said, going over to the tree-trunk to cut her free.

*

As soon as he had cut the rope around the trunk, he tucked the knife into the back pocket of his jeans and promptly forgot all about it. Once again, he was just sweet, kind – if slightly useless with women – Jon, and he had been out walking in the woods when he had stumbled upon this nightmare from hell.

With a cry, Alice thumped to her knees, her big tits swaying violently with the sudden movement. Jon hurried over to her, his erection straining at his underpants.

'Jesus, are you okay?' he gasped, worried that she might have hurt herself with the fall.

'I'm fine,' she sobbed, staggering to her feet.

'No, don't try to stand, you need a moment to recover. Here, let me untie your hands.'

Jon stared in dismay at the beaten, exhausted woman, not believing the nightmare that he had inadvertently wandered into.

What kind of a sick bastard would do this to a woman?

Gripping her shoulders, he gently but assertively encouraged her to sit on the ground. She did so, and tenderly he reached for her wrists.

'We have to hurry, before he comes back. Jesus, I can't believe this.'

Frantically, he tugged and pulled at the rope binding her wrists, working the knots until her hands were free. He winced when he saw the red welts that the rope had left behind on her flawless, white skin.

'Here,' he said, shrugging out of his black hoody and wrapping it around her shoulders.

He was sad to see her beautiful tits disappear from view, but he knew that it was the right thing to do. Gingerly, she inserted one hand into the armhole, then the other.

'Jon?'

'Yes?'

'Fuck you to hell.'

Bright light exploded in his head and he found himself lying on his back in the dirt and the fallen leaves.

'Fuck,' he groaned, the canopy of the treetops closing in above him and his ears ringing like there was a buzzer going off in his brain.

He struggled up onto his elbows, his head throbbing and his world spinning.

Bitch smacked me in the head, he thought incredulously. She fucking punched me.

He could taste coppery blood on his lips and daintily he dabbed at the cut with the tip of his tongue.

She's getting away!

That realization spurred him into action and he clambered to his feet, the ringing in his ears instantly subsiding.

'Bitch!' he roared after her retreating figure. 'You'll fucking pay for that!'

The cunt was ruining his fantasy, it wasn't supposed to be like this. Up ahead, her curvy little arse was visible beneath the edge of the hoody, jolting in time to her pounding feet.

Thanks to her, he may have had a thumping bloody headache, but she was in a far worse state than he was. Plus the bitch wasn't wearing any shoes.

In less than ten seconds, he had caught up with her and rugby tackled her to the ground. She went sprawling, the air leaving her lungs in a hard *oomph*.

His landing, however, was nice and soft.

'You'll pay for ruining my fantasy,' he grunted on top of her. 'You'll fucking pay. Tell me, cunt, how badly do you want to survive?'

'Get off me,' she said, but she was so winded that the words came out in a breathy rush.

Jon flipped her over onto her back, straddling her waist. Her face was a fucking mess, and a wave of anger crashed over him. Why did she have to go and be such a fighter? It only resulted in her ruining her looks far quicker than she should.

'How long will you survive? What do I have to do to you before you beg me to kill you?'

'Fuck you,' she breathed, writhing and bucking beneath him.

Christ, this girl had fire in her belly, he'd give her that.

'I don't think you appreciate how important this story I'm writing is to me. I mean, writing is my life now, and I don't want to go back to my shitty old job in the factory. Okay, so I don't have a mortgage, but the bills don't pay themselves, and I really want to keep writing. But I need you to help me.'

As he was talking, he didn't realize that he had wrapped his hands around her neck. He removed his hands and looked down at her red face and bulging eye.

'Will you help me, Alice? Will you help me understand the human instinct to survive, no matter what? I want to see how long you last before you beg me to kill you.'

Retrieving the knife from his back pocket at the same time as he freed his aching cock, he roughly shoved her thighs apart and drove into her dry vagina.

'You're a little raspy down there,' he said, pulling out for a second to jab the knife inside her cunt.

She let out an inhuman-sounding howl as the hot blood gushed out of her, easing his re-entry. He fucked her hard, her body jerking violently back and forth in the leaves and the dirt.

To his disappointment, he came really quickly, his come spurting against the tide of her flowing blood.

'Sorry I was so quick,' he panted. 'I guess I've been waiting a long time to do that.'

Figuring that he would probably be good to go again in an hour or less, he tucked his soggy cock back into his jeans and got to work on her with his knife, jabbing her lightly with the tip of it all over her torso.

'Whoops,' he said as he sliced off a nipple. 'That one was a little deep.'

She was screaming now, and he balled his fist and punched her in the face.

'Please,' she managed to cry through her fat, ugly, swollen face.

Jon stopped jabbing her with the knife and cocked his head to one side, staring thoughtfully down at her.

'Please? Please what? Please kill you? Or are you pleading to survive?'

She didn't reply for a moment, and just lay there moaning and thrashing her head from side to side. Just when he had given up all hope of her ever replying she croaked out that one, magic word:

'Survive. Survive, survive, survive…'

His heart lurched in joy, for he was witnessing the human survival instinct first hand. This stuff was gold, and would help him no end with his anthology entry.

'Fascinating. Let's see how long it takes you for you to change your mind.'

Alice cried and sobbed and let out guttural wails as Jon got to work slowly killing her with his knife.

*

Later on that evening, Jon was back in his office, sitting in front of the computer. At least his headache had passed. He remembered going to the pub to see Alice, but sadly it had been her night off. Then he remembered walking home and getting the most chronic headache. He had gone straight to bed, waking up just now to write.

Now he felt refreshed, an idea for a story burning bright in his mind. The premise was simple – a man kidnaps a girl with the soul intention of seeing how badly she wants to survive. Yes, it was going to be a simple but effective, gory little story.

He began to type:

The killer moved in closer, the stink of her blood and sweat perfuming her naked skin, making his cock stiffen. Her arms were pulled high above her head, the rope that bound her wrists together looping over the low hanging branch of the tree.

'Will you help me?' the killer whispered in her ear. 'Will

you help me understand the human instinct to survive, no matter what? I want to see how long you last before you beg me to kill you.'

Jon smiled to himself. This was good shit – he could tell that the blank word document wouldn't be blank for long.

Honestly, sometimes he really did wonder where it all came from.

MARY
Written by **J. R. Park**

I've spent all morning scrubbing faces out of the carpet.

A slither of nose, a slice of cheek, a wisp of lip. All caught between the fibres, staring up; looking at me.

These disparate pieces somehow make a whole. A sea of souls that smile in my presence.

Are they happy now?

If so, why do their grins disturb me so?

They hadn't been smiling when I took their lives; when I carved them up into tiny pieces.

I remember them all so clearly. I can picture the contortions of terror that stretched their faces; the twisting influence of agony that screwed their features into nightmarish masks.

Maybe that's all they were.

Masks.

There is more beneath.

There is a light inside us all.

A divine spark.

But I have yet to see proof of this. I have searched. Lord knows I have searched. I have cracked open and pulled apart many husks of humanity. I have split flesh and severed muscle from bone. I have sliced, slashed and separated, to no avail.

The light I seek escapes me.

It should be escaping them.

It should be blinding me with its heavenly brilliance as their screams fade. When peace takes hold, when tranquillity claims them, freed from the binds of the flesh, that's when I'd expect to bear witness.

But it eludes me.

God eludes me, even if the Devil stays near.

At night I hear him, the Devil and his servants. The ghostly damned. The suffering.

They crawl through my house searching for the secret I keep hidden. But they will never find it. Their lost treasures are stowed away in a symbol of God and kept on me at all times. I, however, have grown used to their tricks; their ghastly touch and the terrible visions it inflicts.

I sigh as I look down.

The carpet is a mess. Pink and crusty and lined with lost souls.

My hands are stained. I rub my palms with my handkerchief, wiping the residue from the cracks in my ageing skin.

I'm not expecting any visitors, so the knock at the door startles me.

I am agitated, but then I have been ever since last year when I had taken pity on that poor, young woman. A soul in distress led to a questioning of faith; a need to seek the proof I desired. A desire that still goes unsated.

My usual calmness is a façade, a veneer of control, but one that I cannot evoke right now.

The knocking comes again. My letterbox rattles. They will not leave.

The faces on the floor smile at me, refusing to blink as they follow me around the room with unsettling concentration. I wish I could blind them with a flash of light.

The divine spark.

Once I have it, once I master its power and commune with the Almighty - once I sit by His side - my work will be righteous.

They'll never gaze on me again.

Until then I must bear the burden of the unwanted.

And deal with uninvited guests at my door.

*

'Good morning, have you thought much about heaven?'

My speech is well practised; honed and automatic. It had taken a while for him to answer, and I had nearly given up, but as soon as the old man opens the door, my mouth, already spread into a welcoming grin, begins to move. My words fall out with the sincerity of a doctor and the calming reassurance of an old friend.

By the time I've noticed his white dog collar I've already begun offering the benefits of a place beside Jesus. My words stumble. Falter. My sentences collapse into an awkward silence.

The vicar looks at me with a patient smile as he wipes his hands in a handkerchief. He looks agitated, something more than the irritation of a Jehovah's Witness call.

'A bit of gardening?' I ask in an attempt to change the subject.

'Housework,' he sighs. 'Stubborn stains on the carpet. Always something to clean.'

I laugh. A sign of empathy.

The silence descends again. His clerical attire has wrong-footed me, and unusually I am finding it a struggle to recover. I step to the side, readjusting my position and attempt to see past him into the house. He moves with me, trying his hardest to keep the view blocked.

I'm intrigued by this behaviour. It's like he has something to hide.

'What denomination are you?' I ask, my eyes back on him; trying to settle him down and win his confidence.

'Church of England,' he smiles. 'Do I know you?'

'I don't think so.' I lie. His face has more wrinkles now, but he hasn't changed much. That kindly expression, semi-fraught with worry, still reminds me of my Nan's funeral; I must have been ten at the time. I don't remember his eyes looking so grey, almost silver. Is that an age thing? I change the subject, trying to get back on track. 'How about we pop inside and talk about our faiths?'

I step towards him, expecting the old man to welcome me in, but he stands firm. Our shoulders clash and I stumble into him, nearly falling at his feet.

Father Farrington is surprisingly strong as his hands grip my arms and halt my descent. He pulls me back to my feet. My heart is thumping inside my chest, and his growing smile does nothing to settle my unease.

I stagger backwards, pulling my arms from his grip. Blood trickles down my palm.

Had I cut myself?

I can't find any wound.

It must be from him. My heart pounds as my mind screams at me that there's something wrong. I keep walking backwards.

'Goodbye,' I nervously call. 'It was nice talking with you.'

Another lie, but I hope it doesn't show.

He stays stood in the doorway, that smile unflinching. My eyes stay trained on him until I'm back on the pavement and heading to the car.

As I open the passenger door I still haven't shaken this God-awful feeling. A shiver runs down my spine and I don't know why.

*

Dan gets into the car and his face is ashen white.

'You okay?' I ask him.

'Yeah, fine,' he says. 'Do you know who I was just speaking to?'

I'd watched from down the street but was too far away to make out any detail of the figure in the doorway.

'That was Father Farrington.'

'He's still alive?' I ask, although the statement is merely rhetorical. I think back to my childhood; to the days when I was dragged to Sunday school by my mother, God rest her soul. 'So the whole Jehovah's Witness thing didn't wash?'

'Ha, not really.'

'Big house though. A man of the cloth probably has a treasure or two hidden in there.' I think about church gold and presents from the elders. Paintings and sculptures. The monetary value of these gifts unknown by the stupid priests that view them from a spiritual perspective.

'I tried to get inside, but he was having none of it,' Dan informs me.

I start up the car and pull away, my eyes on the priest's house in the rear view mirror whilst Dan continues to fill me in on the failed con.

'There was no way I was gonna get his bank details to sign up for a piece of heaven.' I smile at this. The con is a simple one, preying on the weak. Convince them of the soul saving value of donating to the church. Give them the spiel about how helping out in this life will reward them in the next. Lay it on thick. If you got inside their house then you already had them. And Dan was the best at that. Silver-tongued bastard. Even if they cancelled their standing order after the first payment, it was still money for nothing. 'I got five sign-ups before the priest,' he reports. 'And Father Farrington wasn't a waste of time.'

From my peripheral vision, I watch Dan pull something out of his jacket pocket. It glints in the sunshine and he brings it closer so I can see what he's lifted. It's a crucifix, about five inches long and dangling on a metallic chain. The cross and the chain both look like solid gold.

'Holy shit,' I nearly lose control of the car as I accidentally swerve in my excitement to gander at the spoils. 'Leave it with me,' I say as I straighten the car back on the road. 'I can shift that, no problem.'

'I bet you can,' Dan smiles. 'Best thing about you, Steve, you know all the right people.'

'Years of being in the business,' I chuckle.

I can't so much see his grin as feel it, as Dan passes me the crucifix. A chill creeps over me. It's heavy. Good. That means it's valuable. I can't believe he managed to pickpocket a priest on his own doorstep.

He's good, I'll give him that.

Smooth bastard.

*

I hadn't laid eyes on Steve for some years, but time hasn't worn away his rugged good looks. It's a surprise to see him enter my shop, but a welcome one.

An even bigger surprise is the crucifix he hands me. It's old and a little worn which already gives me an indication of its worth.

I spend some time looking it over whilst he patiently waits, eyeing up the watches and gold chains in the display cabinets. I tell him it's twenty two carat, and his face stays stoic.

When I explain what that means - the value of the item - he beams.

'I thought it might be worth something,' his grin continuing to grow as the shock fades, 'but that's incredible.'

I don't ask where he got it. I never do. Not with Steve.

He understands that I don't have that amount of cash on me, and accepts a down-payment. He knows I'm good to organise the rest in a few days. His joke about knowing where I live is half-serious, and I'm fully aware of his semi-threat. He frightens and enthralls me in equal measure. I'd never tell him so. He doesn't look like the homosexual type.

I don't want him to leave, but capture his face with a gaze once more before he does. I can save that one for the wank bank later.

Left in the solitude of my own shop I look back down to the wonder I hold in my hands. The crucifix has me entranced. It is beautiful.

When the shop-door bell rings again I don't even look up. I figure it's Steve coming back. Maybe he's forgotten something.

The slurred shouting, the aggression from the other side of the counter, shocks me to attention. As I look up I see the barrel of a sawn-off shotgun pointed at my chest.

I drop the cross and try to slide my hand secretly towards the panic button.

*

The sound of the shotgun engulfs my senses. For a moment I feel like I'm submerged deep underwater, and it takes a while to regain the understanding of my surroundings.

My ears ring in the aftermath of the gunfire, but I don't have time to let them clear. I thrust my hands into the till and pull out the cash from the drawer. I collect up the blood-stained jewellery that's lying on the counter, but I get greedy. Smashing the butt of my gun into a glass display cabinet, I go for the gold chains and diamond rings. An alarm sounds out, wailing through the shop.

The cacophony makes me panic. As I rush to leave the store, I slip on the spilled entrails of the jeweller. Climbing back to my feet I'm covered in blood. I have to get out of sight, quickly.

I rush down the street, trying to get as much distance as I can between me and the screaming alarm.

In my haste to get away, I'm not concentrating. The sweat makes my grip loose, and I hardly notice the trail of bounty I'm leaving behind. When I finally do, I've almost dropped the lot. I don't go back to pick it up. Adrenaline keeps me moving forward.

By the time I stop, hiding out in the shadows of a deserted alleyway, I'm left with a roll of banknotes, a couple of rings and a large, gold crucifix.

An hour later and I'm back at the squat. The money and rings are gone, exchanged for the bag of brown I'm cooking up. But the crucifix stays with me.

Something compelled me to keep it. A little voice in the back of my mind. I finger its golden edges and accidentally slide some kind of hidden catch. The bottom of the shaft pops out, and with a couple of twists I've removed a cap, revealing a secret compartment inside.

A parchment falls from the hidden space and onto my lap. I unravel it to see a familiarly strange image. A symbol that reminds me of another life.

I stroke the coffee-brown cloth and trace over the design. Three elaborate S's entwining at their bases and dissolving into an encompassing circle that surrounds the central motif. The pattern makes me sick as my mind regresses. The smell of the attic where it was first found fills my nostrils. Hidden under some boards and wrapped around a bejewelled ring with the exact same symbol.

I wish it had never been discovered.

Tears fall silently down my face as I remember everything I've lost.

I inject the heroin, hoping to escape the suffocating melancholy and cloying chill that grips my body. I fall back onto my filthy mattress but the usual waves of euphoria do not greet me. The room grows darker. I grip my bedding as the shadows pulsate, leaning towards me as if desperate to caress my soul. Within the darkness there's a sound like moving.

Sliding.

Crawling.

Shapes emerge from the stygian surroundings. The faint outline of heads and shoulders. Hands reach out, dragging these crawling creatures across the floor. They approach from all sides, from all corners of the room. I can hear them groan, a wordless expression of pain; an embodiment of suffering.

As they get closer I see their faces are twisted, frozen at a moment when terror was all they knew.

Their eyes are absent, their fingers stretch forward, feeling the world around them. The blind souls, reaching out, are driven on by a call I cannot hear. But that call is towards me.

I cannot move under the influence of the drug coursing through my bloodstream. All I can do is watch as they grow ever closer.

One reaches me and places a cold hand on my arm. I scream and convulse in fear as my skin turns to ice.

Images flash through my mind. Fire illuminates a darkened room. Torches held by robed figures. A crying baby, defenceless on an altar, screams as a huge snake with human eyes wraps its body around the infant. Its deadly embrace tightens.

I try to break free from the visions but the crawling creatures surround me.

The symbol from the parchment appears on the ceiling, seeping through the plaster. Its curves refuse to stay static. The shimmering image burns into my mind.

This must have been how Lucy felt.

In the distance I hear someone shouting.

'Nobody move,' the voice commands.

A freezing grip takes hold of my head, pulling at my hair as another one of those things creeps closer.

Fingers swarm over me, grabbing my thigh, my chest, my shoulders.

I try to shout but I can't even breathe as a hand covers my mouth.

*

The smell hits me hard the moment I walk into the building. I'm used to the worst of human existence, it comes with the job, but this squat is something else.

I try not to gag as I command everyone to stay still. My order falls on deaf ears. One tries to jump out of the window to flee, whilst another comes forward, giving it a lot of mouth, telling us we can't just barge in here.

I'm not in the mood for this and twist his arm around his back, threatening to break it unless he shuts up. He soon complies.

I think the guy's a little ashamed too. Big man like that being physically bested by a woman.

We quiz him about the robbery and homicide at Appleton's the jewellers. He says he knows nothing despite a trail of dropped jewellery and a number of witness reports all tracing the suspect back here. Control radio in, telling me Father Farrington has called again. That's the fifth time today. I'm growing impatient. I don't have time to take a statement about thefts from the collection box.

A scream from elsewhere causes me to abandon my interview and run up the stairs, homing in on the source of the sound.

By the time I get there Collins is already standing over the body.

'O.D.?' I ask, looking at the bicep tied in a tourniquet and the needle by his side.

'I reckon,' Collins replies. 'Look at the state of his arm. Needle marks all over him. The guy was a full on junkie. I think we've got your murderer too,' he says staring at the golden crucifix lying across his chest. 'Matches the one on CCTV.'

I bend down beside the corpse to get a better look. In his hand is a scrunched up cloth. Only it's not really a cloth. Prising his hand open I see it's a parchment. Really old by the looks of it.

'Any ideas?' I ask, turning to Collins.

He studies the symbol for a moment then shakes his head. 'Not a clue, Detective Harrison,' he replies.

I study the dead man's face. 'That must have been one hell of a trip,' I mutter under my breath as I clock the expression of fear in his face. 'Best send him to the slab and get an official verdict.'

*

'And so finally, a tale of utter tragedy comes to an end.'

At first I don't understand what Dr. Redfern is referring to. He obviously recognises this as I look quizzically at the dead man's face whilst we prepare for the autopsy.

'The body,' he explains with his velvet voice, 'you don't recognise it, Angela?'

I shake my head, feeling ashamed at not knowing.

'This is Marcus Blackmore,' he said looking up at me. 'We had his wife here a year ago. Do you remember? Such a sad case. Lucy Blackmore. Died of an apparent heart attack. She was eight months pregnant. We tried to save the baby, but the experience was too much for the little one.' I swallow back a bit of bile as I recall those events. 'The press had a field day. Some mumbo jumbo about the woman fearing she was possessed and calling for a priest. An exorcism gone wrong. Of course the church denied it and the clergyman in question remained silent on the matter.'

'Father Farrington,' I add.

Dr. Redfern smiled in approval. 'Father Farrington. You know, I think you're right. Can you imagine dealing with such grief and having the idiotic, tabloid press turning it into some sort of freakish side show? The poor husband took it pretty hard. Understandably so; losing both your wife and unborn child in one fell swoop.' I feel a tear collect in my eye as I imagine the pain he must have gone through. I try to take my mind off it as I lay out the instruments, but Dr. Redfern continues. 'Marcus was a good man. We used to frequent the same pub. Had mutual friends, and they always spoke highly of him. But after his wife died he crumbled. There was nothing we could do to prevent it. He lost his job, his house. He disappeared. Judging from the state of his arms it's clear he became addicted to drugs. So sad. So deeply tragic.'

I feel my heart stop for a moment. A sadness overtakes me and I cannot prevent a tear quietly rolling down my face, despite my attempt to maintain a professional decorum.

A cloud of melancholy hangs over me all day. It turns into something more, something akin to panic. I long to return to my baby. I hope she's alright.

The bus takes an age, and my mind keeps replaying the evening Lucy Blackmore was brought in. A day that will be imprinted on my soul forever. It was so sad to see her corpse being wheeled in. A container next to her with a label on it. There was no name. The child had not even been born. Its foetal corpse tossed into a bucket like a piece of trash.

I gave it a name in an attempt to grant it some peace; some dignity. I named her Mary.

I knew I shouldn't have done it. I knew it was against all protocol, but not once have I regretted my actions. Left alone to tidy up and close down the morgue that night, I heard a noise. Unbelievably, when I removed the lid of the container I saw the child meekly moving, calling out to me with an unspoken cry.

The child had survived!

Its body was twisted, its head misshapen, and yet it was the most beautiful thing I'd ever seen.

My job, my office, I was surrounded by death; it was all I knew. And yet here was this miracle. A life reborn. The resurrection of a discarded soul.

Wrapping it in a towel, I smuggled the baby out of the morgue, doctoring the paperwork to report of its disposal. Calling in sick, I took a few weeks off and stayed at home, nursing Mary back to health; caring for her as if she were my own.

The remorse of seeing Mary's father, the guilt that sears through me is almost unbearable. Unlocking the door to my apartment I am thankful to gaze on my darling, my baby. Her beauty defies all other thoughts; washes me clean of all shame and sin.

She's grown so much in her first year. Mary now towers a foot above me. Her head is almost three times the size it once was and the soft, mushy membrane of her skull inflates and falls with the rhythmic meter of her breathing. As I walk into the room she smiles, exposing her sharpened teeth, and although her skull-like features hide her eyes in the centre of two dark craters, I swear I see them light up.

A glistening moisture shimmers over her bloated body, and whilst her legs have thickened over the last few months and can most likely support her bulk now, I'm thankful the tentacles on her back have attached themselves to the wall by that odd smelling, jelly substance that dribbles from their tips. The plaster has swollen and the wallpaper hangs in strips, saturated by my baby's secretions, but the dirty marks in the corner of the living room are a small price to pay. All children make a mess.

I embrace my baby and she cuddles me back. Her hooked talons reach around my body and push me into the mound of her plump belly. I sink into her warmth, my face gently placed against the swirling symbol on her skin; an elaborate birthmark of wavy lines trapped within a circle.

A wave of euphoria fills my being. Love flows through me, and I can feel my soul basking in a sea of serenity; a cocktail of tranquillity and contentment. I feel whole.

Eventually we part from our hug and I wipe away the slime that sticks to my clothes.

Mary gurgles. A sound that grows more crazed the longer she makes it. She's in some discomfort; has been for the last few days.

Even the clawing sounds at the door do little to soothe her. At first, when they started, I was terrified. Blind figures, freakish and ghastly, crawling down the hallway and desperate to attract the attention of Mary. I soon realised they loved her as much as I. Worshipped her. I don't understand where they come from. Souls of the dead, perhaps? Did she have something to do with their demise?

I don't allow them through the door, but Mary likes to listen to their moans of agony; their fingernails scratching against the wooden panelling. The last few nights they have been even more active than usual, but this only seems to irritate my baby.

I wonder what's gotten into her, so consider what we'll have for dinner. What treat would make her happy?

I am aware the physical food which I provide equates to only a portion of the sustenance that keeps her healthy and strong. There is an invisible influence which Mary yields. Ethereal tendrils that are unseen but very real. I am aware of the one that wraps around my mind. I cherish it as if she's holding my hand, and when I move through the hospital, taking an hour each day to watch the screams and suffering of the fresh in-patients at the A&E

department, I know she is finding nourishment in their agony.

I wonder if she has others in her sway? I suspect she does, but what is it like for them? I understand what drives me to gaze upon the horrors of the Accident and Emergency department, but what of any others? What does she make them do? Why do they believe they're doing it?

Absent-mindedly I gaze out of the window. I see a woman across the street staring intently at my flat. I recognise the long, red hair and creases across her forehead. We often report our findings to her at work: It's Detective Harrison.

I ponder for a moment as to what she's doing out there, but the call of my baby frees me from any thought outside of her.

At least it's not the priest this time, I think to myself as I close the curtains on the fading evening sky.

*

The sun's setting, but there's still enough light for me to catch the colour of her ginger hair. It flips my stomach as all red-heads seem to do. Ignoring the distraction I focus back onto the ranting phone, cutting in to stop the instructions I've heard like ten times this evening.

'Okay, okay, looks like he's leaving,' I whisper into the microphone.

'See I told you,' Steve replies, sounding smug.

'And you sure this place is worth it?' I ask.

'Man, you should have seen the gold cross Dan lifted from him,' Steve reassures me. 'I bet you there's a ton more lovely church loot in that old codger's gaff.'

'Okay cool, I'll let you know.'

'Excellent. Look, Tony, I'm not available for the rest of the evening. If you've got any problems give Dan a call.' Typical Steve, doesn't like getting his hands dirty.

As I watch the priest leave, heading to his evening prayers, I step out the car and clutch my bag tightly. The redhead is still across the street. I clock her heading my way through my peripheral vision. I love a bit of ginger and want to take a better look, check out what the face is like, but I dare not. The last thing I want to do is make eye contact and attract attention.

Heading towards the priest's house I make my way round the back with a purposeful stride. No one gives a shit about their neighbours anymore. As long as I look like I should be there, ain't no one going to question it.

Once I'm off the street and in the back garden I place my bag down, pulling out a screwdriver and hammer. The tall hedges keep me secluded, so a few well-placed taps against the lock and a bit of shoulder and I'm in.

Easy peasy.

The first thing that hits me is the smell. It's rancid, despite the air fresheners hanging from the ceiling. Dan never said anything to Steve about this god awful stink. But then the poor bastard hasn't been able to smell good since that car crash three years ago. Right now, I'm thinking he's a lucky sod.

I unzip my bag fully, ready to throw in whatever I can find of value.

Heading through the house I make my way upstairs. Start there and work down.

The bedroom is innocuous enough. No lady's underwear or sex dolls. I'm slightly disappointed, I thought all priests were perverts. There's some oil paintings on the wall, they look fancy so I place them in my bag. The silver crucifix hung beside them follows suit.

Checking under the bed, I pull out a shoebox. Classic. Full of notes. I empty its contents into my holdall then head to the next room. The smell doesn't so much hit me as smacks me round the chops the moment I open the door.

Flies buzz in the dark, and I instantly go for the light switch. My hand finds a cord and I pull on it, revealing a bathroom. The bathtub is dirty. A brownie-red liquid has stained the white ceramics. The flies crawl across the smooth surface, feasting on the residue. It doesn't take a genius to work out that's blood. Looks like he's tried to get rid of it, but that's some serious stains.

What the fuck is up with this priest?

Shit like that doesn't happen from a bad shave.

I walk backwards, allowing a wave of fear to wash through me. My senses sharpen. The house begins to creak, the windows rattle in the wind; every sound is amplified.

I head downstairs and scan a room off to the left. Something glints in the dark. I'm too scared to turn the light on in case I attract attention. Shining my torchlight into the room I inspect the wall. Bingo! There's a table with a golden cup and some silver candlestick holders. I rush over to them and throw them in my bag.

On the table there's a set of ornate daggers. I'm not sure of their worth but grab them anyway. There's a painting on the wall. A symbol crudely drawn.

It catches my eye because I remember the same symbol on a ring Dan showed me; three swirls in a circle. He said he'd swiped it from the priest, same time as he got the cross. He didn't tell Steve as he wanted it for himself. He knows I won't tell Steve either. Me and Dan go way back. Right from school. We're as good as brothers.

The similarity of the symbols on the ring and wall unexpectedly turn my stomach. I don't know why but an awful feeling creeps over me. A sound emanates from behind me. Something's crawling across the floor, scratching at the carpet. I turn and shine my light in its direction, but nothing's there. Another noise, this time above me. On the ceiling?

I throw my beam up. Again empty space.

I've got to get a grip.

Relax.

This place has clearly got me spooked.

Come on Tone, stop being a dick. I berate myself, trying to command some sense back into me.

The noise comes again, across the room. This time I'm quicker as I flash the torch. I catch sight of something moving across the wall, scuttling just out of sight like a startled silverfish. I follow the direction, shining the torch and to my horror I make out a foot. I move the beam forward, getting the measure of my target.

As the beam finally captures the whole of the thing, I see it all and wish to God I hadn't. It freezes, and somehow clings to the wall. A human figure. A woman.

I recognise the coat and boots she's wearing. It's the hottie from the street. Her hair confirms it, and as she turns to stare me down, a pair of silver eyes glow through the ginger locks that cover her face.

I run, but she launches herself and is on me in a second. Her fingers are like claws, clenched and gnarled. She rakes them across my face. My cheek tears.

I flail, trying to push her off, but she's strong; stronger than me.

I swing my bag at her and it spills open, the contents scattering across my chest. The woman strikes again. She clenches my throat and begins to squeeze. Her eyes shine like a pair of twin moons. I gasp for breath. Reaching out, I catch hold of a handle. It's one of the daggers from the mad priest's altar. Without a second thought I thrust it forward, plunging the blade deep into her neck.

She falls backwards as I feel the warm spray of her blood hit my face.

I climb to my feet and shine the light back on her. Her movements slow as her brain starves of oxygen. Her hand opens up and reveals a piece of parchment. Like the ones I saw at the Egyptian section in London's History Museum. As it slowly unfurls I recognise the symbol.

I instinctively pick it up for a better look but panic sets in again. I've made a fucking mess. I've just killed someone!

I pull my phone out of my pocket and ring Steve. It goes straight to answerphone. Shit!

I hear sounds in front of me. Behind me. Things crawling on the

59

floor all around me. A hand touches my arm and I try to scream but an icy sensation sweeps through my core and keeps me silent.

A noise threatens to deafen me. The sound of something crying. A creature in pain. A monster. Its vision takes my mind, appearing behind my eyes but commanding all my senses. It is large. A grotesque mockery of a newborn. It is hungry for the agony of others, for the cacophony of a massacre. I feel its age. It's been waiting. Frustrated by a failed attempt of calling it forth by eager but unprepared followers. Those followers crawl around my feet. They are the damned. The suffering. Their unsuccessful summoning has become their curse, and yet their devotion lives on. But they shall be proved right. The monster will be strong enough within a few years. Then the world will be ready to meet its new master.

I don't know how I know all this, but I do. Like our minds have merged. Its thoughts are my thoughts.

The touch of the tormented blind keeps my head filled with these visions and the symbol throbs in my fist, the aged script channelling the sway of the creature. I can feel its will engulfing mine. A desire to kill, to split flesh in the most prolonged and terrifying ways moves through me like a spreading ink blot. My own murderous hunger appals me.

I drop the parchment, trying to lessen the demonic influence.

Momentarily it works and my vision returns to the darkened room of the priest's house surrounded by the suffering followers that crawl within the gloom. I dial my phone again. This time I call my friend. I try to run, to make my way through the sea of sightless bodies that writhe on the carpet, but within moments I am brought down by cold, grasping hands. I keep the phone pressed against my ear, desperate for him to answer. I need help.

Dan will know what to do.

*

I glare at Daniel as he fumbles for his phone and turns it off. He can't hide his embarrassment, as well he shouldn't. The whole congregation are staring at us!

When the ringtone finally ends he looks up apologetically and the audience turn back to the priest.

I can't believe he did this to me! Why did I even bring him along?

The interruption is quickly forgotten, however, as Father Farrington continues with his sermon. He is mesmerising tonight, so inspirational to watch. I can't remember the last time he looked so enthused with the Lord's word, so at ease and peace with the world around him. Ever since that awful business in the newspapers he hadn't been the same.

Being begged by a pregnant woman, a crazy who was convinced she'd been possessed by a demon, to perform an exorcism. What would anyone do in that situation? He only wanted to help. It's in his nature. He had no idea her delusions would cause a seizure. Kill her and the baby. It had nothing to do with the exorcism. He was just trying to help. To appease her. A spiritual and psychological placebo.

It wasn't his fault.

The mess and scandal took its toll on the poor man. But tonight, for the first time, he seems free from the burdens of the past. His tranquillity and joy is infectious. We are all lapping it up. Every single word.

Except for Daniel.

He keeps fidgeting. Looking uncomfortable. Ever since he laid eyes on the priest it's like he wanted to get out of here. What is that expression, anyway? Guilt? What's he been up to now?

I hold his hand in an attempt to reassure him. After all, he never comes to church with me. But tonight he promised. He made the wonderful gesture of proposing to me, so he'd better get used to it. He'll be back here again a few times, that's for sure. Hymn choices, rehearsals, not to mention the big day itself. Escorting me to St Mary's to tell the Father our good news is only the beginning.

The engagement ring feels large on my finger. Its weight is beautiful. It's unusual but stylish. A three-pronged pattern, bejewelled and centred with the most wonderful diamond. It's a real one-of-a-kind. Daniel did me proud. He must love me so much. I wanted to tell him about the other good news. The little bun in the oven. But let's not take away from this special moment. I'll wait a week and tell him then.

Happiness upon happiness.

The good Lord is truly setting us up for a wonderful future.

Daniel fidgets again, turning his head away from the gaze of Father Farrington. What's wrong with him? Put those sunglasses down, I scream in my head. God, he can be so annoying at times!

I grit my teeth and feel a rage flush my cheeks.

I've been angry all day. My temper has been so short.

I didn't sleep well. Nightmares kept me awake, haunting me long into the day: A band of monks, persecuted and hunted down. I watched their bodies burn in my sleep; so vivid I swear I could smell their scorched flesh. A woman, the last of the order, wrapping her ring in a protective cloth, sealed by magic and hidden in her friend's house. Boarded it up in the attic before she was dragged out onto the street and beaten to death by an angry mob. Her startling, silver eyes gouged out with an ornate dagger.

I feel sick thinking about it again.

Maybe it's the hormones. They say pregnancy does funny things to you.

The sermon ends and I'm still wistful with its wise words; its musings on God's love, His forgiveness and the ability to be absolved through worship from the most heinous of transgressions.

I tell Daniel to stay put whilst I head over to the Father to share our good news.

The priest is delighted when I tell him. Such a warm, sincere smile.

The smile widens when I show him the ring, but for some

reason he's suddenly giving me the creeps. He stares at the exotic pattern, the symbol that encircles the diamond, and for a moment he zones out, his eyes glazing over with a silvery shimmer. They remind me of the woman's in my nightmare. Those beautiful silver eyes, before they were plucked from her skull... I shudder as I recall it once more.

The peaceful air that surrounded the Father all evening evaporates and his body stiffens. His grin falters, dropping at the corners and his cheeks tighten. A sudden intake of air suggests an emotion, but I am unable to fully understand what he might be thinking. He grabs my wrist and a shiver runs through me. My throat goes dry and I'm scared. I can feel myself shaking and I don't know why.

The room appears to darken and I swear I can hear something moving on the floor.

Crawling.

I turn and of course there's nothing there. Nothing I can see.

Silly me, it's probably just my hormones. I'm going to have to get used to this. Instinctively I rub my belly for comfort, smiling as I think about the child inside.

I point to Daniel when the Father asks who the lucky man is.

He smiles again, although oddly his brow wrinkles.

I tell him that Daniel is lovely but I've left him over there as he's been irritating me all evening.

'Never mind,' Father Farrington says as he places his arm around me, his eyes sparkling with that silver shimmer. 'Daniel looks familiar, but I can't remember why. I've been in a blur the last few days. I've allowed myself to deviate from my true mission. Seeing your delightful ring has brought it all back. You've reinvigorated my sense of purpose.'

He takes my hand and leads me away from the main hall into a back room. Even his walk has altered within the last few minutes. It's like he's a different person. Like someone else is in control.

This baby brain really has me thinking the most stupid things!

He opens a drawer, but my attention is taken by the pattern scratched onto the stone floor. Not professionally etched, but hacked into the flooring by a simple knife and an unsteady hand.

'That's the same as my ring,' I announce pointing at the image crudely carved into the ground.

'Don't be too hard on Daniel. The Lord says there is a divine light inside all of us. A heavenly spark. I've been seeking it for some time.' The Father speaks calmly, ignoring my remark. He steps closer with a widening smile. He's hiding something behind his back. Maybe it's a gift. 'Sometimes the light is hard to find,' he continues, 'but I'm sure it's there. Why don't we have a look for yours.'

DOLL FACE
Written by **Peter McKeirnon**

'What is your truth, Abigail?'

'I don't think I have one.'

'Then make this your truth. Do it, do it now. Yes. That's it. How does it feel, Abigail?'

'Warm, Daddy.'

'Good'

Barbara was awake but barely. Her body felt like lead and her eyes so heavy she struggled to open them. She slowly moved her legs and heard the clattering of chains and the pull of something weighty against her ankle. Then she pissed on her leg and passed out.

It was the whistling that brought her round. A low, drawn out tuneless whistle. Lifting her head from the cold floor she brought a hand up to shield her eyes. Finally, with the smallest of blinks, her eyelids parted and she was met with a bright light from a single light bulb hanging from the ceiling. Then suddenly the light went dim and the silhouette of a large man loomed over her.

'You're awake,' he said, with a voice so soft it betrayed his size.

The man leaned in. Inches from Barbara's face he grabbed her jaw with a thick chubby hand and looked her over. She was in a daze, groggy and barely able to see but she could smell him. The odour of stale sweat was overpowering and there was a heat emanating from his groin area and with it came a smell so horrid she struggled not to gag. The man was unclean.

The light shone down from behind his head, darkening his huge face. Barbara screwed up her nose in an attempt to withstand the smell. The man did not seem to notice or care.

'Your eyes, they're still glazed. Your vision will return. These things take time. Especially when you've had twice as much,' he added, looking her over keenly.

Although unable to see, she could sense he was studying her face, feeling his eyes watching her. The man removed his hand from her jaw and Barbara's head fell heavily to the floor. For the first time she was aware of her position and what's more, how naked and vulnerable she was.

'You're shivering. I had to remove your clothes. You urinated all over your dress but don't be embarrassed. It's happened to some of the others too. It appears to be a side effect from the drugs. Along with the loss of feeling and the heaviness you're experiencing. It's not permanent, don't worry. Your clothes should be dry now. I'll go check then I'll come and clean you up properly. They'll be ready for you soon. It's almost time.'

She heard the man's slow, dragging footsteps as he walked away and blinding light again flooded her vision.

She lifted a hand to shield her eyes from the light. 'Time for what?' she slurred with a terrified quiver.

The man stopped at the door, turning to face her. His weighty frame completely obscured the door from view. She strained her eyes and slowly the man came into focus. His dirty black boots. His faded blue jeans which hung straight down from his chunky legs. And his shirt. She couldn't make out if it was darkened from sweat, dirt or both.

He looked at her coldly and then smiled. A smile so big it stretched his enormous face, lifting his cheeks so high his eyes almost disappeared.

'Time for you to meet the family,' he replied with a tone that carried little emotion.

CRR'UNK!

BANG!

CLINK!

With her hands covering her ears she lowered her head to the floor. The unlocking, opening and then closing of the door rung in Barbara's ears. Combined with the intense light she now had a severe headache.

Slowly her vision became clearer and she lowered her hand from her eyes. She was in a room, chained to a wall by her ankles. The room was small with stone walls and no windows. In front of her against the far wall was an old wicker chair and in the wall on her left was a large heavy duty door. She was without clothes, dirty and her body felt like lead.

'What the fuck is going on?' she cried.

She looked to the wicker chair. Between its legs was a bowl, half filled with water. Immediately, as if seeing the water triggered the reaction, she found it difficult to swallow, realising how dry her throat was.

Pushing her hands into the ground she tried to stand but it was no good. Her legs were too heavy. Instead she stretched across the ground; grasping at the floor with her fingers to pull herself forward. Sluggishly she moved closer to the bowl; the slow jangling of chains accompanied her movement. It was the most difficult thing she had ever done.

Finally she made it to the bowl and reached out drinking from it greedily. Large gulps of water hit her dry throat hard and it hurt. Like sharp pieces of rock hitting the back of her mouth. Suddenly she couldn't breathe. Her throat closed over and she was choking. She began to panic; jerking forwards whilst grabbing at her neck.

CRR'UNK!

BANG!

CLINK!

The man came in through the door carrying Barbara's dress.

'What are you doing?' he yelled, bounding over to her.

He sprung forward, at a speed that appeared impossible for his size, grabbing Barbara and kicking the bowl of water away. He forced open her mouth stabbed his fingers inside, deep into her throat making her puke heavily. Watery bile ran down the man's hand and arm dripping onto her newly cleaned dress. He removed his fingers from her throat and Barbara fell forward to the floor, gasping deeply.

'You have to sip! You cannot drink normally, not yet. If you do, your throat shuts over and you start to choke. But I guess you know that now huh? You'll be fine in a couple of hours,' he said. 'But until then, sip!'

The man looked around the room. At the kicked over water bowl and vomit covered floor.

'Look at this mess. You've ruined your dress again. After I'd just got it cleaned too,' he sighed, holding the dress out to look at it properly. There's no time to clean it up again. Oh they won't be happy about this. They'll want you well presented. Looking your best. I'll have to find you something else. I can't give you to them wearing this. Not now.'

'What family, what are you talking about? Why are you keeping me here? Look, please, Mr... let me go. I promise I won't say anything or tell anyone. Just let me go, you'll never hear from me again I swear it,' she pleaded, tears rolling down her face.

The man walked towards the door. Pausing for a moment with his back to her, 'Nobody leaves. Nobody. I'll be back with new clothes soon. Remember, if you need water, sip it. You can't die on me too.'

CRR'UNK!

BANG!

CLINK!

'You can't die on me too.'

Those words triggered a memory. She remembered how she had got there.

*

Barbara hit her head hard then opened her eyes. It was the pain that brought her round. With blurred vision and a pounding headache she struggled to focus. Where the hell was she?

It took a few seconds, but she soon realised she was in the boot of a moving car. She was cramped and could barely move. There was something else in there with her too. Something big restricting her movement. What's more her feet were bound and her hands tied behind her back. Confused and with panic she began to struggle, screaming as loud as she could in an attempt to be heard over the noise of the engine.

'Help! Somebody help! Anyone! Get me the fuck out of here!'

Then suddenly the car stopped with a jolt. Jerking her body backwards she bumped hard into whatever it was that was next to her. She heard the car door open then slam shut, followed by the sound of footsteps heading her way.

The boot opened and the shadowy figure of a large man loomed over her; a full moon brought the only light. The man reached inside and grabbed her with his huge hands, lifting her from the boot and dumping her on the ground. She hit the ground hard, grazing skin from her legs.

Barbara checked her surroundings. A thin fog hovered just above the ground and in the distance was what appeared to be an old farmhouse. Trees surrounded her, rustling in a mild wind.

The man reached down, grabbed her hair and dragged her away from the car, towards the farmhouse. The skin from her legs and feet scraped and shredded against the sharp stony ground.

'Stay here, don't even think about moving,' the man said with a soft haunting voice, as he walked back towards the car, muttering to himself as he moved.

Barbara reached for her skin torn legs. They were too painful to touch. She looked around. The man had left her in the entrance to the farmhouse grounds. The fog was still low but she could see walls to either side of her and right ahead was a large dilapidated house. To the side of the house was an old stone building.

With her hands tied behind her back she lay down, rubbing her rope covered wrists back and forth against the rocky ground, desperately trying to free herself. It was working. She could feel the rope loosening against her wrists as it split and shredded against the gravel.

She heard slow laboured footsteps accompanied by grunts and groans. Out of the fog the man re-appeared and Barbara stopped trying to free herself. The man was dragging something big and heavy behind him. The closer he got the more visible he became. Barbara looked on in terror. He was dragging a body. Wrapped in bin bags and tied with tape. The man dumped the body next to her and caught his breath. She looked at the big man, panting with exhaustion then she shifted her eyes and looked at the body. Now she knew what she had been pushed up against in the boot of the car.

Full of fear she moved her eyes along the body until she reached the head. The impact of the body hitting the ground had ripped the bin bag exposing the face. Barbara became numb. She couldn't move and she couldn't speak as her eyes looked upon the face of her sister.

*

The man, using Barbara's dress, wiped puke and saliva from his hand and arm. Then he noticed a change in her. A change he had seen in others before her.

'You're remembering. I recognise that look. The fear in your eyes. The realisation. I've seen it many times. It means it's almost time. I must clean you up or they won't be happy. I'll be right back and remember, sip if you need to drink. Sip.'

CRR'UNK!

The man stood quietly for a few seconds, facing the open door. Then he spoke.

'The dead girl. She was your friend right? Sister maybe? Yeah. Sister. That's who she was. She struggled too much, she wasn't meant to die. The family don't like it when they die. But sometimes they struggle and, well… accidents happen. If it makes you feel any better. She was better going out the way she did than the way she was meant to.'

'What the fuck does that mean?' Barbara cried.

Turning his head to look at her the man replied, 'You'll see.'

BANG!

CLINK!

Barbara sat slumped against the wall, crying for her sister. The room was spinning and her mind swirling. If she had anything left inside she would have vomited again.

'Why is this happening?' she cried out. 'Why?'

Finding strength she held back her tears and struggled to her feet. Standing for the first time since waking. She looked around the stark room once more. Nothing but the wicker chair, water bowl and the chains that shackled her to the wall.

She hobbled over to the water bowl, taking it to the door. Down on her knees she poured what water remained through the small gap under the door and watched as it trickled back towards her. Wherever she was being kept, she was below ground level.

Grabbing her chains she pushed her feet against the wall she was shackled to and began to pull using what little strength she had but it was pointless. She slumped back down, drained with her back against the wall and her head lowered. There she noticed something scraped into the stone floor. One word.

'FIGHT.'

*

The fog was growing making it almost impossible to see. The man walked towards the farm house, leaving Barbara next to her dead sister. She watched him take a few steps then the fog took him. Frantically she again began rubbing her rope tied wrists against the rough ground until finally the rope snapped and her arms were freed.

Reaching to untie her ankles she heard talking in the near distance, stopping her dead in her tracks.

'Dead? How dead? Is the face ok?' she heard a gruff throaty voice say.

'No, sorry Uncle,' the man replied.

'God damn it man. If you weren't family I would have killed you a long time ago? We need them alive and undamaged. Especially the face. Never touch the face. What about the other one?'

'She's fine Uncle. A few marks on her wrists and ankles but no more than usual.'

'Take her in. You can do what you please with the dead one. Fuck it, eat it, I don't care, just get it off my land.'

Barbara heard footsteps approaching. She desperately pulled at the rope tying her ankles and got lucky, loosening the knot just enough to lift her feet free. She took one last look at her sister and placed a loving hand on her head. Then she picked herself up and ran as fast as her legs would let her. She had no idea where she was going and with the fog so thick she might as well have been blind. She only managed a few yards before a strong hand grabbed her arm.

'It's pointless to run. You can't escape from here,' the large man said as he pulled her into his chest, jabbing a needle into her neck.

*

Barbara, her heart racing, stood facing the door. She was trembling with the wicker chair in her hands. It was her only chance of escape.

CRR'UNK!

BANG!

CLINK!

The door opened and the huge man filled the doorway. He was

carrying a clean dress, a sponge and a large bowl filled with soapy water.

'Found you a dress. I've collected lots over the years. Not as nice as yours but at least it's not covered in puke..'

Barbara brought the chair crashing into the man's chest forcing him to drop the dress and the bowl, sending soapy water spilling to the ground. The man quickly recovered, taking a strong step towards Barbara. As his foot hit the soapy floor he slipped, falling backwards, hitting his head on the ground. The crack of his skull hitting the hard floor was loud enough for Barbara to hear and she watched as blood poured from the back of his head, mixing with water then dispersing into channels. The man was dead.

She pulled at the chains once more but there was no give. Dejected she looked down to her legs. The chains around each ankle were secured by padlocks. The man must have the key.

Frantically she searched his body. Placing her hands inside his pockets she felt a sweaty warmth emanating from his obese body. She retrieved a set of keys and desperately set about trying each one on the locks to her shackles. In little to no time she found the correct key. She was free.

She took the dress and pulled it over her head, stepping over the man to leave the room. Outside the room she found a steep set of winding stairs. It was dark with the only light coming from large thick candles, stuck to the steps by their own wax. Adrenalin pumped through her body and her heart was beating out of her chest. She turned her head and looked down at the dead man and remembered her sister.

'Fucking freak!' she screamed, spitting at his blood soaked head.

She turned away from the man and hobbled out of the room, began her climb of the steps, the cold ground delivering sharp pain to her bare feet.

Reaching the top of the stairs she found herself facing a bleak corridor with a closed door at the far end. The walls, like the room and the stairway behind her, were stone and again, only a few lit candles gave light but now she could hear rain.

Barbara ran to the door at the end of the corridor and pulled on the handle. Locked. She felt a draft. A cool rush of air tickling her feet as it rushed underneath the door. She tried key after key from the set she had taken but none fit the lock. Only one key remained. She placed it in the lock and turned it.

CLICK!

The door was unlocked. Quickly she pulled it open. The first thing she saw was rain as a wind blew it straight into her face, flooding her vision. Then, stepping out of the rain and into the doorway she saw a man, tall and thin with skin creased like nothing she had ever seen. The man gave a thin, evil smile when suddenly and with haste, he stabbed a needle into her neck.

Barbara opened her eyes. Once more she had an intense headache and she felt seasick her mind was swimming so much. Light blinded her eyes. Only this time it felt different. She was not back in the room where she had been captive. She felt warm and to a degree, comfortable. As her vision cleared and the fog in her head dispersed she looked to the light above her. It was a light bulb housed inside a paper chandelier. The chandelier was pink, making the light warm and soft.

She tried to lift her head but couldn't. Her arms, her legs, she couldn't move anything. Barbara's entire body was numb and without feeling. Only her eyes had movement. Even her mouth, open and slobbering, would not say the words she tried to say.

'Help!' Barbara wanted to scream. 'Someone, please. Help me!'

Nothing. She made no sound. Just trickles of drool dribbling down the side of her mouth.

She moved her eyes to take in as much of the room as she could see. There were shelves covering the walls, lined with creepy porcelain dolls.

'I'm in a bedroom. A girl's bedroom,' she thought.

Inside she was crying hysterically. Loaded with fear and distress. Outside she lay still, only her eyes told how terrified she was. Then she heard footsteps and the man with creased skin walked into her view leaning over her so that his thin, weathered and wrinkle lined face was inches from her own. His hand touched her eye, removing a single tear.

'She's ready,' he said. 'Are you ready, Abigail?'

'Ready daddy.' A young girl spoke.

The man moved his head away from Barbara's face and a young girl, dressed like the porcelain dolls that adorned the walls was revealed standing next to him. In her hand was a scalpel. Barbara looked at the girl and the instrument in her hand then she looked at the dolls again, noticing something horrific she had not seen at first glance. The dolls faces were human.

'What is your truth, Abigail?' the man spoke, his eyes fixed on Barbara.

'I don't think I have one.' The young girl replied blankly.

'Then make this your truth,' he replied, turning to the young girl, taking her hand with the scalpel and moving it towards Barbara's face. 'Do it, do it now.'

With the man's guiding hand the young girl sliced the scalpel into Barbara's skin. Starting at the hairline above her forehead then moving across and down to her temple.

'Yes. That's it,' the man smiled. 'How does it feel, Abigail?'

'Warm, Daddy,' the girl replied without emotion.

'Good.'

A TASTE OF MERCY
Written by **Andrew Freudenberg**

The saw quivered as he pulled it free from the almost severed leg. With a grunt of exhaustion he dropped the dripping steel onto the floor and took a deep breath. One final tug on the limb and the last few sinews of connecting flesh broke. It took the rest of his strength to pick it up and carry it over to the growing pile of anonymous body parts. He gasped for air, his chest aching in the thick miasma of slaughter, smoke and dissipated mustard gas.

Marlow wiped his watering eyes with a bloody sleeve and looked around the room. Two colleagues struggled to keep the torrent of eviscerated youth alive. Wilson was attempting a tracheotomy on a boy who was turning blue. Beyond him Lawrence was shaking his head and gesturing for another patient.

'Doctor Marlow?'

The orderly's voice bought him back to his senses. He looked at the young man. Like all of them, his green uniform was almost entirely stained by bodily fluids.

'What?'

He hardly recognized his own voice, so thick was it with phlegm and exhaustion.

'Have you finished with this one?'

A loud boom interrupted their conversation and a shower of dust fell from the ceiling. Activity in the room paused for a few seconds and then carried on.

'Wait a moment.'

Marlow busied himself securing a tourniquet above the cut and then nodded to the orderly.

'Take him away.'

He used the short respite to curse his life and wipe his hands on a filthy towel. They were the first port of call for those patients that wouldn't survive transport to more civilized facilities. Of course treatment here guaranteed nothing. A drunken argument with his immediate superior had secured him a place in this constant hell, right in the trenches with all the other poor fools. He had never imagined that he, with his old school connections and worthy qualifications, would be abandoned to this fate.

There was a thud as a new arrival landed in front of him. He looked down and a chill ran through his aching spine.

'This is a girl.'

The orderly shrugged.

'It's a local, is what it is. Christ knows what she was doing out there.'

Marlow looked at her again. For a split second she reminded him of a waitress at his club back in London and he was temporarily transported to the cozy ambience of that place. She was a pretty thing, no more than eighteen or nineteen, high cheekbones and pale white skin splattered with mud and gore.

He looked down at her chest and sighed. Something, probably an errant shell, had torn her wide open. He could see splintered ribs and, within, her heart, struggling valiantly to maintain a constant beat.

'Is she going to make it sir?'

The orderly's question sounded obscene to him, an intruder on a sacred moment.

'Get out!'

The man frowned and ducked through the low entrance back into the trenches.

'Monsieur...'

Her voice was a fragment of a whisper. She stared up at him with startling green eyes.

'Aidez moi.'

'Don't speak.'

He could see that she was fading as he watched and searched for something useful to do. He removed a fleshy fragment of bone that had broken away from her rib cage and absent-mindedly put it into his pocket. Taking it away revealed a large tear in her aorta. Dark fluid was seeping out in diminishing spurts. It was beyond hopeless.

'Est-ce-que je vais mourir?'

He could barely hear the words above the rushing sound that filled his ears. There seemed no appropriate response other than the brutal truth so he said nothing. He stroked her cheek and waited for it to be over. Recognition, despair and finally acceptance passed over her and then she was gone. He closed her eyelids with the palm of his hand and stepped back. Time slowed as he watched the shadows from the gas lamps flickering across her motionless corpse.

All the clamor in the room dissolved into white noise as he stood staring at her angelic face. Something in his mind cracked and he knew that everything in his world had changed. For months he had repeated the same bloody routine until he could no longer see beyond the mechanics of his job. The thousands of ruined young men that came under his knife no longer touched him emotionally. He saw them as part of this monstrous lunacy in which he was forced to participate. He resented them. Their wounds had scarred his spirit and turned him into a machine. Now this dead girl had awoken something within him, something pure. He grasped her limp hand and gently squeezed it.

'Who are you?' he murmured.

As he waited for an answer that could never come, he noticed for the first time that she was wearing a pendant. He lifted it with his spare hand and wiped off the moisture with his thumb. It was a delicate painting of the Virgin Mary. Although he had long ago lost any religious inclination its beauty moved him almost to tears. He lowered it back down to rest against her neck. Looking at his hand he was struck by how much of her blood covered his fingers.

He stared at his sticky digits. The urge to lick them was overwhelming. His mouth went dry as this alien concept took hold.

'Marlow?' It was Wilson. 'Are you alright?'

He looked down at his fingers and then up at his fellow cutter.

'I'm fine.'

'You look like you've had enough for the day old chap.'

Wilson looked at the girl.

'Christ I hate it when they blow up the natives. Why don't you clean up and get some rest? It looks as if we're through the worst of this round.'

Marlow nodded. He went over to the bowl of pink water that served as a basin and washed quickly.

'I'll try and get some sleep.'

A thick fog had fallen over the trenches and he shivered in the cold night air. All was quiet. He trudged through the mud in a daze, not noticing the few halfhearted salutes that he received. Finally he reached the foxhole that he called home. It offered little comfort other than cover from the rain, but even that was a luxury most didn't enjoy. As a surgeon he could have slept behind the line, but he felt estranged from that world, preferring to simply fall into a coma between shifts.

Once he had crawled in, he lay down in the darkness and pulled his coat tighter around him. Out of habit, he felt in his pockets for his hip flask, intending to down the contents before attempting to sleep. The rum was harsh but it numbed him and took away the foul taste that lingered after a day's work. This time his hand fell on something sharp and hard. He took it out and realized that it was the rib shard that he had removed from the girl's chest.

This was far from the first peculiar item that he'd shoved into his pocket in the heat of the moment. He'd found twisted bullets, shell fragments, and on one occasion several fingers.

He gripped the fragment with an illogical fear that someone would try and steal it from him; this relic was his. He clutched it to his chest and looked around for challengers but found none. He lifted it to his nose and inhaled. It smelled sweet and the odor made him light headed; exhaustion lifted from his body and for the first time in an age, he felt rested. After a while he noticed that he was salivating; his stomach churned. Months of canned beef and beans had taken their toll but this was something more. This was a need that he couldn't explain or justify to himself. Almost of its own accord the rib found itself brushing his lips, touching his teeth...

Reverentially he gnawed some of the raw meat from it. He shook with pleasure and shock as it melted in his mouth. His whole body felt as if it was in the grip of an electric current. He sat up and attacked the bone with vigor, this time without any reservation. Soon it was picked clean and he stuffed it back into his pocket.

He felt weightless. It astonished him how he could have forgotten his own humanity in such a short period of time. This knowledge was a gift; the girl was a gift. She had been sent to save him from himself. It all seemed so obvious now, even if he struggled to understand how this could have come about. It was not that he was undeserving, far from it. It was rather that he would never have expected the universe to serve him in such a thoughtful manner. Of course a part of him knew that he was insane but he was living in a world where normality had been forgotten. She had died so that he could absorb her purity and become someone new. Elation overcame him as him as his concept of reality expanded beyond the filth and murder in which he lived. There had to be a greater purpose in store for him but he couldn't see what it was. He needed to absorb more of her if he was to fulfill his destiny.

The fog was clearing as he stepped back out into the trench. He could see the stars sparkling in the sky above. Corpses were kept in a canvas-covered pit behind the lines and he headed towards the junction that would take him there.

'Good evening Doctor.'

He almost knocked the Padre over as he turned the corner.

'How are you this evening?'

Marlow looked at the disheveled figure with his horn rimmed

81

glasses and dog collar. What could he possibly say to him now? He seemed transparent, two dimensional, almost a walking illusion of life.

'I'm fine', he managed, and carried on walking. The priest watched him walk away, a concerned expression on his face.

The charnel pit was dark underneath the canvas. As his eyes became more accustomed to the light, he could see rats moving about like shadows around him. The girl wasn't hard to find as the space was nearing capacity and she had been thrown on to a heap near the entrance.

He knelt down next to her and breathed in her aroma. He shuddered. She was perfection. Instinctively he knew that her heart was meant to be his. He pushed his hands into her chest cavity and grasped it. With a little effort the muscles and fibrous tissues holding it in place tore, and it came away from her body. Hungrily he sank his teeth into it.

Meat and bloody juices filled his mouth, the overflow running down his chin. It created a collage of textures on his tongue like nothing that he had ever experienced before. As soon as there was space he chewed off more, snorting like a pig as he breathed through his nose. He couldn't recall ever eating anything so delicious.

Lost in reverie he dropped the mangled organ and pushed his face into her. Rabidly he bit at the tender morsels that he came into contact with. He wasn't thinking now, he had passed into a realm of existence that consisted only of sensation. His entire head was now completely covered in her gore. He leant back to take a breath before scooping out a fist full of entrails and jamming it into his mouth.

'Hello?'

Before he could react to the voice he was joined by a lone figure carrying a lamp. The sudden change in illumination dazzled him, sending spots streaming across his vision.

'Doctor Marlow? Is that you?'

The holy man squinted at the bloody apparition before him. Marlow blinked back at him with eyes that were the only white in a sea of dark red.

'What are you doing?'

A low growl came from Marlow's throat. How dare this nobody interrupt him?

'Good God man, are you eating that poor girl?'

The priest gagged and took a panicked step backwards as Marlow leapt. They collapsed into a pile of corpses, the priest desperately trying to detach Marlow's hands from around his throat. The lamp fell and smashed. The two rolled around the uneven surface as one man tried to prevent the other from ending his life. Marlow was unstoppable, his whole body wild with energy. The priest's burst of adrenaline was short lived and soon he weakened. As Marley choked the last vestiges of life from his prey's body he roared. It was an inhuman sound. He had been transformed. This cursed war had rendered him into a broken automaton. He had been lost in the dark but now he was born again as a creature of the light. No one could hold him back again.

He ran laughing from the pit, back towards the trench. A bedraggled quartet of soldiers scattered as he barreled through them.

On reaching the trench, Marlow paused. He looked at the mud filled ditch that had been his home for so long and sighed. There was nothing to achieve here in this dead end. It had sucked the life from his very bones in return for his efforts but now he was free. It was time to leave. He walked up to the foot of one of the rotting wooden ladders that led up over the side and into no man's land. No sooner had he put one foot on the bottom rung than he felt a hand on his shoulder.

'You really don't want to do that old chap.'

It was one of the soldiers that he had pushed aside earlier.

'You look very tired. Why don't you climb down and come and have a cup of tea with us?'

Marlow shrugged the hand away and climbed up another step before glancing back. The tired faces displayed a mixture of concern and distaste. On one hand they were obviously of the opinion that he had lost his mind. On the other they were very aware that to leave the trench would be desertion, if not suicide.

'Come on down. We'll have a nice chat.'

The Doctor twisted round and kicked the man in the nose. His victim cursed and grabbed hold of Marlow's waistband. Holding tightly to a step with one hand Marlow reached into his pocket and found the bone. He summoned all his strength and stuck it into the soldier's neck as far as it would go. He was immediately released as the man fell to the floor. A barrage of abuse followed him as he sprang to the top and leapt into the beyond.

Barbed wire grabbed at his ankles and he almost fell as he stumbled over the rotting departed. Shots rang out behind him as his fellow compatriots attempted to end his flight. One tore through the soft flesh of his upper arm. He ignored the burning sensation and ran on. It felt good to be out in the open. It reminded him of the Heath at home, which in turn made him think of his family. He imagined their delight when he returned and told them of his transformation. He had lost the photograph that he had once treasured but their innocent faces were still crystal clear to him. How relieved they would be that he hadn't returned as a bitter husk, stuffed only with the indignities of war.

A machine gun opened up from the other side and he threw himself to the ground. Bullets flew over his head. He had landed between a pair of recumbent cadavers, one German and one British. He lay between them on his back staring up at the moon and listening to the voices in the night.

'I can't see him anymore.'

'Perhaps Fritz got him.'

'Er ist tot.'

'Wie wissen Sie? Er ist verschwunden.'

Words arrived on the wind in fragments. He breathed in deeply, filling his lungs with the freezing night air. He thought that he could faintly hear a string quartet by Shubert. It had to be his imagination but he let it wash over him nonetheless. The machine gunner had given up wasting ammunition and peace had fallen over the deadly wasteland. Marlow basked in the silence and soaked up the atmosphere. He thought if he could just imagine himself back in London then it would become a reality. He closed his eyes and relaxed. The world seemed to be drifting away from him. He didn't hear the soft thud of the distant mortar launch nor the whining whistle as the shell fell towards him. It was a direct hit and, amidst the fire and mutilation, what passed for sanity was once more restored to the front line.

CHOCOLATE
Written by **Mason Sabre**

With a huff, Rebecca snapped the lid back onto the empty tub. This had to stop. Her daughters' sudden kleptomaniac tendencies were worrying her. Chocolate she understood, but it was other things she couldn't fathom. The empty tub told her that once again, Cynthia had got into the kitchen.

Rebecca opened cupboard after cupboard, surveying the items, taking an on-site itinerary of what was there and what was missing. This week alone she had noticed two tins of air freshener, a bag of popcorn and even a packet of cooked meat vanish from the kitchen. She didn't know why. Cynthia wouldn't give her an answer.

'Who,' she yelled even though she knew, 'has been in this box again and taken the last bar of chocolate I had?'

Her voice echoed around the house, and Cynthia, her nine-year-old daughter, froze with one foot on the bottom step. When Kevin, her older brother, appeared at the top of the stairs, she backed away.

Kevin watched her, tilting his head and listening as their mother continued her rant about not having anything to herself, having to deal with the kids during the school holidays, and their father not lifting a damn finger to help.

He walked down the stairs towards Cynthia; she backed away even more and wrapped her small fingers around the stolen prize in her pocket.

'What are you doing?' he asked her.

'Nothing,' she said, and she shoved the chocolate deeper into the pocket of her jacket.

'It was you again, wasn't it? Give it back,' he demanded when

87

he reached the bottom step. 'It's Mum's, not yours.'

'I don't have it.'

'You're a liar.' As he advanced towards her, she stumbled back, but before she could do anything; he rammed his hand into her pocket and found the chocolate her hand was clutching.

'You don't have it then, do you?' he goaded her as he freed his hand. She swung away, but he caught her arm and tried to pull her hand from her pocket. She yelled at him to get off her, but to no avail. He was determined. That chocolate wasn't hers, and he was going to take it back. He was bigger and stronger than her—she was going to lose the fight.

She didn't even think as she yelled out his name in protest, which managed to bring their mother racing into the hallway to see what was going on.

'Kevin,' Rebecca scolded him, 'what are you doing?'

'Cynthia has your chocolate,' he tattled. 'I was getting it back for you.'

'Cynthia? Is this true?'

Kevin took a step back, a smug smile spreading across his face knowing he had just got her into a lot of trouble. Cynthia tugged her jacket around herself nervously, her hands still stuffed in her pockets. Looking down at her shoes, she shook her head.

'It's in her pocket,' cried Kevin, pointing at her jacket. 'I was trying to get it back for you.'

Rebecca's lips drew into a thin line. 'Turn out your pockets, Cynthia.'

Cynthia didn't want to. That chocolate was *hers*. She stood firm and pursed her lips together, shaking her head once more at her mother's request.

'Turn out your pockets. I won't tell you again. We've talked about this behaviour, Cynthia. It is wrong to steal; you know that. Even if it is just from me, it is wrong to sneak things out and take them upstairs. I'm going to count to three, and then I will come and get it. 1 … 2 …'

'But it's for Roger,' Cynthia wailed. 'He needs it. All the other stuff makes him sick; maybe he likes chocolate. He'll go away if I don't give it to him.'

Rebecca sighed. She didn't know what she was supposed to do about this. Roger was Cynthia's imaginary friend and recently her excuse for stealing. Roger always wanted things, according to her.

She mentally counted to ten. She couldn't understand what had got into Cynthia. It wasn't like her to be this way.

She had even considered putting a lock on the kitchen door, but Steven had said it was a little drastic. 'It's just Cynthia having an imagination; all kids do these kinds of things,' he would say, brushing off her complaints and making her feel foolish. 'Let her have those things. She isn't doing anyone any harm. She'll grow out of it.' Rebecca had tried to plead her case; it wasn't about *what* she was stealing, it was that she *was* stealing. If they didn't do something now, wouldn't Cynthia grow up to think she could just take anything? Steven had it easy. He went to work and didn't have to deal with the kids' correct upbringing.

Rebecca held out her hand and glared at her daughter, waiting for the chocolate to be returned. Kevin sniggered as Cynthia's shoulders slumped and her bottom lip quivered. She slid her hand out of her pocket but didn't look at her mother or Kevin. Slowly, she handed the chocolate over.

'Roger really does need it,' she grumbled one more time before the chocolate was gone forever. The way she said it made Rebecca feel cruel, but she had to do this. It was for Cynthia's own good. She had to learn she couldn't steal.

The chocolate was broken and had melted in the middle where Cynthia had clutched it. 'Go to your room, please. I don't want to see you again until you have thought about your actions and what you are going to do in the future. Stealing is not going to be tolerated.'

'But—'

'No buts. Upstairs … right now.'

Cynthia didn't say anything more. She just sighed and walked back towards the stairs, away from her mother and brother. They didn't know or understand. They didn't care about Roger.

Kevin leant into her as she walked past him. 'Busted,' he whispered into her ear and she lashed out, bashing him with her arm and pushing him out of the way. She raced up the stairs, stomping her feet down as hard as she could with each step.

Two days later, there had been no more incidents—or not that Rebecca had noticed. She watched the kitchen like a hawk. Every time Cynthia moved, her eyes followed her warily.

'Do you fancy going to the park?' Rebecca asked her as she walked by now. 'It's a nice day outside; we might not get another before you go back to school.' She hadn't been out at all, staying cooped up in the playroom on the third floor most of the time. It wasn't healthy. The fresh air would do both of them some good.

'Roger will be all alone,' she said. 'He gets scared by himself.'

'Just an hour. He'll be okay. I promise.'

Rebecca got their coats and began to lock the house up before Cynthia had any more time to protest. It wouldn't be long and perhaps spending a little time together would do them both some good as well. It was worth a shot. Her daughter was changing, and she suspected it was more than just growing up things.

She played, but she kept herself away from the other children. Rebecca watched her and wondered if maybe they needed to get some professional advice before it was too late. What if it were more than just a phase?

As she watched Cynthia playing in the park, one of the mum's from the PTFA came to sit on the bench next to her. Lucy's perfectly manicured hands, perfect clothes and hair, perfect smile, looked nothing like hers—-or any other mother who was currently sitting at home with the kids on the school holidays, just about ready to rip their hair out.

'Nice day, isn't it?' she crooned.

Rebecca nodded and forced a smile onto her lips. It was. 'Yes, lovely day.'

Lucy wasn't really interested, though; she launched into tales of what the last two weeks had held for her and all the drama with her friends. Rebecca found her mind drifting off. How any person could care so much about such insignificant things was beyond her. Lucy's haughty tone said she thought she was better than them all. She had no idea that most of the mothers found her pathetic. She lived in the same neighbourhood; her husband was just a builder, for Christ's sake. She came from a council estate. You could give a person money, but you could never take them common out of them—and no one had with Lucy, that was for sure.

She looked around for Cynthia, deciding to get them both home before she died of boredom from the idle chit-chat. When she realised she couldn't see her anywhere, she jumped to her feet, her heart missing a beat. 'Have you seen my Cynthia?' she asked Lucy, interrupting her irritating monologue. 'She was just here.'

'Er, no—'

Heart in her throat, she started to run through the playground, calling out her name over and over again. She checked the swings, the slide, the climbing frame....

Nothing.

People watched as she started to yell in earnest now, panic rising to fever pitch.

'Cynthia—'

A tugging on her jacket had her spinning around to face some child she didn't know.

'She went to the sweet shop,' the boy said.

She rushed off in that direction with just a quick thanks.

'You're in so much trouble when I find you,' she muttered to herself. She raced from the park, over the road, navigating an elderly woman on a mobility scooter before dashing through the doorway of the said shop.

Cynthia was standing there, head down, the shop owner's hand on her shoulder.

Rebecca's heart sank.

'Oh, no. What has she done?'

The woman behind the counter held up three large, family-sized bars of chocolate. 'She had these in her coat; she was trying to take them. We saw her do it. We were trying to ask for her address, so we don't have to call the police. Are you her mother?'

'I am.' Steven was going to have to face this now, instead of brushing it off as childish stuff. It was one thing to steal from the house, but to sneak off and shoplift? That had pushed it too far. 'How much do I owe you?'

'Nothing,' the woman said. 'We got them back.'

'Ah, no. I want to buy them,'—she glanced at her daughter— 'and then you are going to give these to the donation bags at the supermarket. You will pay for them out of your own pocket money, and you will write this lady here a letter of apology. Do you understand?'

'No.' Cynthia raised a defiant chin to her mother. 'Roger needs them, and you're taking them away. The stupid children can get their own.'

Heat filled her cheeks, flushing with embarrassment from her daughter's words. 'I'm really sorry,' she spluttered with an apologetic smile to the woman. She fished in her pocket for some change, paid for the bars and then hurried Cynthia out of there and back to the house before she could say anything else.

When they got through the front door, she caught Cynthia by the arm before she could run up the stairs to the attic again. 'Not so fast, young lady. You and I need to have a chat.'

'Roger needs me,' she whined.

'Roger can wait.'

'But he'll die—'

'He isn't real. You have to stop this.'

'He *is* real.'

'No, he isn't,' she ground out.

'He is … you just don't believe me. He is … I promise. He's hungry. I have to take him food, and you made it go away.' Cynthia grabbed the bag with the chocolate from her mother's hand and then ran up the stairs to the landing. 'I'll show you.'

Rebecca scowled. 'Now, you listen to—'

'Come on,' she called down to her mother.

She sighed, then followed her up the stairs, across the landing and then to the attic stairs for the playroom. As soon as she opened the door, Rebecca gasped and slapped a hand over her mouth. She had never smelt anything so retched in all her life. Bile rose and stung the back of her throat, her eyes watering from the stench.

'He's a little stinky,' Cynthia said, and Rebecca wondered how she hadn't smelt it before. Then she noticed the canisters, many of them lined up on the window ledge. So this was what had happened to all of the air fresheners.

'There's no one here,' Rebecca muttered exasperatedly, scanning the room and pulling her blouse up over her nose and mouth to get rid of the smell.

'He's over here.' Her daughter opened the bag and took the chocolate out. She removed the wrapper and broke some of the squares off.

Rebecca didn't stop her—if this was the only way to prove Roger wasn't real and to stop all this theft, then so be it.

She watched as Cynthia crept to a door on the other side of the room. When the attic had been converted, they hadn't managed to do it all. Where the roof sloped down, they had decided to wall it off. It could be used as extra storage; it only needed a floor, no walls or anything. So Steven had fitted a door.

As Cynthia turned the knob and pulled the door partially open, Rebecca craned her neck to see better. It was too dark to make out anything, however.

She placed the chocolate just outside the open door and then backed away. Rebecca gasped when she heard movement, and automatically moved closer to her daughter so that she was within arm's reach. She watched the door, wondering what the hell had been under her roof all this time and she had been blissfully unaware. Had Cynthia brought an animal—or worse—some tramp into their house, and he had been living in the attic for weeks?

A strangled cry left her lips when a gnarled ... *hand* came out. But it was no normal hand. It had fingers and nails, but no real skin. Dark, rotted muscle twisted around bones and fingers that moved awkwardly.

Rebecca grabbed Cynthia and stumbled back, pulling her daughter with her.

'It's Roger, see?' A wide smile spread across Cynthia's face. 'I told you he was real.'

Horrified, Rebecca stared at the lump that dragged itself out of the closed off compartment. The head had a dent in it, looking as though something had hit it, and a bloodied socket that was missing its eye. Skin folded back from the forehead, exposing dirty bone. As he lifted his head to look at her, she noticed a gap in the flesh of his throat. He had no legs and just one arm.

She stood clutching her daughter, rooted to the spot, but he made no attempt to move towards them.

'Eat it,' Cynthia encouraged Roger, trying to shrug her mother off. When he made no move to take the offering, her shoulders slumped. 'He doesn't eat anything I bring him. I give him lots of things, but he doesn't want them.'

Speechless and numb with shock, Rebecca tried to back away on rubbery legs, pulling Cynthia with her.

Her child had brought a goddamn *zombie* into their house.

Good Lord.

Blindly stumbling back, she tripped over a small stool and went toppling to the floor, cracking her head off an old side table. Pain shot through her, and her vision went dark. She heard words somewhere far off, but each time she tried to open her eyes, the room spun.

She tried to warn her daughter to get out, but no words left her throat.

'This is what you eat?' Cynthia's cheerful voice echoed in her head.

Rebecca felt a cold, clammy hand snake around her ankle.

'See, Mummy … I told you Roger was real.'

THE CONTRACT
Written by **Shaun Hutson**

Frank Hacket hated hospitals.

He hated the smell of disinfectant and he hated the fact that they reminded him of his own mortality. For many he realized they were places of hope, salvation and belief but Hacket saw them as places of pain, suffering and death. Once you went in, your chances of coming out again were slim as far as he was concerned.

He'd seen that happen with both his parents when he was younger and, more recently, he'd seen it happen with his wife. Just four years earlier she had died after spending three weeks in Intensive Care, the victim of a drunken driver and an accident that should never have happened. Apart from the smells and all the painful memories that hospitals brought back, Hacket hated the places mainly because he couldn't smoke inside them and, right now, he needed a cigarette.

He walked to the lift that would carry him to the tenth floor, glancing to his right and left, noticing that there were patients and visitors seated in the cafe off to his right. They were sipping cups of tea and coffee, exchanging cordial and banal words.

Hacket continued on to the lift, hitting the call button and waiting for it to arrive. When it did he was relieved to find that there was no one in it. He had no desire to be caught in some meaningless conversation with a patient or visitor while he rode to the tenth floor.

He moved to the back of the car, turned his gaze upwards towards the floor indicator panel and watched as each successive floor was reached and then passed. When the number ten was finally illuminated, Hacket stepped out of the lift and turned to his left, heading along a corridor that ended with a large picture window.

On either side of the corridor there were doors, all of them firmly closed.

There was a vending machine about half way up the corridor and Hacket paused for a moment, wondering whether or not to get himself a coffee but he checked his watch, saw that he was running a little later than he'd have liked and decided against it. Punctuality was a big thing in Frank Hacket's life. He hated being late. He hated it when other people were late. To him it smacked of laziness or unprofessionalism and he couldn't abide either of those traits in himself or others.

As he passed the first of the doors, a nurse emerged from the room beyond pushing a small trolley. Hacket stepped aside to let her through and she nodded and smiled by way of acknowledgement. As she tried to turn the trolley she bumped it against the wall and a small roll of surgical tape fell to the floor. Hacket hastily retrieved it and handed it to her. She thanked him and headed off in the other direction, the sound of the trolley wheels squeaking softly until she disappeared into one of the other rooms closing the door behind her. Hacket continued up the corridor until he reached the last of the closed doors.

He walked in without knocking and found himself in what looked like a waiting area. There were several brown plastic chairs arranged around a low table that was strewn with magazines and plastic cups from the vending machine. On one side of this table sat a man in a grey suit, busy with a newspaper crossword, his brow furrowed in concentration. He got to his feet and smiled as Hacket walked in, extending one huge hand in the newcomer's direction.

He was a big man, so broad across the shoulders and chest it looked as if the material of his suit was in danger of splitting due to the amount of muscle and sinew it had to contain. The pen he was holding looked like a matchstick held between his thick fingers.

'Hello, Frank,' he beamed.

'How you doing, Wally?' Hacket asked, gripping the other man's hand as firmly as he could while worrying that his own might be crushed to powder by the vice-like grip.

'Can't complain,' the big man said. 'What about you? Busy?'

'Always busy, Wally.'

The big man chuckled.

Hacket nodded towards the door behind the huge figure.

'How is he?' he wanted to know.

'Not good,' the big man told him, his features softening. 'He's been asking for you.'

Hacket nodded and moved towards the other door as the big man slapped him across the shoulder affectionately with a blow that would have sent lesser men sprawling.

'Has anyone else been in?' Hacket asked.

'He only wants to see you,' the other man explained.

Hacket hesitated a moment longer then opened the door and slipped through as quickly and quietly as he could.

The first sound that met his ears when he walked into the next room was the steady blip of an oscilloscope.

The machine was set up next to the single bed that was in the middle of the room. In that bed there was a figure, propped up on pillows with eyes closed and head bowed. On either side of the bed there were drips. Hacket could see clear fluid making its way from plastic bags into the veins of the motionless recipient in the bed.

The man who lay there was in his mid-fifties but looked twenty years older. His skin was like parchment and the veins on the backs of his hands appeared black against the milky whiteness of his skin.

Hacket stood looking at him, his eyes drawn to the man's chest that was rising and falling almost imperceptibly. The curtains at the large picture window were drawn to prevent the sun from shining directly into the patient's eyes. Motes of dust turned lazily in the single ray that had managed to penetrate. Hacket walked slowly towards the bed, his gaze on the occupant.

The man in the bed didn't stir and Hacket wondered if he was asleep. He looked at the bedside cabinets on either side of the patient. Both had vases of flowers on them and, arrayed around those were cards mostly bearing the legend; GET WELL SOON.

Hacket admired the sentiment but doubted the possibility.

He wondered how long he'd have to wait until the patient woke up. He wasn't pressed for time but he didn't relish the prospect of having to hang around in the hospital for any longer than he had to.

There were two plastic chairs beside the bed and Hacket was about to settle himself on one of these when the man in the bed raised his head.

'I thought it was the nurse come back to take more blood,' the man said, quietly. 'I thought she'd leave if she saw I was asleep. They're good like that.'

'Morning, George,' Hacket said. 'I would ask how you are but I can see.'

'I won't be running any marathons in the next few days, let's put it that way,' the other man said. 'Have a seat.' He motioned to one of the plastic chairs and Hacket seated himself.

George Vaughn lifted a hand to scratch one cheek and Hacket saw the drip attached to it, that clear plastic vein running into him like so many others, each resembling some kind of benevolent circuit cable. The blip of the oscilloscope continued with its weary tone.

'I won't waste your time, Frank,' Vaughn said, trying to take a deep breath but not quite managing it because of the pain it caused him. 'I haven't got much time left to waste.'

'Is it that bad?' Hacket wanted to know.

'What does it look like? It's spread to the other lung and they say it could spread to my brain before the end of next week. I've got less than a month if I'm lucky.'

'I'm sorry, George.'

'Some might say it's poetic justice I suppose. What with the line of work I've been in. Karma and all that. That is what they call it isn't it?'

'Something like that.'

Vaugh coughed, clutching at his chest with one gnarled hand.

Hacket got to his feet and reached for the nearby jug of water. He poured some into a beaker and handed it to Vaughn who finally managed to take a sip when the coughing fit subsided.

'Fucking cancer,' he grunted through clenched teeth.

Hacket took the beaker from him and seated himself again.

'Do you want me to get someone?' he asked. 'A nurse or something?'

'They can't do anything for me anyway,' Vaughn said. 'They just keep pumping me full of fucking morphine but even that's not working as well as it used to.' He sighed. 'Listen, Frank, I've got a job for you.'

'I'd have thought you'd got more important things on your mind, George.'

'This is important,' Vaughn snapped. 'It's a special job. A million if you do it before the end of next week.'

'A million? Who's the target? The Queen?'

Vaughn motioned to the top drawer of the nearest bed side cabinet.

'All the information's in there,' he said.

Hacket opened the draw and took out a small manilla file that he proceeded to flip open.

There were a number of photographs inside. Mostly of a large country house and the driveway that led up to it. Others showed the vast overgrown lawn that guarded the approaches to the house. Most of the pictures had been taken in bright sunlight that only served to illustrate even more starkly how badly cared for the house and its grounds really were. Hacket raised his eyebrows as he considered each one, turning several over to discover there was an address written on them in black ink.

'So the target is here?' he asked, raising one of the pictures.

'He was last seen there two days ago,' Vaughn told him. 'He

moves around a lot but he always comes back to that place.'

'There's no name or description of the guy I'm supposed to hit.'

'You've got the address where he lives. He lives alone. No family. No security. What more do you want? His fucking inside leg measurement?'

'No security? In a gaff like that?'

'He lives there alone.'

'Are you sure your intelligence is right? I don't want to go walking in there and find out he's got half the fucking SAS guarding him.'

'He's alone there,' Vaughn said, coughing. 'Now, can you do the job or not?'

'Have I ever turned one down before?'

'No.'

'Ever fucked one up?'

'No.'

Hacket pushed the photographs back into the envelope.

'So what's he done to you, George?' he asked. 'What's he done that's pissed you off so much you'd order a hit from your deathbed?'

'You never normally ask,' Vaughn reminded him.

'You never normally pay me this much. I'm just checking there isn't more to this guy than you've told me.'

'Just kill him. I pay for the job, Frank. Getting it done is your problem. How you do it is up to you. If you don't trust me you can have half the money now and the other half on completion.'

'I trust you, George. I'll pick up all the money when the job's done.'

Vaughn nodded.

'Just get it done before the end of next week,' he said. He coughed again and the oscilloscope speeded up slightly before settling back into its usual rhythm.

Hacket waited a moment longer then got to his feet. He held up the manilla envelope again then pushed it into the inside pocket of his jacket and turned to leave.

'One thing, Frank,' Vaughn said, almost as an afterthought.

Hacket hesitated.

'As soon as the job's done I want you to come back here and tell me,' Vaughn went on. 'And I want you to bring me something.'

'Go on.'

'I want the index finger from his right hand,' Vaughn said, flatly.

'For what you're paying me, you can have the whole fucking arm,' Hacket smiled.

'Just the finger,' Vaughn insisted. 'The right index finger.'

Hacket nodded then turned towards the door once again, slipping out of the room. As he closed the door behind him he heard Vaughn coughing again.

The huge man in the grey suit again looked up from his crossword puzzle as Hacket entered the room again.

'Did you get it sorted?' he wanted to know.

Hacket nodded.

'See you around, Wally,' he said, one hand on the handle of the door beyond.

'Frank, what do you reckon this is?' the big man said, waving his crossword in the air. "If you get rid of someone, you give them this,' Six letters, first letter is B.'

'Bullet,' Hacket said, smiling. And he was gone.

He stepped out into the corridor beyond, walked to the lift and rode it to the ground floor, relieved that no one had joined him during the short journey.

As soon as he reached the car park of the hospital he reached for his cigarettes, lighting one up and puffing on it gratefully. He watched as an ambulance, blue lights spinning, swept into view then he wandered back to his car. The drive home took him thirty minutes.

*

The house in the photographs was called Westfield Grange.

It didn't take Hacket long to discover that, just as it didn't take him long to work out that it was about three hours drive from him. It was approachable through leafy countryside and several small villages that seemed to vie with each other for which was the most picturesque.

Hacket stopped in the nearest one to Westfield Grange for some lunch, sitting at the end of the bar in a pub called The Three Horseshoes. He managed to get through his shepherd's pie and vegetables without being disturbed. Only as he was enjoying his dessert and another glass of non-alcoholic lager did the balding man behind the bar amble over to him.

'How was your food?' the man wanted to know, busily polishing glasses and then replacing them beneath and behind the bar.

'Very nice,' Hacket told him. 'My compliments to the cook.'

'I'll tell the wife, she'll be glad to hear that,' the man chuckled.

'Do you own this place?' Hacket enquired.

'We run it. We bought the lease about twelve years ago.'

'So you must know what goes on around here. In the village and that.'

'You can't really avoid it.'

'How much do you know about the owner of Westfield Grange?'

'He's not as friendly as the last owner,' the balding man announced. 'The last owner used to have an annual barbecue in the grounds of the house every spring time but no one's even seen this owner.'

'Perhaps he just likes to keep himself to himself,' Hacket offered.

'The lady who used to clean there was sacked not long after he moved in. Hardly anyone visits the place. He got rid of his gardeners too. The place is a real mess now.'

Hacket could certainly have attested to the overgrown nature of the grounds and gardens after seeing photographs of the Grange but he merely nodded sagely and let the balding man go on.

'So he never comes in here for a pint then?' Hacket said, smiling.

'Never.'

'Do you know if he's got any family?'

'If he has no one's ever seen them.'

Again Hacket nodded almost imperceptibly.

'How do you know about the Grange?' the balding man wanted to know.

'I'm a bit of an amateur historian,' Hacket lied. 'I like buildings from that period.'

The other man nodded enthusiastically and Hacket was happy that he'd fallen for the lie so readily. Hacket finished his drink, paid his bill and wandered out to his car.

The drive to Westfield Grange took him another thirty minutes.

He drove past the high stone wall and wrought iron gates that guarded the driveway and grounds of the building then he drove back, pulling his car off the road into a small copse of trees that effectively hid the vehicle from anyone who was passing.

He sat behind the wheel and smoked a cigarette then he clambered out of the car and walked to the boot where he selected the tools he would need for the job. Usually he preferred doing his work from a distance and he favoured a Parker-Hale M85 7.62mm sniper rifle but this time closer contact was necessary so he settled for a 9mm Taurus PT-92, checking the ten round magazine before slipping it into the shoulder holster he wore.

The five inch Bowie Knife he slid into the sheath on his belt.

Suitably equipped, Hacket climbed back behind the wheel of the car and reversed onto the road. He drove along the narrow track to the gates of Westfield Grange and then, leaving the engine running, swung himself out of the vehicle and approached the entryway looking around for surveillance cameras, careful to keep his face hidden from any that might be mounted on the high walls around the grounds. There was an intercom on the right hand pillar and Hacket pressed the buzzer there.

No one answered but, to Hacket's delight, the gates swung open.

He stroked his chin lightly.

This was too fucking easy.

He reached, almost subconsciously inside his jacket and touched his fingers to the butt of the Taurus, as if to remind himself that he could pull the automatic any time he needed to. His heart began to beat a little faster. As he drove down the long driveway he glanced into the rear view mirror and saw the iron gates close behind him.

Was he being watched even now? Surely whoever owned this place couldn't be as lax with security as he appeared to be. This was crazy. Hacket wondered again if he was being set up but, he reasoned, why would Vaughn want to do that to him? He shook his head as if to dispel any such paranoid thoughts, finally bringing the car to a halt in front of the short flight of stone steps that led up to the front door of the Grange.

His feet made crunching noises on the gravel of the driveway as he made his way to the main entrance. He waited there for a second, eyes constantly alert for any movement but there was none. Hacket banged the door three times, using the large ornate knocker set in the centre of the wooden partition. Having done that he ducked back along the side of the building, hurrying past the ivy covered brickwork and finally pausing beside a window.

He used the bowie knife to slide the sash window open a few inches, completing the task by sliding his fingers into the gap and easing the window up until it allowed him to slip inside.

Hacket eased himself soundlessly over the sill, finding himself inside a large and thankfully empty room.

Once again he was struck by the lack of security, wondering how anyone with such obvious wealth could live like this without any apparent concern for this kind of eventuality. Admittedly not everyone faced the prospect of being shot by a hitman, Hacket mused but there was always the danger of burglars. The owner of this place didn't appear to have considered any of those eventualities and, again, Hacket wondered what that person could have done to George Vaughn to merit this kind of treatment.

He moved towards the door of the room, placed his hand lightly on the handle and turned it.

The door was unlocked.

Hacket opened it slightly, peering out into the large hallway beyond. A broad corridor snaked away to his right and left and, as he eased himself out into it he saw that there were indeed CCTV cameras set high up on the walls but they didn't seem to be working. The wide lenses didn't move as he did, the red lights on them didn't blink. Hacket decided that even if they were working they didn't appear to be triggered by motion. Nevertheless, he was also certain by now that whoever inhabited this house was aware of his presence. He slid the Taurus from his shoulder holster and slipped off the safety catch.

Directly in front of him was a large dining room, to his right a corridor that led down to another set of double doors. Hacket chose that particular route, moving quickly and quietly until he reached the doors where he stood listening, trying to catch any sounds coming from beyond.

There was nothing but silence and, again, Hacket wondered if the target was merely sitting on the other side of the doors waiting for him. He gripped the pistol more tightly and pushed doors, both of which swung open.

Hacket ducked back slightly then peered into the room and saw that it too was empty.

There was a staircase rising from the centre of this room and Hacket moved towards it, climbing it swiftly but quietly, the automatic held before him, ready in case anyone appeared before him. The staircase bent to the left and then the right before finally opening out into a landing.

Hacket paused again, seeing two doors before him.

The silence remained oppressive but, he realized, it was also doing nothing to mask his approach.

He moved as quietly as he could towards the first of the doors, closing his hand gently around the handle.

The door opened easily and Hacket stepped inside.

The room was completely devoid of furniture and lit only by overhead fluorescent lights that made him shield his eyes so bright was the cold whiteness pouring from these overhead strips.

The only thing in the room was a child's cradle.

It stood right in the centre of the small room and, as Hacket moved cautiously towards it, he wrinkled his nose. There was a strange antiseptic smell in the air, something he hadn't noticed anywhere else in the house.

More than a little unsettled now, Hacket backed out of the room, closing the door behind him.

He turned towards the next door and opened that too.

It also opened onto another blindingly white room but this one was occupied.

There was one single high backed chair in the centre of the room and, in that chair sat a man.

He had his bowed. His chin was touching his chest as if he was asleep. Hacket couldn't see his face, only that he was dressed in an immaculately pressed charcoal grey suit. If he'd heard Hacket enter the room he certainly showed no signs of acknowledging it.

As Hacket stood there in that doorway he detected that antiseptic smell he'd noticed in the previous room. That smell he hated so much. That stink of hospitals and sick beds. Of wards and examination rooms.

'Is this your house?' Hacket asked.

The man raised his head, looked at Hacket unconcernedly and nodded slowly.

He was in his mid-fifties. An unremarkable looking man with brown hair that was greying at the temples and deep lines across his forehead that looked as if someone had dragged a fork across his flesh there.

'Are you on your own here?' Hacket went on.

The man nodded again, his gaze now fixed on the barrel of the automatic.

'No one else lives here?' Hacket persisted.

The man shook his head.

'Then you're the one I'm looking for,' Hacket told him.

'I knew you'd come,' the man said, a slight smile on his thin lips. 'I knew it would be you.'

'How?'

'I just knew.'

Again the man smiled.

'You have no idea what you're doing,' he intoned.

'I'm doing my job,' Hacket told him.

'So was I,' the man said, his smile fading.

The man held his gaze now and Hacket looked back at him, his own features impassive.

Hacket shot him three times.

He stood there for a moment looking down at the body then he holstered the Taurus and reached instead for the Bowie knife. There was one more task to complete before he left.

*

As the lift bumped to a halt at the tenth floor, Frank Hacket ran a hand through his hair then stepped out into the corridor beyond.

He walked along to the room he sought and entered, hearing talking and even laughter coming from the room beyond that. Hacket crossed to that other door and stood beside it for a moment, listening to the sounds from the other side of the wooden partition. Finally, he knocked once and walked in.

George Vaughn was sitting in a chair next to the bed.

Wally Grant was standing beside him, smiling benevolently at his employer. He also nodded happily in Hacket's direction as he entered but Hacket barely saw the gesture. He was more concerned with Vaughn. Transfixed by him.

Gone was the deathly pallor. His eyes were no longer sunken into their sockets like punctured balloons, instead they looked bright and alert, fixing Hacket in a welcoming gaze as he walked in. Vaughn even got up out of his chair and took a couple of steps towards the newcomer, extending his right hand as an added gesture of welcome. Hacket felt the strength in the grip. A strength he could not have imagined being present the last time he saw the stricken older man.

There was a small plaster on the back of Vaughn's hand. A final reminder of the drips that had been attached to him the last time Hacket had visited.

'Leave us alone for a minute, Wally,' Vaughn said and the big man nodded and retreated from the room, patting Hacket appreciatively on the shoulder as he passed.

Vaughn waited until the big man had left the room then perched on the edge of the bed.

'So, miracles do happen?' Hacket said, smiling. 'You look great.'

Vaughn smiled.

'I feel great,' he exclaimed.

'What happened?' Hacket persisted.

'You did what I paid you for, that's what happened.'

'I'm not with you.'

'The hit. You carried it out.'

'Who was he, George?'

'You didn't guess?'

Hacket shook his head.

'Did you bring me what I asked for?' Vaughn went on.

Hacket reached into his inside pocket and pulled out a small wooden box about the size of a mobile phone. He handed it to Vaughn who opened it and inspected the contents.

There was a slim index finger inside the box. It had been severed at the third

knuckle and the blood had long since congealed on the raw end.

'I don't get it, George,' Hacket confessed, watching as Vaughn ran appraising eyes over the digit.

'I was dying, Frank,' Vaughn told him. 'You could see that. Doctors couldn't help me. Drugs couldn't help me. *You* saved me.' He looked at Hacket and smiled.

'How? By killing the guy in that house? I still don't get it.'

'He would have come for me, Frank. Next week. Next month. But one day he would have walked in here, he would have touched me with this finger,' Vaughn held up the small box and it's grisly contents. 'And he would have taken me. Now do you get it?'

'You're trying to tell me I killed death?' Hacket smiled.

'The Grim Reaper himself.'

'Bullshit.'

'You don't believe me? Just because he wasn't sitting there in a black cloak holding a fucking great scythe?'

'George, come on.'

'Look at me,' Vaughn insisted. 'You saw me before. How do you explain this? How do you think I got better? I was dying the last time you were here. I was waiting for death. But now I don't have to wait any more. You got rid of him.'

'So I'm the man who killed death?'

'Spot on. They should build statues to you.' Vaughn smiled.

'So what now?' Hacket persisted. 'No more famines in Africa? No more refugees drowning in boats? No more casualties in wars?'

'I don't know and I don't give a fuck. I hired you to protect me. No one else.'

'George this is ridiculous.'

'Is it?' Vaughn snapped. 'Look at me. How do you explain what's happened to me?'

'I can't but how come it was so easy? Why has no one tried it before?'

'Fuck knows but you did it. You did what you were hired to do.' He pulled open the drawer of the bedside table and pulled out an envelope which he handed to Hacket. 'And now you're getting paid. Take it. You earned it.'

Hacket took the envelope and slipped it into his inside pocket.

'Not going to check it?' Vaughn asked.

'I trust you, George,' Hacket told him. 'If I killed Death I'm not going to think twice about blowing *your* fucking head off am I?' He smiled, hesitated a moment longer then turned and walked out of the room.

He walked slowly. As if the newly acquired knowledge Vaughn had imparted to him had somehow slowed him down. As he walked through the hospital he glanced at patients wondering if some of them would now survive because of what he'd done.

And yet he knew how ridiculous that supposition was. How the fuck could anyone kill death? How could anyone stop the approach of their own end? How could a man snuff out an entity capable of annihilating entire civilizations? It made no sense.

He was still considering that when he walked out of the hospital's main entrance.

He lit up a cigarette, told himself again that he was losing his mind and walked on.

The speeding ambulance that came hurtling around a corner was doing seventy when it hit him.

Hacket was catapulted a good fifteen feet into the air by the impact.

He hit the ground again with a sickening thud and lay there gazing at the sky, wondering why he felt no pain. It puzzled him even more when he realized that both his legs, several ribs, one shoulder, his pelvis and two fingers were shattered. Hacket concluded that he must be in shock, that was preventing him from being consumed by the agony that would normally have enveloped him.

His right femur was smashed. The jagged end of bone was

protruding from his thigh, dark matter oozing from the centre of the bone. As Hacket looked at it he realized it was marrow. The thought made him nauseous but only a little less than the fact that he had also sustained a massive gash to his lower abdomen that had caused several lengths of intestine to bulge from the bloody rent. Hacket tried to push the slippery coils of gut back into his abdomen, his fingers slipping on the reeking pieces of viscera. His intestines looked like the tentacles of a crimson octopus.

As a nurse and paramedic ran towards him, Hacket turned in their direction.

His head was almost at a right angle, practically touching his shoulder because of his broken spine and gashed neck. The blood that was spurting into the air from one of his severed carotid arteries didn't bother him either.

Hacket got to his feet, the nurse and paramedic now gazing blankly at him. He took a couple of faltering steps, glancing down at his own smashed body, his right leg dragging along uselessly as he shuffled across the tarmac leaving a thick trail of blood on the ground behind. Each time he drew breath he could hear the air hissing in his punctured lung.

'The man who killed death,' Hacket murmured, a twisted smile spreading across his lips.

And he began to laugh. As he did, his head, which was still hanging at an impossible angle, began to move backwards and forwards, the shattered vertebrae grinding together.

When he felt the vibration from his mobile phone he reached for it without thinking.

On the other end of the line was George Vaughn.

'I saw what happened to you, Frank,' he said. 'I was watching from my window.'

'What the fuck is going on?' Hacket slurred, blood bubbling over his lips.

'I told you. You killed him. You killed death,' Vaughn chuckled. 'If you hadn't, you'd be in the morgue now. Enjoy it.'

'But I'm crippled,' Hacket roared. 'I look like a fucking freak.'

'At least you're still alive, Frank.'

'How can I live like this?'

'It's better than dying, Frank. Anything is better than dying.'

Vaughn hung up.

Hacket dropped the phone, allowing it to slip from his shattered fingers.

He stood in the hospital car park and screamed.

DEAD-EYED DICK
by **Anton Palmer**

'Just relax, Mr Smith...' The nurse pushed the hypodermic needle towards her patient's arm.

Don't you fucking say it, bitch!

'Just a *little* pr...'

Don't you fucking dare!

'...scratch.'

Piss-taking bitch!

The nurse smiled at the man on the operating table, a playful glint in her beautiful brown eyes as she stuck him with the needle. 'Count out loud from ten back to one, please, Mr Smith.'

'Ten...nine...eight...' Sleep began to crawl in at the edges of his consciousness. He relaxed and closed his eyes as he continued to count. 'Seven...six...five...'

*

Despite the fact that he was six-foot-three and weighed in at two-hundred and ten pounds of gym-sculpted muscle, Richard Smith knew he was the smallest guy in the pub. From his perch atop a wooden stool at the bar, he took a swallow of his beer and cast an envious eye around the room...

A couple of middle-aged men were enjoying a game of darts at the far end, chalking off mediocre scores while their professional counterparts played, muted and barely noticed, on a too-large plasma screen above their heads.

They were bigger than Richard.

His eyes scanned further. A pair of dolly-birds, caked in make-up, aged anywhere between twenty and forty, sat at a round table, sipping shorts and giggling. One of them, with shaggy, dirty-blonde hair that was either two decades out of fashion or the cutting edge of retro, smiled coyly as he caught her eye before quickly turning her attention back to her friend. Richard continued his perusal of the room. At the table next to the women were two athletic-looking men dressed in sportswear, chatting covertly about league tables and committees. Perhaps, parched after a game of squash at the leisure centre down the road they'd popped in for a refreshing pint and a spot of sports-club-political back-stabbing, Richard mused.

Whatever. *They* were bigger than him.

He craned his neck and shifted on his stool to look behind. A group of male students were gathered around a worn-out pool table, garbed in fake-original T-shirts of bands that had quit or died long before these spotty twats were even born. Necking berry-flavoured alco-pops, they laughed loudly as they regaled each other with their various antics, looking around to see if anyone was impressed.

Fucking students! No one was impressed...or even fucking listening. Wankers!

Still, wankers or not – even *they* were bigger than Richard.

Behind the students, standing in the bay window where the signal was stronger, his mate, Jason was talking animatedly on his mobile phone, sporadically grabbing his crotch. Probably chatting to one of his *women*, deciding which of the bow-legged slags he was going to service later, Richard assumed. Gulping down a few more mouthfuls of ale, he waggled his glass at his friend, indicating it was his turn to get them in.

If he had any fucking money that was.

As Richard let his head relax back around, he caught the eye of the blonde once more. Again she smiled. He paused, just long enough to give her the once-over...good body, nice tits - looked like she could be 'up for it' - and possibly not too fussy...

'Don't waste your time, babe...hung like a maggot.'

The two women melted into fits of laughter as Bridget, the proverbial mutton-dressed-as-lamb, staggered from the ladies, banging against the women's table before crashing into the bar behind Richard, a long liquid belch spewing from her mouth as she tottered on her heels.

'Alright, babe?' She turned to him as she waited for the barman to notice her, 'Ow's it 'anging?' Bridget wiggled her little finger at him and collapsed in hysterics against the bar, her derisive laughter threatening her 'sensitive' bladder despite her recent visit to the toilet.

'Fuck off, you slut!' Richard growled.

Jesus Christ! How pissed must he have been to have taken that home?

As he looked at her now - her tight, leopard-print blouse emphasising nothing more than an obvious muffin-top and a cleavage of sun-bed baked skin that wouldn't look out of place in a pterodactyl's armpit – he felt sick at the memory of their drunken one night stand.

It had been pretty much like all of his 'dates' - everything was fine until they got down to business. Bridget had been all over him in the rear of the taxi back to his place and, as they stumbled through his front door she had virtually ripped his trousers down, immediately taking him in her mouth.

'I'll soon get this little fellow standing to attention.' She'd purred. It only took a minute or two for her to realise that the 'little fellow' was already standing as proudly to attention as he was going to get. Immediately spitting him out with a look of pure disgust on her face, she had dribbled something about *not being a paedophile…* and *having no interest in sucking the dick of an eight-year-old*, before stumbling out the door and slamming it shut behind her.

And *this* was why Richard – despite his height, despite his weight, despite the biceps that bulged through the sleeves of his polo shirt - was damn near certain that he was most definitely, without a doubt, the smallest guy in the room.

As a man, he had *almost* everything: he was decent looking, had a great physique (which he worked hard to maintain), a fantastic house and car, and a big, fat, fuck-off bank balance. The late, Richard Smith *Senior,* had owned a network of used car dealerships up and down the country. From the humble grime of his working-class roots, the man had built a thriving, household-name that had made him a millionaire several times over.

Richard Smith *Junior,* on the other hand, was a work-shy waste of space who had been gifted the position of 'Deputy MD' on leaving college. All he'd had to do for his bloated salary was to visit a few showrooms each month and pretend to understand the numbers while studying the receptionist's figures. When his father died thirteen years later, Richard inherited the house and the money, selling the business to his father's fiercest competitor at the first opportunity.

Yep, he had it all - the looks, the body, the pussy-magnet car...and a free *'micro-penis'* thrown in for good measure. Sitting below that rippling six-pack, he boasted a solid three and a half inches of wrist-slashing shame.

His mate, Jason was the complete opposite. Short, overweight, he was an almost permanently unemployed slob, who showered less than he worked and lived in a flat that was barely more than a mould-encrusted hovel.

Oh, and he had a nine-inch cock that was as thick as a woman's wrist.

Bastard...

The whole thing had started off as nothing more than a drunken joke. Just over twelve months ago in this very pub, Jason had made some crack about how 'money can't buy you everything', grabbing the bulging package that strained his jeans to make sure Richard caught his drift. To be fair, if Jason had known exactly *how* small his mate's cock actually was, he would never have made the joke in the first place. He'd heard from various women that it was 'tiny', but he'd been with some of those women himself and assumed they were talking in relative terms. But, Richard, the worse for alcohol, had taken the bait and by the end of the night, a contract had been drawn up on the back of a beer-stained menu and signed by both pissed-up parties: if Jason was to die – Richard would get his penis.

That was a year ago. Tonight was tonight - and Bridget's caustic remarks were the final straw. When you became the butt of a joke from a leather-skinned old slapper like that, it was time to do something about it. And Jason wasn't really a *mate* – more of an *acquaintance*. Not even that, truth be told - he was just a drinking buddy, a fellow stool-warmer at the Coach and Horses...

Jason's death, two months later, on his birthday, aroused little, if any, suspicion.

Richard had spent the afternoon and evening with him in the pub. Various regulars had bought drinks for the birthday-boy throughout the evening, Richard pacing himself as his friend got ever more intoxicated. By chucking-out time Jason could barely stand, Richard propping him up as they staggered to the taxi, slipping the driver an extra twenty pounds in advance as he saw a hint of '*Fuck off*' on the driver's lips – the man's tired face telegraphing the vision of puke covered seats that his years of experience told him might be the result of taking *this* particular fare.

With the taxi and it's miraculously spew-free seats heading off into the distance, Richard laid his drunken friend on a leather sofa and headed to the kitchen. He took a couple of beers from the fridge and emptied a little of one bottle into the sink, topping it back up with vodka before heading back to the lounge and offering the spiked drink to Jason. With his beer barely settled in his stomach, Jason drifted into a deep, inebriated sleep. Richard watched his slow, steady breathing for a few moments then tickled him under his ribs.

No response. He was out of it.

He squeezed Jason's nostrils together, sticking two fingers down the back of his throat as soon as he opened his mouth. Despite being unconscious, Jason's gag reflex was surprisingly alert - hot, stinking, vomit pouring over Richard's hand within a few seconds. He grabbed the bottom of Jason's T-shirt, lifting it over his unconscious friend's face, forcing vomit up his nostrils and back down his windpipe. His own stomach heaved, both from the smell and the sounds of Jason choking and gagging as he was drowned by the liquid contents of his own stomach. The amount of alcohol Jason had consumed throughout the day had rendered him virtually comatose and while his body fought for every scrap of oxygen, his mind was oblivious, lost to some booze-sodden dream, his eyes remaining firmly closed throughout his final moments.

When it was all over, Richard wept. This was it – he was finally going to get a penis he could be proud of. A weapon rather than a cock. He would never attempt to *make love* to any woman again – he would hammer them raw with his new tool, make sure they knew they'd been well and truly fucked when he was done.

Taking another look at Jason's lifeless body, he picked up his mobile phone and made a call…

Several weeks earlier, a brief internet search and a few minutes of negotiation had secured the services of a Dr Kohl. A former plastic surgeon with experience of transplants, the good doctor had fallen upon harder times since being 'made a scapegoat' following a series of lawsuits and allegations of botched procedures. Now working as an exhausted doctor in a hospital emergency department, it hadn't taken nearly as much money as Richard had expected to bring him onboard.

Richard had converted one of his home's six bedrooms into an operating theatre and recovery room in accordance with Dr Kohl's instructions, ripping out carpets and covering the floor with easy to clean vinyl tiles. The disgraced surgeon, after receiving his first down-payment, had furnished the room with the requisite equipment in readiness.

'It's time. Get down here now.' Richard disconnected the call and waited.

'Choked on his own vomit after a binge-drinking session.' That was the verdict on the death certificate; or words to that effect. The document was perfectly legal and official - signed by Dr Kohl – a professional with letters after his name.

'A fucking rock star's death!' That was the verdict of the less well-educated regulars of the Coach and Horses as they raised a glass to the departed. Several women dabbed tears from their eyes as they shared their memories, slack vaginas weeping into frilly drip-trays as they too mourned their loss.

By a lucky coincidence, or possibly the greatest streak of business brilliance, one of the locals – a retired wing commander with a passion for gardening – chose that moment to enter the bar with a box of his extra-large, home-grown cucumbers.

He sold the lot.

*

When he came to, Richard could feel it pressing down on him. Could feel the weight of the bruised, swollen snake that was taped tight to his belly.

It felt fucking *good*!

He tried to sit up to take a look, but the new addition was heavily bandaged and the sight of the catheter protruding from the dressing, draining blood-infused urine into a bag, made him feel sick, forcing him to lay his spinning head back down.

Several bed-resting days passed before the doctor was happy to remove the catheter and the dressings, allowing Richard to see himself properly for the first time. The base of his new penis was supported in a sort of hammock to minimise against straining the fresh skin and muscle grafts, not to mention the network of blood vessels and growing nerves. Despite his bizarre underwear, Richard could clearly appreciate what he had. Though still swollen and sporting all the colours of contusion from yellow-green to purple and black, the thing literally *oozed* with the possibilities it would now afford its new master. As he stared at his reflection in the bathroom mirror, Richard felt complete for the first time in his life.

He was a whole man.

A *real* man.

No longer would the drunken sluts he picked up gape open-mouthed with mocking laughter. Their lipstick-smothered orifices would be gaping alright, stretched to breaking point as he fucked their faces. They would choke on his length. Gag on his girth. That fucking slag, Bridget would be first. He'd buy her a few drinks, let her feel the goods through the crotch of his jeans then take her back to his place. He'd get her good and wet, let her think her past-its-prime pussy was going to get the fuck of a lifetime, then bend her over and shove it in her arse. Go in dry, balls-deep, ignoring the friction until her blood lubed her channel...

Oh, and she would scream. Scream in agony and then, perhaps, in ecstasy – he didn't care which. And after he was done, she would stagger out of his front door, dripping with his cum, struggling to keep her prolapsing bowels inside. That leather-skinned bitch would *never, ever,* laugh at him again.

As he played out the scene in his head, he felt a tingle of arousal in his loins and looked down at his new dick.

No sign of any erection.

That's fine, he reassured himself. Dr Kohl had told him it could take several months before full sexual function was possible. He had waited thirty-one years for a 'proper' cock - he could cope with waiting a few more months before he got to use it in anger...

When he woke the next morning, his legs were itching like crazy and he crawled out from under his sheets to inspect the limbs.

The skin seemed looser. Saggy, wrinkly. And was it just his imagination or were the hairs thicker and darker than before?

A side-effect of his medication perhaps?

He was on a regime of various drugs – immune system suppressants, painkillers, antibiotics. He picked up the phone next to his bed and dialled Dr Kohl's number, demanding he come over immediately. But even with Richard's money, immediately turned out to be a couple of leg-scratching hours.

'Hmmm...it *could* be a side-effect of the medication...but I have to admit...' Dr Kohl pulled at the flappy skin on Richard's thighs, knees and shins. '...I've never seen it before in any of my other patients. Don't worry - I'm sure it's only temporary...perhaps a nice soak would help with the itching.'

Richard turned off the taps, tested the temperature with his hands then stepped into the bath.

Oh, that feels so good...so warm...so wet...

He closed his eyes and immersed himself, slowly rocking back and forth, the warm water rhythmically slapping against the sides of the tub as it gently washed over him. As he pumped up and down the length of the bath he felt...strange...excited; *aroused*. The sensations were like that of an approaching orgasm, but not confined to his genitals. The feelings filled his whole body and he found himself sliding harder and faster, water splashing over the sides of the bath until the discomfort between his legs forced him to get out.

As he towelled himself off, dirty water sloshing down the plug-hole, a clump of damp hair slid from his scalp.

Shit. Another side-effect?

Dr Kohl had warned of *numerous* side-effects.

Was hair-loss one of them? Possibly...he couldn't recall.

He climbed back into bed and switched on the TV, hoping to find a good movie to distract himself. Maybe the hair loss was normal. People shed a number of hairs every day, didn't they? Perhaps it just seemed like a lot because he hadn't bathed or showered since before his operation. He decided to keep an eye on things and see if his symptoms improved. He didn't want to be seen as some kind of pathetic fucking hypochondriac, running to the doctor every five minutes for every little worry. Besides, Sopa, his Thai nurse would be in soon to check his vitals and cook him some food – he could mention it to her.

Richard assumed Dr Kohl either had a very limited supply of nurses or he was a master of torture - Sopa was a hot piece of ass. She flaunted herself in a uniform that, he was certain, was far shorter than either the NHS or Bupa would allow as she took his blood pressure and temperature. He *assumed* she was fully trained – she *seemed* to know what she was doing - but there was a look in her eyes that told him that maybe, she had paid her way through some Thai nursing school by giving '*massages*' and shooting ping-pong balls out of various orifices.

Richard couldn't care less what she'd shot out of whatever hole – she looked great and knew her way around a kitchen. After eating a dinner of mildly spiced chicken and noodles, he popped his pills and lay, propped up on his pillows, staring at the television screen, dozing on and off until finally falling asleep…

He awoke to darkness.

And pain. His legs were fucking *killing* him.

Switching on the lamp beside the bed he checked the clock on the wall: three-twenty-two in the morning. He swung himself out of his covers and collapsed in a heap on the cold floor. His knees had swollen like two watery balloons, the skin on his legs hanging from his bones like empty, wrinkled sacks.

He thrust his hands to his head in panic.

What the fuck was happening to him?

Running trembling fingers through his hair, great tufts came away. He tried to stand, to get to the bathroom mirror to see the damage but his limbs refused to straighten. It felt as if the muscles in his lower legs were contracting, cramping his feet up tight behind his thighs. The pressure in his swollen knees was increasing, his skin - so saggy on the other parts of his limbs – was stretched tight across the fluid-filled joints. As he stared at his knees his leg muscles contracted again and he screamed as the taut flesh over his patella split open, blood and yellowish liquid flooding out of the gaping wounds. Nausea overwhelmed him as the agony continued – his kneecaps lifting before snapping away as a surge of noodle-like tubers, dripping with bloody slime, burst from beneath the detached bones and cartilage.

Fighting the vomit that rose in his throat, he turned back to his bed, stretching for the phone, slipping as his desperate fingers grasped for it. He fell back to the floor, his head hitting the edge of the bedside drawers with a sickening crack. He slumped into unconsciousness...

Shrill screams woke him, the look of sheer horror mixed with abject disgust in Sopa's beautiful brown eyes, snapping him back to full alertness. He immediately followed her gaze and felt his stomach heave at the sight of what used to be his well-toned legs.

Although his eyes knew what they were seeing his brain temporarily refused to believe the evidence of his optic nerves.

He must be asleep.

Dreaming.

A drug-induced nightmare.

He shook his head and wept. He was very much wide awake. His lower extremities looked like a giant scrotum; legs fused, shortened, bulbous; swollen and rounded inside the hairy sack of angry red skin that puddled on the floor around him. His old ball-bag had all but disappeared into the wrinkly folds of the new - just a rough, dark patch of skin serving as a pathetic reminder of its previous existence. His new penis, which just hours ago had hung long and thick between his thighs had followed suit leaving little more than a smooth nub: no foreskin; no glans; no urethra.

What the fuck? How was he going to piss?

His weeping turned to screams that bounced around the room. Sopa, with her hands clamped over her mouth, either to stifle her own screams or hold her stomach contents in place, ran to the phone and called Dr Kohl, yelling and wailing her observations down the line.

'I'll be there in an hour...do what you can to make him comfortable.'

She dropped the phone and stared at the monstrosity on the floor. What the hell could she do to make this...*thing* more comfortable?

'Help me...' Richard pleaded, his voice thin and weedy.

The nurse stood; frozen. Impotent. Despite her professional training and all the horror and gore she must have experienced in her working life, she seemed unable to bring herself to touch the freak that lay on the floor in front of her. As he gazed back at her, helpless and confused, he saw that she was no longer just focused on what had become of his legs. Her dark eyes were slowly moving up the length of his body, coming to a sickening halt at his face.

Richard slowly put his hands to his head, a cold dread tightening around his bowels like a hangman's noose...

His scalp was smooth beneath his fingers. All his hair was gone. Shit...fuck me...

He gradually let his hands drift down his face. Everything *seemed* in place but something felt different; odd, *wrong*. His nose was flatter, his lips less defined and his lower jaw seemed much wider. He let his digits slide lower...and gasped, breath strangled in his throat, where the skin hung loose like a turtle's neck. He pulled and grabbed at the flaccid folds, the skin on his face tightening as he did so.

What the fuck was happening to him?

This couldn't be normal. Couldn't be just side-effects...

'Help me!' He pleaded with his nurse once more, the woman visibly swallowing her bile-laden disgust at the thought of touching this aberration before slipping her hands into a pair of latex gloves. She crouched beside his chest, deliberately keeping as far away as possible from the hideous sack at his lower regions. Her gloved hands trembled, hovering over her patient's body as she debated exactly where and how to touch him. She couldn't lift his bulk back to his bed and she doubted his testicle-like legs would allow him to raise himself off the floor.

'I want to see...' His voice was now barely audible, his lips almost sealed shut and dissolving into his misshapen face. 'Bathroom...mirror...'

Sopa turned towards the ensuite. She *could* possibly drag him across the smooth floor so that he could see his reflection. Hell, there was little else she could do to help him - the poor bastard seemed to be 'mutating' before her eyes. The nurse stood at his head, bending her knees as she reached under his arms to lift him. She grunted as she took his weight, attempting to raise his upper torso off the floor. As she straightened up she felt the skin on Richard's body slide in her grip. The flesh was loose, slipping over his ribs and gathering in folds under her gloved fingers. She screamed, dropping her patient back to the floor.

Sopa took a deep breath and tried again, ignoring the nauseating feel of the slick folds in her grasp she hauled him, one step at a time, towards the bathroom. With every backwards pace, she had to pause for breath, bending her knees and lowering him slightly before lifting him again and pulling him back towards her. Every time she stopped, the loose skin slid back down his torso a little before being pulled back up towards his head as she hauled on him again. Every movement of his flesh tugged at the skin on his face and head, stretching and tightening.

Richard had stopped screaming. Pain was being replaced by something else. Something that was stiffening his body, his torso becoming thicker, blood vessels pulsing and throbbing under his skin. He could feel his face getting hotter as blood filled his veins and capillaries, his head pounding at the top of his skull.

He felt good.

With each step backwards that his nurse took, his skin slipped up and down. Each movement of his flesh teased and pleasured his nerves until, by the time Sopa had dragged him through the bathroom doorway, Richard could feel his new balls contracting, a warmth flowing through him. As she manoeuvred him in front of the mirror, the skin at his head ripped open.

Sopa screamed and fell back against the wall, pushing Richard away from her, releasing him from her grip.

It didn't matter. He was past the point of no return.

The sensation of warmth was now a liquid heat, surging up through him. The pounding at the top of his head peaked and he moaned in agonised joy as he felt his skull crack and, through his dimming vision, saw a gaping slit open in the bone as a geyser of semen erupted. Huge gobs of white cum splashed against the walls and ceiling, Sopa's screams adding to the transcendent pleasure of his release.

Beneath the shrieks and the splashes and the orgasmic madness in his head, he thought he heard the sound of a ping-pong ball bouncing across the bathroom floor…

*

Richard looked around the room with blurry eyes. Something, somewhere, was beeping.

'Good afternoon, Mr Smith.' A cheery voice. 'You're awake.'

'Where am I?' He gagged as he spoke, a feeding tube filling his throat.

The male nurse stared down at him. 'In hospital, Mr Smith. You contracted a very serious infection following your procedure and have been in a coma for over a week.'

'A coma? But…'

'Shhh…just rest, Mr Smith. The antibiotics have done their job. In a day or two, you can be moved out of intensive care to a general ward to continue your recovery.' The nurse took a clipboard from the foot of the bed and scribbled something on Richard's notes before heading to the door and opening it. He turned his head toward his patient before leaving the room. 'The doctor will be in to see you shortly, Mr Smith. She'll explain everything that's been going on and answer any questions you might have.'

The nurse left the room, quietly closing the door behind him.

Richard could feel it pressing down on him. Could feel the weight of the bruised, swollen snake that was taped tight to his belly. He lifted the sheet to take a look, the sight of the catheter protruding from his dressed appendage inducing gut-wrenching nausea along with a chest-crushing deja-vu.

Not again...not again...

With panicked fingers, he tugged at the feeding-tube, choking and retching as it slid from his dry throat. Raising his head from his pillow, he scanned the room. A wheeled-table sat at the bottom of the bed, a knife and fork placed haphazardly on the brown plastic surface.

He couldn't help but chuckle to himself.

He was in an NHS hospital - trust a tax-payer funded organisation to give cutlery to a comatose patient.

He sat up, pain shooting through his nether regions as he did so and stretched his fingers towards the table, pulling it closer on its squeaking castors. The knife was of no use to him, blunt and rounded – good for cutting mashed potato.

It would have to be the fork.

Richard hauled the catheter from his alien urethra, a splash of warm piss hitting his belly in its wake and he stared for a second into the dead weeping eye. As he pulled the bandages away, the sight of the serpentine tumescence spiked his gut with ice. He took a deep breath and dug the fork's prongs into the stitches at the base of his new penis, blood and thick yellow pus oozing from the opened wounds. Grasping the bloated black cock he tugged as hard as his agonised nerves would allow but the thing held firm. He thrust the fork deeper, squirming as the tines met a meaty resistance, pushing the eating-iron as far as he could before bending and twisting the metal prongs inside his appendage until he felt something give…

Only halfway through a sixty hour week Dr Penny Thwaite was exhausted and stressed as fuck. She'd skipped breakfast after her appetite was anaesthetised by her live-in boyfriend – full of beans with his thirty-five hours a week insurance job - slamming out of the house, whining like a brat over their non-existent sex life. Starving, she had just barely found time to wolf down a tasteless and overpriced chicken salad for a late lunch, silencing her growling stomach for the time being at least.

As she reached for the door to the intensive-care room with her left hand, the fingers of her right rolled constantly around the table-tennis ball that she used to relieve her tension.

She checked her watch. It was 4.40.

An image of Pete flashed into her mind. He would have left work by now and if her suspicions were correct was probably on his way to wallow in the musky bouquet of Tara, the slutty nineteen-year-old waitress from their favourite wine bar.

Fuck Pete! If he was fucking that little bitch she'd cut his fucking…

She opened the door and stepped into the room.

…cock off!

It sat on the table staring at her out of its sightless eye and she felt the blood drain from her face, vomit rushing up to her gullet. The bland meal she had so recently eaten seemed much more vibrant second time around as it splashed over her black, sensible shoes.

Richard sat cross-legged on the gore-soaked bed, his hands between his splayed legs, slicked red with blood, playing with the tubes that hung, glistening wet from the gaping gash where his genitals used to be. He looked at first glance like an irate toddler playing with tomato sauce coated spaghetti, his anguished wails just adding to the effect. He raised his eyes to the visitor at his door and revelled in her gape-mouthed screams.

Beneath his demented cries and the shrieks of the doctor, the sound of a ping-pong ball bouncing across the tiled floor went unnoticed...

BEAST MODE
Written by **Wrath James White**

Week 1. Day 1

Went to the gym on the third floor. It took me a while to find it. In the four years I've lived in this building, the only time I'd ever set foot in the fitness center before today was the day the saleswoman walked me around to impress me with the condo's many wonderful amenities. There were six treadmills, six elliptical machines, three rowing machines, a pulley machine, a couple of adjustable benches, and a dumbbell rack with dumbbells ranging from five pounds all the way up to a hundred. It was pretty intimidating. Probably why I'd never used it before.

I pulled out my new bible: 'BEAST MODE! Six-Week Body Transformation Workout,' written by a guy named Adam Namor, who was a strength and conditioning coach for a couple of famous mixed martial artists This wasn't your normal bodybuilding book. This was supposed to build functional, practical strength and endurance and was based on the workouts of Olympic gymnasts, sprinters, boxers, and wrestlers,.

I turned to the first chapter: 'Week 1,' and read down the list of exercises. I groaned in genuine emotional pain when I spotted 'burpees' and 'mountain climbers' on the list. Burpees reminded me of a sadistic gym teacher I had in junior high school who used to make us run a mile every day in the middle of the schoolyard— in the Las Vegas heat. I hated that bitch. Another likely reason I've avoided the gym for most of my life. Of course, there's also my visceral hatred of jocks, stemming from being a certified nerd throughout high school and college. Anyway, here's the complete list of exercises.

Warm up with a fifteen-minute jog on the treadmill, followed by

15 burpees
15 mountain climbers
15 pushups
15 bench dips
15 pull-ups
30 squats (with light dumbbells or own body weight)
15 crunches
Side plank (30 seconds each side)

Repeat 2 to 3 times.

I made it through once and then promptly vomited into the nearest trash can. I forced myself to do one more set. Then I threw up again. This time I didn't make it to the trash can. Almost regurgitated a third time cleaning up the vomit from the gym floor. That's when I decided I needed to keep a journal of all of this. Have I mentioned that I'm a former smoker, a drinker, and that I'm thirty pounds overweight? Big belly, big ass, skinny arms, man boobs.

This is going to be hard. I haven't even begun the diet yet.

Low-carb, high-fat, moderate protein. It's called the Primal Diet. I found it on an Internet search of 'best diets to get ripped quick.' I liked the sound of it. There was irony to it. What it meant was that I could eat meat, dairy, and lots of vegetables. Only low sugar fruits. No grains. No legumes. No sugar. No alcohol.

It said I should only eat fresh fruits and vegetables. Nothing processed. That was going to be hard under the circumstances.

Luckily, I had lots of frozen vegetables that my ex-girlfriend had left in the freezer. Those would work.

Tonight's dinner: Broccoli and cheese and two burger patties. No bun.

Day 2

Woke up this morning at eight with a loud groan and a few popular words of profanity. My entire body was sore. I took as hot a shower as I could stand. The steaming water felt good on my aching muscles. Afterward, I threw on some boxer shorts and popped in a yoga DVD. After thirty minutes of poses and stretches, I actually felt better. Maybe my ex-girlfriend wasn't such a kook after all.

For breakfast I made a two-egg omelet with onions, mushrooms, bell peppers, and aged cheddar, along with three pieces of beef bacon and a tall glass of milk. I read for a while. Wrote in my journal. Went onto the balcony and looked out at the city, but I found it too depressing. Las Vegas was just one big festering pit of wasted dreams, wasted lives. Someone should have dropped a bomb on it long ago and put us all out of our misery. Fuck this town. I don't know why I stayed here for so long.

I decided to hit the gym early today. Made it through two sets of exercises without throwing up this time. For lunch I had a can of sardines in olive oil and a salad. Dinner was a sixteen-ounce rib eye steak, two hardboiled eggs, and half a bag of frozen green beans. I need to slow down on how much I'm eating. Don't want to run out of food. Working out just makes me ravenous.

Day 3

Ran into the redhead from across the hall in the gym this morning. She looks amazing, but she talks too much. I don't watch the news because I don't want to hear about all the bad shit going on in the world. There's never anything positive on TV. The last thing I wanted was to have to hear a blow-by-blow of the latest atrocities when I'm trying to get my workout in. At least I got to stare at her tits. She has great tits. She was only wearing a sports bra when she ran on the treadmill beside me, and her D-cups were flopping all over the place. I was staring so hard I almost fell off the treadmill. Made it through three sets this time. I felt like the redhead was impressed, though she didn't really let on. I think she may have seen me staring at her tits. Now I feel like a jerk. I wonder if I should apologize.

Found some pork chops in the back of the freezer. They were shriveled and gray, completely freezer burned. No telling how long they'd been there. My ex-girlfriend was anti-pork. I had to have bought them before she and I started dating. That has to make them at least two years old. Probably older. But beggars can't be choosers. Had them with the rest of the green beans. They were delicious. Well, kinda.

Day 4

My body is so sore I want to scream. Did three sets again today. I want to say it's getting easier, that I'm getting stronger. But I think it's all mental. I'm just getting used to the pain. This time I ran with the treadmill on an incline and I used ten pound dumbbells when I did my squats. The redhead was there again. Her eyes were bloodshot. She'd obviously been crying. I asked her if she was okay, and she smiled and gave me a hug. Then she spent twenty minutes telling me about all the horrible shit going on in the world, and her life in particular. I listened, even though I didn't really want to hear it.

I had a hard time falling asleep last night, despite being bored and exhausted. I kept having nightmares about being eaten alive. I could almost feel teeth ripping into my abdomen and tearing out my intestines. I woke up screaming. I did jumping jacks and burpees until I finally collapsed from exhaustion.

Day 5

Only got three hours' sleep last night. I feel like hammered shit. Made another omelet for breakfast. Ate the last of the bacon. Starting to run out of eggs. Gonna have to borrow some from the neighbors. Maybe I'll see if the redhead has some. The workout was much easier today. Progress!

Day 6

Rest day. Spent the day watching porn and reading comic books like I was back in high school. I needed it. Every time I tried to take a nap I kept dreaming about getting torn apart. I'm just too sensitive.

Day 7

Went over to borrow some eggs from the redhead. Finally worked up the nerve to ask her name. Cindy. First Cindy I've met since elementary school. I still think of it as a child's name. She said she used to be a stripper. I guess that fits. I traded her a couple of steaks for three cartons of eggs. I invited her to dinner, but she said she wasn't in the mood for company. Fuck her.

Did a different routine on the treadmill today. I started at six miles per hour, then increased it every tenth of a mile until I got up to eight miles per hour, and then I'd start all over again. My lungs were burning so badly I wanted to stop after the first five minutes, but I made it all fifteen minutes. Tomorrow the workouts get harder.

Week 2. Day 8

Twenty-minute jog on the treadmill.

30 jumping jacks

30 burpees

30 mountain climbers

20 pushups

20 bench dips
Set of 10 dumbbell bench presses with 25 lb. dumbbells
20 pull-ups
Set of 10 dumbbell curls with 15 lb. dumbbells
Set of 10 shoulder presses with 15 lb. dumbbells
Set of 50 squats with 20 lb. dumbbells
Set of 10 lunges with 20 lb. dumbbells
Side planks (1 minute each side)

Repeat 2 to 3 times.

I only made it through once. Had natural, organic, all-beef hotdogs and pickled asparagus tips for lunch. Hamburgers without a bun and salad again for dinner. Checked the scale. I've already lost ten pounds. I guess my body must be in shock going from fast food, beer, and apathy to exercise and zero carbs or sugar. Still have a long way to go.

Day 9

Ran into Mr. Jenkins from the second floor. He didn't look so good. He always looks so angry. I can't say I blame him. Life sucks. I asked him if he had any canned vegetables. He said he hated vegetables. His wife filled the pantry with all kinds of canned food a few weeks before she passed, and he hadn't eaten any of it. Said he'd give me all of them for $100. I don't know what he planned to do with the money, but I paid him. My pantry is full now. There was a really bad smell coming from his apartment. I definitely heard someone moaning. I think I need to keep an eye on Mr. Jenkins. Only made it through one set of exercises again today. This shit is hard!

Had three eggs for breakfast. No bacon. Canned tuna and canned green beans for lunch. Cooked hot dogs and frozen peas and carrots for dinner.

Day 10

Two full sets! Getting stronger! I read that fasting helps your body repair itself, so I didn't eat all day today. I'm going to be so fucking hungry in the morning!

Day 11

More eggs for breakfast. Hardboiled. Ate half a block of cheese, about three-quarters of a pound if I had to guess. Saw Cindy in the gym again this morning. She ran for a full two hours without stopping. I guess that explains that amazing body of hers. She had the incline on 6 percent and the speed at 7.5! I kept up with her (sort of) for the first ten minutes, and then I said, 'Fuck that!' and put it back down to 6 mph and a 1 percent incline for the last ten minutes. I was exhausted when I got done, but I still managed to make it through two full sets of exercises again.

Ran into a kid running through the halls. Kid couldn't be more than ten years old. No parent in sight. I asked him where his parents were, but he ran off. I hope he's okay.

Ate my last steak for dinner today. Starting to regret trading Cindy steak for those eggs. It's just frozen hot dogs and hamburgers from here on out. I do have one pack of frozen chicken fingers, but they're breaded. I could probably scrape off all the breading though.

Day 12

Three full sets! Who's the man? I'm the man. Saw Mr. Jenkins in the hall right after my workout. He looked even worse today. He tried to bite me so I had to crush his skull with a twenty pound dumbbell. Got brains and blood everywhere. I never realized the brain was so pale and squishy. It looked like a big nest of bloated larva floating in cherry Jell-O. Took me almost an hour to clean it all, and then drag his body into the elevator and down to the basement with the rest of them. So glad the power is still working. It would suck if I had to carry him all the way downstairs. Mr.

Jenkins may not have liked canned vegetables, but whatever he was eating, he definitely wasn't missing any meals. Now I'm curious who that was upstairs moaning in his apartment. Mrs. Jenkins perhaps?

Ate canned tuna with lettuce and pickles for lunch, and corned beef hash and canned beets for dinner. I fucking hate beets.

Day 13

Cindy invited me to her apartment for lunch. Steamed carrots and Brussels sprouts with canned beef. It honestly wasn't as bad as it sounds and was still in line with my diet. She had rice with her meal, but I declined. Too many carbs, and rice also contains gluten, despite what the USDA says. Rice and corn farmers had their lobbyists make sure their crops didn't get added to the list of foods that contain gluten. So even though corn has almost as much gluten as wheat, you can put both corn and rice in a product and still call it 'gluten free,' and idiots buy it. I'm no idiot.

Cindy told me she was planning to run the 33.3 miles to Hoover Dam. That's where the roadblocks and barricades start. I asked her if she had any weapons. She didn't. I asked her what she planned to do if she got chased or surrounded. She said she'd just run faster. I didn't tell her how stupid I thought that plan was, because my plan isn't a whole hell of a lot better. Besides, I really, really want to fuck Cindy. I know that sounds so sexist, but I haven't had sex in months. Not since my ex-girlfriend left. I wonder if she's still alive.

Three full sets again today. I can see my bicep and chest muscles developing. I wonder if Cindy notices?

Day 14

Another rest day. Finally! Did yoga again. Getting a little more flexible. At least I can actually touch my toes now. That might also be because my gut isn't as big. Regular exercise and no more beer means no more beer belly. That's one good thing about all this.

After a lifetime struggling with my weight, I finally have the proper motivation to get in shape.

Saw that kid again too. He was running through the halls with what looked like some kind of ninja sword. I think there was blood on it, but I can't be certain.

I decided to take a peek in Mr. Jenkins's apartment. He might have guns in there. He seemed like the NRA type. Pretty sure he was a Republican. I also needed to deal with whatever was causing that smell. Everyone else in the building was too lazy or scared to do anything about it. Most of them never came out of their apartments anymore. That meant I had to do almost everything myself.

They had a tenant's meeting a few weeks ago, right after the building was locked down, to try to get some sort of cooperative effort going to share food and maintain the building. That day I helped my neighbors clean up the building. That's when we decided to use the basement as a garbage dump and morgue. It was the only thing we could all agree upon. There was a lot of bitching and complaining, but no solutions. It was hard getting people to agree on anything during the best of times. You'd think a crisis like this would have brought out everyone's survival instincts, made people more willing to work together for the common good, but it did the opposite. It made everyone more suspicious and self-centered. Myself included. I had never been much of a people person. My neighbors tried having a few more meetings, but attendance dwindled down to nothing. No one cared anymore. Everyone was just out for themselves.

I broke into Mr. Jenkins's apartment, had to kick down the door. There was a woman in his guest bedroom tied to the bed. Definitely not Mrs. Jenkins. This woman was too young and built almost as well as Cindy. Or had been, before she'd begun to rot. One of her breasts had sunken in and deflated like a rotten grapefruit. I can only imagine what Mr. Jenkins had been doing with her. I bashed her skull in with a steam iron and then dragged her to the basement too. I didn't bother cleaning up though. It wasn't my apartment.

I did find a handgun in Mr. Jenkins's place. I knew he was the type. It's a SIG Sauer .40 caliber semi-automatic with three full clips. I guess I'm going to have to teach myself how to shoot. This might just make my plan a little more realistic. I also found a fifteen-pound sledgehammer in the basement when I was disposing of the body. That could definitely come in handy. I'll have to add it to my workout routine.

Mr. Jenkins still had a lot of other canned foods in his apartment. I found more Spam and corned beef than anyone had any right to have. There was also tuna fish and canned chicken. I found a big suitcase and filled it with as much food as it would hold. I figured I was entitled to it since I cleaned up his mess. Well, I got rid of the body at least.

He had a bunch of frozen dinners too, but they were all full of carbs. Every last one contained a fuck-ton of cornstarch and corn syrup. The last thing I needed was to gain more weight. That would have completely fucked up my plans. I need to be increasing my strength, speed, and endurance, not chowing down on hot pockets and frozen pizzas. I left the frozen dinners for some other scavenger to find.

Week 3. Day 15
    New workout.
    30 minutes on the treadmill
    50 jumping jacks
    50 burpees
    50 mountain climbers
    30 pushups
    30 bench dips
    Set of 10 dumbbell bench presses with 35 lb. dumbbells
    20 pull-ups
    Set of 10 dumbbell curls with 25 lb. dumbbells

Set of 10 shoulder presses with 25 lb. dumbbells
Set of 10 tricep extensions with 25 lb. dumbbells
Set of 50 squats with 25 lb. dumbbells
Set of 20 lunges with 25 lb. dumbbells
Side planks (1 minute each side.)

I found an old truck tire in the basement and hauled it into the service elevator and upstairs to the gym. I spent five minutes hitting the truck tire with the sledgehammer like they always show MMA fighters do during their workouts. Let me tell you, that shit is hard! I feel like I say that a lot. It's all hard, I guess. Either that or I'm just a pussy. I guess I need to man-up if my plan is going to work. I need to get tougher, mentally as well as physically.

Back in my apartment, after my shower, I looked up MMA videos on the Internet, trying to learn a few moves. I did my best to practice them and commit them to memory. It was challenging without a partner, and without a teacher to tell me if I was actually doing the techniques correctly. I fell asleep watching Special Forces videos on shooting and hand-to-hand combat. Not sure how much, if anything, I actually learned. But at least I now had some idea how to use the gun I found in Mr. Jenkins's apartment.

Had hot dogs for lunch with a big hunk of cheese. Ate Spam and eggs for both breakfast and dinner, along with half a pack of frozen peas and carrots.

Day 16

Ran forty minutes on the treadmill today. Not jogged. Ran! I thought I was going to die at first. The first twenty minutes were pure agony, but then my lungs just opened up and I could breathe again. I felt like I could run forever. I only stopped because my legs started getting sore. I'm thinking I might try to run to Hoover Dam with Cindy, if she'll wait for me. It's going to take me another ten or twelve weeks to get up to where I can run thirty-three miles though. I don't think we have ten or twelve weeks. I guess it's time to up my mileage. Push myself a little harder. Down another four pounds. Less than four more weeks to go in my six-week body transformation! Hoping I can lose at least ten more pounds while also putting on another ten pounds of muscle. That should make running a lot easier.

Started another twenty-four-hour fast. It does make me feel a lot more ... I don't know ... not to sound like a Scientologist or anything, but—clear.

Day 17

Cindy ran for three hours today! At least that's what she said. She'd already been on the treadmill for more than an hour when I walked into the gym. I pushed myself to run for an hour. Then I did three sets of my workout routine. I'm definitely getting a lot stronger.

I talked to Cindy about running to Hoover Dam with her. I told her I could help protect her. She said I'd just slow her down. Besides, I'd never be able to run 33.3 miles in a week. She was pretty sure she'd be ready to make the trip by next weekend. I told her I'd miss her and she kissed me, right on the lips. I don't think I've ever been kissed by a woman that beautiful before. I almost came on myself.

I hit that tire with the sledgehammer for ten minutes straight with no breaks. My back is killing me!

Had scrambled eggs and canned mushrooms and artichoke hearts for breakfast. I've gotta say, it was pretty fucking delicious. Had tuna again for lunch. Made egg salad for dinner.

Day 18

Found out that kid has been hunting in the building, going from apartment to apartment and killing anything inside that wasn't human. Kid couldn't be more than ten years old. I asked him if he wanted to come to my apartment for something to eat, but he called me a pervert and ran off.

Ran for an hour on the treadmill again today, and I mean really ran! I had the treadmill set for eight-minute miles. Still not as fast as Cindy. She can run seven-minutes miles for eighteen or twenty miles! I'm still proud of myself. I've come a long way from the overweight, antisocial couch potato I was. I watched a DVD of John Carpenter's *The Thing* before bedtime. Had nightmares all night. It might be a good idea to go back to Mr. Jenkins' apartment to see if he has any good DVDs.

Eggs for breakfast again. Tuna and canned spinach for lunch. Hamburger without the bun and canned green beans again for dinner.

Day 19

Cindy knocked on my door this morning. She asked me if I'd seen that kid running through the halls with a samurai sword. I told her I was pretty sure it was a ninja sword, and that he was going from apartment to apartment killing things.

'Things? Those things? Isn't he too young?'

I shrugged. I didn't think his age really mattered anymore. We were all going to die eventually. What did it matter?

I invited Cindy to stay for breakfast. I made us both omelets with canned mushrooms, canned spinach, and American cheese. It would have tasted better with the aged cheddar, but I had already eaten all of it.

While she ate, Cindy talked about running to Hoover Dam again.

I asked her once more why I couldn't go with her. Once again she told me I'd just slow her down. I told her I'd miss her. There was a little twitch in the corner of her lip, and then a tear rolled down her cheek. She quickly wiped it away and then shoved more eggs in her mouth.

Day 20

Had tuna and a hardboiled egg for breakfast. I was on my way down to the gym when I saw that kid in the hallway again.

145

Something is definitely wrong with him. He was hacking at some big fat guy with that sword of his. The guy was bloated and decaying, dripping rot and putrescence. His skin had begun to slip. The kid had already lopped off the guy's legs and was still chopping at him with his sword as the fat guy crawled down the hallway. The boy stayed just out of reach of the big guy's snapping teeth, slinging blood and fetid meat onto the walls, floor, and ceiling as he continued hacking and slicing away at him.

The smell wafting from that guy was enough to gag a maggot. I couldn't understand how a kid could watch something like that, let alone participate in it. I could feel my own sanity slipping away just witnessing this carnage. I was holding on with everything I had, but I could feel my very soul screaming in horror. What the fuck was wrong with that kid? Too many violent video games perhaps?

Splashes of gore coated the boy from head to toe. His face was a dripping mask of blood and liquid rot, but his eyes were flat and dispassionate. He had dead eyes, oblivious to the horror around him. His face was completely expressionless as he chopped at the big guy's neck and shoulders with the sword. When the guy's head finally came loose, dangling from the bloody, ragged stump of his neck like some gruesome cat's toy, I wanted to say something to the kid, tell him he shouldn't be doing that. But I couldn't think of any reason why not, except that I was the one who was probably going to have to clean it all up.

After spending a couple of hours mopping and scrubbing the hallways, I went to the gym and ran for more than an hour, until I almost fell off the treadmill. I skipped lunch and dinner. Just wasn't in the mood to eat.

Day 21

Cindy knocked on my door again this morning. I was so tired. I barely slept last night. I kept thinking about that kid hacking that guy to pieces like he was cutting beef. All the blood and bits of

146

rotten fat and muscles tissue that had littered the walls and floor. God, that shit was fucking horrible!

I was still thinking about it when she walked in, wearing nothing but a bathrobe. She was completely naked underneath! She laid on my couch, opened her robe, and spread her legs, revealing a perfectly shaved pussy. It was one of those moments you read about in the forum section of men's magazines. The type of shit I'd always been certain never really happened to anyone. But there I was, staring at the type of body I normally only saw on the cover of fitness magazines, legs spread, arms outstretched, gesturing for me to join her.

I went to lay on top of her, fumbling with my belt, but she took me by the back of the head and guided my face down between those smooth, freshly shaven thighs. She must have just showered, because she smelled like lavender and vanilla. I licked her pussy until she came. The entire time she kept telling me how much she needed this, and then she thanked me and left. Never touched me. I popped in a porno and jacked off three times, and then ate a couple of eggs and went down to the gym.

One hour on the treadmill, three sets of exercises, ten minutes swinging the sledgehammer, followed by some yoga. I wasn't really feeling any of my DVDs. Luckily, the Internet is still up and running. I watched sitcoms and action movies until I fell asleep.

Day 22

Decided to practice with the gun. Went out on the balcony and shot off a few rounds. Didn't hit much. My apartment is too high up. But I did get the hang of working the safety, using the sites, and not flinching in anticipation of the recoil. I don't want to use up all the bullets, so I guess that was the best I could do.

Did three sets of exercises and ran for an hour. Then I had some canned chicken, canned spinach, and boiled some frozen asparagus.

Day 23

Rest day. Ate some eggs and cheese. Did some yoga. Tried to sleep. Dreamt about the boy chopping the fuck out of that fat guy every goddamn time I closed my eyes. Decided to say fuck a rest day and went down to the gym for a run. Ran six miles. Tired as fuck now. Still can't sleep. Ate two cans of tuna and a can of fucking beets. Ran out of green beans and I'm trying to ration the spinach. God, I fucking hate beets!

Day 24

Saw Cindy in the gym this morning. First time I saw her since she came to my apartment the other day. She smiled and waved, then put on her headphones and jumped on the treadmill. Why are the beautiful ones always such assholes?

I ran six miles again today. I have to say I'm pretty impressed with myself. I've lost more than twenty pounds in less than a month and feel as strong as a fucking ox! I think this might work. Ate a can of potted meat. That's what it was called. Potted meat. Never heard of it before. It was just salty chunks of beef. Dog food for humans. Had the last of the frozen peas and carrots before remembering that peas are fucking legumes! So not exactly in keeping with my Primal diet. Fuck it. One day of carbs won't hurt. Not like I'm eating ice cream and pizza.

Day 25

Cindy knocked on my door again this morning. She was wearing the same robe. Naked underneath again. I started to protest. To stand up for myself. But she surprised me. She dropped the robe, walked right past me into my bedroom. I seriously wish I had cleaned my bedroom. It was covered in dirty laundry and cum-crusted towels. Cindy didn't seem to mind. She laid on my dirty, sweaty, semen-stained sheets, spread her legs, and said those two words every man dreams of hearing: 'Fuck me.' I didn't have to be asked twice.

Neither of us went to the gym today. We stayed in my apartment, fucking, eating, and talking. Cindy said she was leaving tomorrow. She was ready to try to make it to Hoover Dam. I asked her why she had to run the whole way. She could just run to the nearest car and drive to Hoover Dam. She shot that idea down, pointing out that the streets were jam-packed with vehicles, and that she didn't know how to hotwire a car anyway. To take her own car, she'd have to open the garage, which meant unlocking the entire building and putting everyone inside at risk, and then there would still be the problem of the clogged streets.

'What about a bike or a motorcycle?'

Same problem with the motorcycle. No keys, and she couldn't hotwire one. She said she'd thought about the bike, but the streets were littered with glass and debris. Falling off a bike and hurting herself would make her even more vulnerable. Running was her best bet. That's when I told her my idea to fight my way out. That's why I've been doing so much strength training. I figured I could just fight my way all the way to Hoover Dam, or at least until I found a spot where the roads were clear and I could borrow a car. She asked me if I was serious, then told me it was the dumbest plan she'd ever heard. We laughed about it, then had sex again.

I scraped the breading off the chicken fingers and cooked them for us, along with my last can of spinach. I wanted to beg her not to go, but I understood. Staying locked up in this building, waiting to be rescued, wasn't an option. Plus, she'd been following the news, and she was pretty sure the government was planning to nuke the place in the next few days. The only thing saving them so far was a Congress that couldn't wipe its own ass without arguing about it. But soon they would give the order, and Las Vegas would be a big mushroom cloud.

'I don't think you're going to have the time to get in the kind of shape you want to get in,' Cindy said.

I told her about the gun and the two-and-a-half magazines of ammo. My plan was to use the sledgehammer to crush skulls until my arms got tired. Then I'd switch to the small hatchet I'd had since I was a young scout. Then, when I was too tired to fight anymore, I'd use the gun. By then, hopefully, I'd be somewhere safe. Another building, a car, somewhere, and I'd just keep repeating that process all the way to Hoover Dam. She nodded at me and smiled. It was the kind of smile you gave someone to boost their confidence before a contest you didn't think they had any chance of winning. The kind of smile normally followed with platitudes like: 'It doesn't matter if you win or lose but how you play the game.' Only it did matter this time. Losing meant death. Or worse.

'I think you're already pretty badass though. Maybe you can make it.'

Maybe. That's what kept me up all night. Maybe. While Cindy slept, snuggled up against me, I decided I wasn't going to let her go without me. I was going to protect her. I would make sure she made it. It occurred to me that, before all this, a girl like her would have looked at a guy like me and thought, *Not if he was the last man on earth.* Cindy may have thought the same thing about me that first day in the gym. Now we were in bed together, and I was considering risking my life for her. Funny how quickly shit can change. As far as Cindy was concerned, I was the last man on earth.

Day 26

Cindy left without telling me. I woke up to her screams. I ran to the balcony and could see her down in the street, getting chased by dozens of rotting corpses. They were pouring out of the buildings on both sides of the street, out of the stalled cars and busses, out of the casinos, bars, restaurants, and gaudy tourist trap souvenir shops. A massive wave of rotting humanity, flowing through the streets like sewage, heading in her direction. Hundreds of them. There was no way she was going to make it. I grabbed a pair of cargo shorts I'd selected weeks ago to wear when I made my own bid for freedom, the hatchet, the sledgehammer, and the gun. Shoving the magazines into my pockets, I ran down eight flights of stairs, unlocked the front door, and raced up the block.

I heard footsteps behind me and turned to see the kid with the ninja sword running just a few strides behind. I nodded to him and he nodded back as we raced into the fray. Cindy had been cornered against a bus when we caught up to her. I yelled and started swinging the sledgehammer. Skulls cracked and ruptured like week-old Jack-o'-lanterns as iron met bone.

I saw Cindy go down, watched her stomach get ripped open, her organs torn out in fistfuls and consumed. Heard the sound of skin and muscle tissue ripping and tearing, bones and tendon breaking, ghoulish slurping and chewing, mixed with her ear-piercing cries of agony. Her pink flesh stretched like taffy as they tore her apart. She was beyond help. We locked eyes for a moment and a look of utter shock, disbelief, and disappointment crossed her face. I couldn't tell if she was disappointed in herself for not being able to outrun them or in me for not rescuing her. Then her pupils dilated and fixed in place as her life fled.

I heard the boy cry out from behind me. He was getting overwhelmed. The dead had surrounded him, and his sword arm was obviously tired. He was about to suffer the same fate as Cindy.

I fought my way to him, and together we ran back to the condo. We were both covered in blood and rot when we pulled down the security gates and locked the doors behind us. We collapsed on the floor of the lobby, breathing hard, trying to catch our breath.

I thought about Cindy. All that training. All that work, and it hadn't helped her. She didn't even make it a mile. But my training had come in handy. I had killed more than a dozen of those things, and I managed to save the boy. Fucking Beast Mode for real! Who'd have ever thought a guy like me could go from zero to hero in less than a month? Almost a hero, that is. I hadn't been able to save poor Cindy. I remember the look of pain and horror on her face, how her eyes had pleaded with me to save her while she was being ripped apart. That look will plague me for the rest of my life, however long that is.

I closed my eyes and let out a sob. Tears began to flow. Then I heard a sound that made me think I may have just gone insane. Laughter.

I opened my eyes and the boy was sitting up, decorated in blood and bits of decayed flesh, laughing like he'd just had the time of his life. Like he was watching some hilarious cartoon or had just rode the world's greatest roller coaster.

'That was pretty awesome! When do you think we'll be ready to try again?' he asked.

'About two weeks and four days,' I said. 'Give or take. Just until I've completed my total body transformation.'

Let's just hope Congress continues to hold their gridlock. Maybe long enough for me to get the boy into shape too. This is going to be hard.

DEWEY DAVENPORT
Written by Shane McKenzie

—Dad's Acting Funny—

My name's Dewey Davenport. I'm six.

I'm in the first grade and my teacher says I'm real good at reading. I'm good at math too, but my teacher hasn't said nothing about it yet. She probably will tomorrow I think. Cuz I'm real good at counting and adding things together.

I always do good in school cuz my mom says if I don't I'll end up like one of those stinky people who sit on the sidewalk all day and ask for money. To me, it looks kinda fun to live outside and do whatever you want all the time. I bet those guys don't even ever have to take a bath cuz when we see them they're always super dirty. I think, to me, it would be kinda cool to never take a bath. But I don't wanna be stinky. Or hungry. And some of them don't even ever wear any shoes. I bet it's probably pretty hard to walk around all day outside with no shoes like that. Maybe that's why they're always sitting on the sidewalk. I bet if enough people gave them money they'd spend it on shoes.

So that's why I try real hard at school. Mom gets real happy when I do good and when the teacher tells her how good I do. Dad says he's proud of me, but I think he just says that cuz Mom is listening to him when he says stuff. I can tell Dad doesn't really care about my school and my grades and what my teacher says about me. He never helps me with my homework or reads to me or anything like that. But my dad is still a good dad. He plays with me and watches movies with me and lets me eat junk food all the time and stay up late and sometimes he even lets me say bad words because he thinks it's funny when I say them.

Mom gets real mad at him when he does fun things with me sometimes. She says we're not friends, that he's my dad and should act like it goddammit.

Mom and Dad fight a lot. Or at least they did. Mom left on a vacation like a week ago and she hasn't come home yet. Dad says they needed the time apart from each other. I was glad at first because Dad let me stay up late and watch movies and play video games and eat junk food and Mom wasn't there to yell at him or tell him to be better at being a dad goddammit.

But I kinda wish Mom would hurry up and come home already. Dad is fun and everything, but he really isn't very good at being a parent, not like Mom is. He doesn't like to clean stuff or get me to school on time. And he's no help with my homework, and even though I'm real good at reading and math and stuff, other things are hard. Mom always helps me when there's hard things on my homework, but I don't think Dad knows how to do them either.

I don't think he's been taking baths that much. Cuz he always smells and his face hair is never shaved and his eyes are always red and I think maybe he's been wearing the same clothes every day. If Mom was here, she would yell at him and make him shower and make him wash his clothes and shave his face hair off.

The house is getting real messy too because Dad doesn't like to clean like Mom does. All the dishes are in the sink so I have to stick my face under the faucet to get a drink cuz there's no cups for me to use. The fridge doesn't have any food to eat inside cuz Dad don't like to go to the store neither. There's some food in there from the last time Mom cooked, but it's real stinky now and it's got this weird green hairy stuff growing on it that makes me think of boogers and Andrew Watson in my class always eats his boogers and it's real gross so I don't wanna eat Mom's old dinner food or kids at my school might find out and I don't wanna be called booger muncher like Andrew Watson.

It's the smell coming out of the basement that's the worst. There's lots of flies in the kitchen cuz I heard they like to eat gross things and since Dad doesn't clean there's lots of gross things for them to eat in there. They even eat poop. There was a big pile of dog poop at the playground at school one time, and me and my friends watched all the flies crawling on it and eating it and it was real yucky. There were these little white wormy things in there crawling around that kinda looked like rice but Annie Thomas said they were baby flies called maggies or something. She's the one who said the flies like to eat the poop because they like gross things, and that to a fly, dog poop was like birthday cake.

I don't ever like to go in the basement because it's always dark down there even when it's day time outside and I always think there's some kind of monster or creature or smelly people with no shoes down there waiting for me to come down so they can jump out and scare me or eat me or ask me for money. But there never used to be a smell before. Not when Mom was home, but maybe that's cuz she made sure to keep it clean so no stinky stuff could start stinking and no flies would be flying around all over the place.

'Dad, there's a smell coming from the basement,' I told him.

'No there's not,' he said. 'How does candy bars for dinner sound, buddy?'

'I think maybe I'm supposed to eat broccoli or something sometimes, Dad. If I eat too much sweets the dentist told me that sugar bugs will eat all my teeth away and then I'll have to only eat soup and oatmeal all the time,' I said, but I could tell he wasn't really listening to me. And he was smoking in the house. Mom would freak out if she saw him doing that, and I wish she was home to freak out on him cuz the smoke makes my tummy kinda hurt when I breathe it. 'But, Dad, there really is a bad smell in the basement. There's flies all over and it's getting more gross every day. They're having a birthday party down there! Pretty soon the whole entire neighborhood will smell it and then they'll think we're a gross family who don't even take baths ever.'

I really missed Mom. When I thought real hard about her and

155

how she'd been gone for so long, it made me wanna cry but I just held my breath and closed my eyes real hard so no tears would come out. Dad's been acting so funny since Mom left for vacation that I didn't know if he'd get mad at me if I cried the way he used to get mad at Mom when she did.

I guess I did a pretty good job at not crying cuz Dad stood up and smooshed his cigarette right on the coffee table and he looked right at me and smiled real big.

I know my dad loves me cuz parents are supposed to love their kids cuz it's the rules, but he never really told me ever. Not like Mom who told me she loved me every day and always put her hands on her hips and pretended to be mad till I said it back. I always make her wait so I can see her pretend mad face, but then after I say it back, she always smiles at me and hugs me and kisses me all over my face and we always laugh cuz it's hard not to laugh when there's so much hugs and kisses.

But Dad was never like Mom was. So when he smiled at me like that, I knew I did something real good and that he was proud of me. I just pretended his smile was the same as him saying I love you to me.

'Dewey Davenport,' he said and kept smiling at me. 'How'd you get so smart, hmm?'

I shrugged my shoulders at him. 'I don't think you have to be smart or anything just to smell something that's stinky, Dad,' I told him. 'But I am real good at reading. And math too!'

*

Dad made me wait at the top of the stairs when he went down in the basement. I thought it was because he was checking for monsters and smelly people and wanted to make sure it was safe for me to come down there with him. But he was down there for a real long time and I could hear him moving things around and making noises like he was trying to move something real heavy.

156

'Okay, Dewey,' he called up to me. 'You can come on down now.'

But I still couldn't see nothing and it made me scared to go down in the basement when I can't see nothing even if my dad is there. I only walked down some of the steps and then I stopped and couldn't make my feet move no matter how hard I told them to move with my brain.

'Come on, son, we need to hurry while it's still good and dark outside.'

'Where are you? It's too dark down here, Dad. Only bad stuff lives in the dark.'

It felt like I stood there for a long time and Dad wasn't saying anything and my feet still wouldn't work. I started to be able to see stuff around me. Then I heard Dad moving around again and heard the sound of a plastic bag kinda like the sound Mom makes when she's packing my lunch for school and putting all my snacks and stuff in those little baggies.

Then I saw a light across the basement kinda moving around like a sword. It shined me in my face and I put up my hand so it didn't go in my eyes but I still kept my eyes open and I saw Dad standing there holding a flashlight. When he moved the flashlight he shined it on himself so I could see him and he was still smiling.

'Come on over here, buddy, and help me. Do you want to help your dad with a special project? I'll pay you one giant bowl of ice cream. Sound good?'

He was smoking again and the smoke was filling up all the air down there but I kinda liked it this time cuz it helped me not smell the other smell. The other smell was real bad, the worst smell I ever smelled. Even worse than the dog poop in the playground. I used my shirt to cover my nose and my mouth and I walked to Dad pretending that I wasn't scared cuz I wanted him to think how brave I was.

There was a giant plastic bag laying on the ground next to him and another smaller plastic bag that he was holding in his hand.

There was this dark stuff dripping out of the bag in his hand and the giant bag was sitting on a big puddle of wet stuff too. It was still too dark for me to see what it was, but I think maybe it was red or brown. Whatever the stuff was, the flies really liked it a lot cuz they couldn't stop crawling in it. No matter how many times they flew into the air, they would just kinda zigzag around, and then land back in the stuff and on the bags again.

I could tell the real bad smell was coming out of the bags because when I walked closer to Dad, I could smell the bad smell real bad. It made me feel like I was gonna throw up like those times I got real sick and couldn't eat nothing and kept throwing up in a bucket and Mom said I could stay home from school and take medicine and drink orange juice and lay in my bed all day.

'What's in there, Dad?' I asked him. 'I think maybe that's why the whole basement smells so much cuz there's something real gross in there, right?'

Dad kinda laughed when I said that. Then he used his hand that wasn't holding the bag and he patted me on the head. 'Got that right, son. But I'll tell you this. As gross as it is now, it's a lot less gross like this than it has been for the last ten years.'

I didn't understand what Dad was talking about, but I didn't say nothing cuz I was happy he was smiling so much and cuz he patted me on the head to tell me I was doing a good job and I didn't want to mess that up.

'Are you gonna throw it in the garbage so the garbage guys can throw it in their big giant garbage truck? They wear gloves so the stinky juicy stuff don't get on them.'

Dad threw his cigarette on the floor and it landed in the dark red puddle and it made a sound like a snake makes and then the bright orange part disappeared. Some flies kept landing on me and crawling and tickling me but I didn't want them to touch me cuz they were covered in all that stinky stuff.

'No, I think we better take care of this one ourselves, son. Remember how you said it's something really gross inside? It's so gross that even the garbage men won't take it.'

'Flies like gross things. Maybe you can just take it outside real far away so we can't smell it no more and then the flies will eat it all up. Then we're not wasting food cuz there's starving people in Africa and it's not good to waste food. Are there starving flies in Africa, Dad?'

He laughed again and it made me smile to make Dad laugh so much. I don't think I ever made him laugh so much ever.

'You know what else likes to eat gross stuff, Dewey?'

He patted me on the head again. I shrugged my shoulders.

'All the little fishies.'

*

Before we left the house, Dad made me help him put the big giant bag inside another bag cuz he said the first bag had some rips in it. When we picked it up, all this juicy stuff poured out of it and splashed us and got our clothes and our skin all gross and dirty. It made the smell even worse when it got on me and even though I tried real hard not to, I threw up on the floor.

Dad said it was okay and didn't even get mad at me or make me clean it up. Once we got the giant wet bag in the other bag, no more juicy stuff came out and me and Dad carried it outside and put it in his trunk. He had to put the smaller bag in another bag cuz that one was all wet and juicy too. When he was doing it, he told me he didn't need any help but I think I should have helped him cuz he dropped the bag and it opened up and the smelly smell came out real bad. Lots of flies flew up in the air, then landed back on the stuff that spilled out and buzzed and buzzed and crawled all over. I saw more of those maggie things in there too.

It was still a long time till it was Halloween, but it looked like there was Halloween decorations in the bag that Dad wanted to feed to the fishies. Dad and me always loved Halloween even though Mom didn't like it that much and said that I wasn't allowed to eat too much candy and I wasn't allowed to watch scary movies cuz they're not propriate and that Dad should grow up and start thinking like a sponstible adult goddammit.

But I guess maybe that stinky stuff got all over our Halloween decorations and now we had to throw it away. We had great stuff that Mom didn't like. Real scary stuff like skeleton bones and zombie heads and fake people parts and plastic axes and knifes and stuff. I saw some hair in Dad's bag, but it was all wet with the stinky stuff. And one of those fake fingers fell out. It must have been a new one cuz I never saw one with a ring on it before or with the fingernail painted pink. Maybe Dad did that to make Mom mad cuz sometimes he did things just so she would get mad I think cuz the pink color is the same kind Mom uses and I bet she'd get real mad if she knew Dad was using her pink color for Halloween decorations.

But Dad put the finger back in the bag and then tied it all up and then throwed it in his trunk with the other big bag and then we got in the car and drove away.

It was real late and I was getting real tired and I told Dad it was a school night and Mom would get real mad if she knew he was letting me stay up late again on a school night. But Dad didn't say nothing. He didn't even turn on the radio but maybe that's cuz it was late and he didn't want to wake nobody up and get yelled at.

But I wish he would have turned on the radio cuz it was too quiet and I didn't like how quiet it was cuz I could hear the flies buzzing in the trunk.

'Almost there, son,' he said after a long time not saying nothing.

We drove up on a bridge that was real high up that had these real long poles that held it up from the water. It kinda looked like a real big, real long caterpillar with long legs.

Dad drove on the bridge till we were real high up, then he stopped the car and just sat there without saying nothing to me. He closed his eyes and was talking but he was saying it real quiet so I

160

couldn't hear him like he was telling a secret to himself.

'Dad?'

He opened his eyes and smiled at me again. Then he got out but held his hand out at me so I knew not to get out yet. He looked all around like we were playing hide and seek and was making sure the person who was it couldn't find us.

'Okay, Dewey. Come help your dad.'

I got out and Dad opened up the trunk and we pulled out the big bag together. It got all juicy and wet again like the second bag Dad used got holes in it and the stinky stuff got all over Dad's trunk and he said bad words when he saw the mess.

We got the bag to the side of the bridge, but it was real heavy and the stinky stuff was dripping out all over the place and I wasn't strong enough to help that much and the stuff kept getting on me and I didn't mean to but I threw up again.

But Dad didn't get mad, just like before. He told me not to worry and to just stand by the car and tell him if I saw someone coming. I stood by the car like he said and watched but there was nobody there cuz it was late and a school night and everyone was probably sleeping.

Dad made growling noises when he tried to pick up the bag by himself, and even though it was real heavy and it looked like it was maybe too heavy for Dad to pick up, he did it. A bunch of the stinky stuff got on him and he said lots of more bad words but he still laughed and smiled when he was done. I guess we were real high up in the air cuz it took a long time before I heard the splash in the water where the big bag fell in.

Then Dad picked up the smaller bag with the Halloween decorations inside, but he walked to the other side of the bridge to throw that one, and since it was smaller he didn't have any trouble. That one took a long time too before it splashed too.

I was real tired then and my eyes kept trying to go to sleep even though I was still standing up and wearing my day clothes instead of my pajamas. And I wasn't wearing any shoes but I didn't notice

161

cuz I was so busy helping Dad. The street hurt my feet and I hoped all those smelly people who live outside got enough money for shoes soon.

Dad talked some more to himself on the side of the bridge, looking down at the water.

'Dad, can we go home now? I'm real tired and I got a spelling test tomorrow and I want to do good on it. I'm real good at spelling, but Mom says if I don't sleep my brain won't work right.'

'Forget about that, Dewey. Me and you, we're going on a vacation. How does that sound?'

'Like Mom?'

'Better than Mom. Way better. You've got plenty of time for school.'

'If we go on vacation and Mom's on vacation then how will she know where to find us when she comes home?' I asked him when we got back in the car.

Dad turned the car on and made sure we both had our seatbelts on and then turned on the radio and changed the channels till he found rock and roll music cuz that's his favorite.

'The best vacations are the ones where nobody can find you no matter how hard they try. It'll be fun. Doesn't a secret vacation with your dad sound like fun?'

I shrugged. 'Yeah. I guess so.'

'Good. Now let's get out of these stinky clothes, hmm?' he said and then patted me again and smiled real big at me.

'Yeah. But don't forget, Dad.'

'What's that, son?'

'You owe me a big bowl of ice cream.'

He laughed real hard this time and it made me feel real good to make him laugh like that.

'I sure do, Dewey. I sure do.'

It was the biggest, bestest ice cream I ever had. Even though flies kept crawling on it.

ZOLEM
Written By **Tonia Brown**

Erotic asphyxiation.

That's what she called it. Dan called it a whole lot of other things, most of which weren't repeatable in polite company. But Rebecca claimed it was the only way she could reach that precious moment of ecstasy. This constant demand for him to choke her during sex did little to assuage his self-doubts. It was bad enough that he wasn't of good Jewish stock—a point she never let him forget—but as a Southern-born and bred young man, he was nothing if not loyal to his woman. Even if he didn't understand her needs.

Or her culture.

Or her beliefs.

Though he was fairly sure the whole choking thing had nothing to do with her faith. As far as Dan was concerned, there was a huge difference between believing the Sabbath is Holy and wanting yourself choked into an orgasm. But if choking was what Rebecca wanted, choking was what Rebecca got.

Only, on that dreadful night, Rebecca got more than just the old two handed squeeze meant to please. Dan, in a rare moment of blissful timing, happened to reach his peak at the same time his woman did. He ended up putting too much pressure on her larynx, crushing her windpipe beneath his ham-fisted grip and closing off her access to life-giving air forever. After he recovered from his own moment of joy, gasping and sweaty and sated, he found Rebecca as limp as an over-boiled cabbage leaf. And just about the same color.

'Rebecca?' he asked, giving her naked body a shake.

She jiggled a bit, more in some places than others, but otherwise didn't answer.

'Hey, Becka?' he asked. 'You okay, babe?'

He prodded her once more, and again bits of her jiggled—which he had to admit looked all kinds of sexy—but she still wasn't okay. She was far from okay. For starters, she wasn't breathing. Dan was always a little on the slow side, but even he was pretty sure you had to breathe to live. At that moment, it dawned upon the ever-slow Dan that Rebecca was well beyond not okay.

She was dead.

'Holy fuck!' he yelled as he leapt from the deathbed of his beautiful lover. 'Holy fuck. Holy fuck. Holy fuck.'

Dan pranced about in the nude, back and forth all around the pullout couch that doubled as their love nest, wringing his hands and repeating his mantra of blessed sex. After a full minute of this prancing and chanting, and a full minute of Rebecca not coming back to life on her own, Dan decided he had to act. But what could he do? He didn't know CPR, though it would have been no use to try such a thing. She was deader than a can of forbidden ham.

'I gotta get someone,' he whispered to no one in particular. 'I gotta get help.'

In the time it took him to find the phone, selflessness shifted into self-preservation, staying his dialing digits. He couldn't call for an ambulance. They would just call the police. They would figure out what happened for sure. And what would become of Daniel then? Huh? He would be arrested for her murder, that's what. His arrest would lead to a trial, leading to his lifetime imprisonment and his eventual new career as the bottom to some huge cellmate named Steve. Or Carl. Or Buck. Yeah. Buck sounded about right. Being butt buddies with a cellmate named Buck was not the way Dan wanted to spend the rest of his measly existence.

Confused and confounded, terrified and troubled, Dan curled up next to the quickly cooling corpse of his lover, side-spooning his little lady as if she were still alive and well.

'Can't call the cops,' he whispered. 'You understand, don't you, baby girl? Can't let 'em know it were me what did this to ya.' He leaned over her, stroking the silky locks of her long, dark hair. Her empty eyes stared up at him, pleading with him, as if begging him to choke her, just one more time. 'I told you not to make me do stuff like that. I never did like it. Now you know why.' He slipped a hand across her face, closing her eyes, then rested his head on her cold shoulder. 'Oh, Becka. What am I gonna do?'

Tears came upon him in a torrent of wet misery. He knew it wasn't very masculine to cry, but all things considered, he supposed Becka would've forgiven him. The idea of forgiveness turned a few loose screws in his mind, leaving him with an inspiration for a possible source of aid.

Lifting his tear-streaked face to the ceiling, he whispered, 'God, if you're there, please help me. I know what we was doing wasn't exactly the right thing and all. I know we was living in sin, but I loved her, so I figured you were okay with it. You just gotta help me. I didn't mean ta kill her. You know that. Don't you? God? You listenin'?'

Dan got the sneaking suspicion that God wasn't listening. Or if He was, then it was with great disappointment and no intention of helping. Daniel paused in his impromptu prayer to swallow a huge swell of tears and snot before trying a different approach.

'Hey, Rebecca's God? You up there too? I don't know if you're the same one I usually talk to, or some different other guy, but maybe you can help me? Just this once? I promise I'll take real good care of Becka. Didn't I always? Just bring her back to me. I'll even give up fish or potatoes or bread or whatever it is her folks ain't supposed ta eat, if you'll just bring her back. Deal?'

As if in some eerie response to this unlikeliest of prayers, a noise sounded in the hallway just outside the apartment door. Dan scrambled to his feet again, racing to the peephole to see if he could make out the source of the noise. Like any apartment complex, the place was full of nosy neighbors, just chomping at the bit to spread what gossip they could get their mealy mouths around. He worried that one of them had heard all the commotion and called the cops.

Through the fisheye world of the peephole, Dan could just make out the shape of Rebecca's neighbor slipping into his apartment across the hall. It wasn't unusual for the man to arrive home at such a late hour. He was a strange guy. A real weirdo, or so Rebecca said. She always called him that wacko Yid, or the guy into all that stupid mystical cable statistic stuff.

Dan didn't know what a Yid was, or what cable statistics were, but he was very familiar with the word mystic. He had heard the term spoken between the elders in his hometown, when they whispered in hushed voices about the goings-on of backwoods folk magic. He wondered if cable statistics were anything like mountain magic, or if it was more like Voodoo or hoodoo or mojo or whatever it was those deep Southerners got up to down on the bayou.

Maybe. Maybe not.

Point being, did the wacko Yid dabble in the forbidden arts? And more to the point, could he use these mystical powers to bring Rebecca back from the dead? A plan to discover this very thing hatched in Dan's overworked brain. It wasn't the best idea or the brightest plan, but it was all he had to work with. And at the worst of times, something always seemed better than nothing.

Even if that something was so very, very wrong.

Dan got dressed in a flash before he tenderly pulled a robe onto the body of his dead beloved and wrapped her now-bulbous, discolored neck in her favorite winter scarf. After he straightened the covers of their love nest and put away the various toys and accessories lying about—no need to let the neighbor see what naughtiness they had been up to—he made his way to the door again. Dan paused to check that the hall was empty, then slipped out of Becka's apartment and across the narrow hallway until he stood in silence before the weirdo's door.

There he knocked, soft but urgent.

'Coming,' a muffled voice yelled through the worn wood. A few noises arose: a toilet flushing, the shuffling of feet, a cat meowing, then at last the door opened, just an inch. In the shadowed recess of that inch, a figure lurked. 'Can I help you?'

'Hi,' Dan said. 'I'm a friend of Becka's, in twenty four, across the hall-'

'I know,' the man said. 'You're her latest conquest. I've seen you coming and going for the last few weeks. What do you want?'

'I'm Daniel.'

The man didn't give his name, just a deep grunt, followed by, 'What do you want? I'm very busy.'

'I was hoping you could give me a hand. You see, Rebecca doesn't seem well, and she asked if you could come have a look at her.'

'What do you mean not well?'

'Sick. She's sick. Very sick. She said you were the only one who could help her.' Dan added a broad smile to this, hoping this air of hayseed innocence would lure the man to Becka's apartment.

'Me?' the man asked in a strained voice of disbelief. 'She won't even look at me when we pass each other in the hallway. I'm not her type, don't you know?'

'I see. Too ... umm ... bookish?'

'No. Too Jewish.'

Which Dan found a little odd, truth be told, considering she was always reminding him that he wasn't Jewish enough. Women. Whether Jewish or normal, who knew what they really wanted?

The man in the doorway interrupted Dan's thoughts. 'So, why does our little ice princess need me now?'

'I don't know. In the middle of throwing up, she heard you coming home, and when she finally stopped dry heaving, she asked if you'd come see her. That's all I know. I'm just the, um, messenger?'

The guy was silent for a few moments, then said, 'I'll be over in a minute.'

Dan thanked the stranger and went back to Becka's place to wait. True to the neighbor's word, a light rapping rose from the door less than sixty seconds later. Dan welcomed the stranger inside with a flourishing wave and a damned near bow. After he was in, Dan locked the door as quietly as he could. He turned around and grinned widely at the neighbor.

The fellow was short, shorter than Rebecca and much, much shorter than Dan, with his all-American quarterback build. He was a little on the lean side too, looking more like a lanky kid than a full-grown man.

He pushed his glasses up his nose and asked, 'Where is she?'

'She's on the couch,' Dan said. 'Behind me, Mister ...?'

'Oh, sorry, I'm Menachem.'

At the harsh roll of consonants, Dan said, 'Gesundheit.'

'I didn't sneeze. It's my name. Menachem.'

'Emimen? Like that rapper?'

'No, Menachem.' The man gave a frustrated sigh. 'Just call me Adam. Every other goy else does.'

'Why Adam?'

'It's my middle name.'

'Okay, Adam, thanks for-'

'Where is she?' Adam said over him.

'Um, yeah, I have to warn you, though ... she ain't looking none too good.'

Adam nodded and eased Dan to one side. He wrinkled his nose the moment he laid eyes on Rebecca's remains. 'Rebecca, you look terrible.' He glanced to Dan again. 'I don't know what you two expect me to do.'

Dan didn't know either. Luring the man to the apartment seemed like a good idea not ten minutes before. But now that Adam was standing over Rebecca, poking at her corpse, Dan got the feeling he had made a terrible mistake.

'She's cold.' The man rested an open palm against her forehead.

'She's freezing. I would have expected a fever, but she's so cold. You should turn up the heat in here. And she's so pale too. Rebecca? Are you awake?'

'I don't know,' Dan said. 'Take her pulse or something.'

Adam shrugged, reached out and touched Becka on her bare wrist.

A heartbeat passed.

Then two.

On the third, Adam lowered her wrist. 'You need to call 911.'

'What do you think is wrong with her?' Dan asked, hoping he portrayed the picture of innocence in his false confusion.

'We need to get her off this bed,' Adam said. He stood and pulled her up by the shoulders. 'Grab her by the ankles.'

'What are you doing?' Dan said.

'I can't do CPR with her on this mattress.' Adam shoved his arms under hers. 'Now grab her ankles so we can get her on the floor.' He paused in his movements as something caught his eye. He wiggled one arm free, then lifted the scarf to take a peek at the hidden flesh of Rebecca's neck. 'What the ...?' He grabbed the loose end of the scarf and pulled it off in an unfurling loop over her head. The thing unwound, leaving Rebecca's very swollen and now-bluish-green neck exposed. Adam recoiled in disgust, dropping her body onto the bed. 'What is this? What's going on here?'

'It's not what you think,' Dan said.

'What should I think? Look at her neck.'

'It were an accident!' Dan blurted it out before he could stop himself.

Adam gasped as his eyes widened. 'You killed her?' He took a step or two away from the bed. 'You did. You killed her.'

Dan then did what came naturally to any animal backed into a corner; he pounced. He leapt upon the little man, clamping one hand over Adam's mouth and the other over Adam's neck, threatening to choke the man in very much the same manner in which he'd killed his own girlfriend. 'Listen to me, and you listen good. I didn't mean to kill her. It were an accident. She likes it a little rough in the sack, and things got out of hand. I didn't like doing that to her, but she begged for it. Understand?'

Under his forceful grip, Dan could just make out the slightest movement from Adam. A nod? Perhaps.

'Good,' Dan said. 'Now I'm gonna let you go, and you're gonna help me. Understand?'

The slight nod came again, so Dan did as promised.

Adam gasped and coughed and dropped to the floor, clawing at his throat as he drew in lungful after lungful of air.

'Now,' Dan said, 'I suggest you start coming up with ways to fix this. Or so help me, I'll drag you down with me.'

'Fix this?' Adam asked in a dry croak before he coughed again. 'Drag me down? What are you talking about?'

Dan was desperate. He knew what he was threatening was wrong, but he didn't know what else to do. 'We all know that you can't step outside one of these doors without one of your nosy neighbors making note of it. One of them was bound to see you come over here. And when they find Becka like that ... well ... I'll tell them you were trying to help me hide her.'

Adam shot Dan a hateful stare. 'I came over here because you asked me to help you.'

'Yeah, help me to hide the body. And you said yes. That's what I'll tell them.'

'You bastard. Why do this to me? You don't even know me.'

'Because I need your help. You gotta fix this.'

'You don't get it, She's dead. What is it you think I can do for her?'

'Rebecca told me all about your mystical cable statistics and stuff. You can use them to make her better.' Dan fell to his knees on the bed and clasped his hands together. 'I'm beggin' ya. Do whatever it is you do. Please bring her back.'

'Mystical cable statistics ...' Adam's words faded as his hateful look fell into dismay. 'No, no, no. I've been studying the Kabala. It's Kabalistic, not cable statistics.'

'What in the heck is a cawbawlah?'

'It's Jewish mysticism. It's kind of hard to explain, but I can safely say I don't have any mystical powers. Sorry.'

'But mystic is right there in the name.'

'I hate to disappoint you, but I'm just a run-of-the-mill guy who happens to know an awful lot about the Zohar and the Tree of Life. That's all.' He rubbed at the back of his neck, as if embarrassed. 'Technically, I'm not even supposed to be studying it at my age.'

'Tree of Life?' Dan snapped his fingers. 'That's the stuff. Use that tree to bring her back to life.'

'That's not how it works. It's not about life and death.' Adam paused to run his hands through his thick, wild hair. 'I mean it is about life and death, but not the way you're thinking. It's … it's … it's very complicated. Okay?'

'I know you must think I'm stupid, but I don't know anything about what you people get up to. And I don't rightly care to. I just want Rebecca back.'

'You people?' Adam rolled his gaze to the ceiling. 'Geesh, you say that like Jews are a whole different species.'

'Sorry, but Rebecca always talked like you were. Well, she talked like I was, at least. But she ain't talking now.' Dan took up her cold hand and let out a long, tired sigh. He stroked her hair again, the way she used to love. 'I didn't mean to do it. I didn't mean to hurt her. You gotta believe me.'

'I do.'

Dan looked up to find Adam staring at him, a touch of understanding in the man's eyes.

'I know you didn't mean to hurt her,' Adam said. 'But that isn't going to bring her back. Nothing is going to bring her back.'

Dan figured as much, but he didn't want to admit it. As he sat on the edge of the bed, stroking the hair of his deceased lover, contemplating the long and complicated path ahead of him now

171

that he was a murderer, Daniel heard the last thing on earth he ever expected to hear.

'Unless …' Adam whispered.

The whisper was so quiet, so low, that Dan almost didn't hear it. 'Unless?' He dropped his dead lover, jumped up and towered over the little man. 'What is unless? What does unless mean?'

'Whoa there, big guy,' Adam said, backing off from the oncoming form of Dan. 'Don't get overexcited. I just had a thought, that's all.'

'What kind of thought?'

'The crazy kind.' And he did look crazy. The understanding in Adam's eyes had vanished, replaced by a touch of fear mixed with madness.

'Crazy is fine by me,' Dan said. 'In fact, crazy sounds real good. Right now crazy sounds a hell of a lot better than prison.'

Adam fell silent for a moment as he began to pace the room, tapping his chin and giving Dan and Becka an occasional glance. At length, he finally said, 'This is going to sound completely out of left field, but … what do you know about golems?'

'Golems?' Dan wrinkled his nose and plunked back down on the bed. 'You mean like that thing in that movie about the ring? The one with all those little people in it and the guy with that great big staff and long beard and-'

'No, not that.' Adam groaned. 'I mean golems. Creatures of myth? They were servants made from clay by very powerful Jewish magicians.'

'Don't ring a bell. Sorry.'

Adam pulled a chair from Becka's kitchen over to the couch. Sitting down, he explained, 'A long time ago, it was believed that a very holy person, someone very close to God, had access not just to His love, but to His wisdom and His power. They were able to gain a deeper understanding of the dynamic relations between the Sefirot of the Tree of Life. A deeper understanding of how life comes into being. It's rumored that someone with this

172

understanding could shape a creature out of clay and bring it to life with the right series of symbols and words. They animated these creatures to serve God and His people. You following me?'

'I guess so. But what does that have to do with this?' Dan looked down to his sweetheart, who was still quite dead. 'Rebecca ain't made of clay. She's made of flesh and bone.'

'Yes, well, interesting you should mention that, because I've been giving it a lot of thought lately. In fact, I've been preparing a presentation on just this very thing.' Adam gave a short trill of nervous laughter. 'Isn't it odd how the universe provides?'

Dan shook his head. 'I still don't know what you're hemming and hawing about.'

'I'm talking about this. I'm talking about humans.'

'What about 'em?'

Adam leaned back in the chair, crossing his arms and eyeing Dan. 'You read your Bible much lately?'

'Mine or yours?'

'The first part is the same.'

'Really? I always thought you guys had a different book.'

Adam held up his palm, finger spread wide. 'We share the same first five books.'

'You mean the Old Testament?'

'For the sake of argument, yes, that's what I mean.'

'Oh, well, yeah I've read some of it.' Which was to say his momma had read him bits and pieces while he snapped green beans and shucked corn for Sunday dinner.

'Do you know Genesis?'

Dan made a back and forth noncommittal gesture with his hand.

Adam seemed satisfied with this answer. 'What did God use to make Adam?'

'Dirt and soil and …' Dan's eyes went wide as synapses fired and dots connected. 'Clay. He made Adam out of clay. Hot dog! You saying what I think you're saying?'

'Yes. It's my theory that a golem can be created from a corpse. I know it sounds crazy, but-'

'That ain't crazy. No, sir. Makes sense to me.'

'Really?' Adam rubbed the back of his neck as he grinned. 'Because I have a feeling just the idea of it will cause me trouble in my community.

'Just be straight with me. Are you saying you can bring her to life?'

'I'm saying—and honestly I can't believe I am saying this—I have always wanted to try.'

'Wahoo!' Dan yelled and clapped and hugged Rebecca's corpse closer to him.

'But,' Adam said over Dan's enthusiasm. 'I'm also saying that it won't be easy. And you might not be happy with the results.'

'Why? You said you could bring her back. Why wouldn't I be happy with that?'

'No, I said I would try to animate her. She won't be the same Becka as before. She'll be alive, but she won't be. Not really.'

Dan slumped in place, hanging his head as he cradled Rebecca to him. 'Okay, you lost me again.'

'That corpse you're holding isn't Rebecca anymore. Her soul is gone, Dan. Rebecca has gone. She left her clay shell behind, but her essence, everything that made her Rebecca, is gone. I can try to animate that shell, but before I can do this, you have to understand that she won't be the same. Tell me you understand.'

'I understand,' Dan mumbled.

'Dan, look at me.'

Daniel lifted his eyes to Adam's.

'Tell me you understand,' Adam said.

'I understand she won't be Rebecca no more. But I don't understand what good it'll do. Why bring her back if you can't really bring her back?'

'Think about it. Dead like that, she's just a murdered corpse in your bed. But if we can get her on her feet, we can take her somewhere else, away from here, without looking like we're dragging a dead body around. Hell, she can even dig her own grave if you want.'

Dan furrowed his brow. 'I can't keep her?'

'Excuse me?'

'I want to keep her.' Dan pushed her hair back from her swollen face. 'I'll take real good care of her. I always did.'

Adam seemed unmoved by Dan's proclamations of devotion. 'Why would you want to keep her? She'll be a total invalid. You'll have to watch her all the time and take constant care of her. She'll be mindless, only able to perform the most menial of physical tasks …' The man's words drifted away as a new thought captured his attention. Slowly, his face morphed into a mask of disgust. 'Ugh!'

'What?'

'You still *want* her?'

'Yes.'

Adam grinned. 'Kinky.'

'Not like that. I mean I still love her. So get your mind out of the gutter. I just, well, I feel like I owe it to her after I killed her and everything. I won't mind taking care of her forever if I have to.'

'Okay, no judging. I'm just here to help.'

'Then get to helping. She ain't getting any fresher, you know.'

Adam ran back to his apartment to fetch what he called the Book of Creation, which made sense to Dan, considering what they were planning. Hope returned and sharing a cell with Buck seemed less like an ominous and imminent future. At a loss for anything better to do, Dan just held onto Rebecca and thought about what he was signing up for. A lifetime of looking after her. Taking care of her. Setting her to menial tasks. Physical tasks. At the thought of the word, his mind soon wandered into the very same gutter Adam's had moments before.

Could she make love when she came back? Would she? Would she like it if he had his way with her? How would they do it? What would her soulless mouth feel like wrapped around his aching-

'I found my Sefer Yetzirah,' Adam said, barging into the apartment without so much as a knock, interrupting Dan's intimate thoughts. 'But I couldn't find a marker. Do you suppose she has one here somewhere?'

'Sure,' Dan said. 'She keeps one by the phone.'

'Perfect.' Adam dropped the book on the bed and retrieved the requested item.

Dan looked the tome over and wasn't impressed. He expected it to be covered in archaic symbols and hold pictures of demons and half-naked ladies, but all there was, as far as he could tell, was a bunch of gobbledygook symbols that made no sense.

'I was going to use an ink pen,' Adam said, returning to the bed with the marker in tow. 'But I worried it wouldn't write clear enough on skin. A marker will work much better. At least I hope it will.'

'So how do we do this?'

'You just keep doing what you're doing. I'll handle the rest.' Adam opened the book and began to flip through the pages. After a bit, he settled on one, running his finger along the yellowing page. 'Here, this is the passage. Now hold her out to me, and push her hair off her forehead.'

Dan did as asked, watching with wonder as Adam got to his knees and took the marker to Rebecca's flawless skin. 'What are you doing?'

'I'm inscribing the word *emet* on the clay. It means truth in Hebrew.' Adam's flowing script was slow and elegant, but what he wrote didn't look like the word 'truth.' It didn't look like anything Dan had ever seen.

'It don't look like a word. It looks funny. Like Chinese.'

Adam smirked while he carefully worked on his inscription. 'You're not her first, you know. In case you were wondering.'

'I know that.' The ferocity with which Rebecca made love, the woman would've had a hard time pretending to be inexperienced. In fact, Dan had a hard time not imagining that she did it for a living, she loved the act so much. 'She dated other guys before me. I know all about it.'

'No,' Adam said with a chuckle. 'I mean you're not her first goy.'

Dan glared at the man. 'I'm not gay. I thought that much was obvious.'

'I didn't say you were. I said you were a goy. A Gentile. A non-Jew.'

'Oh, you mean a normal guy.'

'Normal?' Adam leaned back on his heels and stared up at Dan. 'Is that how you see us? As abnormal?'

'Well …' Dan shrugged. 'Maybe not abnormal. But I know you're not like me. And I think I'm pretty normal.'

Adam shook his head and sighed. 'You know, you're right. I'm not like you. And if that means I'm abnormal, then I'm glad of it.' He leaned in again to add a few touches to the inscription, making casual talk while he drew on the forehead of the corpse as if it were the most natural thing in the world. 'As I was saying, you aren't her first. She's dated plenty of goyim. It's her thing. She finds the biggest and blondest hicks and takes them home to meet Mommy and Daddy. Shock the parents. Give the yentas something to talk about. She got quite the kick out of it.'

He didn't want to believe the man, but the fact that Dan was himself a big, blond hick confirmed Adam's theory. 'I was different. She loved me.'

'Is that what she told you?'

'What do you know about it? What do you know about her? You said she wouldn't even look at you.'

'I grew up with her.' Adam leaned back again, taking on a sad look as he inspected his handiwork. 'Becka and I went to school together. Used to go to the same synagogue, before she stopped going. We were never close, but we were friends. I'd like to think we still are. Or were.'

'Sorry. I didn't know.'

'There's an awful lot you don't know about me.' Adam got to his feet again and snapped up his book. He stood over the pair of them, reading in silence but moving his lips as if practicing a speech.

Dan thought about his previous words and how they would've felt directed at him. 'I'm also sorry I said you weren't normal. I didn't mean it like that.'

Adam nodded but didn't look up from his book. 'It's okay. No harm done. As they say, suffering is the curse of the chosen people.'

'You see?' Dan snorted. 'Its stuff like that I don't get. Why do you guys go around saying you're chosen? You think you're better than everyone else. That's why.'

'It has nothing to do with that. It's much deeper than just our opinion of ourselves.'

'What? You think God thinks you're better too?'

Adam snorted at some private joke. 'No, no I don't.'

'Then what is it all about?'

'Do you really think now is the best time?'

'Typical. You think I'm too stupid to get it.'

Adam eyed him over the book. 'Aren't you one of those yokels who claim to be saved?'

'Yes. And proud of it.'

'Imagine that.' Adam gave another small snort of a laugh as he returned his attention to the tome. 'Saved, huh? Saved for what?'

'For heaven. The saved are the ones God will keep by His right hand at the end times. When the rapture comes, the saved will be … saved.'

'Isn't that essentially the same thing as being chosen?'

Dan bristled at the jab. 'No. It's different.'

'Why?'

'Because it is! Anyone can get saved, but you guys seem to think only a handful of people are good enough to be chosen.' Dan curled his fingers around the last word and delivered it in a high-pitched whine. 'What makes you so god damned special?'

'Over two thousand years of tradition is really hard to explain to a normal guy.' Adam mimicked Dan's air quotes with one hand.

The action turned to acid on Dan's tongue. 'You're just jealous because we've had a Savior for over two thousand years and you're still waiting on yours.' It was a childish jab, but Dan couldn't help it. The guy had it coming.

After a long sigh, Adam said, 'You know, Jesus might love you, but everyone else thinks you're an asshole.'

Dan blinked in stunned silence before he grinned and said, 'Yeah. I reckon I deserved that.'

'Don't be too impressed. I stole it from a bumper sticker.' Adam read in silence for another few moments, then announced, 'Okay, I think I'm ready. Lift her higher, face up, just like that. Now be still and stay quiet.'

Holding the book in his left hand, Adam lifted his right, fist clenched save for the first two fingers, which he leveled over the corpse. He moved his hand along the length of her body and back again, all while he recited a long passage in some alien tongue. At first, Dan flinched at the harsh consonants and rolling vowels. The guy sounded like he was trying cough up a well-lodged loogie half of the time, while the rest he spent droning and whining through his nose.

A quacking duck made more sense than he did.

Yet the longer Adam recited, the more Dan paid attention, the softer the words fell on his virgin Christian ears. The tone shifted from harsh to melodic, then from melodic to enchanting. Dan closed his eyes as he listened, falling into a semi-trance with the rhythm of the language. In the cadence of Adam's strange words, Dan sensed tragedy and pain, beauty and joy, power and compassion, mirth and reverence and so much more than he could ever put into words of his own.

Daniel reckoned it must be what God sounded like when He talked.

After a long while of reciting, Adam fell quiet and Dan was left in a vacuum of blessedness. One moment he was following the golden words to the feet of his Lord, the next he was tumbling back to earth. He opened his eyes to look up at the Jew, wondering if what he felt was normal, or if it was some kind of trick of the trade.

'What were you reciting?' he asked.

'I wasn't reciting,' Adam said. 'I was meditating.'

'Either way, what was it?'

Adam considered Dan for a moment, then shook his head. 'It wouldn't make sense to anyone but a student of the Kabala. Let's just say it concerns the nature of existence and leave it at that.'

'No, I meant what language was that? It wasn't American.'

'It's Hebrew.'

'Hebrew,' Dan echoed. 'Like you?'

'Yeah. Like me. And Rebecca.'

Dan glanced down at the corpse in his arms. 'I didn't know you guys had your own language.'

'Yes. And I know you probably think it sounds stupid, but-'

'No, no.' Dan looked back up at Adam. 'I'm saying it was nice. Real nice.'

Adam smiled. 'Thanks.'

'I sorta liked it. It was nice. Sounded, you know, special.'

'It is special.' Adam closed the book and ran his hand gingerly across the spine. 'It's been special for a very, very long time. You know, we aren't so different, you and me. I'm chosen and you're saved, but we are both His children.'

'Yeah. I guess so.'

They fell into a moment of shared silence, during which a thousand questions leapt to Dan's mind about Adam's faith. Things he always wanted to know, but had been too proud to ask Rebecca. Things like how they prayed and what they ate for Sunday dinner and why they wore those neat little beanies. Stuff like that. But before he could voice a single word, Becka began to tremble, ever so lightly, in his arms.

'Oh boy,' Dan said. 'Something's happening.'

'What?' Adam asked.

'I think it's working. I think … I think she's moving.'

The book slipped from Adam's hands, tumbling to the floor with a dull thud as he whispered in awe, 'Oy vey… I didn't think it would really work.'

But work it did. Becka shuddered from head to toe in a long wave of undulating flesh. She followed this with a series of stilted twitches, dancing as if some mad puppet master were yanking her strings. Dan hugged her tight, thankful for her return, but scared for what might happen next.

'Hold her down,' Adam said. 'This might be rough on her, physically. We don't want her to break a bone or something.'

Dan held on as best he could, but the twitching turned to jerking, and before either of them knew what was going on, Rebecca was shucking and jiving her way out of Dan's embrace. The more he clutched, the more she fought. Their bed squeaked and squealed under the exertions of the pair of lovers, more than it ever had in the past.

'Hold onto her!' Adam yelled over the squeaking hinges and springs.

'I'm trying!' Dan yelled. 'I just don't wanna hurt her!'

'You already killed her. I don't think you can do worse.'

Dan didn't have time to fire off a retort. Becka all but leapt from his arms onto the floor and set into a seizure of epic proportions. As she whipped and bucked, a thick head of dark foam gathered at her mouth, bubbling and oozing and splattering everything in a ten-foot radius. It tore at Dan's very soul and left him covered in bloody goop. He wanted Rebecca back, but he didn't know she would suffer so much in the process.

Or that it would be so messy.

'Make it stop!' Dan cried as he cowered against the mattress. 'Please, make it stop!'

'Just wait,' Adam said from somewhere at the other end of the couch. 'It'll pass.'

No sooner had he said this than Rebecca stopped jerking. She lay motionless on the floor, tranquil as a corpse ever was.

And she stayed that way for what seemed a very long time.

At length, Dan poked his head over the edge of the bed. 'Is it over?'

'I don't know,' Adam said.

'I think it is.' Dan stared down at her still form. 'Is she dead again?'

'I don't know,' Adam said.

Dan turned back to the other end of the couch, where Adam's voice was coming from. 'What happens now?'

Adam's head appeared over the arm of the sofa. 'I don't know.'

'You don't know? Christ! What *do* you know?'

'Not a lot. It's not like I do this kind of thing all the time.'

'But you said you knew what you were doing.'

Adam ducked behind the couch again. 'No, I said I would like to figure it out.'

'But … you were writing a thing on it.' Dan crawled over to the edge of the pullout bed to where Adam sat with his back to the couch and his head hung low. 'Your words. Your thing. If you don't know what's going on, then what in the heck did you write?'

'There is a far cry between writing and doing.' Adam snapped his head up, his eyes once more alive with the same madness as before. 'And I should add that while I find myself in possession of a fair amount of things to write with and about and on, I've never, and I mean never, had access to an actual corpse. So this is just as new to me as it is to you.'

Dan laid his forehead on the arm of the sofa. The Jew was right all along. This whole thing was crazy. What were they doing here? Rebecca was dead, and Dan was in deep doodoo, and the poor neighbor was just along for the insane ride. It was time to fess up and face facts.

'I should call the cops,' Dan said.

'Maybe you should,' Adam admitted. 'I'm sorry it didn't work out. I've done all I know to do and-'

Over Adam's commiserations, a low and throaty moan rolled across the room.

Adam shot a worried look up to Dan, who in turn stared wide-eyed at him.

The moan sounded again.

Dan rolled over and got to his knees.

The moan repeated. It was coming from Rebecca.

'Do you think-' Dan started.

'Uh-huh,' Adam said, getting to his feet behind Dan.

'So she's-'

'Uh-huh.'

'Then we-'

'Yeah. I think we did.'

Dan leapt from the mattress, all but pouncing on the moaning corpse. He scooped Rebecca into his arms and cradled her tighter than he had ever hugged another human being in his entire life. 'Aw, Becka! Welcome back, hun. I missed you. Did you miss me? I'm so glad you're back. I plan on taking real good care of ya, you'll see. Didn't I always? We're gonna be together forever. I promise.'

Rebecca moaned in response to his promise, this time right in Dan's ear. He leaned away from her, holding her at arm's length as he inspected her reanimated form. Her head hung low, her body limp. The only sign of life she gave was the low and creepy moaning. Whatever sensation the Hebrew intoning brought to Dan, Rebecca's moaning invoked the exact opposite. It wasn't the sound of God. It was an empty resonance.

Hollow.

Soulless.

'Rebecca?' Dan asked. He gave her body a little shake.

She moaned again, lifting her head to face him.

One of the things Daniel used to love the most about Rebecca was her eyes, sexy and soft and always alight with mischief. The eyes that faced him now were anything but sexy. Rebecca's once-soft brown eyes were now milky and cold and lifeless. The moan faded as she sneered and gnawed the air, grunting between guttural growls. Dan thought she was attempting to speak, so he leaned in to hear her better. He didn't fully realize what she was trying to do until he recognized the click of her teeth just a hair's breadth from his ear.

'Sweet Jesus!' Dan shouted, holding her as far away from him as he could. 'She's trying to bite me!'

'No she isn't,' Adam said, crawling across the pullout to join them.

'She sure as hell is!' Dan ducked and shifted, trying to avoid her chomping mouth.

'Keep your voice down or you'll wake the whole complex.' Adam sat on the edge of the bed, watching the pair wrestle. 'Besides, I told you she wouldn't act normal. This is fascinating. I didn't think she would come around so strongly so soon. I assumed there would be more brain damage from lack of oxygen, but she seems almost coherent.'

'She seems hungry.'

'She probably is hungry. Dying is bound to take a lot of energy out of you. Not to mention the whole act of coming back.'

'Yeah, but she acts like she wants to eat me.'

'No she doesn't. She's just acting on instinct. That's pretty much all she has left now.'

Rebecca added clawing to her biting routine. Dan grabbed her by the wrists and twisted her arms behind her back, but she kept on wriggling and biting the air between them, growling and groaning the whole while. Her efforts were weak, but with every second, Dan could feel her power building. The more they struggled, the stronger she got. He said as much to Adam.

'We should tie her up,' Adam suggested. 'At least until we can figure out what to do with her. Do you have any rope?'

'Rope?' Dan asked. 'Who the heck has rope just lying around their apartment?'

'Hey, I don't know what kind of kinky things you guys got up to over here.'

'Nothing that involved rope.'

'Okay. We can use the bed sheets.' Without even asking, the man snatched up the bundle of top sheet beside him and tore off a long strip.

'Hey, now! I bought those special for her. Those were thousand count Egyptian cotton.'

'They still are. Put her in that chair and hold her down.'

Dan struggled to get to his knees and bring Rebecca with him, all while Adam watched. 'You know, you could help a brother out.'

'Of course,' Adam said, snapping out of his fascination to help Dan maneuver the wriggling woman onto the chair. Once she was in place, Adam proceeded to bind her hands behind her, working the tie through the wooden slats at the back of the chair. Out of breath, he rested on the edge of the pullout. 'That should keep her still. Hopefully.'

Dan sat next to the man. 'I don't know. She's awful strong.'

'Yes. Stronger than I thought she would be, but I suppose it's a side effect of the spell. Perhaps. Maybe.'

Rebecca growled and writhed against her bonds like she wanted nothing more than to get free and have at the pair of them. What she would do if she did, Dan had no idea, but he didn't think it would be pleasant. Though at first he was thrilled to have her back again, Dan now found he had mixed feelings about her return. On the one hand, she was alive, sort of, which he supposed got him off the legal hook. But on the other hand, she wasn't quite right in the head—or in the body, since her neck was still swollen to a grotesque degree and her eyes ... well it was best not to look into them for too long. And then there was the way she snapped at the air. And growled. And that awful moan.

Most of all, he didn't know what to do with her now that he had her back.

'What do we do with her now?' Dan asked.

Adam said nothing in return.

'What do we do?' Dan said.

'I don't know,' Adam said.

'Not this shit again.'

'Look, shmuck, you wanted to take care of her. Remember? Forever and ever? Well, she's all yours, buddy.'

'Yeah, but I didn't want-'

Over his words there came the loud and distinct sound of fabric ripping apart. Both men looked back to Rebecca, who now stood on her own two feet, hands clawing the air, throat growling, teeth gnashing.

'Becka?' Dan asked, which was probably the biggest mistake he had made all evening.

Save for killing his girlfriend in the first place.

At the sound of his voice, Rebecca leapt from her stance and fell on him. Dan cried out in surprise and fought the good fight, but in the last few minutes, her strength had multiplied beyond his own. Try as he might, he couldn't hold her back. She landed a bite on his shoulder, bearing down through the fabric until her teeth sank into the tender skin beneath.

'Jesus Christ!' Dan yelled. 'Get her off me!'

Adam ran to him, grabbing Rebecca by her shoulders and yanking her off the bleeding Dan. But instead of letting up, Rebecca bit down harder, through Dan's shoulder, taking a mouthful of red wetness as Adam pulled her away. Dan groped the wound, screaming in agony before he shoved his bloody fist in his mouth to keep quiet. Adam was right. It was bad enough they had raised the dead. No need to raise the neighbors as well.

Adam rolled over onto his back with Rebecca locked in an embrace above him. 'We have to break the spell.'

'She fucking bit me,' Dan said.

'Stop whining. It's not that deep.'

'Not that deep? She bit me, you asshole.'

'Would you just shut up and help me break the spell'

'How?' Dan asked as he held down Becka's kicking legs and tried very hard to ignore the blood pouring from his shoulder.

Adam answered him in a staccato rhythm of words, every syllable punctuated by his struggle with the once-dead woman. 'The aleph in *emet*. The first letter. You have to wipe it away. It will change the word from *emet* to *met*.'

Now, according to his earlier Hebrew lesson, *emet* meant truth. If Dan took away the first letter, did that change the word to lie? Or something else? Despite the situation, his curiosity got the best of him. 'What does *met* mean?'

'Death.'

Death. Which meant, essentially, that Dan had to kill her. Again.

'Do it,' Adam begged. 'I can't hold onto her much longer.'

Dan snatched a shred of binding from the floor and raised it to Rebecca's forehead. He hesitated, just a moment, wondering if he could put her to rest again so soon after just getting her back. His mind was decided for him when his eyes met hers. Dan pressed down, wiping away at aleph as hard as he could.

The aleph, however, wasn't going away.

'It's not going away,' Dan said.

'What?' Adam asked.

'The mark. It's not going away.'

'Rub harder!'

'I am rubbing, but it ain't budging.'

'Here,' Adam said, thrusting Rebecca into Dan's arms. 'You take her and I'll try.'

Dan wrapped his big arms around Becka and stood her up with him, squirting blood all over the pair of them from his fresh pumping wound. Thank God Rebecca was too occupied with her chunk of flesh to put up much of a fight. Okay, maybe it wasn't so much a chunk as a sliver, but still, it hurt like hell. 'I don't think I can hang onto her long. I'm getting woozy.'

'It's probably the blood loss.'

'No shit, Sherlock.'

'Come on,' Adam grumbled as he rubbed at her forehead. 'You're right. It's not coming off.'

'Told you,' Dan said.

'Why won't it come off …' Adam's words faded as if he realized the answer while asking the question. He grunted and asked, 'How stupid can we be?'

'What does that mean?'

'It won't come off because we wrote it in permanent marker.'

'We? What's all this we business? You're the Heeb that used a marker.'

'You're right. I'm the idiot here. After all, I can't expect some fresh-off-the-farm moron to catch my mistakes.'

'Really? You want to start shit with me now?'

'Shut up, I'm trying to think. Not that you know what that's like, I'm sure.'

And that last insult just about did it for Dan. Here he was with a mouth-sized hole in his shoulder, and Mister Chosen was telling him to shut up? That wouldn't do. Not at all. It was time to settle the score. As if sensing his hatred, Rebecca swallowed the piece of meat she had been chewing, freeing her mouth for another bite. Just as Adam turned his back to them, Dan let her go. With a wild growl, Rebecca threw herself onto the man. Adam let out a feminine cry, high pitched and shrill, as Rebecca latched onto his shoulder with her teeth.

'Now, now,' Dan teased. 'Best keep quiet or you'll wake the neighbors.'

A thump from the floor beneath them emphasized his warning.

'Get her off me,' Adam begged.

At first Dan was pleased, eye for an eye and all that. Well, a shoulder for a shoulder, he supposed. But the more Adam struggled—unable to dislodge the woman from the awkward angle on his back—the guiltier Dan felt. Finally, he moved forward to separate the pair, pulling Rebecca away with a satisfying scream from Adam as she took a hunk of his flesh with her.

'What the hell happened?' Adam asked, pressing a crimson-coated hand to his bloody wound. 'I thought you had her.'

'My grip slipped,' Dan lied. 'Must've been all the blood.'

'Is that so?'

'Yeah.'

'Yeah?'

'Yeah!'

Adam sneered.

Dan glared.

Rebecca chewed.

'We'll settle this later,' Adam said. He wound a length of the binding around his shoulder, trying to staunch his wound. 'We need to deal with that first.'

'Don't call her that,' Dan said as he held Rebecca to him, her struggles once again subdued by her mouthful of meat. 'She's still Rebecca.'

'She stopped being Rebecca the moment she died. I don't know what the hell she is now, but she's not Rebecca. I thought the passage would make her into a golem, but I don't think that's what she is either.'

'Do you think the whole *met* thing will still work? I mean, if she ain't a real golem?'

'I sure hope so, but it won't wash off. I don't see what we can do.'

'We'll have to cut it off.'

'Cut what off?'

'That aleph thing. Either that or her whole head. You reckon that might work?'

Adam stuck out his tongue. 'Ugh. That's just gruesome.'

'What else can we do?' Dan bore down harder on her as she swallowed her minute meal and started to growl once more. The weight of her renewed struggle pushed them back onto the bed. 'You best think of something. She's getting frisky again.'

'I think you're right. We have to cut it away.'

'I have a switchblade in my pants, over there.' Dan nodded to the far end of the couch, to his pants slung on the back of the recliner.

Adam fetched the blade, unfolding it as he stood over them. With a trembling hand, he poised the blade against her forehead. But instead of cutting, he whined, 'I don't know if I can do this.'

'Adam, you best start to cutting or I swear to both our Gods, I will beat your ass raw.' What Dan didn't add was that he might just do that anyway, once this whole affair was done.

'Okay. Bear with me. I'm not used to mutilating the living dead.' Adam drew a deep breath, made a few quick motions over her head, and came away with a small square of dripping red.

Just as easy as that, Rebecca fell as limp as before.

Dan held on anyway, expecting some kind of trickery from her after all that had happened. 'Is she dead again?'

'I think so. I think it worked. She's not moving.' Though he took a few steps back as if she would start again any moment.

Dan didn't blame him. 'You reckon I can let her go now?'

'I think so. Try it.'

With a grunt, he rolled Rebecca away from himself and scrambled off the bed. He joined Adam on the other side of the room, prepared to give chase or turn tail and run should her dormant state be just an act. The men stood in the quiet aftershock of the moment, staring at the defaced corpse, the enormity of what they had done settling on Dan like a dark shroud. Before this, she was just the victim of an overaggressive lover. Dan would've gotten accidental manslaughter at the most.

But now?

Now she was drawn on and beaten all to hell and cut open and covered in blood, not all of it hers. This wasn't accidental manslaughter anymore. It wasn't accidental anything.

Temporary insanity.

Maybe.

His future cellmate Buck once again started to seem more like reality and less like a bad dream.

'Well … shit,' Daniel finally said.

'Yeah,' Adam agreed.

'I reckon this is gonna be all kinds of hard to explain to the police.'

'It sure will.'

They shared a collective sigh. Dan grabbed a half finished bottle of vodka from the kitchen. He took a swig, then offered the bottle to Adam. The man hesitated before he took the vodka and downed a gulp. Adam winced as he passed the bottle back to Dan. They passed it back and forth a few, quiet moments.

'How're your digging skills?' Adam asked.

'Usually great,' Dan said. He hissed as he touched his shoulder, the wound almost forgotten in the excitement of killing Rebecca twice. 'But with this, I don't know what good I'll be at anything.'

'I hear ya. I'm not much for manual labor on a normal day, but I'll do what I can.'

Dan shot Adam a surprised glance. 'You mean you'll help me get rid of her?'

'Sure.'

'Why? You don't have to. It's my fault she's dead.'

Adam shrugged. 'I might not have killed her, but I'm as much to blame for the state she's in now. And I know you didn't mean to kill her in the first place. Why should you suffer for an accident?'

Dan was moved by this act of generosity. Adam could've easily walked away from this with his shoulder wound and nothing more. But here he was, offering to stash the body and cover up the evidence. 'No, it's too much to ask. I'll take care of it. You go home and take care of your shoulder. Forget about this night.

191

Forget about me.'

'And that's the real reason I'll help you. Because you aren't asking for it. Humility goes a long way with my people.'

'It does with mine too. Or at least it's supposed to.'

'We sufferers have to stick together, you know.'

'Well, I don't know what to say.'

'Thank you is usually appropriate.'

Dan smiled warmly despite the excruciating pain in his shoulder. 'Thank you.'

'You're welcome. Just don't call me a Heeb again.'

'Deal. As long as you don't call me that gay thing.'

Adam laughed at the request. 'I'll try my best. Though it'll be a hard habit to break.'

'Speaking of habits, I have some questions, if you don't mind me asking.'

Worried he might never get another chance, Dan grilled his new friend about the Jewish faith—the ins and outs of worship, the holy days and the scriptures, even about that neat little beanie—all to the tune of stuffing his mutilated and twice-dead girlfriend into an oversized contractor bag. As they dragged her to his work van and drove her to the woods at the outskirts of town, Dan couldn't help but think how funny it was the way some folks came into your life. He always knew his relationship with Rebecca would never last. They were, after all, from two different worlds. Not that he cared, but she was always reminding him that they were so different.

Yet, chosen or saved, he supposed he and his new friend were the same at heart. Just two guys hiding a twice dead body. That kind of thing was bound to bond folks.

Digging a hole in the weak glow of the headlights was a bother. Especially with each of them sporting a hole in the shoulder. Yet they managed with a bit of teamwork. After they lowered her body into the hole, and Dan began the process of covering the corpse, Adam paused in his labors to say a few words. Adam chanted something in that confusing tongue of his, all but singing as he rocked back and forth on his heels. His eyes closed, the man droned on and on, and Dan found it surprisingly comforting. Just as Dan dumped the last shovelful of dirt onto Rebecca, Adam's chant wound to a peaceful close. Dan stood beside of Adam, staring down at the lump that made the makeshift grave.

'That was kinda nice,' Dan said.

'It's a traditional funerary prayer,' Adam said. 'El Malei Rachamim'

A growl rose between them. Adam glanced down to the grave. The growl rose again.

'Did you hear that?' Adam said.

'Sorry,' Dan said. 'That was my belly.'

'You're hungry?' Adam said. 'After all that?'

'Well, you mentioned mole and it made me think of mole sauce and that made me think of Mexican.' His belly growled again. 'You don't suppose there's an all night burrito place around here, do you?'

'Come on, goy boy,' Adam said heading back to the van. 'Surely there is a bar around here still open. Let's see if we can find something to nosh.'

'Sure,' Dan said. 'And maybe after that we can find something to eat.'

Adam began to laugh then—a genuine from the gut laughter. Dan followed him to the van with no idea what the man found so funny. He started to think about it, almost too hard, and he began to laugh as well.

'What are you laughing at?' Adam said.

'I was just thinking,' Dan said, 'this whole thing sounds like the start to a stupid joke.'

'What's so funny about two guys hiding a corpse in the woods?'

'No. I meant the part about a Christian and a Jew walk into a bar.'

Adam began to laugh again, and this time Dan joined him. They laughed together as they fled the scene, leaving Rebecca six feet under the cold, quiet earth.

THE PIT
Written by **Graeme Reynolds**

It was the smell that I noticed first. A thick, charnel stench that evoked a childhood memory. My friends and I had found a dead cat in the woods behind my house. One of my friends had prodded the animal's corpse with a stick until the feline's body split open, spilling a wriggling mass of white, bloated maggots onto the dark earth. The smell assailing my nostrils was the same sickly sweet stink of corruption that had billowed from the cat, but magnified a thousand fold.

My mind swam with confusion, thoughts sluggish, as if I'd been drugged. I tried to remember where I was and, failing that, tried to go back to the basics. Who was I? I didn't know. Couldn't even remember my name, the memories as ethereal and insubstantial as smoke, dissipating into nothing as soon as I tried to grasp hold of them. I fought through the mind-fog and tried to focus on the memory fragment that I did have – that hot summer as a young boy when I'd experienced the raw reality of death for the first time. What had I been called? What were the names of my friends? I replayed the scene in my mind, but now when I tried to visualise the faces of my companions, all I saw were blank, featureless masks of unblemished flesh, framed with tousled hair.

I tried to open my eyes, but found that my eyelids were stuck together and the effort simply made them water. Instead I brought my right arm up, wincing as the cramped muscles were urged into motion, and wiped the crust from my eyes with a sticky hand. I blinked fluid away, then wiped my face on my arm again in an attempt to bring the blurred scene into focus. I was lying on my back, face tilted to the star-filled sky. It took a few more attempts before I managed to clear my vision and tried to make sense of where I was. Outside. At night. And judging from the clarity of the stars, far from civilisation. There was virtually no light pollution at all, and the milky way bisected the night sky like a scar while the thin sliver of the crescent moon illuminated me in a faint, cool light. The scene could have been considered pleasant if not for the smell. Where the hell was that coming from?

I wiggled my fingers and toes, then tensed the other muscle groups one at a time. My body ached, my muscles burned with cramp and there was a painful area of skin on my stomach that made me wince whenever I moved, but after some experimentation I didn't think that I was injured. At least, not badly. I placed my palms down beside me, my nose wrinkling in disgust at the wet, slimy texture of my resting place, and rolled onto my right side in an attempt to get up.

A woman's face stared back at me. Ragged gaping holes where her eyes should have been. Mouth wide open in an endless, silent scream. Writhing, squirming things glimpsed in the darkness of her eye sockets. I let out a cry of alarm and lurched into movement, pushing down hard in an attempt to scramble away from the corpse, only to find my hands and feet sank deep into the decomposing flesh with a terrible wet slurping sound. My hands buried up to the wrists in cold, wet decay where unseen things slithered through my fingers. The movement released an eruption of foul gas from the corpse, intensifying the stench. For a moment my voice caught in my throat, unable to process the horror of the situation, before my stomach reacted, splashing a jet of sour bile across the dead woman's ruined face.

I scrambled back, hardly aware of anything else but the need to get away from her. Away from those empty eye sockets and the cold swampy texture of her semi-liquid flesh that seemed to suck at my hands and feet. Away from the stink of her dissolution that now seemed to permeate every pore of my being. I could taste it on my tongue. Feel the rot beneath my fingernails. Soaking through my clothes. I was *covered* in her. Contaminated by her remains. I finally managed to tear my gaze away from the corpse and take in the rest of my surroundings. My stomach lurched again and I dry heaved. I was in a pit, perhaps thirty feet across and ten feet deep. And the pit was filled with corpses. Men, women and children in various stages of decomposition. Some were missing limbs. Most had gaping holes in their chests or stomachs, with glistening loops of intestine visible in the moonlight.

The fear and disgust that had been vying for control of my emotions finally gave way into full-fledged panic. I struggled to my feet as the adrenaline surged through me, trying to ignore the crunch of bones and the soft squelching of ripe flesh beneath my feet. I clawed at the sheer sides of the pit, desperately searching for some hand or foothold that would allow me to escape, and finally, when I found no obvious way out, I turned my face to the sky, all thoughts of who had put me there and who might be waiting in the darkness forgotten, and screamed. 'HELP! Please, someone, HELP ME!'

I was about to scream again, when the stillness of the night was broken by a groan from behind me. I span around to face the charnel pit once more, hardly daring to breathe. One of the corpses on the periphery of the pit began to move, rising up from the sea of flesh on stick-thin arms, dripping gore and black ichor. Warm liquid gushed down the inside of my thigh and I felt the scream begin to rise again in my throat before the newly animated corpse beat me to it, emitting a wail of such horror and despair that I was left caught in a state between bewildered terror and aching pity for anything that could make such a sound.

It took a few seconds for me to realise that the shape was not some unholy revenant, but a living, breathing woman coming to terms with the reality of where she was. Something that I myself had only understood scant moments before and was still struggling to accept. Despite the horror of the situation, the knowledge that I was not utterly alone in this terrible place lessened my own panic, and the feeling of relief was palpable.

'Over here,' I called. 'Oh, thank god. I thought I was the only one alive down here.'

Other shapes began to move among the shadows, roused from their torpor by the horrified screams of the woman. More apparitions rising from the ocean of decaying flesh. Three more in total – another woman, a man and what seemed to be a child, adding their screams to the chorus of panic that echoed around the walls of the pit. The relief that I'd felt when I'd seen the first woman began to change into the smallest flicker of hope.

I forced myself into motion, and began making my way towards the others while doing my best to ignore the sensation of cold wet flesh giving way beneath my feet and the sounds of brittle bones crunching under my weight. I called out to them. 'The walls are lower here. If we help each other, we can get out.'

My words didn't seem to have any effect at first, but slowly the others seemed to understand what I was saying and began making their way towards the area that I'd indicated. The roots of a large tree were protruding from the edges of the pit and those would, I hoped, give us a way to escape.

The man made it to me first. He appeared to be middle aged, perhaps in his early sixties at most, but in reasonable shape all things considered. His face was drawn, with a hollow, haunted expression that I was fairly certain mirrored my own.

'Here,' I said, 'I need your help. Give me a boost and I'll climb out, then help the rest of you up.'

The man looked straight through me, his eyes glassy with shock. I felt a small surge of impatience with him and snapped, 'Listen, I don't want to spend the rest of the night in this stinking pit. I'm sure you don't fancy it much either, so snap out of it and give me a bloody boost.'

With that, the man seemed to regain some of his senses. He stepped closer and shook his head, as if to clear his mind. 'Yes... right... of course,'

He pressed his back against the walls of the pit and linked his hands, boosting me up so that I could grasp hold of the tree roots. My hands were slimy with decay and slipped on the wet wood on my first attempt. The only thing that prevented me from losing my grip and falling back into the pit was the sheer determination that I would *not* allow that to happen. The thought of tumbling into that mass of rotten flesh was almost too much to bear. I tightened my hold on the roots and hauled myself skywards, ignoring the aching in my limbs and the flare of pain from the sore skin patch on my stomach when it brushed against the rough wood. I clambered out of the pit and collapsed onto the damp grass, feeling warm tears stream down my face. I'd made it. I'd escaped. I was still alive.

I experienced an almost overwhelming urge to run. To get far away before whoever had put us down there returned to finish the job. I got to my feet and tried to ascertain the best escape route through the trees – to locate a trail or animal track, but the moonlight didn't extend beyond the first row of pines and I honestly had no idea of which way I needed to go. I could hear one of the women crying in the pit below me, and I sighed with exasperation. I had to get them out, if for no other reason than for the comfort and security of having other people around me. There was a lot to be said for strength in numbers.

I lay flat on my stomach and peered over the rim of the pit once more. If anything, the view was even worse from this angle. There could be hundreds of dead bodies down there, all of them seeming to have suffered terrible wounds. Now that I'd had a few lungfuls of fresh air, the stench was like a physical barrier. If I hadn't already emptied my stomach, I felt certain that I would have thrown up again, which would have been unfortunate for those standing directly below me. Instead I fought down my gag reflex and dangled my right arm down into the pit. 'Here, grab hold of my arm' I said to a pale faced, blonde haired woman who seemed to be on the verge of having a breakdown, 'Grab hold and I'll pull you up.'

She didn't move at first and I wasn't sure whether she was

going to be able to pull herself together enough to follow my instructions. Then, after receiving words of encouragement from the man, she allowed him to hoist her up high enough for me to grab on and help her out of the pit. I wasn't sure if she was heavier than she looked or my ordeal had left me weakened – probably a combination of the two – but the task was much harder than I'd anticipated and I was uncertain as to where I was going to find the strength to pull the others to safety.

The child was helped out next. A little boy perhaps nine or ten years old. He managed to control his fear long enough to clamber out and the blonde woman gathered him into her arms where he began sobbing. The sound irritated the life out of me and I feared that it would attract the attention of whoever had put us in the pit in the first place. Part of me wanted to push him back over the edge to shut him up, but I forced the thought away and chided myself. I might not be able to remember who I was, but I knew that I was not *that* sort of person. He was just a kid, coping with a terrible ordeal. All things considered, he was holding himself together well. I just wished he'd do it quieter.

The older woman came next. Her wrists felt as thin and brittle as twigs as I reached down for her, and I seriously worried about them snapping under the strain of being hauled upwards. I remembered the way that the bones of the corpses below had crumbled and splintered under my weight as I'd made my way across the pit, as if they had somehow been weakened. I pulled her up as quickly as I could, grateful for the absence of anything more than a grunt of exertion from her. She rubbed her arms once she was clear of the pit, then sat alone some distance from the younger woman and the child, with her back to me.

I turned my attention from the old woman, back to the pit's final living occupant. The old man. He was going to be the most difficult one to extract. Not only was my strength fading, my arms and shoulders burning with the effort expended to drag the others to safety, but there was also the matter of reaching him. There was no one left to boost him up, and I dared not reach too far for him in case he ended up dragging me back down there with him. He looked to outweigh me by a couple of stone at least. There was something else, too. A feeling. An ingrained dislike of the man that I couldn't quite rationalise, as if he'd done something terrible to me in a dream that had been carried over to the waking world. He must have sensed my reticence because he put his hands on his hips and regarded me with a look that would have curdled milk. I overcame my revulsion and, bracing myself against the roots, extended my hand to him.

He reached up, but the distance between our outstretched hands was too great. He huffed, and began searching for a foothold in the wall of the pit. After a few moments he located a piece of stone protruding from the earth that he was able to excavate until it provided a makeshift step. Steadying himself against the crumbling earth with his hands, he planted his foot on the stone and launched himself skywards with more power and agility than I would have judged him capable of. I grasped his hand as he reached for me and tried to pull him up but damn, he was heavy. My arms felt like they were about to snap off at the elbow. The old man's feet scrabbled against the soft walls, desperately trying to find purchase. I couldn't do it. I felt his hand slipping from mine and, as he flung his other arm around to grab me, he fell backwards onto the pile of corpses with a wet crunch.

'You fucking moron,' he bellowed as he hauled himself out of the decomposing bodies, 'you did that on purpose, didn't you? Bet you thought that was hi-fucking-larious. Well, Sunshine, do it again and see what happens to you when I get out of here.'

There it was again. That feeling of utter detestation towards the older man. Something about the way he spoke just set my teeth on edge. I still couldn't remember so much as my name, but one thing I was certain of. I *knew* this man, and I hated him to my core. I forced my rising anger down and kept my voice level. 'It was an accident. You were heavier than I was expecting and your hand was slippery. That's all. Now, come on. Let's try it again.'

The man glared at me and I got the distinct impression that his feelings towards me were not too far removed from my own, even before I'd dropped him into a pit of rotting bodies. Still, when he scrambled up the side of the pit this time I managed to maintain my grip on his arm and drag him to safety, even though there was a little voice in the back of my mind telling me to let him fall again, just to see the expression on the bastard's face.

The five of us lay by the pit in the wet grass, not speaking for a while. The old woman was still off by herself, gazing into the middle-distance and the boy was curled up against the younger woman, his sobs gradually subsiding to a soft sniffling. I was just glad of a chance to recover my strength. The escape had taken more out me than I'd expected and all I really wanted to do at this point was sleep for a week or so. I closed my eyes and took a deep breath. Big mistake. My nostrils filled with the stink of decay once more and another wave of nausea crashed over me, forcing me to roll over onto my side and dry heave in painful spasms until tears streamed down my face. That made my mind up. No matter how exhausted I felt, I needed to get the fuck away from this place.

I got to my feet and tried to take in my surroundings. We were in a clearing surrounded by pine trees. There was no sound beyond the rasping breaths of the old woman and the soft sobs of the boy. No nocturnal animals moving through the undergrowth. Not even the hoot of a hunting owl. Perhaps the rotting stink of the pit had put the animals off, but I suspected that ordinarily the opposite would be true. Scavengers would have been drawn to the pit in search of carrion. Which meant that there was probably another reason why they were keeping their distance.

The ground had a slight declination to the right of where we sat and I decided that heading downhill was as good a direction as any. I turned to the group and said, 'I think we should get moving. I can't stand the stink of this place and I'd rather not risk whoever put us in that pit coming back.'

The younger woman got to her feet and walked over to my side, the boy still holding on to her for dear life. 'I agree. I can't stand to be here for another second. Do you have any idea which way we should go?'

'My best guess is that way, in the absence of any trails. There are more likely to be people, roads or even a river we can follow the lower we get.'

The old man glared at me and put his hands on his hips again. 'And who put you in charge, Sunshine? Why the hell should we all follow your lead? I say we get to higher ground and see if we can spot some lights to head towards.'

I pushed down the almost overwhelming urge to punch the prick in the face, not least of all because he was bigger than I was and in my weakened condition I was not at all convinced I'd come off best in a physical confrontation. Instead I gave him a smile that was closer to a sneer and said, 'If you see any lights, then they'll most likely be the way I'm walking anyway, and to be honest, I'm not sure I've got the energy for the climb. Do what you want. I don't give a shit. But I'm going this way.'

I didn't bother to wait for a reply and just started walking towards the treeline. The younger woman and the child followed me after a moment's hesitation, while the old woman remained where she was, apparently lost in her own world. Fuck it. The old bastard could take care of her. It wasn't my problem.

The younger woman touched my arm, 'Slow down, please. We can't keep up with you.'

I let out a breath that was equal parts relief and exasperation. My self-enforced march away from the clearing was not quite a 'stomping off' but it was close and I didn't really have the energy for it. I did however want to be as far away from that pit as I could get, as quickly as possible.

I forced myself to relax and gave her what I hoped was a reassuring smile. 'Yes, sorry. Of course. I just… you know…'

She touched my arm and tried to return the smile, an

unconscious gesture that seemed familiar. 'I know. I feel the same way. I had to get away from that place. I just wish we hadn't left the others behind.'

I shrugged. 'He made his choice. I wasn't going to stand there and waste time arguing with him. I got the feeling that he'd have gone against anything I said on principle.'

The woman sighed. 'I know, I think you're right. But I just wish you'd tried a little harder with him. You two always...'

I stopped walking and gripped her hand. 'We always what? Can you remember anything?'

She shook her head. 'No. Just for a moment there I had a sort of déjà vu feeling. As if we'd had this conversation before. It felt like I was on the verge of remembering something, but it's gone again. Sorry.'

'It's alright. I think some bastard drugged us and it's messing with our memory. It'll come back to us in time I think. I've had a few flashes as well.'

We lapsed into an uneasy silence as we continued through the trees, following the slope down. It became impossible to keep track of time. I'd tried counting our steps but my mind was still fuzzy and I lost count before I reached a hundred. We could have been walking for twenty minutes or two hours, our concentration focused on picking a path through the dark undergrowth. Each of us lost in our thoughts. Trying to process the horror of what had happened. Trying to remember who we were and how we'd ended up in such an awful place. None of us really wanting to know the answer.

Then we heard the scream.

It started off as a roar of defiance and rage before descending all too quickly into a howl of terror and pain that ended as abruptly as it had begun. It didn't take a genius to realise what had happened. The old man had encountered our assailant, tried to take him on and had lost. Badly.

The woman gripped my arm hard enough to make me wince,

her eyes wide with barely contained panic. I did my best to keep my expression stoic and hide my own terror. The old guy had been bigger and stronger than me and, from the sound of it, he had lasted seconds in a direct confrontation. That didn't bode well for my chances.

'We'd better keep moving,' I said, avoiding her gaze.

'But shouldn't we go back for them? They could be hurt and need our help!'

I shook my head, 'Sound carries a long way at night. They're probably miles away by now. We'd never find them and even if we did, I don't know that we'd be much use. The best thing we can do for them is get out of here and find help.'

The lie burned in my throat. It hadn't sounded as if they'd been miles away. That scream hadn't seemed like it had come from very far away at all.

The tension between the three of us became palpable after that. The boy kept lagging behind, necessitating a number of stops while the woman tried to persuade him to keep up. She wouldn't even acknowledge me anymore, which suited me fine. I wasn't in the mood for small talk and I was otherwise occupied with scanning the woods and straining my ears for any sounds of pursuit. The forest remained dark and silent, however this didn't calm my jittery nerves one bit. Quite the opposite in fact. When we came across a fallen tree, I spent a few minutes and a significant proportion of my strength reserves tearing a heavy branch free. One end, where it had been attached to the trunk was thick and would work fairly well as a makeshift club, while the opposite end was split into a vicious, jagged point. It might not do much against whoever was hunting us, but it made me feel a hell of a lot better.

We continued on like this for some time. Without a horizon I couldn't see if there was the tell-tale lightening of the sky to indicate the approaching dawn. I felt like we should have seen something by now, but the mind is adept at playing tricks, especially in times of stress. All I knew was that the star lit sky that

I glimpsed through the towering pines seemed to be as dark as it had been when I'd woken. The despair was building in the pit of my stomach. I could feel acid burning the back of my throat and surges of adrenaline sporadically swept through my system causing my heart to race and a cold sweat to bead across my body. I was experiencing a fight or flight response without any obvious or immediate threat to respond to. Then I saw the light through the trees.

I almost fell to my knees with relief. Light meant people and people meant a telephone or maybe even a car. I grabbed the woman's arm and pointed. 'There's a light. Over there, through the trees. Look.'

She smiled then, for the first time since we'd awoken. 'Oh thank God. I thought we'd never get out of these woods.' She took my hand in hers and gave it a light squeeze, then turned to the young boy to tell him the news.

He wasn't there. There was no sign of him. The woods were dark and silent. An ice finger of fear traced a line down my spine. If he'd been taken, it had happened right under our noses without a sound. I gripped the stick so hard my knuckles turned white and whipped my head around, searching for any indication that we were next.

The woman began shouting for him, her voice shrill with panic and desperation. I put my hand over her mouth and shook my head. Whoever had taken the boy clearly knew exactly where we were, but I didn't want her shouting to disguise their approach. There was no way I was going down without a fight.

'Shh. Look, he's probably just seen that light and run on ahead. I'm sure he's OK. And even if he's not there, we can get help. Get the police out with a helicopter and dogs to help look.'

She looked uncertain, but after a moments hesitation followed me towards the light, albeit reluctantly. She kept looking back over her shoulder, hoping to see the child racing to catch up with us. I knew better. We were being picked off, one at a time and it would not be long before our pursuer returned to finish the job.

As we drew closer to the light, I tried to temper my eagerness to be out of the woods with caution. I still had no idea what had happened to us. For all I knew we could be walking straight up to the front door of the psychopath responsible abducting us in the first place. The nagging voice urging me to be careful struggled to make itself heard over the clamouring chorus of hope that filled my mind. It was all I could do not to break into a sprint and, from the looks of it, the woman was experiencing a similar emotional surge, hers amplified by concern for the missing child. After a few dozen paces she lost all pretence of restraint and began crashing through the undergrowth towards what we hoped would be salvation. I kept my distance and maintained my steady pace, keeping my wits about me. Weighing up whether her rapid, noisy progress through the woodlands would make her a more likely target for attack or whether our mystery assailant would choose to remove the armed male from play first.

It didn't take long before she vanished from sight, although I could still track her progress by the cracking of branches and rustle of bracken. That continued for perhaps another thirty or forty seconds before the woods fell silent again.

My muscles stiffened as the fear did its best to immobilize me. I urged my leaden limbs into action, tightening my grip on the branch until blood trickled through my clenched fingers. My progress slowed further, each foot placed with deliberate precision. Pausing after each step to listen for the stealthy approach of the bastard that was hunting me, but only hearing the hammering of my heart and my own ragged breaths. I continued like this for what felt like hours but in reality was probably only a few minutes, until the woods thinned and I came to a dirt road. The woman was standing in the middle of it, looking up at an illuminated sign.

I walked up to her and put my hand on her shoulder. 'Are you OK?'

She turned around, her face a mask of fury, and slapped me so hard I almost lost my footing. 'You prick! You fucking bastard!'

I backed away from her and raised my arms, 'What the hell? What did I do?'

This enraged her further and she advanced towards me, raining a fusillade of blows down on my face and chest, 'What did you do? What did you fucking do? YOU MADE ME LEAVE THEM!'

Her punches were coming with such speed and ferocity that I was struggling to block them. Instead I gave her a shove that rocked her on her heels, and took a couple of steps back to put some distance between us. 'What the hell do you mean? Leave who?'

She gave me a look of utter contempt. 'I'm going to find my son. You stay the fuck away from me, you piece of shit. If I ever see you again, I'll fucking kill you!'

I watched her turn and walk towards the sign, then disappear from sight. I had no idea what the hell was going on. Leave them? Leave who? The old man and woman? She knew that had been the old bastard's choice. She'd fucking been there! I looked up at the sign –a gaudy, cheerful monstrosity that read 'Welcome to Galloway Forest Retreat' and was flanked by a painting of a happy family that would not have looked out of place in a 1950's postcard. The name of the place seemed familiar, though. As did the sign and the inane, grinning expressions of the people on it. I'd seen it before and I was sure that I'd thought the same thing the last time I saw it.

Only the last time I was here, bright sunshine had been filtering through the trees. I'd been in a really fucking bad mood. And I'd been in my car.

It was as if someone had turned on a tap in my head as the memories came flooding back. Jane, my wife bundling Scotty, her son, into her car with a tear streaked face, telling me that when she got back, if I wasn't gone, she'd call the police. The red rage that threatened to consume me replaced by something much colder, calmer and utterly implacable. A determination that she was not going to walk away from me like that. That she wasn't going to just piss off with her fucking parents to that shitty caravan park. I wasn't going to let her have the last word. I was going to drive up there. Be there when they arrived and if that patronising tosser of a father didn't like it then I'd ram my fucking fist down his throat. I'd give the lot of them a surprise they wouldn't forget in a hurry.

Shit.

I could remember driving up here, ready to do god-knows-what. The place had been deserted when I got here, which had seemed odd considering the time of year, but I'd been too consumed with rage to pay it much thought. I remembered parking the car up and chain-smoking cigarettes while I waited for my family to arrive. Then… nothing. My memory was still patchy but at least I knew who I was, I knew where I was, and most importantly, I remembered where I'd parked my Audi.

I could hear Jane, still screaming for Scotty somewhere in the caravan park. Fuck her. Fuck them all. If she wanted me to keep away then she could stand there and watch as I drove out of this shithole. If she was lucky, I might even alert the emergency services once I made it back to civilisation. But maybe not. Divorces were messy things and the last thing I wanted was her getting her hands on my pension fund.

I made my way through the deserted caravan park as quickly as I could. I'd not noticed on my previous visit, but the signs of violence were plain to see now with the benefit of hindsight. A barbeque lying prone on the grass with the half cooked burgers lying in the ash. A caravan door flapping in the wind. A bloody hand print on the white plastic facia of a mobile home. Death had come to the Galloway Forest Retreat, and it had come with such speed and ferocity that none of the residents seemed to have escaped. The sooner I was far from this place, the happier I'd be.

I reached the centre point of the caravan park - an ornamental fountain sited within a gravel enclosure and tried to get my bearings. I knew that I'd parked at the very rear of the place so that my car wouldn't be noticed by Jane, but the caravan park was like a rabbit warren and my memory was still patchy at best. I chided myself for not taking more notice of the road names when I'd arrived when I noticed that Jane wasn't shouting for her son anymore. That could only mean two things. Either she'd found the snot-nosed little shit, or the most likely option, that her yelling had drawn the killer to her like a moth to a flame. I needed to hurry. I selected the trail to the left of the fountain and began jogging down it. I would have sprinted if I'd been able. My strength reserves were close to being completely depleted and the nausea from before had returned with a vengeance. Sweat trickled into my eyes and my clothes clung to my body like a stinking wet dishcloth.

I stumbled through identical looking roads, past rows of white caravans, mobile homes and tents, trying to calm my laboured breathing and my pounding heart. I couldn't help but notice the damage now. Tents torn open. Half a rag doll lying in the grass with its stuffing stretched over a good three or four feet. Overturned picnic benches. In many ways, the woods had been better than this. The absence of life in a place that should have been filled with it was far more disturbing than the dark and silent woods had been. It made my skin crawl and the hairs stand up on the back of my neck. The panic was rising in me again. Where the fucking hell had I parked the car?

There was a hum in the air that I hadn't noticed before. A deep vibration in the ether that I felt rather than heard. I'd experienced this before and been similarly confused the last time I'd felt this, but couldn't quite bring the memory fragment into focus.

By the time I remembered what was responsible for that sound, it was far too late for me to be able to do anything about it.

They flew from the edge of the forest straight at me. Dozens of the bastards. Jet black apart from a splash of red across their segmented abdomens and bright yellow compound eyes. As big as my fucking hand. I swung my branch wildly. I couldn't miss. The air was thick with them and the impact of my makeshift club was satisfying, as was the spray of yellow ichor from the wasps ruined bodies. For a second or two, my terror was balanced with an adrenaline fuelled elation. They'd taken me by surprise the last time, but this time I was ready for them and I wouldn't stop hitting them until every last one of the fuckers was ground down into a sticky yellow paste beneath my feet. For a precious moment I felt invincible. That I had met the enemy and they were nothing but oversized bugs. They had no idea who they were messing with!

Of course, that feeling of confident superiority didn't last long. There were too many of them, and my assault burned through the last of my strength reserves in a matter of seconds. One got past my branch and landed on my shoulder. I instinctively dropped my branch and grabbed hold of it, crushing its armoured thorax between my fingers. Then another landed on my chest and stabbed a stinger as thick as my little finger straight into my flesh.

That was all it took. One single sting and I was out of it. My nerve endings lit up as if someone had stripped the protective sheath from every axon in my body with a blunt Stanley knife. My muscles went into spasm. I couldn't breathe. Couldn't move. Hardly noticed it when my body hit the ground like a felled tree. The last time this happened, just over twenty four hours ago, I'd been out like a light and stayed that way until I woke in the charnel pit. Perhaps my body had developed a partial immunity to the venom because this time I didn't lose consciousness right away. I stayed awake long enough to see the wasp that stung me crawl across my stomach and plunge the fat stinger into my flesh once more. It stayed there, its black wings shuddering, while the stinger seemed to be pulsating. It wasn't injecting me with more venom. It was laying its eggs inside of me!

I wanted to scream. To smash the parasite into pulp, slice my stomach cavity open and dig the eggs out of me, but my body was not mine to control. Then, as the monstrous insect finished impregnating me, the venom finally completed its work and I lapsed into unconsciousness once more.

The Bright summer sunshine streaming through the trees was what brought me out of my fugue state. The sun shone straight into my eyes, making them water and causing enough discomfort that it woke me up. I tried to shield my eyes with my arm but found that I couldn't. I couldn't even turn my head or close my eyes. My body was on autopilot, following the invisible pheromone trail of the swarm into the forest, with my consciousness an unwilling passenger. Judging from the position of the sun, it had been up for at least four or five hours, which meant I was probably drawing close to my destination by now.

Sure enough, the trees thinned, then parted into an all-too-familiar clearing and I stood at the edge of the pit once more. Only it wasn't a pit. Not really. I'd assumed that this had been a dumping ground for corpses, when infact its true purpose was a nest. A place where the wasp-creatures offspring could gestate deep within their food source.

I could see Jane lying below me, reunited once more with her son and her parents. Their faces wore what would have been a peaceful expression if it were not for the fat larval grubs chewing their way out from their eye sockets and boring holes in their cheeks.

I felt something shift within me, like a mass of eels within my stomach and realised that it had always been too late. The larva had been growing within me before I ever opened my eyes and saw this place. I teetered on the edge of the pit, then tumbled over the edge, landing beside the ruined corpse of my wife. I gazed up at the clear summer sky, unable to move and unable to save myself from what was about to happen. Strangely, I'm not sure I would have even tried if I'd been able. Perhaps it was an effect of the venom, but I was almost looking forward to it. I'd always wanted to be a father and now I was going to get the chance to be there for another living thing in the way I'd never managed to be with Scotty. It was a beautiful day to become a parent.

HIPPOCAMPUS
Written by **Adam L. G. Nevill**

Walls of water as slow as lava, black as coal, push the freighter up mountainsides, over frothing peaks and into plunging descents. Across vast, rolling waves the vessel ploughs, ungainly. Conjuring galaxies of bubbles around its passage and in its wake, temporary cosmoses appear for moments in the immensity of onyx water, forged then sucked beneath the hull, or are sacrificed, fizzing, to the freezing night air.

On and on the great steel vessel wallops. Staggering up as if from soiled knees before another nauseating drop into a trough. There is no rest and the ship has no choice but to brace itself, dizzy and near breathless, over and over again, for the next great wave.

On board, lighted portholes and square windows offer tiny yellow shapes of reassurance amidst the lightless, roaring ocean that stretches all around and so far below. Reminiscent of a warm home offering a welcome on a winter night, the cabin lights are complemented by the two metal doorways that gape in the rear house of the superstructure. Their spilled light glosses portions of the slick deck.

All of the surfaces on board are steel, painted white. Riveted and welded tight to the deck and each other, the metal cubes of the superstructure are necklaced by yellow rails intended for those who must slip and reel about the flooded decks. Here and there, white ladders rise, and seem by their very presence to evoke a *kang kang kang* sound of feet going up and down quickly.

Small lifeboat cases resembling plastic barrels are fixed at the sides of the upper deck, all of them intact and locked shut. The occasional crane peers out to sea with inappropriate nonchalance, or with the expectation of a purpose that has not come. Up above the distant bridge, from which no faces peer out, the aerials, satellite dishes and navigation masts appear to totter in panic, or to whip their poles, wires and struts from side to side as if engaged in a frantic search of the ever-changing landscape of water below.

The vast steel door of the hold's first hatch is raised and still attached to the crane by chains. This large square section of the hull is filled with white sacks, stacked upon each other in tight columns. Those at the top of the pile are now dark and sopping with rain and sea water. In the centre, scores of the heavy bags have been removed from around a scuffed and dented metal container, painted black. Until its discovery, the container appears to have been deliberately hidden among the tiers of fibre sacks. One side of the double doors at the front of the old container has been jammed open.

Somewhere on deck, a small brass bell clangs a lonesome, undirected cry – a mere nod to tradition, as there are speakers thrusting their silent horns from the metallic walls and masts. But though in better weather the tiny, urgent sound of the bell is occasionally answered by a gull, tonight it is answered by nothing save the black, shrieking chaos of the wind and the water it thrashes.

There is a lane between the freighter's rear house and the crane above the open hatch. A passage unpeopled, wet, and lit by six lights in metal cages. MUSTER STATION: LIFEBOAT 2 is stencilled on the wall in red lettering. Passing through the lane, the noise of the engine intake fans fills the space hotly. Diesel heat creates the impression of being close to moving machine parts. As if functioning as evidence of the ship's purpose and life, and rumbling across every surface like electric current in each part of the vessel, the continuous vibration of the engine's exhaust thrums. Above the open hatch and beside the lifeboat assembly point, from a door left gaping in the rear house, drifts a thick warmth. Heat that waits to wrap itself round wind-seared cheeks in the way a summer's sun cups faces.

Once across the metal threshold the engine fibrillations deepen as if muted underground. The bronchial roar of the intake fans dulls. Inside, the salty-spittle scour of the night air, and the noxious mechanical odours, are replaced by the scent of old emulsion and the stale chemicals of exhausted air fresheners.

A staircase leads down.

But as above, so below. As on deck, no one walks here. All is still, brightly lit and faintly rumbling with the bass strumming of the exhaust. The communal area appears calm and indifferent to the intense black energies of the hurricane outside.

A long, narrow corridor runs through the rear house. Square lenses in the steel ceiling illuminate the plain passageway. The floor is covered in linoleum, the walls are matt yellow, the doors to the cabins trimmed with wood laminate. Halfway down, two opposing doors hang open before lit rooms.

The first room was intended for recreation to ease a crew's passage on a long voyage, but no one seeks leisure now. Coloured balls roll across the pool table from the swell that shimmies the ship. Two cues lie amongst the balls and move back and forth like flotsam on the tide. At rest upon the table-tennis table are two worn paddles. The television screen remains as empty and black as the rain-thrashed canopy of sky above the freighter. One of the brown leatherette sofas is split in two places and masking tape suppresses the spongy eruptions of cushion entrails.

Across the corridor, a long bank of washing machines and dryers stand idle in the crew's laundry room. Strung across the ceiling are washing-line cords that loop like skipping ropes from the weight of the clothing that is pegged in rows: jeans, socks, shirts, towels. One basket has been dropped upon the floor and has spilled its contents towards the door.

Up one flight of stairs, an empty bridge. Monitor screens glow green, consoles flicker. One stool lies on its side and the cushioned seat rolls back and forth. A solitary handgun skitters this way and that across the floor. The weapon adds a touch of tension to the otherwise tranquil area of operations, as if a drama has recently passed, been interrupted or even abandoned.

Back down below, deeper inside the ship and further along the crew's communal corridor, the stainless-steel galley glimmers dully in white light. A skein of steam clouds over the work surfaces and condenses on the ceiling above the oven. Two large, unwashed pots have boiled dry upon cooker rings glowing red. From around the oven door, wisps of black smoke puff. Inside the oven a tray of potatoes has baked to carbon and they now resemble the fossils of reptile guano.

Around the great chopping board on the central table lies a scattering of chopped vegetables, cast wide by the freighter's lurches and twists. The ceiling above the work station is railed with steel and festooned with swaying kitchenware.

Six large steaks, encrusted with crushed salt, await the abandoned spatula and the griddle that hisses black and dry. A large refrigerator door, resembling the gate of a bank vault, hangs open to reveal crowded shelves that gleam in ivory light.

There is a metal sink the size of a bath tub. Inside it lies a human scalp.

Lopped roughly from the top of a head and left to drain beside the plughole, the gingery mess looks absurdly artificial. But the clod of hair was once plumbed into a circulatory system because the hair is matted dark and wet at the fringes and surrounded by flecks of ochre. The implement that removed the scalp lies upon the draining board: a long knife, the edge serrated for sawing. Above the adjacent work station, at the end of the rack that holds the cook's knives, several items are missing.

Maybe this dripping thing of hair was brought to the sink area from somewhere outside the galley, carried along the corridor and up the flight of stairs that leads from the crew's quarters. Red droplets as round as rose petals make a trail into the first cabin on a corridor identical to the communal passage on the deck above. The door to this cabin is open. Inside, the trail of scarlet is immediately lost within the borders of a far bigger stain.

A fluorescent jacket and cap hang upon a peg just inside the door of the cabin. All is neat and orderly upon the bookshelf, which holds volumes that brush the low white ceiling. A chest of drawers doubles as a desk. The articles on the desktop are held down by a glass paperweight and overlooked by silver-framed photographs of wives and children at the rear of the desk. On top of the wardrobe, life jackets and hardhats are stowed. Two twin beds, arranged close together, are unoccupied. Beneath the bedframes, orange survival suits remain neatly folded and tightly packed.

The bedclothes of the berth on the righthand side are tidy and undisturbed. But the white top sheet and the yellow blanket of the adjacent berth droop to the linoleum floor like idle sails. There is a suggestion that an occupant departed this bed hurriedly, or was removed swiftly. The bed linen has been yanked from the bed and only remains tucked under the mattress in one corner. A body was also ruined in that bed: the middle of the mattress is blood-sodden and the cabin reeks of salt and rust. Crimson gouts from a bedside frenzy have flecked and speckled the wall beside the bed, and part of the ceiling.

Attached to the room is a small ensuite bathroom that just manages to hold a shower cubicle and small steel sink. The bathroom is pristine; the taps, shower head and towel rail sparkle. All that is amiss is a single slip-on shoe, dropped on the floor just in front of the sink. A foot remains inside the shoe with part of a hairy ankle extending from the uppers.

From the cabin more than a trail of droplets can be followed further down the passage and towards the neighbouring berths. A long, intermittent streak of red has been smeared along the length of the corridor, past the four doors that all hang open and drift back and forth as the ship lists. From each of these cabins, other collections have been made.

What occupants once existed in the crew's quarters appear to have arisen from their beds before stumbling towards the doors as if hearing some cause for alarm nearby. Just before the doorways of their berths, they seem to have met their ends quickly. Wide, lumpy puddles, like spilled stew made with red wine, are splashed across the floors. One crew member sought refuge inside the shower cubicle of the last cabin, because the bathroom door is broken open and the basin of the shower is drenched nearly black from a sudden and conclusive emptying. Livestock hung above the cement of a slaughterhouse and emptied from the throat leaves similar stains.

To the left at the end of the passage, the open door of the captain's cabin is visible. Inside, the sofa beside the coffee table and the two easy chairs sit expectant but empty. The office furniture and shelves reveal no disarray. But set upon the broad desk are three long wooden crates. The tops have been levered off, and the packing straw that was once inside is now littered about the table's surface and the carpeted floor. Mingled with the straw is a plethora of dried flower petals.

Upon a tablecloth spread on the floor before the captain's desk, two small forms have been laid out. They lie side by side. They are the size of five-year-old children and blackened by age, not unlike the preserved forms of ancient peoples, protected behind glass in museums of antiquities. They appear to be shrivelled and contorted. Vestiges of a fibrous binding have fused with their petrified flesh and obscured their arms, if they have such limbs. The two small figures are primarily distinguished by the irregular shape and silhouette of their skulls. Their heads appear oversized, and the swollenness of the crania contributes to the leathery ghastliness of their grimacing faces. The rear of each head is fanned by an incomplete mane of spikes, while the front of each head elongates and protrudes into a snout. The desiccated figures have had their lower limbs bound tightly together to create a suggestion of long and curling tails.

Inside the second crate lies a large black stone, crudely hollowed out in the middle. The dull and chipped appearance of the block also suggests great age. A modern addition has been made, or offered, to the hollow within the stone. A single human foot. The shoe around the disarticulated foot matches the footwear inside the shower cubicle of the crew member's cabin.

The contents of the third crate have barely been disturbed. In there lie several artefacts that resemble jagged flints, or the surviving blades of old weapons or knives of which the handles are missing. The implements are hand-forged from a stone as black as the basin that has become a receptacle for a human foot.

Pictures of a ship and framed maps have been removed from the widest wall, and upon this wall a marker pen has been used to depict the outlines of two snouted or trumpeting figures that are attached by what appear to be long, entwined tails. The imagery is crude and childlike, but the silhouettes are similar to the embalmed remains laid out upon the bed sheet.

Below the two figures are imprecise sticklike figures that appear to cavort in emulation of the much larger and snouted characters. Set atop some kind of uneven pyramid shape, another group of human figures have been excitedly and messily drawn with spikes protruding from their heads or headdresses. Between the crowned forms another, plainer figure has been held aloft and bleeds from the torso into a waiting receptacle. Detail has been included to indicate that the sacrificed figure's feet have been removed and its legs bound.

The mess of human leavings that led here departs from the captain's cabin and rises up a staircase to the deck above and into an unlit canteen.

Light falls into this room from the corridor, and in the half-light two long tables, and one smaller table for the officers, are revealed. Upon the two larger crew tables long reddish shapes lie glistening: some twelve bodies dwindling into darkness as they stretch away from the door. As if they have been unzipped across the front, what

219

was once inside each of the men has now been gathered and piled upon chairs where the same men once sat and ate. Their feet, some bare, some still inside shoes, have been amputated and are set in a messy pile at the head of the two tables.

The far end of the cafeteria is barely touched by the residual light. Presented to no living audience, perversely and inappropriately and yet in a grimly touching fashion, two misshapen shadows flicker and leap upon the dim wall as if in joyous reunion. They wheel about each other, ferociously, but not without grace. They are attached, it seems, by two long, spiny tails.

Back outside and on deck, it can be seen that the ship continues to meander, dazed with desolation and weariness, perhaps punchdrunk from the shock of what has occurred below deck.

The bow momentarily rises up the small hillside of a wave and, just once, almost expectantly, looks towards the distant harbour to which the vessel has slowly drifted all night since changing its course.

On shore, and across the surrounding basin of treeless land, the lights of a small harbour town are white pinpricks, desperate to be counted in this black storm. Here and there, the harbour lights define the uneven silhouettes of small buildings, suggesting stone facades in which glass shimmers to form an unwitting beacon for what exists out here upon these waves.

Oblivious to anything but its own lurching and clanking, the ship rolls on the swell, inexorably drifting on the current that picked up its steel bulk the day before and now slowly propels the hull, though perhaps not as purposelessly as first appeared, towards the shore.

At the prow, having first bound himself tight to the railing with rope, a solitary and unclothed figure nods a bowed head towards the land. The pale flesh of the rotund torso is whipped and occasionally drenched by sea spray, but still bears the ruddy impressions of bestial deeds that were both boisterous and thorough. From navel to sternum, the curious figurehead is blackly open, or has been opened, to the elements. The implement used to carve such crude entrances to the heart is long gone, perhaps dropped from stained and curling fingers into the obsidian whirling and clashing of the monumental ocean far below.

As if to emulate a king, where the scalp has been carved away, a crude series of spikes, fashioned from nails, have been hammered into a pattern resembling a spine or fin across the top of the dead man's skull. Both of his feet are missing and his legs have been bound with twine into a single, gruesome tail.

YOU CAN GO NOW
Written by **Gary McMahon**

The dinner party was winding down. It was that time of the evening when only the stragglers remained; everyone else had either retired to bed or left in a taxi, vanishing drunkenly into the night. The lights were turned down low. Whisky was sipped from crystal glasses. Logs in the fire popped and fizzled.

'I heard this story the other day,' said Jim, breaking a rare silence.

'Oh, no...not one of your smutty ones, is it?' Jane laughed, flirting, as usual.

'No. This is a scary one.'

'Ooooh,' shrieked Tammy, smiling. 'I like scary stories.'

Matt slid his fingers into Gemma's palm. She closed her fist, holding onto him, pretending that it was all real and that she could feel something.

'So there was this woman brought into the emergency room. She was all shaken up, eyes wide and staring, shaking like crazy. She'd gone into catatonic shock.'

He took a sip of whisky; Gemma thought it was a ploy to heighten the tension: Jim was always such a drama queen.

'So,' he continued, 'they bring her in and we get her into a room, take her vital signs, then get her comfortable. A shot of sedative brings her back to us and she starts to talk. After a little while she's fully lucid, telling us what happened.'

Jane's phone started to ring, shattering the mood. 'Sorry, gang,' she said, glancing at the screen. 'Fuck, it's my ex.' She swiped a finger across the screen and put the phone away in her handbag. 'Please, do go on.' The expression on her face was mock-serious; she was trying to pretend she wasn't drunk again.

'Okay, so this is what she tells us:

'She's at home alone; her hubby is out working the night shift. She orders a pizza and opens a glass of wine, watches a movie. Hell, for all I know, she probably has a quick finger-stroke while she's watching Dirty Dancing.' He laughed, his eyes flashing. 'Anyway, she falls asleep on the couch and wakes up around 2am. She remembers the time because she has her iPad right next to her, with the clock displaying.

'She hears a noise. Has the impression that she's already heard it – that the noise was what woke her. Still bleary and half asleep, she gets up and staggers into the kitchen. The lights are off and she doesn't bother switching them on. No reason to be afraid. She's used to her own house.

'So, like I said, she walks through the kitchen, then into the dining room, listening to the noise. It's a banging sound, like the cat flap makes when her pets come and go. She has two cats so this is something she's used to hearing. Only this time it's louder, as if something heavier than her cats is hitting the flap. She thinks it's probably the big tom that stalks the neighbourhood after dark.

'Once in the dining room she can't see the bottom of the French doors, where the cat flap is, because the dining table blocks the view. So she walks around the table, approaching the doors. And that's when she sees it.'

There was another dramatic pause, followed by another slow sip of whisky as he smiled around the rim of the glass.

'What? What did she see?' Gemma was gripping Matt's hand so tightly that she was surprised he didn't call out, or at the very least try to pull away his hand.

'A small, thin man: a midget. Completely naked. Bald and glistening, like a grub or something. He's wedged himself in the cat flap with his arms trapped by his sides, and the sound is because of his struggling. He opens his mouth but nothing comes out, just a dry hissing sound. He has no teeth, just hard, ridge-like gums, like a beak. His eyes are large – too big for his head, and spaced too far apart, like fish eyes: one on each side of his skull.

'The woman screams and he hisses again; then starts to struggle backwards – he was struggling forward before, trying to get inside. He squirms backwards out of the cat flap, writhing away into the dark garden…

'The woman called the police, and they had to break the door down when they arrived because by that time she'd gone into shock.'

'Wow,' said Jane, wide-eyed. 'That is so cool. Is it an urban legend?'

Jim shook his head. 'Fuck off. It really happened. I was there when she told the story. It wasn't a friend of a friend of a friend. I heard it all.'

'Bullshit,' said Matt, standing, tugging Gemma to her feet. 'And on that note, I think it's time we made our exit. But by the door, not the cat flap.'

Everybody laughed, using his weak joke to break the mood.

In the taxi home, Gemma realised she was a lot drunker than she'd thought. The world was a smear of light outside the car; the darkness kept trying to flood in. 'I feel sick,' she said, lurching as the taxi stopped at a red light. The reality was, she didn't feel anything. She rarely did.

'Not in my cab,' yelled the driver, peering over his shoulder.

'It's okay,' said Matt, rubbing Gemma's arm. 'She'll be fine.'

Before they went to bed that night she asked Matt to check the cat flap three times. Just in case. She made herself sick in the toilet but she wasn't sure why.

'I wish that prick hadn't told that story.'

'It's fine,' she said, trying to reassure him. 'You know I have a low tolerance for scary shit. It's one of the things you love most about me.'

His smile was hollow; there was nothing behind it but another kind of darkness, one that lived inside of people. She'd seen it many times before and would see it again. It was the darkness he retreated into when he was having his affairs, the shadow-land where he told himself that what he was doing wasn't that bad. There was a similar kind of darkness living inside her.

The next day she called into the office and told them that she was sick. Her boss was reasonable about her absence, telling her to take some rest and get better. Feeling slightly guilty, she hung up the phone, took her morning pill, and had a long, hot shower, trying to wash off the stink of the bad feelings Jim's story had invoked.

She wasn't poorly; she was just tired. Tired of the crappy dinner parties; of Matt's seedy double life; of her inability to tackle him about the problems in their marriage... She used to cut herself, back in the day, when she thought it might help her to feel something other than weak. She stopped doing that when, finally, she admitted to herself that it wasn't working. Now she just floated around in the bell jar of her life, dry-swallowing her daily pills and pretending that nothing really mattered.

At lunchtime she made a sandwich, and then stared at it on the plate. She even touched it once, twice, three times, before giving up and throwing it in the bin. She couldn't remember the last time she'd eaten a decent meal without throwing it up again afterwards.

Social media was a bust: nobody interesting was around today. She watched some YouTube videos that were meant to be funny but were really just dull and then logged off, feeling disconnected from the world as well as her own feelings. It was a familiar sensation, one that she'd grown accustomed to. She didn't mind; there was no pain. Everything was just a crashing bore.

She prepared a cold dinner that only Matt would eat and then waited for him to come home. An hour after he was due back from work, he called to tell her that he was working late and didn't know what time he'd eventually get away.

'A few of us are considering sleeping here at the office. This deadline...it's so fucking tight. You know how it is, this business. Deadline is king.'

'Okay. That's fine. I'll see you tomorrow.'

'Thanks, babe. I'll make it up to you. We'll spend some quality time together at the weekend.'

But they never did. There were always friends around: friends and parties and anything to make sure they never spent any time alone, because if they did they might have to admit that they had nothing whatsoever in common and their marriage was – and always had been – a sham.

She waited to see if she could feel anything, but, as usual, there was nothing there. That hollow darkness, just like the one behind Matt's smile, churned inside her; a storm of shadows, a black turmoil that she could not even feel. She knew it was all that remained of the baby, the one that never had a chance to live, but the thought offered no comfort.

She opened a bottle of wine. Before long, it was empty and she had to open another.

She woke without realising she'd even been to sleep. The noise came again: a loud, flat slamming sound, the cat flap, either opening or closing with sudden violence.

Gemma got up, almost sleepwalking; she padded out of the living room and into the hall accompanied by a vague sense of inevitability. The lights were out. The darkness was comforting. She moved into the kitchen, past the centrally located sink and work surface, through the door and into the conservatory. Something pale glistened in the darkness at the foot of the conservatory doors – small and thin and maggot-like.

Gemma stopped and crouched down, her knees straining from the movement. She wasn't afraid. 'Hello there,' she said.

She saw the top of a bald head, which turned to reveal a face. Narrow cheeks, a small, moist, lipless mouth, two huge eyes spaced much too far apart on the head.

'Why are you here?'

This felt like a dream but she wasn't sure if it was. Everything was so ill-defined, so lacking in hard edges, that she just went

227

along with it, still unafraid, not even worried - which was a new sensation, because usually she was scared of everything. Or pretended to be, to get Matt's attention.

The small, thin figure opened its mouth to show her its toughened gums. When it hissed, spittle splattered like rainfall. It hissed again, but still she was not afraid.

'What do you want?'

The thing shuddered, as if a small electrical current was passing through its body, and then it slithered backwards out of the cat flap, moving quickly away from the door.

The last thing she saw was its face. Those massive eyes.

Matt's bags were packed and waiting when he came home the following morning. She was perched on the end of the bed, two suitcases at her feet, hands held daintily in her lap, when he trotted up the stairs and bundled through the door.

'I'm sorry,' he said. 'It couldn't be helped.'

'You can go now.' She glanced at her feet, at the suitcases.

'What?'

'You didn't even care enough to have a shower. I can still smell her cunt on you.' It was a lie, of course, but she knew how much he hated that word and the casual profanity would hurt him.

'What are you talking about?'

'You can go now. I'm fine.'

He approached her, hands raised and clutching at air; he didn't know what to do. 'Listen. I had to work late. We all did.'

She stood and slapped him hard across the face. Time halted: he stood there with a shocked look on his face; she stood opposite him with her arm outstretched, the palm of her hand stinging. This was the first thing she had truly felt without faking in a year, since the baby that never was.

'You can go now,' she said again, moving slowly around him and leaving the room.

Sitting in the conservatory, she heard him come down the stairs, hauling his suitcases. He stopped; she knew that he was looking back, at the kitchen door. But he didn't dare say a word. He just opened the door and left.

Gemma made herself a cup of coffee and sat in the garden to drink it. The birds were singing. The sky was blue and clear, but there was a chill in the air. She didn't mind the cold. It made her skin tingle, as if her body was coming back to life. The darkness inside her belly retreated, as if it was afraid of the light.

That night she left the conservatory doors wide open, inviting it inside.

She sat in the little armchair outside the utility room and waited, cradling a blanket in case it got too cold. The night bloomed, dark flowers opening in the sky. The nearby traffic noise decreased, and then stopped altogether. She wasn't sure how long she sat there – didn't care – and after what seemed like a long time or no time at all, it slithered into the doorway.

'Come in,' she said, not moving to get out of the chair. She didn't want to scare it away. 'I won't hurt you.'

As it moved slowly on its belly, like a snake, over the threshold and into the conservatory, Gemma could see that it had no legs. The sexless body ended at the pelvis in a narrow nub of flesh, like a fish's tail. It had no arms, just flaps of sinew that resembled arms if they were held tightly to its sides. The thing was little more than a torso and a head. It seemed unfinished rather than deformed, as if it had been sent out into the world too early: the unfinished product of a disinterred god.

It writhed and slithered to her feet, then stopped, turning up its head to look at her. The eyes were large and wet; they shone like mirrors in the dark. Gemma rested a hand on her belly, sensing the emptiness beneath the skin, and rubbed, slowly, in a small circle.

The thing opened its mouth and hissed softly; but this time it wasn't an aggressive sound. It was a sound of enquiry, a question.

'Yes,' she said. 'He's gone now. So we can be together, if you'd like to stay.'

It struggled to climb up her legs, and sat in her lap. Its skin was clammy, but she didn't mind that. There were worse things than clammy flesh, more unpleasant experiences to endure. She should know; she had been through a lot of them.

She stood and carried it upstairs. It was lighter than it looked, as if its bones were hollow. She could feel the flesh sliding over whatever thin skeleton it had beneath.

Everything was ready. She had spent the day preparing for its arrival. Getting the cot down out of the loft was the trickiest part, but she managed to manhandle it down and into the room they were always planning to use as a nursery until she lost the baby. The toys she'd kept in black plastic bin bags, unable to throw them away. She'd never told Matt they were still in the house – he believed her when she told them a charity came to take them away.

She placed the thing in the cot and covered it with a soft blanket. There were kittens on the blanket, and clouds.

'Go to sleep,' she said.

The huge eyes blinked slowly – much slower than normal human eyes. It was disconcerting to see them slow-blinking on each side of the head, but she would grow accustomed to these small differences.

She knew this wasn't her child – wasn't a child at all, not in any way that she could ever explain – but it would serve as a temporary stopgap to fill the void in her life, the empty spaces where something should have lived and breathed and loved.

'We'll get used to each other, you and I, but we can't tell anyone about you. It's our secret.' She passed her hand across its face, caressing its moist cheeks. The bones shifted beneath the skin; an unpleasant sensation. 'For now...'

Gemma switched out the light and locked the door when she left the room. She didn't think it would try to escape, but she needed to prevent it from moving around the house in the night until she decided what to do with it.

When she went to bed she fell asleep immediately. Her dreams were filled with kittens and clouds and writhing things with pale skin and large eyes that took forever to blink.

She drifted in and out of sleep, unsettled. The sudden changes in her life were taking effect; she could not seem to relax. She got up in the dark and stood outside the nursery. A hissing sound came from behind the door.

She had no idea what she was going to do, but she knew she was going to do something. The time for being a bystander to her own life had passed; this was a time for action.

There was a knife in her hand but she didn't know where it had come from. She had no recollection of going downstairs to fetch it, but she must have done because the knives were kept in the kitchen drawer. She was either half asleep or half awake: the distinction didn't matter.

'You can go now,' she whispered, sooner than she expected to. 'I think we're finished.'

Before she'd gone to bed, she had an eye on the long game: she thought that it might take years for the changes to finish taking place. But she was wrong; she was different now, and able to cope on her own. She didn't need a husband, or a dead baby, or a thing that had come to replace them both. She realised that now. The truth was within reach: the truth about everything. Throwing out Matt had been a watershed moment. Everything afterwards was just part of the wreckage.

She opened the door and stepped inside.

'Please,' said a voice that was familiar but garbled, as if it was coming from a distorted mouth – a mouth that had had its teeth knocked out, or was stuffed full of cotton. 'I'm sorry.'

Hush,' she said, walking forward and raising the knife. Reality threatened to intrude but she pushed it away. The darkness inside her spewed out between her legs, staining the floor and turning the room black. It washed across the floor, a dark flood, obscuring everything. Black waves, breaking on a desolate shore.

Briefly, before the blackness took it away, Matt's face overlaid

231

that of the thing in the cot, and the lifeless, bloodied face of a baby that never was overlaid them both. Then those other faces were replaced by hers, and she was smiling.

'I said, you can leave now,' she whispered, for the last time.' 'I don't need you anymore. I don't need anyone.' She wasn't even certain there was anything there. It felt as if she was talking to herself. This whole thing could have been a hallucination of some kind, a vision brought on by stress.

The black tide ebbed and flowed, washing away her old life and pouring through new wounds in her body. Newborn feelings and sensations twitched at the edges of experience as she raised the knife high above her head.

Then, at last, she felt something – truly felt it.

The only problem was, she had no idea what it was.

DOWN THERE
Written By **Ryan Harding**

I

Kendra didn't like the woods.

Back home—she still couldn't bring herself to think of Centerville as 'home'—they had lived in a neighborhood bordered by other neighborhoods where you could see houses in every direction. She knew the woods only from the school bus ride. They creeped her out, especially mornings when it was still dark outside. Russell would watch them with the same longing he'd show at a toy store, which was par for the course from a spaz like Russell.

Anything could be back there! he said.

Exactly why she didn't want to go anywhere near them.

Naturally he was happy about the world of trees so close to their new house. Kendra suspected her parents even chose this one in part because of the little brat's enthusiasm for the woods. Another house they considered was more like their old one in location if not size, which would have also sucked by virtue of being anywhere but Clayton, but at least there weren't miles of trees behind it.

Maybe she could lay as much blame on Gwendolyn.

When the real estate agent showed them the house, Kendra made the mistake of eye contact with a girl riding her bike in the street, who rode over to ask if they were moving in. Kendra shrugged, bit back the *I hope not* on her tongue, and mentally urged her to pedal off into the sunset, but her mom and dad locked in and started pumping the girl for information about the neighborhood (liked it but more kids would be really cool, hint, hint), the school system (great, she had learned all kinds of neat stuff), even the weather (hot in summer, snow in winter, who knew), and her name (Gwendolyn Marie). Kendra's mom embarrassingly introduced her as if Kendra wasn't standing there in earshot praying for a sniper.

Gwendolyn Marie, that's such a pretty name, her mom said. Don't you think so, Kendra?

Sure, if you didn't mind someone losing interest and strolling half a block by the time you spit it all out.

Her parents then shared a knowing look, and Kendra's heart sank. They might as well have stenciled SOLD on the sign then and there.

Two weeks and hundreds of miles later, they moved in to the single story home with a sticky-looking brown paint job on Sycamore Lane. Pros: Summer vacation lasted until Labor Day in Centerville. Cons: Everything else. The isolation from the blockade of trees made it feel like a colony on another planet.

'Kendra, why don't you go out and play with your new friend?'

That was a mom's logic. A girl with a stupid name you talked to one time is automatically your friend because she's your age and she rides her bike past your house in some weird pattern that probably spells out I AM EXTREMELY LAME PLEASE COME OUT AND PLAY.

'You can take your brother out to the woods.' Another mom trademark, *can* as *will* in disguise

'I already share a room with the little creep. Do I have to take him on a play date too?'

Her mom's eyes narrowed. 'Your brother is *not* a little creep, Miss Kendra Jane. It won't kill you to take him out there.'

No, I'm not that lucky.

But she didn't say it. She'd edged a toe across the line complaining about the sleeping arrangements and didn't need the whole 'your father never asked to be downsized lecture' a third time.

Her mom smacked an animal figurine down on the étagère. 'It's either play outside or finish unpacking. How's that grab you?'

Unpacking enhanced the awful permanence of Kendra's nightmare. 'Guess I'll say hello.'

Her mom couldn't resist a parting shot as Kendra departed. 'Honestly! Try to think about someone besides yourself for a change!'

Oh, you mean like all the friends I had to leave behind in Clayton?

The front door opened again seconds after she emerged, and Russell followed.

Gwendolyn looped around on her bike to intercept them, already smiling, a dark haired girl with wide eyes. She also had braces, which was a little ominous. Kendra didn't want to enter a new school situation befriending one of the kids everyone made fun of since that could put her in the crossfire too, but a new school would be less scary if Kendra made a friend in advance. Gwendolyn didn't seem much like her friends back home, but maybe she would turn out to be cool.

'Hey, Kendra,' she said as she pedaled up. 'Wanna see the woods?'

II

The woods swallowed them immediately and utterly. It was another world with new sights, sounds, and smells. Colors, too—deeper within, some leaves had begun to redden with the early touch of fall. Within two minutes there was no trace of their street at all.

'This is awesome,' Russell announced. His head swiveled back and forth as though thinking, *And this is mine...all mine.*

'I love it,' Gwendolyn said. 'I come back here a lot.'

Except when you're riding your bike in front of my house, hoping to be noticed, Kendra thought. She'd kept a rein on her sarcasm so far, though, trying to determine boundaries.

The trees seemed endless in all directions until everything began to look the same, much to Kendra's growing uneasiness. It seemed awfully easy to get lost. She would swear they'd passed the same fallen log at least three times. They walked several minutes with the accompaniment of distant sounds—things falling, things breaking, like signals of their approach.

She also thought she sensed someone stepping behind a trunk from the corner of her eye. A couple of times a branch would be waving when she turned to look. *Hi, Kendra...yes, there's someone back here. Come and see.*

'It's a little eerie,' she said.

'Pretty cool, huh?' Gwendolyn said. 'Did you know a girl from another school disappeared here last year?'

Russell's swiveling head stopped and whipped back to her. The woods didn't look quite as awesome to him now. 'You mean they never found her?'

Kendra had no obligation to hold back on her brother today. 'Yep, that's usually what they mean by disappear. Kind of like how your brain seems to have disappeared.'

'Shut up.'

'She really did, though,' Gwendolyn said.

'What do they think happened to her?' Kendra said.

'Well, some kids say she failed social studies and ran away from home.'

Kendra saw another waving branch, closer this time. The tree trunk wasn't big enough to hide anyone but she walked faster anyway until she caught Gwendolyn in the lead.

She tried to sound nonchalant. 'Do you ever see anyone else back here?'

'Not really. There was some creepy looking guy with a beard just walking through one time. I don't think he saw me.'

Great.

'Is social studies hard?' Russell asked. He would probably face it in third grade next week.

'It is if your brain disappears,' Kendra said. It was practically muscle reflex these days.

Gwendolyn gave her the metal smile. To Russell, she said, 'Don't worry about it. I don't think that's what happened anyway.'

Russell smirked at Kendra like he'd somehow 'won' an argument.

'No,' Gwendolyn continued, 'I think the Woodsman took her.'

'The Woodsman?' Kendra repeated. Bad enough her parents dragged her to Centerville, but was there some serial killer picking off children here too?

She pictured her parents researching on the internet before the move.

Oh, wait, he just slaughters little girls. At least Russell will be okay.

And hey, if anything happens to Kendra, we can cash in her college fund and get Russ a cool car when he's old enough!

Win/win!

'Yeah, you don't know about the *Woodsman*?'

Kendra resented the mild implication she was uncool for not knowing about a psychotic lumberjack or whatever he was. 'We just got here, remember?'

'But he's everywhere,' Gwendolyn said. Kendra could see now she hadn't been critical after all, just puzzled by Kendra's ignorance. 'I mean, in all the forests.'

Kendra shrugged. 'No, sorry.' Guess he hasn't opened up a chain back in Clayton, she thought.

'He has a lot of names,' Gwendolyn said. 'Maybe you know a different one.'

'Oh,' Kendra said. 'Yeah, maybe.' But she doubted Gwendolyn's woodland boogeyman was operating in Clayton under the alias 'Steve' and she somehow forgot about it.

'But why would he take that girl?' Russell asked.

'It's just a story, spaz.'

'It's not made up,' Gwendolyn said. She looked astonished

anyone could doubt it, although 'astonished' was kind of a default mode with her perpetual wide-eyed expression.

Russell looked at Kendra hopefully, willing to be called a spaz again if she would just reassure him about the fictional nature of the Woodsman. She rolled her eyes where Gwendolyn couldn't see, but he did not seem comforted.

'I'll show you where he is,' Gwendolyn said. 'Come on.'

She led them without any noticeable change in direction that Kendra could see. It had probably always been her intended destination from the moment she took charge back by the house.

The foliage grew thicker in the following minutes, taking away the brunt of midafternoon sunlight.

Shadier, Kendra thought, but the word hiding behind that was *darker.*

The random splintering of branches in the distance that had become almost subliminal to her gradually intensified. A strong wind which had not been in evidence at any earlier point in their exploration stirred the boughs. Pine cones and acorns clattered through a maze of limbs in a circle that seemed to be closing in tighter on them.

The whole thing had to be made up, of course, right down to the missing girl, but understanding this couldn't quite make it actually feel that way to Kendra. She wanted to suggest they turn back but there was no excuse that wouldn't seem like she was freaked out. She wasn't, not quite, but feeling so cut off from everything here, it was a little easier to accept that Gwendolyn's story could be real after all.

'Here.' Gwendolyn pointed.

There was an arch of trees. It couldn't be accidental. All of the other trees around them had sprung up independently with no sense of proportion. The branches intruded on one another and the spaces between their trunks could be several yards or merely feet.

The arch was perfectly symmetrical, gnarled ash-colored trees with no leaves and strange growths that made Kendra think of tumors. Some of the protrusions looked to have formed around human heads. The room between each tree in the line was a perfect three yards. The column extended for twelve trees on both sides with just enough space within for Kendra, Gwendolyn, and Russell to walk side by side until past the halfway point. Gwendolyn stopped them there. The trees ahead grew closer together until the end when there was only space for one person at a time.

It's like a doorway, Kendra thought.

'If you go through there,' Gwendolyn said, gesturing to the end of the column, 'you'll see him.'

A few yards past the last two trees, there was a hole in the ground.

'He comes up from the dark, and if you don't bring an offering, he takes you back with him.'

'That's why he took the girl?' Russell asked.

'Probably.'

Russell took a step forward, searching through his pockets. Kendra's hand instinctively went to his shoulder to stop him. She shook her head. He gave her a look that said, Now *who's being the spaz*.

This was silly. Nothing would happen if she let him walk through there, and she wouldn't see anything if she followed him, either.

And we definitely won't see him if we never walk through it in the first place.

She studied the hole closer, standing tiptoed and leaning forward. 'That's not even big enough for one us to get in there. How could a man do it?'

'But he's not like us,' Gwendolyn explained; slowly, like Kendra was feeble-minded. 'He can be anywhere in the woods, or anything. He could be as tall as the trees and he can also get down below.'

Kendra thought of something vaguely human shaped contorting, breaking itself down with collapsible limbs to slip deep

239

into the earth. The shade grew much colder on her skin. No, he wasn't real, of course not...but if he was less unreal, was he poised beneath them now, ready to emerge from the deeps if one of them took another twenty steps forward, crawling along in some spidery fashion in an ebb and flow of crackling shifting bones?

'Have you ever seen him?' Russell asked Gwendolyn.

'I...I'm not sure.' Gwendolyn frowned. 'I thought once, maybe, over there.'

The tree she indicated stood well away from the arch, visible in the three yards between the gnarled trees nearest to Kendra. A knothole gaped in its trunk like a porthole to observe their archway.

'He was inside the tree?' Kendra meant for it to sound skeptical (and not more than a little mocking), but it came out wrong and nearly sounded declarative, like part of her mind believed it even if the rest resisted.

'It was a face,' Gwendolyn said. 'I think.' She stared intently, like it might still be there to help her find the words. 'Not how it'd look if one of us was looking out, though. More like the pattern inside the tree had a face you could see if you looked at it long enough. I know I saw its eyes. They were moving.'

Kendra silently urged Gwendolyn to snort sudden laughter. You should see your faces! Oh, man, I really had you guys going! By the way, nobody at school likes me!

Instead she shook her head, still solemn. 'I don't know. I walked over and it didn't look like anything by then, but until I got really close, I could see that face.' She sounded disappointed for its loss rather than frightened by its appearance.

Russell frowned. 'Hey, what's that?'

He took off running toward the oak with the knothole. Kendra followed, mainly to get away from the arch. Apparently there was no hard and fast rule about cutting through the line of trees since Gwendolyn came along too.

Russell knelt and picked something up from a mound of leaves.

It was a doll that had taken a beating from the elements, its white dress damp and filthy. The plastic girl with curly blonde hair looked stoic about her predicament, a smudge on one cheek like a bruise and deep red lips to form a small heart-shaped mouth.

'Is that yours?' Kendra asked Gwendolyn.

'No, I've never seen it before.'

'Let's give it to the Woodsman!' Russell said.

Kendra doubted a homeless girl would condescend to rescue this battered thing from the trash, but Gwendolyn nodded and said, 'Good idea.' She accepted the doll from him, in the lead once more, and let it dangle from her hand as she walked.

They worked their way back to the entry of the arch rather than cutting between its trees to where they'd stopped. This time they walked beyond the halfway point, eventually falling into single file with Kendra in the middle. She kept her eyes on the doll to avoid the approach of the doorway. Its blue eyes returned her stare, blank and soulless.

Gwendolyn stopped four trees from the end. The snaps and crunches of the surrounding forest continued with the occasional call of a bird, but it all sounded somehow muted from within the column.

'Have you done this before?' Kendra asked when Gwendolyn didn't move after five seconds.

Gwendolyn shook her head, not turning around. The doll gazed at something unseen behind them. Kendra wondered if the face in the knothole watched Gwendolyn so impassively.

There was no face!

She didn't doubt Gwendolyn saw one, though, if only a trick of light and shadow. If she looked back now, would she see it too?

'Just toss it into the hole,' she suggested, an easy compromise which wouldn't require Gwendolyn actually stepping through the passageway.

Russell made an exasperated noise behind her. 'But we won't know if he took it.'

Kendra's stomach flipped. They would have to come back here again, just to see.

Gwendolyn advanced carefully as though walking to the edge of a cliff.

'Great Presence of the Woods, we offer this to you,' Gwendolyn said, loud enough to carry. She delicately set the doll down before the threshold, then turned and hurried back to Kendra and Russell.

'We'll come back tomorrow to see if it's gone,' she said, softly now as if they were in a church. She and Kendra walked back through the arch with more haste. When Kendra turned to chart Russell's progress, she saw him casually walking backwards, as if hoping to something reach out from the hole to claim their offering.

III

Neither of them slept right away that night.

After several minutes of waiting for sleep, Russell said, 'Do you think he took the doll?' It was the first they had spoken of it back in the house.

'Of course not.'

'Why not?'

'Duh, he's not real.'

'But Gwendolyn saw him!'

'Think about it, Russ. If she really saw his face in that tree, why would she keep going back there all by herself?' Kendra had pondered that question all night, though instead of comforting her as evidence of a hoax, she'd found herself thinking, *Because it's making her come back...because it wanted her to bring us.*

Russell stayed quiet long enough she thought he'd gone to sleep, but at last he said, 'He's real. I bet he's coming out of the ground right now.'

IV

'It's still there,' Gwendolyn said the following afternoon, clearly disappointed.

It was right where they left it, a flash of white at the foot of the 'passage' where nothing would happen if they walked through.

Aw, man, the terrifying thing in the woods is just a story after all. Bummer!

Kendra could finally loosen up. Her chest had felt tight all morning, especially when the walk here already seemed impossibly familiar despite the lack of distinguishing landmarks (she was sure she could find the arch without Gwendolyn now).

The three of them approached the apparently rejected offering. Kendra made it a point to find the knothole. Nope, nothing there, why would there be? She let Gwendolyn spook her yesterday, that was all. The only scary thing now was starting a new school with a friend who saw faces in tree trunks and left broken dolls for the 'Great Presence of the Woods.'

Total freak show. And probably known for it by everyone at school.

'Hey, do you see that?' Gwendolyn asked. She sprinted the rest of the way to the doll. Heart heavier in her chest, the tightness settling back in, Kendra hurried to catch up with with Russell in tow.

'Look.' Gwendolyn pointed to the doll. Its dead eyes and ruby heart-shaped mouth looked no worse for the horror of the thing in the earth. The dress was a different matter. It was damp when they left it before and grimy, but the moisture had a distinctly crimson cast to it now right over the chest.

Russell reached down to yank the dress up to the neck.

'Oh God,' Kendra said.

Gwendolyn's hand flew to her mouth. She looked away in a hurry.

The doll's chest gaped uncovered, hollowed out, the resultant

243

cavity filled with blood of a quite similar shade to that of its lips. There were other things inside too, islets of glistening pieces of tissue. At first Kendra thought a trick of light reflected in the blood had her seeing things, but realized something was moving inside it after all. Tiny whitish-yellow slivers writhing within the hole.

Maggots.

Kendra looked away too, eyes watering, gorge rising. She took deep breaths until the worst of it passed, vision in and out of focus as she searched for distractions. A falling leaf, a sycamore tree, the bushy tail of a squirrel like a sail as it dashed between a cluster of trees.

'What does that mean?' Gwendolyn kept her hand close to her mouth in case she needed to clamp it back to keep from being sick.

'I don't think he liked it,' Russell said. He continued to peer into the cavity as if trying to see his reflection.

'Come on, Russ, you don't need to be looking at that.'

He shrugged at her, as if to say *Just because* you *can't take it*... But he abandoned his vigil and joined Kendra and Gwendolyn.

'Did you do that?' Gwendolyn asked.

Kendra thought she meant Russell, and then realized even more absurdly, she meant Kendra herself.

'You're asking if I stuffed that doll with *gore* and…and…' She couldn't get the word out but she saw them in her mind, the swarm of grubs. 'No! Did *you*?'

'No, I swear!'

There hadn't been enough pieces for identification but someone obviously dissected a small creature and tossed the stuffing into the doll.

Either that or a woodchuck threw itself on a grenade.

Gwendolyn seemed sincere in the denial, her face curdled. Kendra couldn't picture her coming back last night to do something so sick as darkness spread over this secret world. The arch was the last place in the world she'd want to be in the dead of night, though there was an undeniable fascination at the prospect as well. A desire that didn't seem to belong to her any more than her familiarity with the path here, to feel the caress of the night air with a prism of bone-shaded moonlight glowing through the gnarled pillars in a land cast in shadow.

And him waiting to bestow his favor beyond the arch, down there.

'Oh, cool,' Russell said. He had wandered back to the doll.

She and Gwendolyn turned, careful not to look at the ground, though Kendra thought she heard the moist sound of those slivers squirming in the blood anyway.

Russell examined one of the trees at the threshold to the hole.

'Don't you go through there!' Kendra said.

'Duh.'

A knife protruded from the tree trunk on the left. Its handle shared the weathered appearance of the doll, something potentially lost back here for months. A dark stain shadowed the trunk around the groove, like the tree bled from the stab wound. The blade stuck at an angle where its handle pointed to the ground. At the doll.

Russell reached for the knife.

'Don't touch that,' Kendra said.

He made the trademark *uh!* sound she despised. 'Why not? He gave it to us!'

'Then he should have asked mom and dad first. You know they'd never let you keep a knife.'

Russell turned up his lip in pout mode. Kendra almost preferred to look at the doll instead.

Gwendolyn's eyes popped. 'Do you think he really left it there for us?'

'No,' Kendra said. 'Come on, it was probably that creep you saw with the beard. I bet he's watching us.'

She didn't believe it, though, not at all, and was too shaken to appreciate the irony that some nut spying on them and leaving mutilated trinkets would have been a relief.

Gwendolyn and Russell didn't appear to buy it either.

'Okay, then why give us an offering? Russell's nothing special. He doesn't even brush his teeth half the time.'

'Yes, I do!'

'It's not an offering,' Gwendolyn said softly. 'You know it's not.'

'Did that girl really disappear last year?' Kendra asked, desperate.

'Yes, I swear to God!'

Kendra sighed. 'Come on.' She grabbed Russell's shoulder to coax him away from the knife and the passage, toward the mouth of the arch.

'What are we going to do?' Gwendolyn asked as they walked.

'There's nothing *to* do,' Kendra said. 'We just need to stay the hell out of the woods.'

'I'm telling mom you're swearing,' Russell threatened.

'But we didn't do it right,' Gwendolyn said. 'If he's giving us another chance and we're just walking away…'

'We didn't walk through the last trees,' Kendra said. 'And you never have before, right?'

'Never.'

'There you go. We don't owe him shit.'

Russell renewed his threats. Kendra ignored him. She did not glance back at the arch, and absolutely would not look in the direction of the knothole.

V

'You suck,' she told Russell when their parents sent him to bed—a full hour after they forced Kendra since he was as good as his word about reporting her profanity. She also had the pleasure of being grounded tomorrow.

If he hears you talk like that, he's going to think it's okay to do it too, Mom said. You need to think about how you influence him.

Kendra answered with token nods, remembering her dad's

246

colorful phrases about the bosses from his old job, and how those 'cocksucking fucks' would rue the day they told an asset like him to hit the bricks since they 'couldn't find their own assholes if they followed the big rubber dick.' Nothing she'd ever repeated, so maybe the whole influence thing was a bit overrated.

'Sorry,' he said now.

Though she kind of wanted to smother him with a pillow while he slept, she didn't mind sharing a bedroom with him tonight given what they found today.

Her bed faced the large windows above his, with a view to the trees. He would be first in line if something crawled out from the woods. It would have served him right, too, the little tattletale, and she almost told him so, but soon lost herself in thoughts of the woods themselves, how she and Russell could open those windows and go there now when it was so dark. She knew they could find the arch.

He would be there, *come and see.*

Kendra awoke hours later from a dream of falling endlessly and sat up in bed. A leaf became stuck to the window while she slept. The backyard glowed in the moonlight, the front line of trees visible at the border of the woods. Past them several black shapes seemed to move as clouds rushed past the night sky.

Another leaf settled on the window.

Kendra squinted. Were they actually leaves or some kind of insect, like a butterfly?

She slid out of bed and crept to Russell's side of the room, unknowingly adopting the same pose with which she examined the hole beyond the arch. They were black shapes against the moonlight but she thought they had to be leaves.

As she looked, leaning slightly over Russell's bed, others began to float to the window, as if propelled by a leaf blower. Though concentrated in a specific pane of glass, they did not land in a scattered fashion where one covered up another. One would land apart from the others, followed by another beside it, gradually obscuring the pane in a mostly oval shape. It was like watching the formation of a vertical jigsaw puzzle with pear-shaped leaves. When the leaves settled to complete the shape, they moved en masse, like someone tilting their head to see at an angle, amidst a flurry of light scraping sounds against the window.

Kendra jerked back, twisted, and dove into her bed, yanking the covers over her head. The bristling sound continued, like the head or face sought every corner of the room. She thought she heard the sound of more leaves lighting on the window too, perhaps providing additional shape. A neck, shoulders, chest, arms. She knew if she were to turn on the bedroom light, she would find the leaves to be multicolored, able to effect eyes, a nose, a mouth in a crude, horrible fashion.

She stayed under cover, shaking, heart bouncing this way and that like a ball tethered to a paddle, filled with an urge to scream—anything to drown out those seeking, whispering sounds which she feared would become actual words if she heard them long enough.

After untold seconds, a great whooshing sound consumed the night, like a giant snake slithering through the woods to shake all the trees from here back to the arch.

He could be as tall as the trees.

'Kendra?' Russell called, sleepily.

'Go back to sleep,' she said. 'You're dreaming.'

She stayed with the covers pulled overhead the rest of the night.

VI.

She awoke early to find her mom in the kitchen sipping coffee, the sun bright through the windows and the world sane.

'Oh, getting an early start on going nowhere, I see.'

Kendra smirked without much enthusiasm.

Russell wasn't far behind, joining them in the kitchen before Kendra finished her breakfast. When their mother went back to her bedroom to work on the last unpacking, Kendra took hold of

Russell's wrist.

'You can't go back in the woods today.'

That *uh!* sound again. 'Why?'

'It's not safe.'

'But I'll go with Gwendolyn.'

She thought of Gwendolyn wringing her hands. We didn't do it right…if he's giving us another chance—

She tightened her grip. '*Especially* not with her. I mean it.'

'Ow!' He pulled his arm away, rubbing his wrist. That damned pout again. 'You can't make me.'

'I'll tell Mom you're swearing,' she said.

An empty threat since even if he had, she'd probably ground Kendra for putting those words in his head in the first place. It seemed to do the trick, though. His shoulders slumped.

'We'll go tomorrow,' Kendra said. She meant it to be a lie, but found the idea agreeable. Yes, they could go back there and get the offering right this time. The knife would still be there—

Russell left the kitchen with exaggeratedly heavy steps.

'I'll be watching,' Kendra warned.

She did, too. Per Mom's orders she worked on unpacking her room, but every few minutes she went to the front of the house to make sure Gwendolyn and Russell stayed on the street. They rode their bikes, sometimes trading. Kendra filed that away to tease him about a pink bike for his birthday.

They kept an eye on the house and caught Kendra at her vigil several times until resigned to the fact they'd go nowhere today but in circles. Even then she kept watching.

They talked, but Kendra couldn't hear any of it even with the window cracked. She wondered what Gwendolyn said to him, what they planned.

They stared at the woods.

VII

Russell insisted they talked about school and people in the neighborhood, nothing at all about the Woodsman. He stuck to that story when pressed.

Me and you don't talk about it, so why should she?

A logical question, and probably one Gwendolyn coached him on this afternoon. She got nothing from him.

After dinner, their father finally set up the computer they all shared so that evening Kendra did some searching in her allotted thirty minutes (she'd get a full hour tomorrow when no longer grounded).

The Woodsman had many names, as Gwendolyn said, and was believed to be many things; demon, shapeshifter, Wendigo. Some called him the Stickman, Daimon, the Dweller of the Deep Woods. Accounts of his appearance, origins, powers, and objectives varied. Nothing in the lore about a mystical arch of trees. The subject of blood sacrifices received little coverage in the articles she found, though she wasn't sure what she expected. A how-to guide?

She confirmed the disappearance last year of a girl in the bordering county, Sarah Putnam, last seen near the Cedar Bluff Woods playing with her doll. Pictures showed a redhead with a wide smile interrupted by two missing teeth in the top row. Just a year older than Russell. No description of her doll, but Kendra could guess what it looked like. Maybe a boy with a knife went missing another time.

Kendra doubted she would sleep with the uncertainty of tomorrow looming and the memory of last night's horror at the window, but she nodded off soon after Russell turned in. If not for the breeze on her face, she may have slept on through the night.

She expected to find a monstrosity comprised of leaves hunched over her bed, blowing the breath of early fall into her face, but the room was empty of anyone else—including Russell. The chill air of night found her through his open window.

Kendra clambered out from under the covers, quickly trading

her pajamas for clothes in her hamper.

She thought of Gwendolyn leaning over to confide in Russell while they played this afternoon.

Come out tonight after everyone's asleep, Russell. Meet me at the trees…you know which ones. And you can't tell Kendra, okay? We'll get it right this time. Something small. I know what to do.

She used the illumination from her cell phone to find an older pair of shoes in the closet rather than risk waking her parents by going to the front door for the ones she usually wore. Her mom wouldn't so much as entertain the possibility that a new school might possibly suck for Kendra, so the existence of some leaf demon living in a hole out back probably wasn't going to fly.

Kendra crawled through the window and dropped to the grass. She ran in a crouch to the cover of the woods, and after stumbling in places where moonlight didn't give her enough guidance, she at last felt far enough from the house to use her cell phone as a flashlight.

Terror and exhilaration consumed her, the feeling she'd entered a forbidden place contrasted with a sense of belonging. The trees past the moonlight were black towers, artifacts of a dead world. All around her, sounds of rustling, snapping, cracks, collisions. She saw faces everywhere now. Anything she saw in the pale light of the moon or the blue glow of her phone took on vaguely humanoid (or inhumanoid) features—moss growing on one tree, a fallen bird's nest, a collection of fallen pine cones, the whirls in the bark of a trunk. Glimpses from which she wished to avert her eyes, but the caricatures dissolved almost as soon as they formed, to recede into the deeper darkness ahead and await another spotlight.

She yelled Russell's name. It didn't matter to announce her presence. The Dweller already knew, and Gwendolyn would see her light anyway.

No answer. Only the scuttling, knocks, and sighs that had followed her the whole way, the breathing of the forest.

She reached the arch. The tumor trees regarded her, as though curious how she'd proceed. The moonlight revealed most of the column, but at the end of the path was a void.

'Russell?' she called into the darkness.

She heard something in the black. A whisper of movement or maybe just a throat accustomed to a different idea of language.

Kendra advanced. Every part of her screamed to run, but that other influence held her to the path. It wanted her here, and something in her that wanted to be wanted responded to it eagerly.

As the trees drew closer to her on either side, the darkness ahead continued to deny her like a living black drape, concealing its secrets. Past the arch, a ray of moonlight found the hole. It seemed to stop dead at the opening, revealing nothing.

'Answer me, Russell, you little asshole!' Kendra shouted. She'd take the grounding tomorrow and be glad, if he'd just respond.

Heart straining in her chest, she revived the light from her phone. Its glow revealed the knife last seen embedded in the trunk, now bloodied from tip to hilt as though dipped into the doll's gaping chest and tossed aside. Farther up in the path of her light, she found shoes and legs in a pair of jeans.

Russell.

Another step showed the upper half of the body, the arms stretched out in cruciform with the skin of the chest removed in an imperfect circle to display the organs beneath, as diagrammed with the doll. Rather than the hodgepodge of anatomical debris, though, everything remained in its proper place here with mushroom-colored ropes of entrails still neatly tucked within the abdomen. Above those, an assortment of shimmering sacs and tissues to which Kendra could initially supply no name, although the single beat of one darker-shaded structure announced itself as the heart.

Kendra clamped a hand over her mouth, nearly fumbling the phone. Her haste to take the light away from the grotesque sight afforded her a view of the rest of the sacrifice.

Gwendolyn's face did not suggest the blank expression of the doll. The wide eyes appraised Kendra as though she were responsible for this humiliation of the flesh from which Gwendolyn somehow had not yet succumbed. Blood bubbled from a puncture in her throat.

Whatever the plan, Russell surprised her.

'Hel…' Gwendolyn managed, a sound so slight as to be the wind.

Kendra turned the light away toward the trees bordering the offering, where a large, imperfect oval of skin hung. She dropped the phone and merciful darkness absorbed the nightmare images once more, save one—that of an impossibly tall and gangly shape maneuvering past the gnarled pillars in silhouette. Its movements were shuddery as it came to the edge of the arch, between Gwendolyn and the hole in the earth. Its size diminished as it slipped through the threshold to claim its sacrifice, a shadow sinking within a shadow. Kendra heard Gwendolyn's body slide across the grass through the portal of the trees.

'Great Presence of the Woods, we offer this to you,' Kendra shouted.

The shape sank once again, into the hole. Kendra saw more and more of this as clouds rolled past to emit more moonlight. Gwendolyn seemed to hover above the entrance, and then her limbs flailed as something manipulated her in impossible directions with a series of grueling snaps. Something splattered, like a bucket of wet sponges poured out on the ground. The earth accepted her, Gwendolyn the shape of some boneless sprinkler toy with tentacles both tucked and poured into the abyss.

Kendra found her phone, searched briefly with its light, and a moment later began her walk home. The leaves and the moss were now just leaves and moss. No faces.

She thought of Russell's eagerness to provide the offering, the first among them to try to take the blade. Was the face at the window even meant for her? Maybe it wasn't a warning at all, but a blessing.

Russell had left the window open for her when she found her way home. She pocketed her phone and as quietly as she could, she twisted the knob of the spout in the back of the house to wash the blood off the knife in her other hand.

Perhaps the Dweller would remain sated and not call either of them back to the arch. If the day came when another offering was necessary, though, Kendra would take her mom's advice and not think of herself for a change.

LETTER FROM HELL
Written by **Matt Shaw**

Delivered by Hand

Dear Mrs. Williams,

You do not know me and I can but only apologise for this unwelcome intrusion during these difficult times for you. With the News channels hounding you and constant police activity buzzing around your home, I can only imagine that you wish to be left alone - not welcoming further intrusion from people unless it is to do with what happened to your young daughter, Hayley.

I have been watching the events unfold via journalistic sites on the world wide web, television broadcasts and - of course - in the papers. Something like this to happen is shocking wherever it takes place in the world but, somehow, it feels worse given the fact that it has occurred in our own little community. I cannot begin to imagine the stress and worry you are currently feeling and wish there was a way for me to take away the pain for you. I do not have any children so know not of the bond between parent and child but - when little Keith Bennett disappeared, murdered by Ian Brady, I felt the same feeling of empathy for his fretful mother that I feel for you. And - to this day - I can picture Jamie Bulger's mum running around that shopping centre frantically searching for little Jamie, hoping to find him somewhere. I wonder, had she found him, would she have hugged him tighter than she had ever done so before or would she have stood and berated him for wandering off? My guess is a mixture of both. An outward display of anger brought about by the relief of finding him and at her own stupidity for taking her eyes off him, if only for a minute.

A minute is all it takes.

Anyway, like I said, I do not like the idea of you sitting at home and waiting by the telephone in the hope that someone rings with news. With that in mind, perhaps if I tell you my story, you will manage to find some kind of peace?

My name is Laurence Tope. I am seventy-three years old but sometimes feel as though I am older. Times were different when I was younger - we used to go out without feeling the need to lock the front door, children used to play unsupervised in the streets and neighbours knew one another. Nowadays, kids can never stray far from the parents, doors and windows are double-locked and everyone is too busy with their head in their phone, computer, or other electronic device to know the names of the people living on their street. It was a simpler time when I was growing up and - in some respects - all the better for it. That is not to say it was always easy though. Companies struggled and people were continually being laid off. My own father, a man named Norman, lost his job leaving our family of six living in poverty. He was a hardworking individual, a good man. It was not his fault what happened - just one of those things. We went from having three meals a day to just two and - sometimes - one of those was nothing more than gruel without even crusts to mop up the plate. Father's mood changed for the worse the longer he remained unemployed. Daily he would go out seeking work and daily he would return home rejected. The once loving family unit became fragmented as he took his frustrations out on us. First he would shout and then he would hit. My brothers took the beatings worse than me. I guess that's one of the good things about being the youngest but it did mean my brothers grew to resent me, looking upon me as the favourite child.

I was not the favourite though. I believe father would beat them first for no other reason than they could take a harder beating than I could. He was a big man and I was not only the youngest but also the skinniest. The runt of the litter, you could call me. One punch from him and I would have probably gone down, never to stand again. My father was a frustrated man, he was not a fool.

As the weeks turned to months, father was no longer able to afford the rent of our modest home and we were forced to move to new abodes. My brothers and I were crammed into the one room and my sister slept in the bed of my parents. My sister - like me - avoided the beatings. If any of the children was to be labeled as a favourite, it would be my sister with the way father seemed to dote upon her. Yet even so we could often hear her crying during the early hours of the morning but she would never discuss as to why. Most of the time she would even go so far as to say we had imagined it, my brothers then teasing me that the new home was in fact haunted. Years later I can guess as to what was really happening during the early hours of the day.

Despite the new home, we were still living on the poverty line. Father was bringing in money only occasionally with odd-jobs here and there. The jobs could have been anything - painting, decorating, gardening, whatever it took to bring in some much needed income and put food in our bellies. Every night, before we ate, he would make us say a prayer. Thankful for what we were about to receive. We all joined in with the words but the sentiment was never there. How were we to be thankful to a God who had let our family sink to such depths? Surely we should only be thankful if father turned to us and informed us of a new full-time job, a better pay and - pushing our luck - the right to move back into the home we all missed? It doesn't seem fair, or right, to thank a God who has forsaken you and yet we lied if only to keep the beatings at bay.

As time went on, father seemed to stop seeking full-time employment. He had gotten used to the late mornings and ability to be his own boss. There was no one telling him what to do, there was no one he needed to answer to. For a man who had worked his entire life, since a young child, it was blissful - although I only truly appreciated this since retiring myself. I collect a pension but, like my father before me, I also still keep fairly active with the odd job here and there for my neighbours - people I took the time to get to know despite a weariness, or reluctance, on their part to begin with.

The money that came in - from my father's odd-jobs - was never the same as what he had received when working for a company but at least it was something. We could tell mother wasn't happy - so could father - but she never outwardly said anything. Their relationship, once warm and full of love and life, grew cold and dark. As time went on, in an evening, father would sooner cuddle with sister as our favourite shows played through on the wireless as mother kept herself busy in the kitchen - always pristinely clean. This was our life now and - just as we had lived a life before - it was one that we seemed to settle into. There were differences, yes, but we were still a family.

Weeks turned to months, months to years. Father managed to keep the roof above our head doing his little jobs here and there. My oldest brother moved out, joining the forces, and that also helped to ease the pressure as it meant one less mouth to feed. It did have a knock on effect that meant, if a beating was due, I was now in the firing line too. I was still a slight man compared to some but was now, at least, big enough to take a beating should father have so desired. And sometimes I did, often through no fault of my own. I just happened to be there.

Occasionally father would bring a little extra home in his pay packet. With the extra money came a story that he had won it gambling. His bloodied knuckles hinted towards another, darker, alternative as to how he secured the extras though. Again, no one said anything. For one - it meant there was more income for the house and - for another - no one wanted to accept the beating for daring to question his word. It wasn't just money that he brought home either. Sometimes he would bring us the freshest of breads, the juiciest of fruits and - occasionally - the tenderest meat imaginable. Those were good days where, with the extra food, he would also walk in with a beaming smile across his face. For a moment, if only for the evening, our old father returned to us.

I clearly remember father sitting at the head of the table as mother brought in the luxurious food for us. He would engage us, recounting stories of how he came by such culinary delights. The baker needed the windows cleaned and, along with the usual payment, he would offer up bread fresh from the ovens. The grocer needed some sanding to be done and did as the baker - first the money and then the fresh fruits of father's choosing. The butcher needed a hand with deliveries and - on days where they were heavier than usual - father would be permitted to choose a choice cut of meat as a reward for his hard work. It was never expected from his point of view but, and you could tell by the mood he returned to us in, it was always appreciated. People looking out for one another. Something else you tend not to find in this day and age.

Those nights - when everyone was happy and laughing, enjoying foods we were no longer used to receiving due to rising costs - those were the nights that helped to shape me into the man I am today but not for the reasons you may believe. You may believe me to be a kind, gentle soul with empathy and compassion for others but that is not the case. You see - what father said had been a lie. The hard work and the kindness of others within the community did not line our table, or stomachs, with the goods we feasted upon during those happier times. The baker, the grocer, the butcher - they did not give further reward to father for a job they had already paid him to do. We gorged because my father took. He stole for us what our family was missing. Luxurious foods that we had long since forgotten sat in our bellies due to my father breaking the trust of those he worked for. They would leave him to his task and he would fill his bag with whatever would fit. The laughs at our table - usually dark and full of despair and unanswered woes - were there due to ill-gotten means just as the laughs at my own table in recent weeks... Echoing through my house through similar means. My father stole to make our family seem happier. Following his lead - and not for the first time - I stole to make my own home brighter. And, for a time, your daughter did offer me a brightness of which I thought I would never tire.

Hayley was a beautiful girl. From the moment I saw her playing in the park, smiling with her friend, I was truly captivated. Her eyes dazzled with life and intelligence and - for her age - she was well spoken and polite. A credit to you and your husband. I knew, from the moment I saw her, I had to have her.

She was not hard to take. A little white lie, when you popped across the road to the shop to fetch a drink, that you needed her and I was to take you to meet her immediately. She didn't know you were only across the road with your last words to her being that you'd be right back, and not where you were going. For all she knew - you had popped back to your home to fetch something. In her defence she took a little prompting to get into the van. Some reassurance that I was a friend of the family and was only doing as you had asked. She didn't even get me to tell her your name. Apparently knowing her own name - thanks to you calling it - was enough to prove I knew you.

Poor little Hayley did scream when she realised I had lied. I promised her though, if only to silence the screams, that I would be letting her return to you after an evening with me. I told her that I was lonely and wanted some company and this was the only way I knew how to get it. I didn't explain this to her but watching the way my father treated my mother - it damaged me for my own relationships in years to come and when I did manage to find one, it never lasted long.

Hayley eventually calmed soon after. I guess it was the thought of going home, back to you and your husband, that filled her with a sense of hope. We spent the evening together and I must confess, I kept her up way past her bedtime. I made her tell me jokes and stories about your family (and it does sound as though it was a lovely family to be a part of). The way she told them, even through the fear, made me smile.

I know she has been out of your life for a couple of weeks now and I know you are missing her terribly but please rest easy in the knowledge that her suffering lasted no more than an evening. The day I took her, I already told you that I kept her up past her bedtime. We were talking and she was making me laugh. I think it is important for you to know that I did not have sex with her. She died a virgin. That's not to say she had it any easier though.

As the evening progressed, she kept asking when she was going to return home. My answer was always the same: I would free her in the morning and - at the stroke of midnight, a new day, I did free her. I placed my hands around her neck and started to squeeze. Her eyes were wide with fear and she scratched and clawed at my hands with those tiny, dainty fingers - her nails drawing blood from my own flesh. Wounds that, even as I type, are still etched onto my skin. Your daughter, as young and fragile as she may have appeared, put up a fight. Know this though, she went home choking, crying, and scared. Had I not cut off her voice, I believe she would have been calling for you right up until the last minute. The way she spoke of you beforehand, she loved you greatly.

That night I laid with her in bed. I did not touch her. We were simply in the same bed. I stayed up for most of the early morning hours, looking at the beauty that would never age and never become ruined with the harshness of the world we live in. You may not feel so, but I did your daughter a favour. And you: I did you a favour too - not having to watch your child grow and become corrupt through outside influences of which you have little to no control.

The following morning was when I took a sharpened blade to her flesh, cutting in manageable chunks which would be stored in both refrigerator and freezer.

Tonight, as I finish this letter, I also finish the last of her - saving the best until last; her tender derriere. Not a single part was wasted although, being perfectly honest and open with you, some sections were certainly tougher to stomach.

As stated at the start of my note, I told you that I wanted to bring you some peace and I truly hope that this letter does just that. You now know what happened to your little baby girl. Eight years old and forever innocent. You can stop looking now, she sleeps with the Angels - as do I by the time you read this.

I have grown weary of this world and recent news from the doctor has suggested my remaining years (if I was 'lucky') are to be painful and heavily medicated with little chance of beating the poison within my body. I see little point in carrying on, stomach full of tablets and radiation flooding my weakening system. Seventy-three years is a good innings.

As I write my final words to you, I have already prepared the pile of tablets which will send me on my way. Your daughter went to the other place in a panic: Squirming, kicking, scratching, desperate. I shall venture there peacefully in my sleep.

Until our paths cross in the next life, I wish you nothing but the best and - again - hope that this letter brings you some kind of peace. What was done was not for personal reasons against you and your family. What was done was out of a need.

Kind Regards,

L. Tope.

EYE FOR AN EYE
Written by **Matt Hickman**

Per Aeternitatem

The man awoke abruptly, and the terror immediately set in. He could sense no feeling in his body. He attempted to wiggle his toes, nothing; total detachment. His world was blacker than black. A numbing sensation had crept down the back of his throat, and the sour, bellicose taste of blood had begun to settle in the lining of the sore tissue within his mouth.

Summoning all of the exertion that he could muster, he slowly pulled his eyelids apart with an audible rip, and a revolting tearing sensation, somehow separating the solidified, sticky gunk that had sealed them shut.

He was unable to move his head, unable to move any of his limbs. His entire body lay motionless - paralysed. The dead weight of his cranium was somehow being supported from below. Blinking the gunk away from his eyes, he dared a glimpse at his surroundings.

He was in a large room; it resembled an archaic hospital theatre. The illuminous strip lights that were positioned directly above him shone brightly into his eyes, making him squint.

He lay on a grimy medical gurney, his torso bare apart from a filthy, ripped blanket that had been positioned over his waist, barely covering his groin. The lights above the bed were the only ones lit, illuminating him like a centrepiece within the dark room.

Through pained eyes, he continued looking around the room, within his eye line. He spotted a door on the wall opposite – shut. To the right of the bed hung a series of tall mirrors that ran horizontally along the wall.

Positioned on the wall, above the door, hung a round, analogue clock. The time read 6:05. The man had no idea whether it was day or night.

On the left hand side of the bed stood a stainless steel bench, with a vast array of medical apparatus. The tools were lined neatly but were old, rusty and filthy; adorned with dried blood and clumps of what looked like rotting muscle and flesh.

The tools were accompanied by a medium sized glass jar, filled with transparent liquid that contained an ugly looking, pink organ.

Is it mine? Did someone perform surgery on me?

The man felt a wave of nausea slowly begin to creep up from his stomach, it flooded over him. Attempting to move again, his limbs refused to co-operate.

Have I been drugged?

As he slowly digested the layout and contents of the room, he couldn't help but feel he recognised the room, had been there before.

Only, it looked different somehow.

In his peripheral vision, to the right, he caught his reflection in the mirror. His head had been shaved. A thick, leather strap restrained his neck, holding his head down to what resembled a leather pillow, which elevated his head slightly, allowing him to look around.

The top of his arms were also strapped to the bed with similar leather straps, bound and looped over his biceps. Both of his arms were connected to an intravenous drip, both of which stood on opposing sides of his bed. Glancing further down, he saw that his ankles were bound in the same manner.

He wasn't going anywhere.

Well, that and the small fact his body was totally paralysed.

Mixed emotions of fear and dread ran through his ice cold veins, but being strapped down wasn't the main thing that concerned him. Checking his reflection in the mirror, his whole body looked like a roadmap of scars. From head to foot, he was covered in savage looking cuts, lacerations and burns. The wounds had since healed over, making his skin look like a horrific tapestry of pink, red and purple.

How long have I been here?

Attempting to cast his mind back, he desperately racked his brains to think of something, anything that could give him the slightest indication to his current predicament.

Nothing, a total blank.

Over a hidden loud speaker came a calm voice. 'Oh, good, I see that you're finally awake.'

The man's eyes searched around the room frantically, attempting to locate the position of the speakers. He failed to spot anything.

Is that voice inside my head?

As if on cue, the door on the far wall started to open inwards, creaking under its own weight, straining the rusted hinges. In the dark, he could barely make out the silhouette of a tall, thin man standing in the doorway. He tried to call out to the stranger.

Nothing.

The voice in his head spoke again.

Do not try to speak, you have no need to communicate verbally.

Besides, you no longer have the means.

Panicking, his eyes darted over to the steel table, at the contents of the jar. His heart thundered inside his chest upon realising that the organ floating in the clear liquid was his tongue.

The voice in head addressed him again.

Don't be afraid, I'm a doctor. I'm here to help.

The dark outline of the figure in the doorway slowly started to walk towards him. As the light from above the bed began to slowly cascade over his figure, he gradually came into view.

The doctor was a fairly tall, lanky man. He had a long, gaunt, pale face with sunken cheekbones. His long black hair was slicked back tightly over his scalp, and held in place with either product or grease and sweat.

The man gasped inwardly when he noticed the doctor's eyes. The sclera were totally black, they held no expression, pure black orbs, devoid of any gleam from the overhead lighting. They were cold and predatory like a shark. He wore nothing but a filthy lab jacket, smeared with dark red and brown stains, which hung down to his thighs. Upon his bare, filthy feet, he wore a pair of white, plastic, open topped overshoes that left a bloody footprint with every squeaky step he took.

The inner voice addressed the man.

Don't try to speak, use your thoughts, and I will be able to interpret them.

I don't understand. Why am I here? How did I get here? I don't remember a thing.

A smile crawled across the doctor's face, it portrayed no feeling or affection. It was neither friendly nor malicious.

I'm here to help you, and you're here to help me. All will become clear in good time, my friend.

The doctor turned from the man, and selected something from the bench. He turned back around, holding a filthy scalpel. The light reflected from the tip of the blade, the only part of the tool that wasn't smothered with rotting gore. He held it aloft, the handle was smeared with dried blood.

I just need to check something.

Reaching over, he snatched the prisoner by the wrist, and then changed his hand position so that he was gripping his thumb. Using the scalpel, he made a short incision into the flesh on his thumb. A slick trail of blood immediately began to flow from the cut.

The doctor looked back at the man.

Did you feel anything?

The man replied, still bemused as to their form of communication.

No, I didn't feel a thing.

In that case, I will need you to give you something to help with the pain.

But I didn't feel any pain.

The doctor turned and snatched a syringe from the bench, immediately injecting it into the catheter on the patient's arm. A surging, bolt of lightning struck his thumb where the doctor had made his incision. It was complete agony. He tried to scream.

You seem to have misunderstood, I needed to give you something to enhance the pain.

The patient looked at the doctor blinking the tears from his eyes, they streamed down his cheeks and neck.

But I thought you were here to help me?

Oh, I am. I'm here to help you remember, and remember you will. For you see, the answer to why we are both in this place is right there, inside your head.

He pointed to the man's temple with his bony index finger.

We just need to extract it, but all in good time.

The doctor turned and grabbed a pair of surgical pliers from the bench. He leaned towards the man, and gently rested his wrist on top of his head. He stroked his forehead with his thumb, almost affectionately.

Please take a little solace in the fact that anything that I have to do to you, I will not enjoy. You see, you were assigned to me, and that is all I know. I have my instructions.

Before the man could respond, the doctor clutched his head with one hand, then grabbed his two front teeth with the tip of the pliers and violently yanked upwards, immediately snapping the incisors off, and tearing them from the gums in one fluid motion.

The doctor looked at the man, a small dribble of blood and spittle running from the centre of his own mouth.

That wasn't too bad, but this may be a touch worse.

Grabbing a small surgical file from the tool bench, he started filing away at the exposed nerves left behind from the extracted teeth. The pain was harsh and instantaneous, the patient's head nearly exploded with searing agony. The doctor continued to grate the file backwards and forwards over the nerves, a grimacing look across his own face.

In the patient's mind, there was a bright blue flash, the pain slightly abated as a vision began to form inside his mind's eye. Slightly distorted, and lacking in colour and finesse, came the image of two young people; a man and a woman meeting for the first time.

The woman appeared shy, but accepted the man's offer to buy her a drink. They started chatting and soon realised that they had many things in common. The timeline of the vision accelerated, and before long, they had fallen in love; they laughed, they hugged, they were destined to be together. They both knew it as they stood at the altar with the priest, taking their wedding vows.

'I take thee, Steve.'

'I take thee, Wendy.'

As their lives together progressed, they purchased their first house, and had the inevitable conversation about starting a family. Wendy started a new job and things were looking promising.

In a split second, the vision vanished and the man was snapped back from his reverie, lying back on the bed in living agony. He looked around; the doctor was sat next to the bed on his rump, his hand covered in Steve's blood, his own face swollen and purple.

The doctor stood and approached Steve unsteadily.

I hope that was as good for you as it was for me. What did you see?

Steve looked back at the man, his body alive with pain.

I remember, but I don't understand, it was me and my wife.

Nothing of me?

No.

The doctor reached over to the bench and grabbed a stainless steel chisel and hammer. The type used for chipping through bone. He held the tip of the blade against Steve's elbow.

Then I must continue.

The doctor swung with the hammer, connecting violently with

the head of the chisel. A huge clang of metal upon metal echoed around the room. Immediately his own arm went limp, he loosened the grip on the chisel and the white sleeve of his coat blotted into a dark, wet, red patch. Attempting to ignore the pain, he grimaced and continued to smash at the chisel with the hammer. The streams of blood that flowed down his own arm matched that of Steve's exposed bloody elbow, as the steel continued to find a route further into the man's appendage. Torrents of crimson splattered the coat in thick squirts and began to pool and congeal on the floor beside the bed.

The chisel had been hammered into the limb at an angle, and was now protruding into the flesh at the joint, by several inches. Each blow gave off a sickening thump, and the clanging sound of steel against steel. The prisoner watched as it buried itself further into soft tissue. The pain from Steve's arm bolted round his body with every strike, igniting every pain receptor with white heat.

In his mind's eye, he screamed in agony.

Another solid strike with the hammer and chisel, and another bright blue flash ignited behind Steve's eyes. This time, Wendy sat in a restaurant opposite another man that Steve didn't recognise. He found their body language alarming; open. The couple were very touchy, very flirty. It made him feel sick.

Immediately, another image appeared; Steve with Wendy at the Christmas party, when he was introduced to the man. His name was Alan. A selfish, jumped up sonofabitch. He paid no attention to Steve whatsoever, but spent the whole evening leering after his wife. After the party, it had caused a massive argument between them. Steve was adamant that there was something going on between the two of them, but Wendy tried to reassure him he was just being paranoid.

He snapped at her, 'And what about the restaurant?'

She pleaded, 'It was just a business lunch, you've got to believe me, there's nothing going on.'

Steve snapped from his trance, and found himself back in the room with the doctor. Blood was gushing from the gaping hole in Steve's elbow spilling all over the bed and floor, gathering in sticky puddles. The chisel now only protruded a few inches from the joint. The doctor dropped the hammer with a solid thump, his arm covered in his own blood. It had soaked his entire sleeve and began to drip from the cuff to the floor.

He turned to face Steve. 'Well?'

Steve recalled the events from his memories, reciting them, in his mind, back to the doctor, who sighed impassively. Turning back to the work bench, he selected another item; a bone saw.

'It would seem we need something a little more extreme to jog that futile memory of yours.'

Before Steve had a chance to protest, the doctor started to run the blade of the saw across the bridge of his knee. At first, the teeth couldn't find purchase, but he continued to saw, adding downward pressure back and forth. After a few strokes the blade started to cut through the first layer of skin and flesh. Internally, Steve screamed as the doctor's face and lab coat were spattered with warm arterial blood. He didn't stop with the saw, and continued with the pressure. He continued sawing through muscle, even when his own leg gave way, a thick, jagged cut tearing across his own knee. He continued to saw, struggling to slice through cartilage and bone as he knelt in his own gushing blood.

Just as Steve was about to pass out from the pain, there was another blinding, blue flash.

Steve watched the vision of himself entering a house. The house looked familiar; he soon realised it was. It was early afternoon, the sun was shining, and there wasn't a single cloud in the sky. He had taken the afternoon off work to surprise his wife, and he had stopped off on the way home to buy her some flowers.

As he arrived home, he spotted a strange car parked on the driveway. With his curiosity sparked, he let himself in with his key. He found himself creeping up the stairs as quietly as he could. He heard animalistic grunts and moans coming from the master bedroom, and immediately, suspected the worst. He kicked open the bedroom door to witness his wife, naked, on all fours, groaning in pleasure, as Alan fucked her from behind.

Neither of them noticed Steve. He stood there in disbelief watching the two of them go at it like rampant animals. Wendy was the first to spot him, her initial reaction was hostility. She jumped off the bed, nude, pointing her index finger towards him aggressively. She screamed at him that he wasn't a man and he didn't satisfy her. She claimed she wanted a divorce, and that she and Alan had already made plans to move in together. Alan just stood behind her, covering his modesty and tubby, hairy stomach with a pillow, a smug look plastered over his face. Wendy stopped raging at Steve, and the smug look fell from Alan's face, when they realised that he was holding a large kitchen knife in his right hand.

Steve found himself lying back on the filthy hospital bed, which was now drenched with a mixture of his and the doctor's blood. The bright lights above the bed had started to flash on and off intermittently, as if short circuiting, throwing strange shadows and images around the room. The doctor knelt next to him on the floor, with his head resting on the side of the bed next to his own. Steve's right leg had been sawn through at the knee; he was rapidly losing blood. He desperately tried to recall the vision he had witnessed.

Was that somehow the reason that he was in this room, being subjected to this cruelty?

Doctor?

The doctor wearily lifted his head from the bed, a thick sheen of sweat plastered across his face causing his greasy black hair to stick to his forehead.

He looked at Steve through his lifeless, black orbs.

I don't understand, I was told that if I followed my instructions, that the key to solving this puzzle would be revealed.

Steve looked at the man, trying to weigh him up. It seemed like the doctor had just set out to butcher him, but at the same time he was inflicting the same wounds upon himself, it made no sense.

Who gave you, your instructions?

I'm not sure. As I entered this room through the door, I just knew. I have no recollection of anything beforehand.

Steve looked at the doctor.

Just do it.

At first, the doctor didn't understand, but after a few seconds, he gave a slight nod in confirmation. The doctor dragged himself over to the work bench and selected the large surgeon's knife. He wiped it down the sleeve of his lab coat in attempt to remove the residue of dried blood that covered the blade.

Slowly, he pulled himself up onto his remaining leg, blood quickly gushed out from the severed stump of his other, splattering and sluicing all over the floor. He held the long surgical knife up above Steve's chest, with his right hand holding the blade parallel to his body. He proceeded to carve a large piece of fatty flesh from the man's stomach. Blood squirted in every direction as he continued to hack away. His hands, arms and face were speckled with fountains of red. Both men started to shake and convulse, as the doctor continued to slice through the muscle and viscera, cutting it away using the razor sharp, serrated edge of the blade. As he sliced through to the lower portion of the abdomen, with his last remaining shred of strength, he tore away at the large chunk of meat, leaving behind a large gaping hole. Torn edges of skin, muscle and flesh were left exposed. The doctor's lab coat remained a soggy, red mess.

Steve's body went into shock, and he choked on his own blood. The doctor threw the discarded piece of flesh onto the floor beside the bed and collapsed, his face hitting the floor with a wet crack.

Dead.

As Steve drifted into a dream, he was faced with a scene of pure horror; the mutilated bodies of his wife and her lover Alan lay before him in his own bedroom. Blood coated the furniture, the walls, even the ceiling. Both bodies had been butchered, their throats slit. Their hands and feet had been hacked away and strewn around the room. This had been no accident, or crime of passion, this had been an act of brutality and vengeance. Standing immobile in the bedroom as the blood and gore soaked into his white carpet, he began to sob. He heard the police cars approaching from a few streets away. A neighbour had overheard the screams and shouting, and had called the cops. In just a few seconds, they would be busting down his front door.

Rependo

17:00 - The man inspected the food upon his plate. It looked like one of the finest cuts of steak he had ever seen, a beautiful piece of rib eye, cooked to culinary perfection - medium rare. Just enough to keep the taste, without too much blood running through the meat. The plate was also dressed with accompanying potatoes, vegetables and sauces. A large glass of Dal Forno, Valpolicella stood next to it, just as he had ordered.

He took a small sip of the wine and savoured its fruity flavour and aroma. He took a cut of the steak and placed it into his mouth. He started to chew but couldn't bring himself to swallow. Instead, he spat the half chewed morsel back onto the plate. Picking up the glass, he knocked it back in three large gulps. It had been a while since the man had drank and the alcohol immediately went to his head, giving him a warm, fuzzy sensation.

He lay down on his bunk and stretched his legs out as far as they would go. In his mind, he replayed the sequence of events.

The capital murder trial had gone to district court. His original plea, that the murder of his wife and her lover was a crime of passion, had been rejected. The jury had voted that the crime hadn't been committed from a sudden impulse, but had been an act of pre-meditated murder.

As per the law in his home state of Texas, the man was sentenced to death by execution. He was incarcerated in the

Polunsky Unit in Livingston. He had been on death row for nearly seven years. Despite appealing twice, and having both appeals overturned, the man had received a letter two months ago, stating that he was to be executed by lethal injection.

Today.

Yesterday, he had been moved from his normal cell on death row with the other inmates. He was placed into a holding cell next to the execution chamber. As he was escorted from his cell, the jeers, shouts and taunts from the other prisoners filled the halls as he walked by.

'*Dead man walking!*' they taunted.

Items were thrown from cells as he walked past, escorted by the guards. Cups filled with urine, toilet rolls, even parts of soiled bed sheets that had had been ripped up and set on fire. The prisoners seemingly became more vigorous by the news of an execution of one of their own.

Not that the man really considered himself one of them.

During his time, he had done his best to keep his head down and steer away from contact with any of the other convicts.

He had been given the opportunity to order a final meal from the prison chaplain, anything at his request. He had chosen the steak and the wine. He didn't find it surprising that, when the meal was delivered, he wasn't able to eat. There was no escaping from the fact; the man was going to die, and the thought terrified him.

The chaplain had visited the prisoner the previous day to introduce himself. He was a pleasant man, worn, in his early forties. The prisoner thought he may have been a little young to cope with the burden and responsibility of such a role, but he seemed to carry it all in his stride.

They had gone through the exact details and sequence of the execution. The man was to be transferred to the execution chamber at precisely 18:00. Once the details were finalised, he would be given an opportunity to provide a final statement. Here, he could address any family members attending. He would then be given the lethal injection and his body would be pronounced dead, approximately thirty minutes after the start of the procedure.

The chaplain explained that the procedure itself should render the prisoner unconscious within about ten seconds. Then the drug, a combination of barbiturates, would stop the prisoner's breathing and then proceed to shut down the body's organs. For all intents and purposes, it was quite humane. He stated that the only known side-affects were a funny taste in the mouth, and a cold sensation at the back of the throat.

He lay on his bunk for about twenty minutes deep in thought, before being disturbed by the sound of a sliding bolt. The prison chaplain entered his cell. He quickly glanced around the room, making a mental note that the steak had not been touched, but the large glass of wine had been consumed.

He wasn't surprised.

'So, Steve, is there anything that you would like to speak to me about before you are moved to the execution chamber?'

Steve pondered. He thought he would have so many questions to ask the man but his mind came up blank.

'Not really, we ran through all of the details yesterday, and there's no getting out of this.'

The chaplain nodded in confirmation

'Is there anything that you would like to confess?'

'Well, we all know what I did, it was murder. The only thing that I can say is that regardless of what the jury thought, it wasn't pre-meditated; it was a moment of anger and betrayal.'

The chaplain considered his statement before answering.

'You know, Steve, in the eyes of the Lord, murder is murder. Motive or circumstance matters not. If you take another man's life, you have committed the ultimate sin.'

Steve shook his head.

'Come, we don't have much time. Let us pray.'

At exactly 18:00, two guards entered the holding cell, and placed the prisoner in steel handcuffs. The chaplain escorted all three men to the execution chamber in silence. The chamber itself was simple enough. It consisted of a single medical gurney, with a viewing gallery on one side, behind mirrored glass. This allowed families of the victims to oversee the execution.

Steve stared at the glass; he pondered whether there would be anyone he knew peering at him from the other side. He doubted it, perhaps a few independent witnesses, and maybe some medical trainees.

Beside the bed was a small medical workbench, kitted out with medical wipes, syringes and needles. As he entered the room, he was hit with the sensation of dread; it sent an icy chill down his spine.

This was it.

He was gestured toward the medical gurney where he lay on his back, his body had started to shake uncontrollably. He started to sweat profusely and his breathing became shallow and erratic. Thick leather straps were fixed around his neck, arms and ankles to keep him secured in place.

The warden instructed the doctor to hook up the intravenous drips into the arms of the prisoner. One line for each arm. The doctor started to make the necessary connections, and administer the drugs into each bag, along with a saline solution.

The doctor was a fairly tall, thin man, with a long, gaunt face, and sunken cheekbones. His neck long, greasy black hair was brushed back tightly over his scalp. Once he had finished setting up the injections and checking the medication and equipment, he nodded to the warden that he was set to proceed. All that remained left to do was to administer the injection itself. The warden offered the prisoner the chance for one final statement before the execution.

Steve cast his mind back to the chaplain's words whilst they were alone in the cell; '*You know Steve, in the eyes of the lord, murder is murder. Motive or circumstance matters not. If you take another man's life, you have committed the ultimate sin.*'

He looked at the doctor and smiled.

'I'll see you in Hell.'

The time on the clock on the wall read 18:04.

The man awoke abruptly, and the terror immediately set in. He could sense no feeling in his body. He attempted to wiggle his toes, nothing; total detachment. His world was blacker than black. A numbing sensation had crept down the back of his throat, and the sour, bellicose taste of blood had begun to settle in the lining of the sore tissue within his mouth.

Summoning all of the exertion that he could muster, he slowly pulled his eyelids apart with an audible rip, and a revolting tearing sensation, somehow separating the solidified, sticky gunk that had sealed them shut.

He was unable to move his head, unable to move any of his limbs. His entire body lay motionless - paralysed. The dead weight of his cranium was somehow being supported from below. Blinking the gunk away from his eyes, he dared a glimpse at his surroundings.

He was in a large room; it resembled an archaic hospital theatre. The illuminous strip lights that were positioned directly above him shone brightly into his eyes, making him squint.

He lay on a grimy medical gurney, his torso bare apart from a filthy, ripped blanket that had been positioned over his waist, barely covering his groin. The lights above the bed were the only ones lit, illuminating him like a centrepiece within the dark room.

Through pained eyes, he continued looking around the room, within his eye line. He spotted a door on the wall opposite – shut. To the right of the bed hung a series of tall mirrors that ran horizontally along the wall.

Positioned on the wall, above the door, hung a round, analogue clock. The time read 6:05. The man had no idea whether it was day or night.

THREE BLACK DOGS
Written By **Daniel Marc Chant**

Evensong was in progress. N'kaelu stood by a stone angel and listened to the white folk sing about what a friend they had in Jesus. He was buoyed up with pride over the fact that they were singing the Lord's praises in the church he had helped to build.

N'kaelu loved the Church of St. Jerome. He also loved the people of Upper Ridley who worshipped therein, even the ones who had shown him little by the way of kindness.

Sometimes he was sad that the colour of his skin and his status as a slave excluded him from entering the church, but he took solace from knowing he was watched over by the Great Spirit and would one day be in Heaven.

When the service was over, N'kaelu watched the congregation coming out of the church. He stood at a respectful distance, beneath an oak tree whose mighty branches allowed very little moonlight to fall on his ebony face. Here he was but a shadow amongst shadows, unseen and unnoticed.

Soon, all the white folk were gone, all except the priestman who remained a while inside the church, getting it ready for the morning service. Still hiding in the shadow of the oak, N'kaelu watched as the gas lights in the church went out.

The priestman, his way lit by a lantern, eventually came out and hurried off into the night.

Now it was N'kaelu's turn to pray. He got down on his knees in front of the church and spoke to the Creator in his native tongue.

Oh mighty spirit who loves even a humble sinner like me, many thanks for bringing me out of the darkness of Africa. Slave that I am, yet am I more blessed than my brothers and sisters who live beyond your grace.

Blessings please for the Big Lady Chieftain Victoria and to all the folk of her mighty empire. Blessings too for my master, Lord Maxwell, who freed me from the chains of sin and ignorance.

Amen.

A rustling sound told him he was no longer alone. Looking over his shoulder, he was not surprised to see a black dog standing in a clump of long grass. It was a fierce-looking brute, forever showing its teeth and giving him a look that said he might be the beast's next meal.

The first time he saw a black dog in the graveyard, he'd been sure his time was come and was mightily afraid. But the dog hadn't attack him, nor had the other two who showed up later.

Night after night, the dogs prowled the graveyard, keeping their distance and growling at him whenever he came close. His few attempts to befriend them had ended in failure, and now he was content to live and let live. He knew so long as he left them alone, they would do the same for him.

At midnight, a woman came to the lych gate. She carried in her arms something wrapped in a blanket.

N'kaelu hurried to the gate but made no attempt to go through. It had been a long time since he'd left the church grounds – a fact that might have troubled him except that he never gave it any thought.

'Will you let me into the church?' asked the woman. She was dressed in peasant garb yet had the bearing of an aristocrat. A headscarf obscured her face but not her beauty.

N'kaelu was taken aback by the question. 'Madam, I will not stop you entering should you wish to do so.'

'That's not enough. I need your express permission.'

'But, madam, do you not know the house of the Lord is open to all?'

'Your dogs bar the way.'

N'kaelu looked over his shoulder. The black dogs stood in a

row in front of the church. Their demeanour made it clear they did not like the stranger.

'Madam, these dogs are wild,' N'kaelu explained. 'They are not my dogs.'

'Please! I am pursued by wolves. I must find sanctuary!'

Thinking of what might be in the bundle and thinking it must be what the wolves were after, N'kaelu became alarmed. 'Then I invite you in. Don't worry about the dogs. If you are with me, they will not harm you.'

The woman was at last satisfied. Keeping her bundle close to her, she hurried through the lych gate. As she approached them, the dogs sloped away with their tails between their legs and disappeared among the gravestones.

'You must come in with me,' said the woman as they reached the church door.

'No, madam. I cannot. It is forbidden.'

'Forbidden? Did you not say this church is open to all? Don't be foolish. If you stay outside, the wolves will get you.'

N'kaelu pondered. He did not want to desecrate the church, but neither did he want to be eaten by wolves. It occurred to him, as it should have long ago, that as a good Christian, there ought to be no impediment to him entering the building, especially as there were currently no white folk to offend with his presence.

Hoping God would forgive him, he pushed open the church door and stepped aside to allow the woman past. She shook her head, indicating he should go first.

As he stepped into the church, N'kaelu's breath caught in his throat. A life size crucifix stood behind the altar, fooling him into thinking he was face to face with Jesus in the flesh. He very nearly threw himself on the floor but the truth caught up with him in time to stop such foolishness.

Seeing the woman walking down the aisle to the altar, N'kaelu hurried after her.

'Madam,' he said. 'Is there anything I can do for your child?'

'No,' she replied. 'My child can take care of himself.'

'May I ask, in what language you speak? We seem to be talking neither my own tongue nor that of the white man, and yet we understand each other perfectly. How is this possible?'

'In God's house, are not all things possible?' The woman placed her bundle on the altar and unwrapped it.

N'kaelu was appalled by what was revealed. 'Madam, this is a holy place. You must not desecrate it.'

'Come now, N'kaelu. Does God not love all his creatures? And isn't true that of all the creatures on this Earth, only the sons and daughters of Abraham are sinners, for all others know not of good and evil and therefore cannot sin. In which case, this pup, who was but a few short hours ago nursing at its mother teat, is innocence incarnate. How then can its presence here be a desecration?'

'You are right.' N'kaelu felt ashamed. 'The birds of the air and the beasts of the land are beloved of God. I am sure they are welcome here.'

Turning her back on the puppy, the woman began walking back up the aisle.

N'kaelu pursued her. 'Madam, you are surely not going to leave that puppy here? I have not the wit nor the means to take care of it.'

'It is as I said, N'kaelu. My child can take care of himself.'

'You know my name?'

Stopping in her tracks, she smiled and touched his cheek. 'Do you not recognise me, N'kaelu? Did I not haunt the dreams of your youth? Did you not wake often screaming my name? Or should I say the name you and your tribe knew me by?'

With a sinking feeling, N'kaelu realised he had been tricked. He watched in silent horror as the she-demon (for such she was) departed. There was no compunction on his part to try to stop her for it was best that she be gone.

Outside, a storm burst forth. Lightning flashed and thunder rumbled. It seemed to N'kaelu that the tempest was especially for him, a judgement from on high.

Whatever the dog was, it was surely not of this world. He remembered the spirit animals of his childhood, waiting out there in the dark, prowling around the village, seeking a chance to steal the souls of the unwary.

The thing on the altar had to die.

N'kaelu turned, ready to do whatever it took to destroy the hellhound, but there was no sign of it.

Lord Harvey Maxwell was woken by the storm, as were most folk living in or near the village of Upper Ridley. Only those who were deaf to the thunder or closer to death than to life slept through it.

Although he considered himself a rational man and not the least superstitious, Lord Maxwell could not shake a feeling that the storm was not altogether natural.

The time between the storm ceasing with startling suddenness and the break of day could not have been more than a heartbeat. By that time, Lord Maxwell had been bathed and dressed by his servants and was passing time reading a book in his library.

The unexpected silence caused him to put aside his book and walk to the window, where he threw open the curtains and looked to the sky. His house, Hoxton Hall, was built on a hillock, giving him a grand view of the surrounding countryside. He searched in vain for a gap in the drab, ominous clouds. It was only in the distance that the grey gave way to a touch of red as the sun did its feeble best to banish the gloom. Between the house and the sunrise stood the Church of St. Jerome, his gift to the people of the locality. Having provided both the land and the funds for its building, and having also overseen its construction, he regarded it as his ticket to a comfortable life in the great hereafter.

The church seemed to shimmer as if surrounded by swarms of mosquitos. Above it, the clouds were especial dark and ominous.

There was a knock on the door. 'Enter,' he commanded, turning from the window.

Landseer, his elderly butler, answered the summons. 'Breakfast is ready, sir.'

'Did you sleep well last night, Landseer?'

'No, sir. I did not'

As Maxwell followed Landseer to the dining room, he felt compelled to ask, 'Does this day feel right to you, Landseer?'

'Right, sir? I'm not sure what you're getting at.'

'Neither am I. It's just – oh I don't know. There's something about today that seems so wrong.'

As was his custom on a Sunday morning, Lord Maxwell walked to church accompanied by Landseer, who was equipped with an umbrella should the Heavens choose to open once more. Usually the walk lifted his spirits, but on this occasion, it proved to be a joyless experience. It wasn't just that the rain had made the path treacherous with mud and other detritus, or that the sky was overcast. What truly vexed him was an unshakeable certainty that each step he took was a step closer to some unnameable evil.

He was about halfway to the church when he was struck by a sudden realisation. 'The bell,' he said to Landseer. 'Why is the church bell not ringing?'

'I was wondering that myself, sir,' said Landseer. 'Perhaps the bell tower is flooded.'

'Not possible. I oversaw every stage of the construction of that church and I can assure you the drainage is more than adequate.'

'Then I can offer no explanation as to the bell's silence.'

Lord Maxwell's apprehension continued to grow and was in no way alleviated when he saw the crowd gathered at the lych gate.

Father Orwell was addressing the crowd, motioning with his arms in an unmistakable gesture of reassurance. He spoke in his pulpit voice, making his words clearly audible to Lord Maxwell.

'There is no cause for alarm. Despite appearances, there is undoubtedly a rational explanation for this.'

The vicar's declaration was met with an excited clamour from the crowd as everyone spoke at once and expressed varying degrees of disbelief and aggression.

Arriving unobserved, Lord Maxwell cleared his throat very loudly. 'Gentlemen! Ladies! What is the meaning of this unseemly display?'

The crowd fell silent and turned to Maxwell. Father Orwell heaved a great sigh of relief. 'Thank Heaven you're here, my lord. Now perhaps we'll get a solution to this problem.'

'And what problem might that be, Father?'

'Nobody can enter the church grounds.'

'Why? Have you forbidden them to do so?'

'It's not an easy thing to explain – at least not without sounding like a lunatic.' Father Orwell raked back his thin white hair. 'I think it best that you see for yourself.'

'See what? Why the mystery?'

'Please, your lordship. See if you can step through that lych gate.'

'Well, of course I can. What's the matter with you, man?' And so saying, Lord Maxwell made straight for the gate - and walked into what felt like a brick wall. Astounded, he stepped back and tried again. Once more his effort proved both fruitless and painful.

'Well, I never!' he exclaimed, rubbing an injured knee. 'That's the damnedest thing.'

'It's the same for all of us,' explained Father Orwell. 'No one is able to go through the lych gate.'

'Then we must take the back gate.'

'It has been tried – to no avail.'

'Well, has anyone tried climbing over the wall?'

'There have been several attempts, and all have ended in failure.'

'This be the work of the Devil,' piped up Billy Fisher, a farmhand generally held to be the village idiot. 'That what it be.'

'It is no such thing!' barked Father Orwell, his face taking on the aspect it assumed whenever he preached hellfire and damnation. 'This is a house of God! The Devil wouldn't dare!'

Pandemonium descended on the congregation as people voiced their own opinions on the matter. As usual in such a situation, everyone talked while nobody listened.

Lord Maxwell's nerves were already frayed for want of a decent sleep. The last thing he needed now was this ungodly assault on his eardrums. 'Enough!' he cried in his most lordly voice. 'Is this any way for good Christians to behave on a Sunday?'

Embarrassed, the parishioners fell silent.

'That's better.' Lord Maxwell took a deep breath and decided on a course of action. 'There is a chapel in the grounds of Hoxton Hall. If Father Orwell is agreeable, we shall celebrate mass there. In the meantime, I will send one of my servants to the Bishop and one to the Royal Society in London to see what they make of it all. I have no doubt we shall have this mystery cleared up in no time.'

That the service was something of a shambles was hardly surprising given the make-shift nature of it. Twice, Father Orwell lost his train of thought while delivering his sermon and had to start again, much to the dismay and displeasure of the entire congregation.

When the last prayer had been said, the last hymn sung and the congregation dispersed, the vicar accepted Lord Maxwell's invitation to join him in the library for a glass of sherry.

'Well, this is a fine to do,' said Lord Maxwell reflectively as the two men sat nursing glasses of fine Amontillado. 'I have racked my brain for a scientific explanation and drawn a blank. As much as I would like to, it seems I cannot yet rule out the supernatural as a possible cause.'

'Yes,' concurred Father Orwell, sighing heavily to signify that his agreement was a reluctant one. 'There's no doubt in my mind that strange forces are at work.'

'You think the church haunted?'

'I think something evil has taken up residence in it. Only I am puzzled as to how this can be given that the place is protected by church grims.'

This pronouncement took Lord Maxwell with enough surprise to cause his sherry to go down the wrong way. After a brief fit of coughing and spluttering, he said, 'You cannot be serious!'

'But I am, my lord. Very serious.'

'Let's be clear about this. You're talking about ghost dogs. Right?'

'You know of the church grims then?'

'I grew up in these parts. I know all the local folk tales and superstitions.'

'You aware then that not all grims are dogs. They are often the souls of the departed.'

'Now don't tell me we have such a grim at St. Jerome's.'

'You recall, I hope, the slave whom you liked to call James but who much preferred his birth name of N'kaelu.'

'Stop right there, Father Orwell. This won't wash with me.' Lord Maxwell turned to his butler, who was in the process of dusting a pile of books. 'Did you ever hear such nonsense, Landseer?'

'With respect, m'Lord, I do not consider it nonsense, as I know for a fact that it's the truth. Indeed, I played no small part in N'kaelu becoming a grim.'

'Explain yourself, Landseer.'

'As you know, m'lord, my family has a very long history in these parts. What you may be unaware of is that I come from a long line of – for want of a better word – warlocks. Certain secrets have been passed through my family from generation to generation. Not only am I the inheritor of wisdom more ancient than you could imagine, but I am also the seventh son of a seventh son, a fact which endows me with powers of a special kind.'

'Pah!' Lord Maxwell felt anger bubbling up within him. He knew the folk hereabouts were a superstitious bunch, but he'd expected better from Landseer. 'So you cast a magic spell on a corpse! Is that what you're saying?'

'Yes, m'lord.'

'Sacrilege, Landseer! There's no other word for it. And you, Father Orwell, were complicit in the act. I shall write a strongly worded letter to the Bishop about this. Perhaps it's time you thought about departing for pastures new.

'Now both of you leave me. I have much thinking to do.'

Lord Maxwell spent the rest of the day brooding in his library. He ate little, drank too much and slept fitfully. He was standing at the window, looking out over a landscape at once both familiar and alien to him, when the sun went down. It came as no surprise that as darkness fell so did the rain. It was immediately followed by a vicious flash of lightning and rolling thunder that sounded to his ears like the call of some lonely, gigantic beast.

Desiring brandy to dispel his melancholy, he rang for Landseer. When that worthy did not answer, he decided then and there to give the old butler his marching orders.

For his part, Landseer was in no position to answer his master's summons. An hour earlier, he had departed Hoxton Hall and was now standing by the lych gate in defiance of wind and rain.

Any who witnessed his behaviour – and thankfully there were none – might have thought him mad. Whereas a sane man would have been expected to seek shelter from the storm, Landseer held his ground in the middle of the road and let the elements do their worst.

As he closed his eyes and raised his arms, any doubts as to his insanity should have been dispelled, yet if madness there was, it was no ordinary madness.

Landseer began to utter a litany, softly at first but growing steadily in volume. 'O diaghus ulmens agus dhèe,' he chanted. 'Na inferis tha oleac spioradan dhomh ghal ab idhar hurilem

seomar ghlanadh mus na. Obsecro chuideachadh agrann sevaco emura...' He did not know what the words meant for their meaning had been lost centuries ago. As a youth, he had been taught the litany by his grandmother who'd also been ignorant of their meaning. 'Aon lag sgus agir oith uidhche fhad sa laoichadh, mar cuid de aon gu dhair lipadh, homcholaich aig mo agus dad dhuilleat..'

As the storm intensified, so did the chant. Landseer spoke the same words over and over until he was no longer hearing them as words but as a noise as elemental as the wind. He sensed long dormant spirits rise from the ground and gather about him. His body becaming a receptacle for primeval energy that repulsed the rain, leaving him impossibly dry while the world around him grew ever more sodden.

'Na inferis tha oleac spioradan dhomh ghal ab idhar hurilem seomar ghlanadh mus na. Obsecro chuideachadh agrann sevaco emura!' Landseer clapped his hands, producing a sound not unlike a cannon. It was answered by a flash of lightning that struck the lych gate and split it in two. The concussion thus produced knocked Landseer off his feet but he was quickly up and through the ruined gate and into the church yard.

Almost at once, he spotted the three black dogs cowering against the wall of a catacomb.

'Mab,' he said, 'Urb and Lofraghn. Come to me now. I have need of your help.'

The black dogs pressed themselves harder against the wall. The terror in their eyes was incandescent.

Landseer knew the dogs of old and had witnessed their courage for himself. Whatever cowed them now, he realised, must be truly frightening.

He crouched down before them and began to soothe their nerves with a lullaby sung in the strange and cryptic language of his ancestors.

Despite the pounding of the rain and the howling of the wind, N'kaelu heard the lullaby. At first, he took it to be just one of the dozens of noises manufactured by the storm but the rhythm and melody soon convinced him otherwise.

He was lying in front of the altar beside the crucifix, which had been cleft in two as if struck by a giant axe. All around him were signs of violence that had no place in a church. Scattered on and among the pews were the shredded remains of hymn books. The christening font looked to have had a sledge hammer taken to it. The pulpit, an ornate piece crafted in India from mahogany inlaid with ivory, was now little more than matchwood.

N'kaelu had a vague memory of witnessing the destruction, though the more he thought about it, the less he remembered. It was like a dream that had lingered too long.

He had but a vague notion of when and how the destruction had occurred, nor could he decide how long he'd been lying on the floor. Perhaps it was only a moment; perhaps it had always been so.

Trying to make sense of it all, he decided he was in the afterlife, in that place the white folks called Limbo, which was neither Heaven nor Hell.

The words of the dying Jesus came to him: My God, my God, why hast thou forsaken me?

Convinced he was trapped for all eternity in a desecrated church that nobody would now visit, his mind had descended into a slough of despair. All hope had left him, but now it was slowly returning, lapping around him like an incoming tide.

The melody – haunting, melancholic – told him that things could change, that perhaps his God hadn't forsaken him after all.

Slowly, carefully, he got to his feet and turned towards the door. When last he had tried to open it, it had refused to budge despite his best efforts. Now it stood wide open.

The storm was raging as fierce as ever. Trees danced frantically in the wind. The rain looked like an endless series of veils.

And yet, inside the church, all was calm.

The she-demon's black puppy sat in the porch on its haunches with its back to him. It was now fully-grown and packed with powerful musculature.

N'kaelu was gripped by a certainty that the hellhound was waiting for something or someone.

Meanwhile, the melody grew louder, and whereas N'kaelu found it soothing, it seemed to have the opposite effect on the dog, which let out a dismal howl and tensed as if readying for a fight.

A figure walked towards the door. At his side were the three black dogs, slouching and baring their teeth in a decidedly predatory manner.

The hellhound prepared to pounce. N'kaelu was sure it would launch itself at the black dogs, thus initiating a fight that was bound to be savage and terrible. But then the hellhound started to topple, and with a desperate scrabbling of its paws, only just managed to stay upright. It's head, however, dropped.

A moment later, the creature lay on its side and was recognisably asleep.

Lightning illuminated the face of the approaching figure, allowing N'kaelu to recognise him as Landseer the butler. He and the dogs stopped a few feet from the door, and the melody abruptly faded.

Landseer peered into the church. 'Is that you, N'kaelu?'

'Yes, boss. It is I – N'kaelu.'

'Quick! Invite me in. We don't have much time.'

Remembering the lesson of the she-demon, N'kaelu was wary. 'No, boss.'

'No?' Landseer was perplexed and annoyed. 'Don't be stupid. Your very soul is at state. If you don't let me in, you are destined for Hell.'

The mention of Hell caused N'kaelu to rethink the matter. Thanks to the guile of the she-demon, his imminent damnation was a near certainty. Landseer, by dint of having put the hellhound to sleep, was clearly a great magician and might be able to save him. 'OK, boss. You may enter.'

'And the dogs.'

'Not the dogs.'

'Listen to me, N'kaelu. Thanks to you, the Devil himself has a foothold here and is on his way. Unless we do something, Satan will have your soul!'

In his time, N'kaelu had had few dealings with Landseer, but he knew the man was no liar. Unlike many of the white folk who proclaimed their love of Christ and a desire to do good, Landseer actually seemed to mean it. 'OK, boss. The dogs too.'

'You must say their names: Mab, Urb and Lofraghn. Invite each of them in turn.'

'Mab, you may enter. Urb, you may enter. And you, Lofgrahn, are welcome in the house of the Lord.'

'And now me, N'kaelu. Say my name and bid me welcome.'

'You are welcome, Mister Landseer.'

Stepping around the sleeping hellhound, Landseer led the black dogs into the church. 'Do you believe in magic, N'kaelu?'

'Like Jesus and them loaves and fishes?'

'Like the things your witch doctors did.'

'That ain't no magic, boss. The priestman says it's all nonsense and trickery.'

'Well, the priestman would, wouldn't he? But he knows damn well it isn't true.' Landseer marched up to N'kaelu. 'You must tell me how that hellhound got into the graveyard.'

N'kaelu backed away, fearful that the truth was so outrageous it would earn him a thrashing for lying. Then again, if he said nothing, a thrashing would surely follow on the heels of his perceived insolence. He opened his mouth to plead ignorance in the matter, but something in the way Landseer looked at him compelled him to tell the truth. 'A she-demon came to the lych gate, and just like you, she demanded to be allowed in. I swear, boss, I did not know she was a she-demon. She said she was being chased by wolves, so I let her in.'

'Oh N'kaelu, you insufferable fool. There are no wolves in

these parts.'

'I'm sorry, boss. I did not know.'

'Well, what's done is done, and now it's up to you to undo it.'

'Me, boss?'

'You allowed the hellhound into the church, so only you can kill it.'

'No, boss. No!' N'kaelu was no coward, but neither was he a fool. How could he, a mere slave, be expected to dispatch one of the Devil's own? 'You got the magic. You do it.'

'I cannot. Once a demon dog has found its way onto holy ground, only a grim can destroy it.'

N'kaelu had never heard of a grim. Perhaps it was another of the words used by the white folk for people with his skin colour. 'Let's leave this place, boss, while we still can.'

'Poor, poor N'kaelu. You still haven't worked it out, have you? You cannot leave this place – not now, not ever – except that the Devil comes and takes you to Hell.'

If Landseer thought his words would stir N'kaelu into the right sort of action, he was quickly disillusioned.

N'kaelu's eyes widened into saucers as the reality of his situation came home to him. For a moment, he stood trembling. Then, with a terrified scream, he ran from the church, jumped over the slumbering hellhound and headed pell-mell for the ruined lych gate.

'Stop!' Landseer shouted after him. 'It's no use!'

N'kaelu made it as far as the gate but no further. He had a sensation of being punched hard in the face and then he was lying on the ground in an ungainly heap. Fear propelled him to his feet and forward again.

This time, when he hit the invisible wall, he managed to stay upright.

By now his terror was beginning to give way to anger. What had his fellow Christians – these so-called men of God – done to him? What gave them the right? Bad enough that they steal him away from his people. Now they were denying him his place in Heaven!

He ran along the path that circumnavigated the grave yard and attempted to leap over the wall. A moment later, he was face down on the ground with Landseer hurrying towards him.

'N'kaelu! Don't be a fool! You have to kill the dog. It's your only chance of escaping damnation.'

'Damnation, boss? Am I not damned already? I will never see my people – my family, my friends or even the land in which I was born – again. Where is the salvation I was promised? Where's my Heaven?' Needing a vent for his anger, N'kaelu sprang to his feet and charged headlong at Landseer. At the moment he should have made contact with the butler, he tried to seize his midriff – and found himself stumbling on with nothing in his arms but fresh air.

Coming to a halt, he saw something that caused him to forget about the butler. A fresh helping of dread threatened to overwhelm his senses as he watched the hellhound rise groggily from its sleep.

'Hurry!' shouted Landseer from behind. 'Kill it now before it wakes up completely.'

But N'kaelu could see no prospect of defeating the hellhound. As the beast began lumbering towards him, he turned and fled.

He sprinted between gravestones, weaving this way and that, knowing it would be to no avail - there was no escaping his doom. As he leapt over a freshly dug grave, the hellhound pounced and slammed into N'kaelu's back with the force of a cannon ball.

He somersaulted twice before hitting the ground. Unable to arrest its flight, the hellhound disappeared into the dark but was soon coming back, walking with the leisurely pace of one who knows they've won and all that's left is to deliver the coup de grace.

There was no use running.

The hellhound circled N'kaelu. It was in no hurry to end its sport.

Of a sudden, the wind dropped. The relative silence that

followed was broken by what sounded like a hundred twigs being snapped at once. A moment later, the sound came again.

And then again. And again.

With a fresh frisson of terror, N'kaelu realised he was listening to the footsteps of something very large.

'He's coming!' Landseer cried. Cowering behind a large gravestone, he was on the verge of hysteria. 'In the name of all that's holy, N'kaelu, don't just lie there. Save us! Save us both!'

N'kaelu had no intention of obeying Landseer or any other white man – not now, not ever. They were liars, every one of them. He despised them all.

And still the footsteps came on.

The hellhound was by now at N'kaelu's side. He could feel its breath on his face.

'Kill me quick,' he said to the beast. 'Let's end this now.'

Lightning struck the bell tower. Masonry crashed through the church roof. A large chunk of stone tumbled earthwards and landed between N'kaelu and the hellhound.

Startled, the hellhound turned and fled.

The near miss snapped N'kaelu out of his lethargic frame of mind. Looking up at the church over which he had laboured from dawn to dusk for over two years, he raged at its perdition. His anger brought him to his feet, ready to face the hellhound, who had rediscovered its courage and was racing towards him.

With a mighty cry that gave voice to his warrior ancestors, he charged at the oncoming beast. Almost as if they were obeying the dictates of an unseen choreographer, they both leapt into the air at the same instant.

For a long moment, it seemed neither of them was beholden to gravity. They might have risen above the church and even into the clouds had not their progress been checked by the collision of their bodies.

N'kaelu wrapped his arms around the hellhound's midriff and held on for dear life. Momentum put them into a spin.

The hellhound snapped at N'kaelu's neck. N'kaelu felt teeth scrape his skin but not draw blood. Letting go of the beast, he pushed it away.

They plummeted together, hitting the ground with a force that would have destroyed them but for their unearthly nature.

The impact sent pain shooting through N'kaelu's body and left him stunned. He was horrified to feel the ground sway and to see the church toppling towards him. By the time he realised the church's movement was an illusion caused by dizziness, the hellhound was upon him.

N'kaelu gripped the creature's throat with both hands and squeezed. Claws ripped into his stomach and chest, sending brilliant shards of pain through his being.

He knew he couldn't keep the beast at bay for long and wondered at the fact that he could do so at all. It was playing with him, he realised. Letting him use up all his strength before finishing him off.

Beneath N'kaelu, the ground trembled. A shadow fell over the already dark graveyard. From the corner of his eye, he glimpsed something huge and apelike lumbering towards the church. It stopped at the lych gate, waiting for N'kaelu to be banished to Hell so it could enter the graveyard and lay claim to the church.

"Mab! Urb! Lofraghn!' Landseer didn't so much shout the words as spit them out.

The grim dogs attacked the hellhound.

All at once, N'kaelu found himself caught in a melee, a maelstrom of teeth and claws and fur. A great glob of blood slapped him in the face, causing one eye to close and remain closed. Some made its way into his mouth. It tasted of death.

He saw the hellhound sink its teeth into the neck of one of the grim dogs and toss it aside like a toy. The dog tried to make it back to the fray but after limping pathetically for two strides, it fell on its side and made no effort to get up again.

Meanwhile its two companions were not letting up, despite

being in a terrible state. Both had suffered heavy wounds that exposed muscle, gut and bone. One managed to clamp its jaws onto the shin of one of the hellhound's front legs. This distracted the hellhound just enough for the other to seize a rear leg.

The grims spun the hellhound in a full circle and halfway back again. Thrashing frantically, it broke free to exact a terrible revenge on one of its attackers. It lunged at it and came away with a large junk of belly in its mouth.

Awash with pain, N'kaelu could do nothing but lie on the ground. The grims had fought ferociously, but they were no match for the hellhound.

N'kaelu considered praying but his pride wouldn't let him. He'd thought that as a good Christian, his sufferings would pave the way to Heaven. How wrong he'd been. The white folks had lied to him. Their God had no place at His side for the likes of N'kaelu.

The fight ended with a whimper. Rolling on his side, N'kaelu saw all three church grims lying in a triangle of carnage. Two of them were undoubtedly dead. The third twitched; if it wasn't already dead, it soon would be.

The hellhound limped towards him, dragging a loop of entrails along the ground. It bared its teeth, allowing a great deal of blood to escape. When it reached N'kaelu's side, it lowered its head so it was literally face to face with the African. Its breath was sweat and sour, a mixture of corrupted flesh and vinegar.

N'kaelu braced himself for death, but it didn't come.

Without warning, the hellhound closed its eyes and breathed its last.

The thing at the lych gate bellowed in anger and frustration. Defeated, it turned and headed back to whatever ungodly place it had come from.

The rain stopped.

Scarcely had the new day broken than a small crowd was gathered on the road outside the Church of St. Jerome. Word had quickly gotten about Upper Ridley that last night's storm had damaged the church and the villagers all felt a need to see for themselves.

Sure enough, the bell tower was a jagged finger of blasted masonry and there were several holes in the roof. The lych gate looked to have been struck by lightning and would need to be rebuilt.

Although it was quickly established that it was now possible to enter the graveyard, nobody felt inclined to do so until Father Orwell turned up. Bolstered by a post-breakfast glass of sherry, he put his faith in the Lord and climbed over the ruined gate.

It was only when he reached the church and went in that his parishioners found the courage to do likewise.

They found Landseer's body next to Lord Maxwell's family mausoleum. No one was convinced by the coroner's verdict of death by natural causes, but neither did they care to dispute it.

They also came upon the hideously mutilated corpse of a black dog. Father Orwell insisted that it must have been struck by falling masonry and the people of Upper Ridley hastened to agree. Shortly thereafter, an unmarked grave appeared at the northern edge of the graveyard. Nobody thought to ask why.

At the Bishop's insistence, Father Orwell performed an exorcism of the church and its grounds. Those who attended the service declared afterwards that Father Orwell's heart wasn't in it, which is perhaps why to this very day the graveyard remains haunted by the ghosts of an African and three black dogs.

CHECKOUT
Written by **Amy Cross**

Monday
   Bored.
   Beep!

*

Tuesday
   So bored.
   Beep! Beep!

*

Wednesday
   Beep!
   I am so -
   Beep!
   - friggin' bored. Still, at least tomorrow's Thursday. *He* always comes on Thursdays.

*

Thursday
   Oh my god, he's so hot. Like, I swear he's even hotter than before. Oh my god, how is that even possible?
   I love Thursday evenings, because he always comes in just before the supermarket closes, and I'm always the only one on the tills. So he's always mine.

As he sets his items on the belt, I make sure to sit straight and smile. When he's not looking, I check my hair. I know it's dumb to care, but John A. Sinclair (I totally read his name on his loyalty card back when I first met him, months ago, but not 'cause I'm obsessed or anything, just 'cause I was curious) is like the hottest guy I've ever seen in the flesh. I'm not obsessed, I just like him. I know he's way out of my league, but a girl can't be blamed for checking a hot guy out, right?

And he's buying steak tonight, with a bottle of red wine.

He's such a classy guy. He never buys the cheap stuff. Barely even daring to look at him, I start scanning his items. Damn, why am I so shy?

Beep!

Beep!

Maybe I could say something. Just a -

'John!'

Suddenly a woman comes running up behind him, giggling as she puts a hand on his arm. She sets a second bottle of wine on the belt before leaning up and kissing the side of his face. As she does so, her boobs almost spill out of her way-too-low top. Seriously, what kind of person would go out dressed like that? I'd never have guessed that John'd go for someone who looks so slutty.

'Is it okay if we get a second bottle?' she asks, kissing him again. 'For later, just before I suck your..'

She leans closer and whispers something in his ear. Just as I think I might be able to make out what she's saying, however, she glances at me. I immediately look down at my register, and I can feel myself starting to blush. As I get on with scanning their items, I decide not to look at her again. She's trash.

Why's he with such a slut?

*

Friday

He's back! Two days in a row. That's unusual, but I'm not complaining.

And he's alone this time. Maybe he dumped that slutty woman already. I mean, he can do *way* better than her.

As he reaches me and slides his card into the machine, I open my mouth to say hello, but suddenly I notice that he's not buying his usual high-quality wines and fancy food today.

He's buying rope.

And extra-strength black bin bags.

And three large knives.

Beep!

'Would you like a 5p carrier today?' I ask.

'Sure,' he mumbles, but he seems distracted. Skittish. I guess he's just having a bad day. Even hot guys have bad days.

*

Saturday

Seriously, three days in a row? What did I do to get so lucky?

As I finish serving the previous customer, I take care to fix my posture. I really need to start washing my hair every day if he's going to come so frequently. After a moment, however, I realize that he looks a little disheveled and tired. There are bags under his eyes and he keeps glancing over his shoulder, almost as if he's worried about someone watching him.

Plus, I think he's wearing the same clothes as yesterday. The same clothes as the last *few* days, actually.

'How are you today?' I ask, but he doesn't reply. He's still looking over his shoulder, still acting as if he's nervous.

Glancing down at his items, I find that today he's buying matches.

Lots of boxes of matches.

Beep!

And lighter fluid.

Beep!

And more bin bags. He's picked up, like, five rolls of the thick ones, and each roll is thirty bags. That's a lot of bags. Plus some wooden spikes from the camping department.

Beep! Beep! Beep!

'Would you like a 5p carrier?' I ask, trying to smile but not quite managing.

He stares at me, clearly confused.

'Would you like a bag?' I ask again. 'They're.. they're five pence.'

After a moment he shakes his head slightly, and his eyes twitch, so I give him a carrier. I don't even charge him.

I want to ask him if he's okay, but I don't quite summon the courage. He seems very distracted and busy, and I'm sure the last thing he wants is to make small-talk. After all, even though he looks so exhausted, he's still incredibly hot and attractive, and I'm just a checkout girl. I guess I'm not his type.

*

Sunday

'Pass the crisps, love.'

Rolling my eyes, I pass the bowl of crisps over to Dad as the episode of *Motorway Cops* continues.

I can't wait to get back to work tomorrow. I hope John comes in again.

*

Monday

John doesn't come in tonight. I'm on from three in the afternoon until closing, and I keep an eye out, but there's no sign of him.

Well, he doesn't usually come in on Mondays anyway.

*

Tuesday

'Hi,' I say, unable to keep my heart from fluttering as John reaches my checkout, 'would you like -'

Before I can finish that sentence, I'm stopped by the foulest stink I've ever smelt in my life. John looks more disheveled than ever, still wearing the same clothes from several nights ago, but now there's a really disgusting stench of, like, body odor and fluids and I don't even know what else. He kinda looks a bit like a tramp.

I try to smile, but suddenly I notice something smeared on the front of his shirt. Something dark. Red, maybe, or brown. It's almost like something from a horror film, but I know horror films don't start like this in supermarkets.

And then, as if he realized that I noticed the stains, he closes his jacket a little.

'Yeah,' he mutters, his voice sounding hoarse and gravelly, as if he's been shouting a lot, 'I need a bag.'

Looking down, I see that tonight he's buying more bin bags, plus some knives and an electric saw. I guess he has something big and hard that he needs to cut up. *Really* big and hard.

A few minutes later, once I've finished serving him, I watch as he heads out of the store. As soon as he reaches the parking lot, he breaks into a jog, eventually running away into the darkness. He sure seems jumpy these days.

*

Wednesday

No sign of him tonight.

In fact, it's a totally dead night, so I just sit at the till and stare out the window, watching the parking lot in case he shows up.

*

303

Thursday

No sign of him.

Beep!

That's odd. He usually *always* comes in on Thursdays. I wonder where he is?

*

Friday

Still nothing. Maybe he went on holiday. I bet he looks good in the pool.

*

Saturday

Sitting at the checkout, with no customers right now, I can't help staring out the window and watching the dark parking lot.

I guess he isn't coming tonight, either.

*

Sunday

'Pass the crisps.'

Sighing, I pass the bowl of crisps to Dad, before looking back down at my phone. I'm not cyber-stalking John or anything. I'm just trying to find him online. Unfortunately, all his profiles are locked down tight.

I'm not obsessed. I'm just genuinely worried, that's all.

*

Monday

Staring out the window, I watch as a man and a woman head over to their car. I'm so bored tonight, sitting here and serving one or two customers per hour.

Suddenly hearing footsteps, I turn just in time to find that another customer has come to the checkout.

And then I freeze as I realize that I recognize her.

It's that tarty woman who was here with John Sinclair last week, and she's even still wearing the exact same clothes. Her boobs are totally bursting out of her top, so much that I think I can even see a hint of nipple. She's smiling, too, as if she remembers me.

I should look away, but for a moment I can't help staring at her neck. She looks.. I don't know, like, burned or something, with big bloodied charred skin and several cuts. And now that I'm looking properly, I realize her clothes are torn in several places.

Forcing myself to stay totally professional, I look down at the conveyor belt, only to see that she's only buying one thing tonight.

Tooth picks.

And when I look back up at her, I see that she's grinning more than ever.

*

Tuesday
No sign of John. Or that slut.

*

Wednesday
Still no.

*

Thursday
I'm not obsessed, but where *is* he?

305

*

Friday
  Something must have happened.
  Beep!

*

Saturday
  This feels wrong. Like really wrong.

*

Sunday
  'Are you here on your day off *again*?'
  Startled, I turn away from the computer and see that Brenda from produce has come into the break room. I quickly log off and get to my feet. I was hoping nobody would see me tonight, but fortunately I've already got what I came for.
  'I just forgot something,' I tell her, slipping the piece of paper into my pocket. 'I'm off now.'

*

Shivering on the street corner, I look up the steps toward the dark house. This is 212 Fitzcrombie Road, which the address registered to John's loyalty card. I don't even know why I came. It's not like I'm going to go up to the door.
  Well, maybe I'll go to the door, but I won't knock. Slipping through the open garden gate, I make my way up the steps and stop at the door. I listen for a moment, but there's no hint that anybody's inside, although the door has been left partly ajar.

I won't go inside, but I might knock, just to check nothing's wrong.

Knock! Knock knock!

I wait. No answer. There's no way I'm going to snoop, but maybe I should take a quick look inside, just to be sure. The door creaks as I push it open, and I step into a dark, dank-smelling hallway.

'Hello?' I call out. 'Is anybody here?'

Again, there's no reply.

I'm not going to stay for long, but something seems wrong here so I start making my way toward the door past the stairs. I hesitate when I get there, but then I dare to peer through the crack and I see John sitting at the kitchen table.

Except..

He looks so thin and sick, like he's wasting away.

'Hello?' I call out tentatively, barely daring to speak at all. 'Are.. you okay?'

He doesn't answer, but I can see his eyes twitching. He's definitely alive.

Pushing the door further open, I step into the dark kitchen. It's so cold in here, and there's garbage everywhere along with puddles of dark liquid on the floor. It stinks, too, like garbage and something rotten.

'Are you okay?' I ask again, taking another step forward before stopping as I see that he's completely naked, and that chunks of flesh are missing from all over his trembling body, leaving exposed bones as well as sections of muscle that are hanging down from his skeletal arms and ribs.

And then I realize that somebody's right behind me. Turning slowly, I find myself face-to-face with the slut from earlier. She grins at me, and I'm horrified to see that she has two sharp, pointed teeth.

'Well,' she purrs, as she lowers a toothpick from her mouth, 'you *are* a curious little thing, aren't you?'

LOCO PARENTIS
Written by **Kit Power**

This is my magic hammer. Like it? I know, nothing special to look at. Probably got one just like it in your own toolbox at home. Still, this one is different. It has special powers.

With this hammer, I can make people tell me the truth.

Just recently, that's come in very handy.

I'm the caretaker at the school. Mr. Ross, the kids call me. Been there almost as long as the building. I know 'em all - the kids, the mums, the dads. Families. They come through the gates, every morning, and I'm there. Words of encouragement, sometimes, or the odd telling off if needed. I run a tight ship at that gate. It's the only way. Respect, that's the key. That's the key.

You really get a sense of the kids. Even just that, what, five minutes a day. Yeah. You see a lot. The ones that'll be okay, the ones that'll do good. The ones that are just born trouble. I know you're not supposed to say that anymore, but it's true. There are wrong 'uns out there, make no mistake. And I can spot 'em every time.

Truth is, they got a look. The wrong 'uns. Not meant to say that either, but it's a fact. It *is* a fact. Something around the eyes. Line me up a hundred kids, give me a good look at 'em, I'll tell you which one will be the little bastard that thieves from the tuck box, or pulls hair for fun. The one that'll poison the class hamster, if he thinks he'll get away with it.

They got a look. Guilty. Can spot it a mile off. If you know how to look.

I know. Always have. Adults too, come to that.

Anyway.

Little Freddie, now, he was okay. Bit of a noisy little bastard, could be a bit pushy, but basically an alright kid, you know. He'd smirk when he said 'Mornin', Mr Ross', but not a really mean one, more just a bit cheeky. I'd often say 'Got my eye on you, boy', or similar, but grinning right back. Like that. Mum almost always dropped him off, sometime a mate's mum - little Ellie Farmer lives on the same street, sometimes her parents'd drop him - but never dad. It's the kind of detail you notice, in my job. They'd drop him at the end of the road, let him walk down the cul-de-sac by himself. He liked that, made him feel grown up - you could tell by the way he puffed out his eight year old chest, the swagger he'd put on as he walked past me through the gates solo, while the other kids all hung on to some adult's hand. Not Freddie. Freddie didn't need to hold anyone's hand.

Anyway, that morning, there was something very different about him. Head down. Sniffing. Not crying, but he had been, you can tell, there's a look. Don't think I'd ever seen Freddie cry, except that time he fell from the monkey bars after hanging by his legs like a bloody idiot. All the sodding forms I'd had to fill out on that one, just for being the first aider on scene. Bloody nightmare.

'What's wrong, mate?' He looked up at me, and his look struck me cold. Stone cold. His eyes. They had bags under them, almost dark enough to be bruises. And so sad. No, not sad. Worse than that. Blank, somehow. No spark. Kid had had the sparkle knocked right out of him.

'Nothin'.'

'It's okay, mate', I said, trying on a smile. 'You can tell me.'

He shook his head, then turned his gaze back to his feet, not breaking stride. He was about to walk right by me. I didn't know what to do, so I did something I'm not supposed to, and I put my hand out. 'Hey, Freddie…'

'Get the FUCK off me!' he yelled. His high voice almost broke as he swore. I snatched my hand back, like I'd been burned. It sort of felt like I had. He'd looked back up at me as he said it, and his eyes were blazing suddenly. Then he was head down and legging

310

it, disappearing into the throng.

I was shocked, I can tell you. I didn't know what to do. I looked around, wondering who else had seen or heard it, but it was just before bell and the traffic was thin. A few kids and parents filed by, but none of them looked at me funny. I've been shouted at by kids at the gate before - rare, in a nice neighbourhood like this, but it does happen - and there's a look about other parents and kids when it does. It's the 'pretend I didn't hear that' look. It's like a flashing sign, once you've seen it once or twice. This time, with Freddie? Nothing.

So, I mean, there's protocol. Obviously. And technically I'd already not followed it, by not following Freddie in and taking him to a teacher to report him.

There's the reason you say you do it, then the real reason? Well, the reason I'd give - if I had to, which I wouldn't, because nobody saw anything, but - the reason I'd give was, with no-one seeing it, if he said it hadn't happened, I'd be up the creek, especially with not pursuing it the second it happened.

And, you know, that's all true. But it's not the real reason.

The real reason was just the look in the kid's eyes.

He was hurt. Bad. You could see it. Anyone could. Can't remember ever seeing a kid hurt like that. Not too many things can do that. Death, obviously. But no way the kid would be in school in that case, normally. If it was someone close enough died for the kid to be in that state, he'd have stayed home. A pet, maybe?

Or something else?

I really wanted to talk to him. I thought about it all day, but basically, it would only have compounded the fuck up of not reporting it in the first place. Plus, you never put yourself alone with a kid. Ever. That's why I like working the gate so much - you get the one-to-one interaction, but it's all out in the open, nowhere to hide. Safe. Talking to Freddie without reporting it? Not so much.

So I said nothing, and I did nothing. And when it was the end of the day, and I saw him walking out, I waited until he was past me before calling out 'See you, Freddie'. He didn't reply, but his step picked up just a notch.

*

It bugged me. All night. I ended up losing sleep over the little sod. His eyes. That sadness, that pain. I couldn't figure it out.

The next day he was the same - worse, even. Pale, and like he hadn't slept again. Plenty of pace in his step, but all the puff and swagger gone. It was horrible to see, honestly. Made me feel a bit ill. So I did a really stupid thing, I asked a really dangerous question.

'Everything all right at home, Freddie?'

I pitched my voice low, under the crowd, but timed it well. I know he heard. His face went white. Not pale. White. Like he was made out of bone china.

And he sprinted past me.

I think it was then that I decided to get to the bottom of it. Just the look of him, his reaction to me. Something. Something badly, badly wrong.

So I looked up his home address - turns out once you start doing stupid things, it quickly becomes a habit, don't you agree? It was easy enough to do, the office girl always goes for a walk at lunchtime and leaves her computer on.

I really couldn't tell you what I had in mind, honestly. I mean, if talking to Freddie on his own was a stupid idea, under the circumstances, what was going to his house? It was a sacking offence, that's what. And I'm doing it why? What did I think I was going to learn? Did I think I'd see an empty dog kennel, with a flag at half mast, problem solved?

I didn't know. Not on the surface, anyway. But underneath.. Well, let's just put it like this: when I drove over there after lunch, I took the white van I use for my handyman side gig.

And for the first time in a long, long time, I travelled tooled up - with this hammer in my pocket.

Because deep down, I did know. Really.

*

The house was nice - just off the main road into the estate, set back with its own driveway. Big hedges hid the house from the rest of the street. As I entered the road, I glanced about, and couldn't see anyone about - no dog walkers, no cars on driveways. A working street. The road curved soon after it started, so only a couple of houses were overlooking the driveway anyway.

What I'm describing here are habits, right? You get how that works. Stuff you've gotten so used to doing, you keep it up long after your reasons for doing it have stopped. It's just how people are, I think. Creatures of habit.

I pulled in on impulse. It's a white van, and I had my overalls on, business cards in my top pocket. I'd never cold-called for business - never had to, to be honest - but I knew people did it. Wouldn't help me if word got back to the school, of course, but it gave me an out in the moment, at least.

I felt totally calm as I walked up to the front door. I know how that sounds, but I'm not bragging, that's just how I remember it. As I rang the doorbell, I remember glancing over my shoulder, confirming that the front door was concealed from the view of surrounding houses by that hedge.

Like I say. Force of habit.

He opened the door, and right away, alarm bells were ringing. He wasn't dressed, for starters - middle of the afternoon, and he was in a dressing gown over a t-shirt, and - I hoped - shorts. His hairy calves poked out under the hem of the gown. Barefoot, too.

'Hello, mate', I said, putting on my best for-customers smile.

'Can I help you?' His voice was rough, like he'd not had much sleep, or been drinking. Or both. His accent was posh, you know, but he was stubbly and his hair was a bit of a state, and his breath was rank.

I looked him in his bloodshot eyes, and said 'I'm a local handyman, just wanted to pop by and see if you had any work you needed doing…' I let my eyes drift up to the house as I did so, keeping it casual. Like I was assessing the gutters and that. Really looking for an excuse to bring his kid up somehow. And I got one. '..I do all sorts, you know, guttering, carpentry, decorating…'

'We don't need anything like that right now.' No 'thank you'.You get me? Agitated. Like he wanted to get aggressive. At least, wanted shot of me, for sure. The bells started ringing louder. What did this cunt even do for a living? Home in the middle of the day, in a robe. Disgraceful. Missus doing all the running around, dropping the kiddie off, then going to work. It's not right, is it? It don't add up, There's nothing wrong with this feller, he looks fine, healthy.

All this going through my head. I think I knew then, to be honest. At least on a gut level. But I played it supercool as I said 'Can I give you my card? Just in case your son trashes the joint!' I flash him a grin at that, and he just fucking recoils. Visibly. Pulls back, sorta shrinks up, like a turtle. He's worried. Fucking scared, even.

'My son?' Like how the fuck do you know I've got a son? And what about it?

Guilt. I can spot it a mile off. Work the gate as long as me, you can see it, clear as the lines on your hand. Adults think they get better at hiding it, but they don't. It's just other adults start ignoring it. Because it's not polite to call other adults on their bullshit. So you pretend not to notice it, and in the end you really stop noticing.

Only I didn't. I don't. I see it.

I fucking see it all.

I point up at the bedroom window, casual. 'Walking Dead poster. My boy's a nut, too.' My voice was perfectly even as my hand slid under my coat.

He looked up. Like I knew he would, even though the angle was wrong for him to see.

The hammer was in my hand and connecting with his skull before he even began to look back down. You know when you're spreading butter onto a cracker, and it snaps in your hand? It made a noise just like that. Felt it right up to my shoulder.

He dropped like a sack of shit.

*

I don't mind telling you I was a bit worried at first. But I found the pulse in his neck quickly and it was strong and steady. I drove the van off the drive, reversed it back in, loaded him in the back. Drove out of town, and found a quiet layby. Pulled in, got in back. He was still out cold, so I got to work with the gaffer tape. By the time I was done, he was trussed up like a turkey and going nowhere.

I made it back to the gate with plenty of time to spare. Did the afternoon bell routine, goodbyes and see-you-later's and got-my-eye-on-you's. It's as natural as breathing to me, that patter. Could do it in my sleep. Didn't even break stride for Freddie, just kept it rolling, even though he didn't reply. No worries, lad, I thought. Don't you worry about a thing.

He ain't going to hurt you no more

After, I just sat in the van and thought for a bit.

I knew what he was, that piece of shit in the back of my van. I knew what he'd done. I read the papers, I know his kind. And the guilt on him - might as well have been wearing a t-shirt with a photo of him doing it. Not a doubt in my mind, what he was.

So I knew I had to end it. End him. Course I did. No problem with that - no more than stomping a spider. Try and hide the body after, hope for the best. But at least the kid'd be safe. Freddie. Either way.

Or, would he?

That's the thing, innit? These fucking paedo animals, they hunt in packs, don't they? Rings, they call 'em in the papers, always a paedo ring. They find each other on the internet. Share photos. Share victims. My mind goes back to Freddie. Did this sick fuck do something like that?

I thought, only one way to find out for sure.

*

I took him to this lock up of mine. It's a good spot. The concrete walls muffle a shitload of noise. There's only one way in to the complex, and I've added a padlock to it so I'll hear the noise if anyone does try and get in. I doubt they will. It's long term storage. Quiet spot.

I backed the van in first. Then opened it up, and pulled him out. He stank. Fucker had shat himself. He was well taped up, arms tight to his sides, legs wound together. Must have used half a roll on him. He looked like a mummy, sort of.

He lay on his back, chest heaving. Looked like he'd been crying. His nostrils were going nuts. I grabbed a box cutter, and crouched down by his face. He flinched back, eyes wide. A runner of snot shot out one of his nostrils. Tears in his eyes.

I smiled. Told him to stop fucking about. Said I was just going to cut the tape. He stared at me a long time, before nodding slowly, and held still. I managed to get my finger under the tape - his skin was hot and slick with sweat - then slid in the blade between his skin and the tape and cut it, pulling it to one side, clearing his mouth.

He heaved in a huge breath, then turned his head and threw up.

I told him it was all right. Stroked his hair until the heaves stopped and he got his breath back. He got the shakes after that. I waited until he'd got them out of his system. Then he asked me what was going on. He stammered, like he was trying not to cry.

I hadn't really thought about what came next, not in any detail. But as I leaned back, I felt the handle of the hammer in my inside pocket rest against my stomach.

I took it out. His eyes went wide, then he started crying and babbling, just a lot of pleases and what have you, no real sentences. I put up with it for a minute or so. Then I brought it down on his kneecap, as hard as I could.

He screamed, spit flying out his mouth, His whole back arched, and somehow he managed to flop over onto his side, facing away from me. The screaming turned into coughs, then more heaves. I let him, not trying to calm it this time. Eventually, it stopped. Then there was just sniffs and quiet sobs.

'I know what you did,' I said. 'You can't lie to me.' I lowered the hammer in front of his face, so he could see it. He yelped and shrank back from it. I grabbed a fist full of his hair and put my mouth by his ear.

I said, 'This is my magic hammer. Do you know why it's magic? Because I can use it to make people tell me the truth. So now, *you're* going to tell me the truth. Okay?'

He nodded, the movement held back by my fist in his hair.

I said, 'Okay. Good. How long have you been fucking your kid?'

He said, 'I haven't...' and I brought the hammer down on his hand, which was strapped to his side. The sound this time was like popcorn popping.

He yelled so loud his voice squeaked out for a second or two. I gave him a minute. Once he was back to sobbing through his gritted teeth, I tried again. I said, 'I know. You understand? I know. You just need to tell me how long. Okay? Just tell the truth. It doesn't have to hurt anymore, it can stop, but you gotta tell the truth. Now, how long?'

He was just panting. I gave him a few seconds, then raised the hammer.

'Just started! I swear! I swear it was only once...' He started crying again.

He kept up the crying as I got the whole story out of him. I only had to use the hammer twice more - once on his leg, one on his stomach - and by the end, I had everything I needed to know.

Circles, you see. Well, you know, don't you? It's always a ring with nonces, innit? They know their own, somehow, that's what I think, like gaydar but for kiddie fiddlers. Anyway, point is they never seem to act alone, and sure enough, he hadn't, and bit by bit, I got it all out of him - a list of names and addresses of all his sick bastard mates.

And then, one by one, I got them down here, and my hammer did its magic, and they confirmed the story I'd been given by paedo number one. Can't hide the truth, can you? Always comes out in the end. Once they got a dose or two from the hammer, they all fell into line all right. Worked my way through the whole ring. Whole nest of filth scum. Like killing rats. Termites, even. All rolling over on the others, giving up each others names.

Seven names in total. Six of them have bled their last out down here. In pain. I hope it followed them wherever they went after.

Which brings us to you.

See, I know everything. I know you were the ringleader behind the whole group. They told me it, all of 'em, while they still had teeth in their skulls to talk with. I know about all the filthy, disgusting things you've done, to little Freddie. And all the others.

Yeah. I know about them, too.

Well, I have one tiny bit of good news for you. I don't need you to tell me anything. I already know it all.

That's where the good news ends, though. Because now, me and my hammer are gonna make you pay for what you've done. I've done a few of these now, and I reckon you're gonna last a good few hours. That's the plan, anyway. I don't give a fuck what happens to me after. If they find a jury that'll convict, they can throw away the fucking key.

I can see the guilt on you. Could see it a mile off. You're going

to pay for what you've done. You're going to pay.
Right fucking now.

IN THE FAMILY
Written by **Adam Millard**

Most people remember the worst events from their childhood as vividly as the day they occurred; a particularly nasty dog bite, the finalisation of their parents' divorce, the first taste of a certain food that would serve only to put them off forevermore. For me, it was the day Granddad melted.

I was eight years old when it happened, and barely out of my *Joe 90* pyjamas. I liked everything most kids did back then—*The Bionic Woman, M*A*S*H, Mork and Mindy*, Hot Wheels, Micronauts, View-Master. I got through more red-and-white Gran Torinos than Starsky & Hutch ever had during their entire four-season run. As well as liking the same things as my peers, I was frightened of the same things, too. I believed a man lay in wait beneath my bed at night, anticipating a momentary lapse on my part and the unintentional offering of a cold, uncovered foot. I believed the world would end at any moment, thanks to 'those filthy Russians', as my father used to call them, and often wondered what it would be like to reach a hundred-million degree Celsius in less than a millisecond. I tried not to think about the creature living in my cupboard, with its innumerable arms and legs and tentacles and teeth sharper than razors.

And while those things, as ridiculous as they sound now, were terrifying to me then, it turned out I had far stranger things to worry about.

It was a cold day in January; I remember it well, for the needle-free Christmas tree still sat at the end of the driveway awaiting collection and there was a terrible frost, so thick one might have mistaken it for snow. School was back in full-swing, and it was there I had spent much of that day, no doubt learning about

Egyptians or acute angles or something equally banal.

'Don't just leave your coat there,' my mother said as she led me into the house. I wasn't sure whether it was colder inside or out. Our family operated on a strict budget, one which did not stretch so far as to have the gas-fire running all day long. My father, a man with whom I am now estranged—*does he even know what's happening to me? What's about to happen? Is he even still alive?*—worked occasionally in factories and warehouses, but he was never employed in one place long enough for the family to accrue anything like savings. Which was why, as my mother and I returned from school that day—she chain-smoking for warmth and I looking forward to smashing cars together in my bedroom, despite its inclement temperature—it came as no surprise to discover my father unconscious on the sofa, a half-finished bottle of whiskey in his hand and his lips curled into a sneer as he fitfully slept.

My mother didn't acknowledge my father—at least, not that I can recall now, though it was a long time ago—and neither did I. All I remember was her instructions: go upstairs, get washed, because after tea my grandfather, her father, was paying us a visit.

Now I was excited, for it wasn't every day Granddad made a social call. Unlike my father, my granddad was a very busy man, despite his advancing years; my mother often regaled me with tales of her father's travels, how his trips to China, Australia and Ireland had made him one of the highest earning salesmen in his company. If you were to ask me what it was my granddad sold, even now I wouldn't be able to tell you, for I don't think it was anything tangible like encyclopaedias or windows. No, my granddad was a seller of the invisible, the imaginary, the non-existent—shares, insurance, emotions.

Post-haste, I rushed upstairs to wash and change while downstairs my parents argued about the usual—my father's drinking, my mother's nagging, the fact that we had no money and would likely perish before spring. I had a knack of blocking out their voices; years of practice allowed me to mute them at will, and as I prepared for the arrival of my granddad—I couldn't wait to hear from which foreign country he had just returned, what strange and exotic dishes he had eaten and the beautiful women he had encountered along the way—I turned up the volume on my tape-deck to drown out their arguing even more so.

Half-an-hour later I was sat downstairs, clock-watching, even though my mother had given me no specific time of Granddad's arrival. My father sat opposite, a can of beer in one hand and a smouldering cigarette in the other. The over-spilling ashtray resting upon the arm of the chair gave the house its distinct aroma.

That of a crematorium.

Mother stood at the corner of the room, rearranging something in her breakfront, dusting at things with a chamois and humming miserably to herself. We were not what some would call 'a happy family', but we were a family.

I remember that moment thinking: I hope 'those filthy Russians' get around to nuking us soon.

When there came an enthusiastic knock upon the door, my mother closed the breakfront doors and smiled beatifically. 'That'll be him!' she exclaimed, and off she went to let Granddad in. As I went to stand, excited and practically bouncing to my feet, my mother said, 'Sit down, Jim,' as she walked past. I did as I was told, which, for an eight-year-old, was something to be admired.

'I don't know why *he's* here,' my father muttered, sucking noisily on his beer-can. 'Fucking old bastard, just trying to show me up, he is, with his job.' If my mother heard him, she didn't show it.

Granddad was a large man for his age; tall and stocky, with not an ounce of fat on him. And as I wrapped my tiny arms around him, and he snatched me up from the carpet into what must have been the tightest hug ever to pass between two human beings, I could have sworn I felt rippling muscles beneath his overcoat.

'Jimmy!' he said, swinging me this way and that. 'You're

getting so big! Must be all that calamari you're eating, huh?'

I had no idea what calamari was (it sounded like a desert to me) so I changed the subject as quickly as I could. 'Where have you *been*, Granddad?'

We sat as mother set about making sandwiches and father opened a new packet of cigarettes and seethed from his armchair. Granddad told me all about his most recent trip to Istanbul, and I listened intently as if he were proffering me the meaning of life. To me he *was*.

'I made more money in my three weeks in Turkey than most people make in a year,' he told me. I was perched upon his knee, which trembled ever-so-slightly as he animatedly told his tale. 'I also ate my fair share of köfte and drank more Rakı than most Turks do in their lifetime, but the less said about that the better.' He laughed, I laughed, and in the corner my father hissed disapprovingly. I remember hating him for that, for mocking Granddad so openly. It was, I thought, a good job Granddad didn't notice, for my money would have been on him to put my father through the living-room window, and make no mistake about it.

Mother returned with the sandwiches. 'Get off your granddad's knee, Jim,' she said. 'He doesn't want you all over him like some… some parasite. Reckon he's had enough of that in Turkey.'

I didn't know what she meant by that, but it elicited a hearty laugh from Granddad, so it must have been something funny.

We ate our sandwiches, and I listened fixedly as Mom and Granddad caught up on each other's lives. The couple of times Granddad tried to engage my father in polite conversation proved fruitless; the look my mother shot my father suggested there would be further arguments tonight, once my grandfather had departed.

Something to look forward to, I thought at the time.

It was during one of Granddad's little stories—this one involving a Kurdish fella named Ahmet and a stolen motorcycle— that The Melt first began to manifest, and I knew something incongruous was happening.

The entire left side of my grandfather's face became listless, his one eye slipping down his face as if he had unceremoniously been transformed into a Dali painting. My mother, shocked beyond measure, slapped a hand across her mouth, but it did nothing to stifle her scream.

What shocked me the most, however, was not my mother's panicked shrill or the fact that my grandfather's fingertips were now stretching toward the carpet like strings of melted cheese; it was the calmness with which Granddad seemed to be handling the whole thing. He looked almost… *tranquil*. As if he had not only been expecting this to happen, but had known the exact time and place it would occur and had already made his peace with it.

'Oh, no, no, no!' My mother's mournful cries filled the room as Granddad's head tilted to one side and his ear slipped down onto his shoulder before dissolving in a hiss of bubbles.

A nightmare, I remember thinking. It had to be a nightmare, one from which I would waken in a pool of adolescent sweat, sobbing until the terrible images went away, if they ever would.

But when my father staggered half-drunkenly to his feet and said, 'Oh, shit! Is *this* what it looks like? Oh, honey, I'm so fucking sorry!', I knew I was not dreaming.

Before his face became wholly liquefied, Granddad turned to me and grunted something or other. I wouldn't find out what he said until many years later, the message relayed by my mother over a semi-burnt Sunday lunch, and so I stared back into my grandfather's liquescing face with a mixture of horror and confusion.

As my father rushed from the room—the sound of him vomiting from the kitchen a few seconds later was barely audible over the sizzling and hissing of my grandfather's rapidly-dissolving body— I remember sniffing the air and thinking how bitter it tasted at the back of my throat.

'Get out of here!' my mother screeched at me, and not for the first time judging by her tone. 'Jim! Get the fuck out!'

But I was paralysed, unable to look away, my brain working overtime as it tried to figure out what was going on.

The huge man that had been sitting opposite me just a moment ago was now just a heap of smoking clothes and an indiscernible human-like thing wearing them. My mother was on her knees, sobs wracking her entire body; she was no longer watching the tragedy unfold, but I was. I had to see what happened next, what my Granddad would do to escape his ostensibly gruesome fate.

It's a magic trick, I recall thinking, for my grandfather was fond of the old penny-from-behind-the-ear caper. Any moment now, I thought, he would appear from behind the armchair, a satisfied grin stretching from one side of his face to the other. *Ta-da! Don't ask me how I did it. I shall never tell.*

If only. The thing that had once been my grandfather's head blackened and slipped down into the collar of its shirt; the silvering hairs upon the top of its pate were aflame, and yet the clothing didn't catch fire as the body was consumed from within.

A puddle of pink flesh, tinged here and there with a much more vibrant crimson blood, surrounded the armchair. There came a steady *drip, drip, drip* as more flesh melted and oozed from my grandfather's trouser-leg, trickled down over his immaculately polished shoes and onto the carpet below.

I realised I was up on the sofa now, standing, staring down at the mess as if I had just seen the tail of a rat disappear beneath one of the chairs. And mother was crying uncontrollably, and in the kitchen father was throwing up and mumbling something about how he'd never wish this on anyone, not even *that* old prick.

I was screaming at my mother, begging her to tell me what was happening. She was screaming back at me, telling me to 'Get the fuck out of here now, Jim! Please!' It was chaos.

So, you can perhaps see why that day stuck with me throughout my entire life.

I'd like to say it was a one-off inexplicable occurrence.

Alas it was not.

Seven years after Granddad melted, at the aforementioned Sunday lunch, mother stared across the dinner table at me, her eyes glazed over, her mouth opening and shutting, as if she knew she wanted to say something, though quite what was beyond her.

It was just the two of us now—as it had been for the past five years, ever since my father disappeared in the middle of the night without so much as a goodbye or a hastily-scribbled note of apology—and mother and I seldom spoke during meals. Instead we ate our food, maudlin, deep in thought or without thought altogether. Meals, like many of our day-to-day undertakings, were necessary things, not to be enjoyed but to be carried out in order to survive. I can't remember what we ate that particular Sunday; like I said, all I know is that it was overcooked to the point of being carbonised. It could have been anything there on my plate, for I wasn't really hungry or interested. I simply pushed it around, apathetic, nauseated, wearied.

Then mother finally managed to get her words out, and everything changed once again.

'It will happen to us too,' she said.

I looked up from my plate, grateful for the respite and yet not for her choice of words. 'What?'

My mother sighed before continuing. 'What happened to your granddad,' she said. 'It will happen to me, and it will happen to you.' The way she said it—cold and emotionless, like some sociopathic vampire—caused gooseflesh to rise up on my skin. Before I could reply she went on. 'It's been in our family for centuries. Generations of Frewers have melted over the years; it's only blind luck and the fact we have children young that we're still here today.'

I listened to her, fork in hand, and it took me a while to digest what I was being told. That I carried some sort of melting gene and would succumb in much the same manner as Granddad had, but not before I watched the same thing happen to my mother.

'It can't be true!' I said, dropping my fork. It clattered against the edge of my plate, chipping the porcelain. 'What happened to Granddad was—'

'The Melt,' my mother simply said, as if it were a pretty average way to die, like suffering a stroke or falling down a flight of steps. 'There is no explanation for it, no rhyme or reason why it only affects our family. It just *is*. I've read journals written by our ancestors—they called it The Deliquescing, but I prefer The Melt; why put a frilly bow on it? —describing how they witnessed the deaths of their parents, their grandparents, their children—'

'Wait!' I said. 'Their *children*? You mean this thing can strike at any moment, regardless of age?' That terrified me; I was yet to lose my virginity. It would be just my luck to start melting at second base.

'It doesn't happen often to the young,' my mother said, forking sweetcorn into her mouth and chewing agitatedly. 'Once or twice, from what I've been told and what I can glean from the history books. Don't worry yourself about it. You will probably live a full and healthy life.'

'Until the day I suddenly start to dissolve!' I said. My mother drained her wine glass and regarded me with no small amount of concern, as was her wont. 'Why now?' I said. 'After all this time?' I had spent the last seven years questioning her, trying to figure out what had transpired that evening in the living-room of our old house—we'd downsized after my father left, for my mother could not afford the mortgage on her own, which I didn't understand, since my father was hardly King Contributor—only to be met with silence or, worse, my mother's wrath.

'It seems like something you should know,' she said, shrugging a little. 'You're sixteen next year, and I'm not getting any younger. You're old enough to understand... at least, I *hope* you are.'

And yet even though she had finally told me the truth, I still did not understand. Were we freaks? Was this a more widespread affliction, and the only reason it had not been brought to light was because of how downright embarrassing and ridiculous it was?

328

'It's why Dad left, isn't it?' I'd always wondered why he'd gone, and now I knew. It was because he didn't want to be there when his wife evaporated, leaving behind only a gory mess and a puddle-stain on the carpet.

'It wasn't because of me,' said my mother. 'I'm sure he would have *loved* to see me go through The Melt.' She laughed a little, though it was nervous and wretched. When she composed herself once again, she said, 'He could never be there when—if—it happened to you. Said it would kill him to see that.'

Bullshit, I thought. My father had been a wastrel, about as emotionally inept as a person could be. I fancied he just didn't want to have to sponge his son up from the floor, for it would be the most work he'd had to do in years.

But my mother was adamant that was why he left, and who was I to argue? I could melt away at any given moment; arguing over something so trivial seemed like a waste of valuable time.

'Live your life,' my mother said, each word punctuated with a slight pause. 'That's what your grandfather said to you the day he...' She trailed off there, lip quivering slightly. Of course, it had been impossible to discern Granddad's words back then, what with his teeth falling from his frothing lips and his tongue slipping to the back of his flesh-sealed throat.

After lunch, I retired to my bedroom, where I spent the rest of the afternoon in tears, wondering what I had done to deserve such a curse.

People dropped down dead all the time, and at all ages. An embolism, heart attack, stroke, thousands of people every day succumbing to indiscriminate infirmities. And yet it was the manner of my fate which concerned me.

To melt away, to feel the flesh slip from my bones and the organs liquefy within me, was a terrifying prospect. I could only think of one death as grisly; that of being burnt alive.

I had to do something to prevent my seemingly inevitable demise. There had to be someone out there that knew of the condition, that knew how to counteract it. But there was not. I spent three years searching, researching, approaching so-called medical experts and specialists. Many of whom laughed me out of their offices, for the condition I described was, according to their considerable expertise, just not possible. People don't melt. Don't be so absurd, and don't let the door hit you in the ass on your way out.

I interviewed university scholars, made appointments with witnesses to victims of spontaneous human combustion. In a Mexican village called Araras I met with several unfortunate souls whose skin was gradually melting due to a condition known as xeroderma pigmentosum, but as I sat there, unable to look into the dying eyes of the plagued villagers sitting opposite, I knew there was a vast difference between our diseases. Mine was yet to manifest visibly, and yet I could already feel it, a discomfiting warmth deep within, constantly reminding me of my inescapable end.

I was twenty-three when my mother melted, and absent from the country at the time. I had recently uncovered a tribe in Nigeria whose chief had recently—according to issue 165 of *The Fortean Times*—disappeared during the night. The tribe discovered, in his bunk, nothing but a thick puddle. Unfortunately, while I was out there on the Gulf of Guinea, it became apparent that the puddle was the only connection between our diseases, for the chief returned to the village while I was there, as right as rain and healthier than most octogenarians. The puddle, it transpired, was sap from the tree creeping over the chief's bunk. And the chief, who was wont to disappear for days, weeks, and even months at a time on hunting expeditions, had apparently returned with a roan antelope and enough meat to, if rationed properly, feed the entire village for a month.

Frustrated, I returned to England, to the house which I shared with my mother, and there she was.

Where she had been.

She had died in the kitchen; a sink filled with filthy plates and dishes suggested she had gone through The Melt doing the washing up.

I didn't know what was more upsetting, that my mother was gone or that she had gone performing such a menial task.

I picked up the apron—the nightie, the marigolds, and the slippers—from the lino, being careful not to get any of my mother on my hands, and placed them into a refuse sack. I didn't cry, didn't heave or hyperventilate as I worked at the flesh puddle with a mop and bucket. In a way I was glad, for now I no longer hated her for birthing me, for knowingly passing the family curse down to me.

She went into the sink with the dirty bucket-water, and as she disappeared down the plughole—nothing but malformed skin and ashes—relief washed over me.

That was all a very long time ago, and now I can feel The Melt working away at me. Some days it feels like heartburn—nothing more than an uncomfortable sensation in my chest—while other days I am in agony. What's surprising is that I'm being warned, that I can feel the disease going about its business inside of me, and I often find myself wondering whether Granddad experienced the same portending pangs. If he did, he'd hid it well right up until the moment he dissolved all over our living-room floor.

Any day now.

I can already feel my organs shifting and one side of my face appears gaunt, the skin there loosening, coming away from my skull like the peel of an overripe tangerine. Every now and then I get pins and needles in my limbs, though that might just be old age or the fact I haven't left my apartment for months. I don't want to be outside when it happens, don't want to be a newspaper headline or a *Fortean Times* article. I'm hoping it is many months before I am discovered, but that all depends on how thick the ceilings are in this building, for I have visions of the old woman downstairs looking up toward the pink patch blossoming across her Artex ceiling and clicking her tongue as she wondered how much it was going to cost to put right.

Any day now.

My left eye is slowly closing and it hurts when I blink. It's becoming increasingly difficult to breathe, and I've spent much of the morning peeling the dead fingernails from my withered hands. For some reason, The Melt for me is not as spontaneous as it had been for my grandfather. I envy him for that, and sometimes wonder whether my mother went quickly or if it crept up on her, too, like a cancer, teasing her, promising her, *soon, soon, soon.*

Any day now.

I'm ready.

THE PRIEST HOLE
Written by **Guy N. Smith**

Rachael was uneasy, more so tonight than at other times when her son, Tom, was away staying with his girlfriend. Since her husband, George, had left her for another woman those nights spent on her own had become scary although she would never have confessed it to anybody. She tried to tell herself it was silly, she was just pandering to her imagination, all due to the backlash of a broken marriage.

The small farm surrounded the large house, a somewhat rambling building which dated back to the early sixteenth century, Maybe even earlier. Rachael knew that it was definitely haunted even though Tom scoffed at the suggestion. Footsteps in the night, occasionally she heard distant voices, indecipherable but definitely angry like people were quarrelling. She always locked her bedroom door, not that it would keep out ghosts but it made her feel slightly safer.

Worse, during his attempts to renovate the house Tom had discovered a priest hole in the kitchen ceiling. She found it decidedly creepy. Only last week he had chipped the plaster away but had not yet opened the hatch.

'Leave it for now, Tom', she had pleaded with him. 'Maybe just plaster it up again and forget about it.' This was something else which she could do without, a spooky hole in the ceiling dating back centuries.

'We'll see', he grinned. 'I'll maybe take a look inside whilst you're out doing the rounds with the sheep.'

'Please yourself but I don't want to see up in there. Don't do it today, though.' She shuddered involuntarily.

The house was rumoured to be haunted according to some of

the locals. All manner of other strange things had happened in recent weeks. Wild boar had appeared in the locality. They were rumoured to have travelled up from the Forest of Dean where the population had expanded, taking over new territory, replacing their ancestors who had roamed the surrounding forest several hundred years ago.

Then there was that Big Cat which she had twice glimpsed in the upper field adjoining the neighbouring oak wood. It was a huge black beast stalking the edge of the wood in search of a rabbit or deer. Or food of any kind, maybe even a human if it chanced upon one. Indoors or outdoors it had become scary living here. Like something awful was going to happen.

Sometimes at night she heard a shot ring out in the forest. That was undoubtedly deer poachers. God, how she would like to sell up, move down into the village at the foot of the hills. But she had to think of Tom, the small farm was part of his living along with driving for the haulage firm in the nearest town. For his sake she would stick it out, at least until he married his girlfriend and they lived here together.

A low growl came from beneath the table. Sheba, the ageing sheepdog, had heard something outside or maybe she just thought she had. Rachael lifted the table cloth, saw how the dog was trembling. Another growl. Something was scaring her. Something…outside. Maybe it was the wild boar snuffling round the house. Or that leopard or whatever species of feline it was. But whatever was out there could not enter the house. Thank God!

'It's all right, Sheba', she leaned down to stroke the trembling dog. 'It can't get in here…'

Suddenly there was a knocking on the door, faint but urgent.

Who could it be in the depth of a winter night, miles from habitation? It wouldn't be Tom, he had his own key, but in any case he was staying overnight with his girlfriend.

The tapping came again, now louder and with an urgency that demanded a reply. Like Sheba, Rachael began to tremble.

Sheba growled again, louder this time. She cowered even further under the table, her tail between her legs.

There was only one way to find out. Rachael rose and crossed to the window beside the door. The security light would doubtless have come on enabling her to see her nocturnal caller.

The light was not on. That was strange. Perhaps the bulb had blown.

'Who's there?' Her voice was shaky, barely audible.

'Open up!' A demand rather than a request. The voice was cracked, undoubtedly that of an elderly person.

'What d'you want?'

A long pause and then 'I'm lost. It's starting to snow.

Undoubtedly it was a stranger staying in the area, a rambler who had lost his way in the surrounding hills. She could not ignore his plea for help.

'Just a minute'. With trembling fingers she turned the key, kept a foot behind the door as she edged it open a few inches. Now the light from the kitchen fell on her nocturnal visitor.

She could tell at a glance that he was elderly, with stooping shoulders and a frayed overcoat that almost reached down to his ankles. A broad brimmed hat shaded his face. Undoubtedly he was harmless, she tried to convince herself, and she could not slam the door shut in his face and leave him to the mercy of the elements. From time to time ramblers who were not familiar with the area became lost. Not that he looked like a hill walker by any stretch of imagination.

'You'd better step inside.'

He shuffled through the open door, made no attempt to wipe his booted feet on the mat nor to remove his headgear. Snow cascaded from the latter in his wake. Now she could see his heavily lined, wizened features, almost skeletal, adorned with a wisp of grey beard. His eyes seemed to recede into their sockets. Long thin bony hands with ragged dirty fingernails clutched a heavy stick. Rachael closed the door behind him.

'Would you like a cup of tea, mister…?'

She thought his head nodded on a scrawny neck. He made no attempt to remove his headgear as he shuffled his way to a vacant chair at the table. Sheba's growl changed to a low snarl.

'I'll put the kettle on. Are you staying locally?'

He did not reply, lowered his thin frame into the chair.

'Do you remember the siege of Hopton Castle?' A sudden unexpected question in grated tones.

'I don't remember it, of course, because it was several hundred years ago but I've read about it. It was during the Civil War.'

'Or the sacking of Linley Manor?'

'I've read about that, too. It's not far from here.' An icy shiver trickled up her spine. Linley was a neighbouring mansion and had been sacked by the Revolutionaries. It had been rebuilt later.

'Many were slaughtered, Royalists along with those who fought a just cause'. His head was uplifted towards the hatch above, his expression sending another chill through her. Tom had cleared the crumbling plaster, exposed the heavy trapdoor. Her visitor stared fixedly up at it, he was trembling violently. It was probably due to the intense cold outside, she tried to convince herself. There was something distinctly unnerving about him.

He stood up, bent almost double, using his stick to support himself. Behind him, propped up against the wall, was the step ladder where Tom had left it.

'Tom, my son, says it's a priest hole. He's going to take a look inside it. I'm expecting him home any time now.' A lie but she was becoming increasingly afraid of her nocturnal visitor.

Without so much as another word he shuffled across to the step ladder and began to drag it clanking across the stone flagged floor.

'What are you doing?' Her trembling voice was little more than a whisper now.

He did not reply as with no small amount of difficulty he set up the ladder beneath the closed trapdoor. Shakily, he began to mount the steps, still clutching his heavy stick, wobbling. She found herself praying that he would fall, lie in a helpless heap on the floor. Then she would call the doctor, have him taken away to hospital.

Somehow he held on, mounted a shaky step at a time. He banged the rusted catch with his stick and at the third blow it yielded. The heavy door plunged downwards on rusted hinges, missed him by inches, swung and creaked.

Then, with unbelievable agility, her visitor pulled himself up. An excited whisper came from his thin cracked lips as he secured a grip on the frame of the open gap.

'My son will be home any time now.' God, if only Tom wasn't stopping away overnight.

The stranger appeared unaware of her presence down below him. He swayed unsteadily as he levered himself upward on his precarious hold. Rachael gasped as a stale, putrid odour exuded from the open space. God, it was vile, like something had been trapped in there rotting for centuries.

Her visitor's bony hands gripped the edge of the exposed gap, his stick clamped beneath an arm. Somehow he found the strength in his frail body to pull himself up and seconds later he had disappeared through the opening. His breathing was rasping, louder than before.

If only Tom was here. She edged her way across to the telephone. She would call him, beg him to return as quickly as possible,

Oh, Gods, the phone was dead!

Muttered, indecipherable cursing came from up above. A cloud of dust billowed from the opening. The booted feet appeared, seeking out the ladder steps. Except that they were no longer the footwear which he had been wearing upon his arrival, instead calf length leather boots. His coat had changed from that original shabby and well worn rainproof to one of high quality leather. The scrawny fingers gripping the rungs were now strong and supple.

Then she saw the face, younger and full bearded but that, too, was different. The wizened flesh had become supple skin; age and decay were gone, in their place a countenance which was years younger, the very epitome of evil beneath a wide brimmed leather hat.

It was a lithe form which descended the ladder and the hand which had previously clutched a heavy walking stick now grasped a long bladed shiny sword which clanked on the rungs.

Sheba was whining her terror beneath the table. Rachael backed away, a scream on her lips. An icy cold hand gripped her, sprawled her across the table and the face which was thrust within inches of her own depicted hatred and fury, an expression of sheer evil.

'Where is the treasure?' He was shaking, his voice barely audible in his mounting rage, foul breath emanating from his slobbering mouth almost making her vomit. 'Where have you hidden it, bitch?'

She tried to speak but no words came. Now the sharp point of the sword pricked her throat.

'Royalist thief, where is the treasure we took from Linley Manor?'

His other hand was groping her body, squeezing her breasts until she cried out in pain, then exploring her lower regions, ripping her jeans and underwear from her.

'Tell me or you die'

The point of his sword pricked her throat and that was when she fainted, drifted into blissful oblivion.

*

It was daylight when Rachael regained consciousness. She was still sprawled across the table and beneath her the ageing sheepdog was whimpering. Slowly everything came back to her, had her glancing fearfully around the room. There was no sign of her nocturnal visitor, thank God! It must have been an awful nightmare and she had fallen asleep at the table.

Her neck was smarting, her clothing was rumpled and her breasts and thighs were sore from that vicious groping. She pulled up her jeans, rushed to the mirror. There was a slight scratch on her slender neck! She shuddered, thought she might throw up. Up above her the hatch of that dreadful priest hole hung open, the foul stench still emanating from it.

Somehow she made it across to the telephone. To her relief it was now working. She dialled with a trembling finger and Tom answered almost immediately. She needed him more now than she had ever done since she had raised him.

*

'I'd better take a look up there', Tom glanced up at the open hatch as he poured his mother a strong coffee. 'You probably fell asleep and had a nightmare.' His explanation was not convincing to either of them.

The stench was overpowering as Tom mounted the aluminium steps. He hesitated before hauling himself up through the open space and his hands were trembling. Christ, what the hell had been going on here last night?

'Oh, my God!' Rachael heard his shout as he disappeared from view.

Up above Tom stared in horror and disbelief at the scene portrayed in the light which filtered up from below. A human skeleton, clad in what were surely the remains of Roundhead clothing dating back to the Civil War, was sprawled across the dust laden wooden floor. The head was partially severed, probably from a sword blow, propped up and seeming to snarl at him. The arms were uplifted as if it a futile attempt to ward off the sharp blade which had ended its life.

Certainly no Royalist, the body was undoubtedly that of a Roundhead, murdered by his colleagues as they quarrelled over looted treasure. There was nothing else except a layer of filth which had gathered over the centuries. Doubtless this had happened after the sacking of Linley Manor when the thieves had returned for their ill gotten treasure.

It was all conjecture but it figured according to local legend. Yet there was no logical explanation for his mother's night of terror only the supposition that the slain thief had returned in an attempt to regain the loot of which he had been deprived by his vile confederates. There had been a quarrel and they had murdered him. The treasure was long gone and would probably never be found.

'I guess we'd better phone the police'. White faced and shaking Tom descended to the kitchen. 'A theft and murder dating back centuries which will never be solved, I guess. Like your experience last night, for which there is no logical explanation, let's hope that that's the end of a centuries old looting and treachery by Roundhead villains.'

JUST BREATHE
Written by **Jaime Johnesee**

Just breathe. You can do it, you've got this, it's gonna be okay.

These words have gotten me through more than I can tell you. They've been right, been wrong, and been nothing more than a mantra to help me focus but, they've been there.

It sounds stupid to ascribe helpful qualities to words but those words have kept me going when so many would have given up. Probably should have given up.

The pain, burning into me causing me to crash back into myself. More pain as he poured rubbing alcohol on my skin and set it to light.

When done properly, only the alcohol burns and it feels really cold even though you're on fire. Tonight, he was angry and wasn't doing it right.

Tonight, I burned, over and over. My punishment for smiling too much around his friends. He poured alcohol a third time and the pain that ripped through my body broke me and I fell to my face before he could light it.

A boot to the back was his supportive way of saying he was done. Damaged nerves shot lightning across my back and skin sloughed off from where he'd kicked me and the cooked layer of my back pulled away from the rest of the meat.

That's all I was now. Meat.

Just breathe, you're gonna get through this, everything is going to be okay.

I moved to the bathroom to clean what I could reach, gagging when large chunks peeled off. He wasn't going to stop. It would never get better. I needed to run and there was no time like the present.

He has a bunch of methheads over he has been trying to convert to Snort. With so many people over I could sneak out easily but, where to go? Staring at the ruins of my back I decided on going to the hospital.

Fuck this shit.

I left the bathroom and took a right into what would have been a bedroom but instead held an outdoor hot tub and astroturf flooring. The occupants of the vomit strewn jacuzzi were too obliterated to notice me. I scraped through the eternally-stuck-open window, leaving bits of flesh on the frame behind me.

Good. Cops can verify I was here. I began the slow walk through the woods to get myself some help. Branches drag their limbs through the raw ruination of my back. And I wished I'd grabbed a towel or something to cover the wounds.

It grew ever more uncomfortable made worse when a few bugs stopped to nibble some dinner, a couple had become stuck to the raw, weeping muscle. Not the muscle, my muscle.

Just breathe, you can do it. You've got this. Everything is going to be okay.

Then I heard dogs. Lots of dogs, and me a walking rib roast. Great. Just fucking great. I made the brilliant choice to go through a wild blackberry thatch; the thorns tearing into me hopefully would serve to keep the dogs back.

I kept moving, slowly but steady. With all my injuries I wasn't making as much progress as I'd hoped. It took a couple hours before I walked into the town limits and began to see signs of life.

My back started hurting worse then, as if coming back to reality snapped the nerves in place and the pain grew. Several cars drove past, honking at me to get out of the way; gibberish was all that spilled from my mouth.

I wanted to scream for help or collapse and be done with it but I moved on. I needed help and would have to get it for myself. I felt lucky when a cop car rolled up behind me and let go with lights and sirens.

'Ma'am, do you need some help?'

Oh, yes. Need help. Please help. What came out was a strangled cry that sounded more like a terrified raccoon than human.

He saw the full extent of the injuries to my back and gasped, 'Holy Jesus, did someone hurt you, Ma'am?'

I squawked and nodded, still unable to process everything fast enough to speak. The decision to leave Jimmy had been huge. He had broken my self esteem first that had made it easier to break other things from there on.

He'd never expected me to build it back up a scrap at a time. Over time I managed to carve myself a well-battered but solid foundation of knowing who I was and liking the core of me.

I hadn't expected it either. Took way too long to come to this day but everybody has a breaking point and, sadly, being cooked alive was mine.

I felt ashamed that I had stayed so long. I still felt I needed him, however sick that might be. He wasn't always a monster, that came with the drugs. When I'd met him he'd been sweet and caring and a little possessive. Over time I'd become nothing more than a toy to sit on his shelves and bring down when he wanted to play.

This was not the life I wanted and tears flowed from me as the officer told me he had called for EMS and a detective. I mostly sobbed but, when he stared into my eyes, I got the feeling the cop understood I was trying to thank him.

'I promise they'll find whoever did this to you. You don't have to be afraid of him or her.' He offered me his jacket and I shook my head no and pointed at my back. Couldn't he see I didn't want anything on it?

'No, for your front.' He held the jacket up to his chest and I understood and flushed red as I accepted the coat and covered myself.

I was feeling a little calmer and finally spoke the name of the bastard who'd tormented and broken me over and over for a year, 'Jimmy Mecklenburg.'

'The dealer?'

I nodded.

'He did this to you?'

'n'more,' sobbing again.

'Jesus. Come sit down and wait for the EMS, you're safe now. I promise you.' I believed his words, his eyes held genuine concern. I sat in the car, my back turned into the center of the backseat my legs hanging out onto the shoulder of the road.

He walked around the front of the cruiser and I hollered, 'Don't leave me, please don't leave me alone.' I was terrified and I let it show.

'Hey, you're going to be okay. Just breathe, you can get through this. You've got this.'

I gaped at him, how did he know my words? I was suddenly comfortable and aware of everything looking fuzzy. He asked me which hospital I preferred but in the haze of safety and care I gave in to the darkness.

A hollow clanging sound pulled me out of it and back into a very uncomfortable reality that I had no intention of remaining in when I saw what awaited me. I was back in the kitchen of the house I had escaped.

They had me tied to the filthy formica countertop and someone had shoved their sock in my mouth. I'd never felt more broken and empty in my life. There was no hope. Even my treasured words failed to ignite that spark.

I just didn't want to live anymore. If this was to be my life it was better to be cold and in the dirt, which was probably what they were aiming for anyway.

There have only been a few times in my life where I wanted to give up and, every time, someone stepped in unknowingly and gave me that bright spark of hope to keep going.

There was nobody to help this time. As I tested my bonds and found them secure I knew, without a doubt, I would never leave here alive. I also knew that the pain that awaited me would be unending and monstrous.

The formica was warm beneath me but definitely not comfortable. I kept my eyes mostly closed and looked around, doing my best to read the situation I was in. The cop who brought me here was the kindly fellow who had followed the ambulance to the hospital. He was talking to Jim and the few methheads who hadn't run when the police pulled up.

'If you can't keep them here, Jimmy, you shouldn't be allowed to have them.'

'Fuck you, DeTesta! You're the one what gave me the idea for this.'

'Bitch, you can complain all you want but when there exists the possibility of my business being ruined by your extracurricular activities I have to put my foot down. Kill her and be done. Know this, if one of your little games fucks up my pharmaceutical dealings I will fucking fry you all.'

'Don't have to be a dick about it,' Jim slurred.

'Apparently I do, or do I have to remind you she was seen by several fucking people, Jimmy? You're damn lucky I found her first. Clean up your mess, and don't ever leave me another, you hear?'

'Fine. Fucking nag.'

'Don't fuck up, Jimmy.' The cop walked out the front door without so much as a backward glance at me.

I had to get him to untie me or I was as good as dead. I stayed quiet and pretended to still be out cold. It wasn't easy, the way they had me tied forced my raw and shredded back to arch painfully against the rough hemp ropes they'd used.

I waited for them to kill me. Stayed as still as possible, so much so that a cramp was starting in my right calf. I couldn't reach it to rub it out so all that lactic acid began chewing on my muscle and it took my mind off my back for a bit.

I opened my eyes just a bit wider to see what was going on, and because I needed a break from the pain and outside stimuli would be most welcome. Except it wasn't. What I saw was several people in various states of being stoned.

They didn't seem troubled by my presence which let me know they were pretty far down their rabbit holes and there'd be no help from any of them.

Just breathe. You're going to be okay.

I opened my eyes completely and Jimmy noticed me.

'Oh, look who's awake! How ya doing, sleeping beauty?' one of the tweakers started poking at me as he talked. 'Looks so real, like real meat.'

'It is.' Jimmy just grinned at the poor kid's terror and confusion. These were emotions he was excellent at harvesting, he knew just how to milk it.

The tweaker poked at a piece of the already cooked portion of my back and it slid off. He lifted it to his lips and took a bite. I gagged and did my best not to vomit since I had a sock in my mouth and no desire to aspirate.

'It *is* real meat!' he declared, looking at me like I was a bacon cheeseburger.

'Don't eat her too fast, boys. You might get a stomach ache.' Jimmy's chuckle caused me to shudder. He was going to feed me to them and they were so fucked up on Snort I had no doubt they'd eat me alive.

'Oh, darlin', you shouldn't have run. I can see why you did but, now I have to make you really hurt. Why do you do this to me? I liked you.' He clucked his tongue and looked at me as if I were a four year old kid stealing cookies. 'Gonna have to teach you a lesson. One you'll remember into your next life. I am your god now.'

Blasphemous asshole. Is what I wanted to say, it came out garbled due to the sock. The tweaker picked another piece of fried flesh off my back and I fought to keep control of my sanity.

Just breathe, you can do this. You've got this.

Another drug addled fuckwad approached and began picking at

me along with his buddy.

'Yer tasty.' He continued picking and said no more.

I couldn't say anything on account of the gag in my mouth. Had I been able to, I probably would have tried to remind them I was a fellow human being and they were acting like zombies.

It wasn't long before they had peeled my back right down to the raw muscle. I was terrified and it only got worse when the one grabbed a knife and decided to try my thigh. They really were going to eat me alive. There was no way out of this.

I felt the knife slid through my flesh and I screamed. The sock fell away and I took that opportunity to yell.

'Help! Zombies! They're motherfucking zombies!' It was all I could think to yell.

A couple tweakers came rushing into the kitchen and, when they saw their friends carving me up like roast beef, they took up the cry yelling, 'zombies' and began shooting.

I was winged by a bullet that killed the fellow who knifed me. It passed through the meat of my arm and I cried out.

The meth-head that shot me seemed to finally realize what was going on as he stumbled around looking at me and whispering fuck every so often.

'I'm gonna call an ambulance for you. Fuck, man, I didn't sign on for this shit.' He pulled a cell phone from his pocket and started to dial when Jimmy came in and slapped it out of his hands.

'She don't need an ambulance. Just a shovel.'

I disagreed with him, but I was tied to a counter so, my disagreement didn't get me far.

'No, man, she's like, really hurt. Look at her!' A tweaker with a heart of gold. Aw.

'She's my property, not yours, and I say no ambulance.' Jimmy grabbed the bloody knife the other two had used to carve my thigh and cut my ties. 'Get up.' He pushed me off the counter and I fell to the floor in a pained heap.

'I am not cool with this, yo!' My saviour druggie turned and walked out muttering, 'This shit is not what I wanted for my life.'

You and me both, pal.

Jimmy grabbed me by the wounded wing and hauled me to my feet as he pointed a gun at my face. All of the pain hit me in a huge wave and I vomited all over his shoes.

'Stupid bitch!' His gun-free hand snaked around my throat and he pulled my face closer to his. 'I am going to fucking end you. Can't believe you went to the cops. I loved you and you went and narc'd on me.'

I should have been quiet or begged for my life; I've never been good at quiet, or begging. The gun was in my face and I was angry.

'Fuck you, you piece of shit! You call what you did to me love? That's not love, that's sickness. You're a fucking psychopath and I wish like fuck I had never met you.'

Just breathe, you're going to be….

BANG!

RAINTOWN SAM
Written by **Craig Saunders**

Years go by. People change their first names, but surnames, their family names – they live on. They're passed down, generation to generation. Place names, too, they stay the same for a long, long time, but they move around just like families do. Some are lonely towns and cities, like no other, like they're born out of mud with no father or mother or siblings. They're individual, unique. Raintown's not a special name at all. More of a nickname, maybe. The place has a real name – Harold's Ford – but people who've lived a while down there, under the hill and between the streams, they call it Raintown, just as locals might call their place Junktown, or something-Ville if they were American.

You'd expect it to rain all year round in a place purposely called Raintown, but it didn't. It rained just same as other small towns and villages around this country called England.

When the circus came to town, though..then? Oh, it rained. It started in '83, and it was in those thirteen days of rain that the Rain Clowns brought their show.

*

Sam Dunwich – just like the place, he'd tell people – was a drinker, and not a very good one, if dedicated at least. Four of four front teeth were missing – two atop, two from the bottom. Sam tended to become violent and angry when he'd been drinking.

Dunwich's a real place, too, down by the Suffolk, but Sam didn't know that. Never had, never would. Like anywhere else, it's a name that travels, isn't it? Either way, Sam was a man who didn't know much of much. On the dole, laid off from a

349

neighbouring town, a violent bottle covey looking sort with tattoos on his neck and knuckles (back in '83, when most people didn't have that kind of ink, and if they did people crossed the street). He was the kind of man your typical office worker wouldn't mess with, but really, Sam Dunwich wasn't quiet the psycho in whose boots he swaggered, but mostly made of yelling, and bile, with a couple of scrawny arms that looked glued on. He got by on bluster most places, but the Lionhart in Harold's Ford (he didn't think of it as Raintown back then, and not many did) wasn't most other places.

The first time through the short, country door, on which Sam wasn't ever in danger of cracking his head, he drank seven pints and tried being a tosspot with the landlord. Sam hit the floor with three teeth some way across the scrappy boards. A boot and the fourth tooth joined the rest, skittering away through the blood and spit on the wood from his mashed lips. He looked up, dizzy from all the shit kicking and not the beer to see an old guy standing over him. Not angry at all, and he didn't shout.

'My pub, son. My rules - drink, don't be a cunt. That's it. Anything else, I don't give a fuck. You want to shoot up in the john, go right ahead. Have a wank in there if you're up to it. Won't be the first or last, I 'spect. Pick yourself up, figure out if you want to drink or be a cunt.'

Sam, forty-four years old, jobless, no kids, no wife, no girlfriend, one stint of easy-enough-time for assault (just another fight in a pub, but some ponce thought it was worth piles on a hard wooden chair before a judge) had only just arrived in Harold's Ford, where he'd lucked on a cushy number with an old widow who needed a lodger and didn't seem fussed how much, or when, he paid. He wasn't likely to do better and he was smart enough to understand that.

Smart enough to know the Lionhart was the only pub in town that'd have him, too.

He sat up, one hand on the floor and one to his mouth. There was plenty of blood but enough beer in him for that chill whistle through smashed teeth to be nice and far away.

'Drink,' he said and walked a little sideways back to a battered table with cardboard coasters damp with beer and maybe even older than the woman in a bikini on the calendar hung behind the bar.

The landlord nodded, went back to the bar. Old guys with pale ale and bitter in mugs like the glass walls at the swimming baths shrugged or sniffed or did nothing and turned back to stare at nothing in front of them, or down, and drink.

Sam caught a soggy beer mat. 'Don't bleed everywhere, eh?'

Sam nodded, drank the rest of his pint out of bloodymindedness. That set his teeth yelling. He had another, and then took a Teachers back to his seat and the warmth was better. After a while it wasn't bloodymindedness which made him sit there 'til he was good and drunk, but being an alcoholic and not the best at that. He wasn't particularly good with anything.

But, it turned out, Sam might have been average at everything except being a shitty person, but he was really good at not dying.

*

Seventy-five years old, one arm missing and all his teeth (Sam had falsies, but only wore the top set because he figured looks don't matter when you're seventy-five and never getting laid again 'til you're in the dirt).

It might be a different landlord in the Lionhart but it was the same old Sam, if a little wiser, half as many arms, and teeth which weren't all his.

His fist ached, but nothing seemed broke. The lad on the floor whose face made Sam's fist ache couldn't have been more than twenty.

'Leave him be, Sam,' said the landlord. 'Quit it with that shit.'

'It's Raintown, sunshine,' said Sam, ignoring the landlord who

351

was as close to a friend a man like Sam ever gets.

A couple of the old boys who'd been around in '83 nodded in agreement with Sam.

The lad – a nipper – stood and reared up though he didn't need to. He was bigger at twenty-whatever than Sam had been at forty-four, and certainly now. Sam had his pint in his thick glass mug and didn't want to put it down so he took three strides forward (old, but nothing wrong with his legs), and smiling, he nutted the little prick. Missed his nose and caught a bottom tooth in his forehead. Literally. A bit of broken tooth jutted from Sam's wrinkled head.

The kid crumpled.

'Drink or bleed?' said Sam. Same choice a landlord gave him once, thirty-one years ago.

The present landlord nodded, caught the lad's eye, and tapped a big wooden sign with immortal words in black right across it. Drink, don't be a cunt.

The calendar might be gone, the old landlord, most of the old fellas from the eighties, the nineties, the noughties, but those words lived on.

Sam held out his hand. The kid swore, spat a bit of blood, but he swallowed the rest and took Sam's hand.

'Drink,' said the lad.

'Have a seat, young man,' said one of the old fellas. He has a bent old dog-end of a rolly in his mouth.

'Can't..got my arse kicked by a one-armed granddad.'

'You're alright,' said Sam and patted the lad. 'I promise I won't tell.'

'Maybe Sam here'll tell you 'bout his arm,' said the landlord, happy enough to give the lad a pint and a beer towel for the blood as long as the tenners kept sailing over the bar.

'The teeth,' said Sam, plucking out his falsies, 'I lost right here. The arm..?'

'Got a tooth stuck in your head,' said the landlord.

Sam plucked out the tooth. 'Want it back?' he said, holding out the tooth.

'No, ta,' said the lad.

Sam pushed a carrier bag with a newspaper in closer to his seat and nodded for the kid to sit, too. Sam always had a newspaper. The other old boys figured he read the paper every day, but he didn't – he just bought a newspaper everyday.

As Sam put the tooth there on the bar, that little white shard took him back, way back, through time, distance, place, like a photo or a song or a smell can, back to when he was a man down on his luck and that spell of misfortune all of his own making.

Down on his luck, but up, maybe, because carnies and circus folk are tight with each other, but they paid cash and Sam's arms were scrawny but more than good enough for a bit of lugging.

*

Saturday, Friday's kicking done, wind whistling through teeth Sam couldn't sort 'til Monday when he could figure out where a dentist might the-fuck-be, he wandered out his single room, ate two sausages and four eggs and drank tea when it was close enough to tepid. The sun shone, big bright shiny bastard hurting his whole face. Those big vans and lorries with rigs, big tops, caravans with performers, a bus, a couple of cars, were parked all around and out on the village field where kids would've played football ('til they got old enough to drink cider and frig each other off in the dark).

'Got work?' he asked.

A man, more tattoos than Sam, and maybe more ink than skin, held a sledgehammer and a pole.

'You don't look up to much.'

'Strong enough,' said Sam, talking without four teeth at the front still a novel thing for him.

'Talk to Michael. Red and white trailer. Knock.'

Sam nodded, walked, knocked.

353

Michael was the ringmaster, or announcer. Sam wasn't sure. The guy had a big moustache and Sam though he looked like a fair bit of a cunt.

'Twenty quid a day,' Michael told him. 'Two weeks. Lugging shit and you feed yourself. Good?'

They took turns nodding this time.

Saturday evening. The ringmaster, the compare, announcer, said the first words while he twirled a baton. Michael wore a crumpled red jacket with tails, and his long moustache was waxed.

'Ladies and Gentlemen..welcome to the worlds' famous Circus of Storms! Behold the GROTESQUE! The FANTASTIQUE! Fresh from Europe, welcome France's favoured sons and daughters..the MIRACULEUX of Le CIRQUE DU TEMPETE!'

Sam sniffed and went outside and it rained and the rain didn't stop until closing night.

*

There were fewer punters by closing night and the grand finale, but that was nothing strange. Even in a big town business tails off by the end of any road show, and Harold's Ford wasn't a big town.

On the twelfth day, the day before Friday night and the last big hurrah, the man with more tattoos than skin brought his big old sledgehammer down on a long steel peg which held the many ropes around the big top. Sam Dunwich didn't know the man's name, and hadn't asked. Neither of them particularly cared. The man was bastard strong and Sam struggled to keep up, but he wasn't a pussy, either, and keep up he did. He ached, but he was paid daily and at the end of this week he'd have a sweet £260 tucked away, minus beer and chips and battered sausages and £50 rent for the month.

Sam held the peg, all three feet, nice and steady. Those pegs held up the big top. They weren't camping pegs, but solid and heavy. The sledgehammer at the end of the man whose name Sam didn't know drove those things about two feet into the dirt.

They'd done this routine night after night, and every morning, because it always rained when the circus came to town, but in '83 it bucketed and blustered. The ground was sodden and squelched, sucked at Sam's shoes. Everything was damp.

Twelve days, out in the rain, cold but not grumbling, Sam and Sledgehammer went round the old big tent and slammed the pegs back into the dirt. This time, the blow sheared

away, angled, came down and smashed Sam's right hand. The head was 8lbs of steel. It hit just about three or four inches from his wrist. It destroyed the radius, the ulna. The force shattered carpals and three of his fingers snapped when his hand came free of the peg and slammed into the wet earth. It tore tendons from hand to elbow, veins, arteries, capillaries..everything there was to smash was smashed all to fuck.

Sam observed as much, but nice and calmly, he thought.

'Smashed that all to fuck, didn't you?' he said, down there with his hair plastered to his face in the pouring rain.

'Fuck. Sorry. Sorry..sorry.'

'It alright,' said Sam, who looked at the hand flopping at the end of his arm with a weird, stunned, bemused turn of his tight, mean lips. 'Fine. No problem.'

'Jesus. Oh..Jesus fuck.'

'Don't worry,' said Sam.

It took him about seven minutes before he figured out what had happened. He figured out his hand wasn't coming back when he was in the red and white trailer, screaming. Michael, the one with the waxy moustache, held Sam down and put a thick old stick which looked like it'd been chewed by a dog between Sam's broken teeth.

'We look after our own, right?'

Sam thrashed, but the rain didn't stop and neither did the breadknife with crumbs still on it.

Crumpet? Scone? Toast? Marmite sandwich?

He remembered thinking that. Remembered thinking, too, that at first the man called Michael didn't have his red coat on, and that later, he did.

*

'Leave off, granddad. Pyscho carnies? Bollocks.'

Sam shrugged. 'Weren't the carnies.'

'What, who cut your arm off?'

'No..they cut my arm off alright. Saved me. Maybe. Then. But it was a kid called Leon saved my life.'

'Wait..I'm..'

'Lost?'

The lad nodded. He drank his beer, stared at his tooth on the bar.

'That's still yours,' said Sam.

The lad shook his head this time.

'Sam,' said the last of the old timers. Everyone nodded, nobody shook hands. Why bother? It wasn't that much different from lodging with each other. They lived in the pub, even if they slept elsewhere.

Sam took a breath and took out a tab, which he offered but no one took and he didn't mind that.

'Don't want it? Might be able to glue the bugger in?'

'Nah.'

'Fair enough,' said Sam, and covered the tooth with the beer-sodden towel, like a sot's shroud, so he didn't have to keep looking at it.

R.I.P., another tooth gone too soon.

'Where was I?' said Sam. 'Yes. The carnies saved me, for while.'

'Saved you from what? Loony trampanzees?'

The landlord snorted.

Sam shook his head, and pointed to a small colourful flyer on shiny paper which was propped at the end of the bar.

'Ain't called Raintown for no reason...started with the Rain Clowns.'

'Fuck off, now you're just taking the piss. The circus? The same circus here, opening tomorrow night?'

'Sure.'

'Same one?'

Sam nodded. 'I'm not going.'

'Rain Clowns? Balls, you old bastard.'

Sam's look was sober enough. 'Balls to you, sunshine. Fucking things ate my hand.'

*

Sam woke up not on the twelfth, but on that last night, the thirteenth. He wasn't in a red and white trailer, either. He didn't remember that being damp, and cold, and black.

Something right up above him was making a hell of a ruckus, like he was under floorboards, but the big tent was on dirt. It had to be the big top, because he could hear kids laughing and cheering, but the sound drifted back and forth – not because they were moving, or because he was. He sort of drifted away from them. That was more like it.

His teeth, still not fixed, sang up when he stuck awake for longer than a few minutes. Maybe that was because it was a pain he was used to, and he was expecting it, so he looked for it first. A friend in a crowd you might hunt out, rather than going to talk to a bunch of strangers you don't know.

Jeering, clapping, laughing. Like the clowns just finished their show, flappy shoes and pratfalls and buckets of water and shit.

I'm under the big top. I can't be..but I am, just the same.

Somewhere dark and damp. Echoing. A smell like..

He remembered once, up north, going on a holiday before his mum left his dad before his dad killed her.

Where was it?

He remembered V's, or W's, carved into the walls. 'Wards against witches!' said the tour guide, turning off the lights and kids and adults both screaming like they'd farted lumps.

Poole's Cavern. That's the smell. Was that holiday the last time he remembered smiling?

Sam frowned. The last time? No, he'd smiled since. Sure. Of course I have.

Nothing down here but bats.

He lay facing up, back cold on the ground. Colder underground, he remembered. Same temperature, anyway. No sun. No seasons under the dirt.

He remembered pools of pure, crisp water, and thinking that his thirst hit him. Not for beer or whiskey or whatever else, but for water. His head thumped with a headache more from dehydration than being shitfaced.

He sat up, pushing with his hands like people do, but wonky because one of his hands wasn't there and falling sideways.

No other sounds down there except Sam's scream, bouncing back at him from the chill walls and the deep pools he couldn't see, but he knew they were there. Of course they were. He could hear them. Wet and slimy, smell and sound both.

Can't hear cave water, can you? Maybe a drip, once in a while.

Lot of rain. Probably pouring somewhere down here.

It's not a drip.

More of a shh..slshh. A chshk hsk.

Sam was good and freaked out, hurting and confused, and still not entirely comfortable enough with the stranger at this shindig to acknowledge him, and why the shifty, smug looking bastard made Sam stagger sideways instead of getting the fuck up.

'Someone there?'

The words didn't come out right.

'Thumwun?' was how it sounded, because of missing teeth and probably shock and certainly a fair bit of blood he couldn't really spare.

'Chsk.'

Someone else with their mouth all wrong. A different stranger, but not like the one he didn't want to talk to. This one spoke his language. This one held up a can of Tennants and a packet of tabs.

'Alright mate!'

Sam liked this one.

The other pain was a jealous sort, though, and distracted him with a pain like he'd never known, all the way up his arm, his shoulder, his head, eyes, ears, but down, too – unwelcome, inappropriate introductions. His guts and hips and balls even hurt.

I'm out, still. I'm dead. I'm in hospital. I'm on a seven-day bender with strippers and won the fucking pools.

All the stupid shit people tell themselves when they're in pain and scared in the dark.

'Fuck is it? Who the fuck is..is..'

There was a sickening, sucking, slurping sound of something licking his stump and he didn't seem to care. He'd won the pools and that sound wasn't something in a dank cave, but a gob job and a can of lager.

*

'Then? Then?'

Despite himself, his age, his temper and the times, the kid wanted to know where the story went.

Sam didn't have an ending, though. He shrugged and drained the last of his beer. He quit drinking when he was tired now, rather than passed out or skint. Times change a man, maybe not entirely, but in small ways and some of those important.

'Woke up. Turns out that kid – Leon? – he pulled me out. He still lives in town. With his mother. Not right in the head. Mental. Brain damage. Whatever. Scarred him, didn't it? Poor bastard.'

'Fuck? Is that it? What was it?'

'It was a Rain Clown. I never saw it. Thirteen people went missing in '83. That summer that kid Leon's girlfriend got killed. I lived. She died on the last night..not me. It should have been. But it wasn't. Thirty-one years it's been and even though it's a small town I never see him. Guilt, I guess. You believe that?'

'Fuck do I.'

The landlord put his busy-work down and looked at the young man. 'You all done drinking now? Sam? I'm closing up.'

'Don't believe me?' said Sam as he rolled up his pinned sleeve. There, above an untidy old ragged red stump, all around..red marks like dots, still fresh as the day a thing with a maw round and full of teeth sucked and licked at Sam's blood and marrow.

'I can still feel them. I feel them in my sleep and during the day.'

Sam fell quiet.

'Bullshit.'

'Fuck is it,' said Sam.

The lad stood, left his beer with an inch in the bottom and shook his head. He paused, like he was going to say good night, or thank Sam for the story, or something. Maybe he thought better of it. Sam remembered the lad was missing a tooth and not everyone forgives as quickly as an alcoholic might have, once upon a time.

He left without saying anything.

'That's that, then,' said the landlord.

'Seems so,' said Sam.

*

The Lionhart was still a dive, but this landlord washed up the glasses and the towels at the end of the night. When he picked up the towel – Fosters – over the tooth, the tooth wasn't there, but a small pool of something that stank and looked like rot and slime.

The landlord didn't see it. Sam did. He wiped the bar with his sleeve, still unpinned, and stood.

'I believe it's time I fucked off, too. Night.'

'Night, Sam,' said the landlord as Sam pushed open the door to the night.

A light rain, just a precursor, already fell. Once, Sam seemed to remember liking the rain. Not so much anymore.

He checked his watch. Saturday morning. The first day. In the light from over the swinging, hanging sign for the Lionhart there was a trail in the shingle car park where hardly anyone ever parked, right out onto the quiet road.

Thirty-one years is a long time to hold onto a grudge. Long time to hold onto a bread knife he might have gone back to get from a red and white trailer after the kid saved him and everything got weird.

Tonight, thirty-one years late, maybe, but rain doesn't stop in Raintown, neither does memory, and neither does getting even. A man gets used to not dying, especially when he's got one hand and a stump which has teeth marks all the way round.

Sam followed the trail with a bread knife in his hand, and one he'd never cleaned. People thought he was a nut, because wherever he went Sam always took a carrier bag, and always had a newspaper inside he never once read. He figured no one ever took him for a current affairs kind of fellow.

I'm not, he thought. Last time I kept up with current affairs was '83.

Maybe it's time to start. Maybe I will go see that kid after all, thought Sam. Maybe I'll be able to look him in the eye and have something right to say.

Sam walked along a wet, slug trail in the rain and clenched the old knife in a hand with thirty-one years to get strong enough for two.

THE END IS WHERE YOU'LL FIND IT
Written by **Michael Bray**

Autumn was in full force, leaving the pavements a carpet of crisp yellows and the trees bare and skeletal as winter made its relentless approach. Sophie had always liked this time of year when the air starts to bite a little against the skin. She clung to Sam's arm, glad she let him talk her into a Saturday morning walk. It was a little after ten and the streets were quiet. They were meandering, enjoying the cold and each other's company.

'Fancy a walk in the park?' Sam said, half turning towards her as the trees rained gold around them.

Sophie nodded. She knew the park and was familiar with it, yet she still felt a pang of anxiety. Sam knew the signs and squeezed her hand. 'It's fine if you don't want to. It was just an idea.'

'No, I'm fine. The park sounds nice.'

The park was empty apart from a couple of old people walking dogs. Often on a weekend, it would be full of people sitting on the grass or children swarming over on the playground area, but the cold weather had driven most indoors. The park was surrounded on three sides by trees with the entrance and road on the fourth side. A small park with a picnic area sat at one side with markings for football and rugby fields painted more towards the centre for when the local Sunday league teams would play, although it seemed there were no games scheduled for today. Although Sam and Sophie passed the park most days on the way to their respective places of work, they rarely visited it, life generally proving too busy for the most part, which made the chance to relax one they fully intended to make the most of. Like everywhere else, the trees were shedding their leaves and had left a carpet of gold and brown on the ground. As Sophie looked at it framed against the pale blue sky, she wondered why she had neglected to come for so long.

'This is nice,' Sam said as he led her through the gate. She followed and linked arms with him as they walked around the path edging the park. They were silent for a while, passing benches and waste bins, as well as the occasional green painted exercise machine installed by the council to encourage people to get out and exercise.

A small dog approached and sniffed them with enthusiasm, their owner nodding as they crossed paths.

'It's so quiet here.' Sophie said.

'I prefer that, though. It's like we have the place to ourselves.'

They were now at the back edge of the park, the expanse of grass now to their left, the trees to their right. Sophie was lost in thought, enjoying the silence, when Sam stopped, snapping her back to the present.

'Look at this,' He said, pointing towards the trees.

It would have been easy to miss. There was a narrow path disappearing into the tree line. Beside it, a small faded white sign read: *Sunshine Park.*

'I didn't know there was another park here. Shall we go take a look?' Sam said, taking a few steps towards the path.

Dread.

Sophie hated new places. She had an overwhelming fear of getting lost, and even though this was in her local area, a place she knew well, there was no escape from the butterfly feeling in her stomach which fluttered and rolled.

'I don't mind,' she said, not wanting to cause an issue or a problem. She knew Sam would understand if she were reluctant. They had been together for a long time and he was well aware of her fear of unknown places. Maybe because it was her local area and they lived less than a mile away, this wouldn't count as something she should be afraid of yet, something in her gut told her not to go down the path. She was sure, even though they hadn't been to the park for a while that the path wasn't there last time they visited, although it was possible she was wrong. It could have been out of sight of just unnoticed. It could even have been newly installed since they last visited. She tried to recall how long it had been since the last visit and guessed it was four years or more. She approached the sign, the grubby white steel rusting on the edges, the once vibrant black lettering faded and washed out. She touched it. The steel was cold and clammy, and she had the urge to wipe her hands on her jeans.

'You okay? We can just carry on walking, it's no big deal,' Sam said, putting his hands into his jacket pockets.

And she knew he meant it, and that was one of the things she loved about him. He understood how she felt and wouldn't make a fuss or cause drama if she decided she didn't feel comfortable enough to try it. She told herself it was stupid, that it was just a path to another part of the park. Nothing to worry about and if she couldn't conquer a small fear such as this, there was little hope she ever would.

'No,' she said, turning towards him and forcing a smile. 'Let's go take a look.'

She linked arms with him and they started down the narrow path.

II

Sophie's fears were unfounded. The narrow path curled for a short while through the trees before dipping. Beneath them, surrounded by a natural bowl of trees was the second park which from their vantage point looked spectacular caught in the light of the sun.

'Wow, how did we not know this was here?' Sophie said as they started down the sloped path. As they neared the park, Sophie's ears popped. The last time it had happened was when she was on an aeroplane. She turned to Sam to tell him what had happened and saw he was frowning.

'What's wrong?'

He looked at her and grinned. 'Nothing, it's just I don't understand how this place is here.'

'We've probably just missed it, that's all,' she said as they made it to level ground.

'No, that's not what I mean. I don't get the geography. I always thought Asda was on the other side of the park. Not this place.'

She paused to consider. There was indeed an Asda supermarket next to the park. She stopped and looked around her, craning her neck back towards the hill they had just descended then looked at Sam again. 'Yeah, I get what you mean. I think our sense of direction is off a little, though. The path here was curved, remember? I don't think this place is behind the other park directly, but next to it.'

'Oh, it's not a big deal, it just threw me off. Clearly, it's here, as we're standing on it, but for a second it threw me off.'

'What do you want to do?' Sophie asked, looking at the park. It was similar in design to the other one, but because of the fact that it was in a natural bowl of trees, it was more intimate and quiet. A path made of gravel instead of concrete curled around the edge of the park before disappearing into the tree line. Further ahead, they could see where it came out on the opposite side of a small reed filled pond. Ahead, they could see a woman jogging, her luminous lycra pants blinding in the sunlight. She followed the curve of the path into the trees and they were once again alone.

'It's nice here,' Sam said, already forgetting his concerns. 'What do you want to do?'

'We're here now, let's walk around it, then we can go home.'

'Sounds like a plan.'

A gentle breeze brought the subtle smell of fresh grass and flowers to them, and Sophie chose that moment to look at Sam, his features framed against the pale sky. They began to walk, and later, she would remember that moment, that decision not to turn back there and then, and how Sam still wore that ghost of a frown that said something was still bothering him.

III

'I can't believe how quiet it is here.' Sam said as they stood by the pond. A couple of ducks swam in lazy unhurried circles at the other side of the water, leaving ripples behind them.

'Yeah,' Sophie said, 'it's quiet.' There was no birdsong, no sound of traffic from the road. She suspected it was in part due to the nature of the surroundings, the lower elevation and trees filtering out all ambient noise. Still, it was enough to unsettle her and she was starting to wish they had just ignored the path to the second park and stuck to what they knew.

'Come on, let's carry on then we can get home,' Sam said, perhaps sensing her discomfort.

She was glad he said it as the more time she spent in the park the more uncomfortable it made her feel. He took her hand and led her around the path into the trees. The light of the day was swallowed by the branches, giving the entire place a foreboding feel. As with the rest of the park, no birds sang, in fact, now that she was actively listening, Sophie couldn't hear any sound other than the ones they were making. The path curved through the trees, the ground at either side a carpet of brown leaves. Even Sam had grown quiet, and she wondered if he had tuned into the unique vibe of the place. They followed the curve, and although it wasn't something they vocalised, both of them were glad to see the sunlight scattered across the path that signalled they would once again be in open air. They increased their pace, neither having to speak yet instinctively knowing what the other was feeling. They reached the warmth of the sun, its golden rays warming them. Sophie felt herself relax, only then realising how tense her body had been.

'I don't understand.' Sam said.

She opened her eyes and focused on him. The frown had deepened and beneath it, she saw something new. Something she hadn't witnessed before. She could see fear. There was no need to ask what was wrong. Just looking around gave them their answer. They should have been by the pond, the gentle curve bringing them out on the other side so they could follow the rest of the path around towards the way they had entered. She wondered if they had gone the wrong way, or if the path had gone in a different direction to the one they had expected, but she instantly dismissed each notion. The path went the way it should have, the curve following the contours of the unseen pond. As they exited, it should now be to their left, the way they had come across the water beyond it. Only now, as they looked at it, there was no pond. Where it should have been was an expanse of grass and a small picnic area comprising of half a dozen wood tables. The path they had walked when they entered the park was also gone. Instead, neatly cut grass stretched away into the distance behind them. The path they were on stretched out ahead of them before dipping out of sight downhill.

'I don't...I...' Sam looked at her, struggling to find the words. 'What's going on here?'

Sophie would have replied, but her brain was too preoccupied to action such petty things as conversation. She was staring at this new landscape, knowing it shouldn't be there, and what she was looking at was impossible. She tried to speak, failed, then licked her lips and tried again. 'Let's go back. I want to go home.'

'Yeah, I think that's the best idea.'

They turned to retrace their steps, both of them staring and trying to figure out what was going on. There were no trees. No path. What had been there seconds earlier was now gone. In its place was a green painted fence, its top ringed with barbed wire. On the fence was a faded sign, the screws holding it in place rusty and weeping brown streaks down the façade of the sign. Even so, they could see the words printed there.

NO ADMITTANCE. ACCESS TO PARK STAFF ONLY.

Beyond the fence, more open fields stretched as far as they could see.

'I don't understand,' Sam muttered, looking around as if the answers would be scattered on the ground around him.

'Sam, what do we do now?' Sophie said, hearing herself as if from some distance away. she thought it was because of the situation, and how it was her way of tuning out to what was happening, but as she listened to Sam repeat how little he understood the situation, she realised it wasn't her brain causing her to sound distant, it was this place. The air was different and words and sound carried differently. She remembered how her ears had popped when they first followed the path to get to the park and wondered if that was when they had stepped out of the ordinary and into whatever strange world they had entered.

'I don't understand, we didn't stray from the path.'

'Sam,' she said, trying to get his attention, but Sam was struggling to deal with the situation in his own way and as men were apt to do, was trying to figure out a solution. He had his hands on the green painted metal fence, shaking it as if touching it would break some illusion.

'Sam?'

'It's not possible. The trees were just here…'

'Sam, are you listening to me?'

'Then the pond. Why isn't it there?'

'Sam,' she said again, grabbing his arm. He looked at her, broken from his loop of disbelief.

'What do we do now?' He asked.

She had no answer. She had never seen him like this. He had always been confident, always able to solve problems and do so without drama. Now, though, in the face of something nobody would even have any hope of handling, he was close to breaking. She couldn't blame him. She was close to that place too, the fear in the back of her throat a thick, bitter thing she could taste.

'I know,' he said, turning away from the fence, eyes bulging as he took in the new surroundings. 'We'll call someone. Call for help.' He took his phone out of his jeans pocket and stared at the display. 'Mine's dead.' He said. 'What about yours?'

She took hers out of her bag, knowing before she looked it was pointless. Even though the phone had been fully charged before they came out of the house, now the display was blank. She held the power button to try and restart it without success.

The two of them stood and stared at their new surroundings, the silence like a physical thing clinging to them.

'That woman.' Sophie said, turning to Sam, hating how dull and muted the words sounded as they came out.

'What woman?'

'The jogger in the luminous leggings. She never came out.'

'Sam looked at her, the words still not sinking in. she sighed and explained in more detail.

'When we were walking towards the pond, there was that woman jogging head of us.'

'What about her?'

'She never came out of the other side of the pond either.'

'Don't say that. She probably did, we just didn't see her. It's not like we were paying attention to her.'

Sophie was paying attention, though. Even then, something about the vibe of the place had felt off to her, and so she had subconsciously made a note of the jogger and knew she hadn't come out on the other side of the pond when she had gone into the trees. She looked around, wondering if she too was here in this new place, hoping against hope to see those dazzling lycra pants further down the path, but they were completely alone.

'I want to go home. I need to get out of here.' Sophie could feel herself starting to lose it. Everything was starting to unravel for her and she didn't know how to handle it.

'Let's keep walking. Try not to worry just yet.' Sam said, the words empty and without meaning. Knowing there was no other choice, she allowed him to lead her further down the winding path past neatly trimmed grass and flower beds. They didn't speak, but unlike the peaceful quiet of earlier, this was a tense silence. The deeper they got into the park, the more they knew the geography of it was impossible. It simply couldn't fit in the world they had come from before her ears and popped and the silence had smothered them. With every moment that passed, Sophie could feel the tension rise, and with it, the fear which crept into her with the growing cold. It was as she was in this half daydream state that Sam stopped walking. She blinked and looked at him, then followed his line of sight.

There was a man on the path.

He was standing by a rose bush, hands clasped behind his back, balding head gleaming in the sunlight as the breeze fluttered the ring of snow coloured hair which remained. He hadn't yet seen them and seemed lost in smelling the pink roses.

'We'll ask for help.' Sam said, stepping forward. Sophie grabbed him. She looked at the man in front of them and the fear and tension increased a notch. Something didn't sit right, her internal warning system screaming that there was a problem. She wondered if it was the way his spindly frame seemed almost arachnid or the way his shadow stretched out on the concrete path ahead of her, freakishly malformed and elongated by the lowering sun. Or maybe it was the fact that he didn't appear to be lost or trapped in the same way they were. He looked like he belonged there, part of wherever it was they had stumbled into.

'What is it?' Sam said, frowning at her. Although it made sense in her head, she knew it wasn't something she would be able to explain to Sam in a way he would understand. She lowered her eyes to the concrete, unsure what do.

'Just wait here, I'll go talk to him, okay?'

She nodded, even though it wasn't okay. Not at all. She didn't want to be left alone, even if it was only ten feet or so between them and the man. But she also didn't want to be near the flower sniffing stranger, so she hung back, agitated and shifting her weight from one foot to the other as she watched Sam approach the man. They spoke for a few seconds, and Sam gestured towards her then turned back to the man. After a few seconds, Sam waved her over and she approached, setting eyes on the old man for the first time. There was no hostility in his eyes, and it took her a few seconds to realise that wasn't all. There was no *anything* in there. His eyes were like those of a doll and she suppressed a shudder.

'I understand you two have lost your way?' the old man said, his voice brittle and dull. He folded his slender hands in front of him and smiled. 'We get that a lot. It's a much bigger place than people think.'

'Can you point us to the way out?' Sam asked. Sophie wondered if he got the same sense about him she did and was grateful to have him there.

The old man exhaled and looked around. 'Well, the end is where you find it, son.'

Sam and Sophie exchanged glances. The old man was straight faced then chuckled. 'Relax, it was just a little joke and not one you would get.'

'Can you help us?' Sophie said.

The old man pointed a withered finger down the path. 'Keep going that way. Stay on the path and you'll find your way back to where you were.'

Sam and Sophie exchanged glances, bringing another dry chuckle from the old man. 'Not so confident I see?' The old man shrugged 'I get that. Easy to get yourself turned around in here. It's bigger than it looks.' He paused, flicking a shrivelled pink tongue tip against withered lips. 'Tell you what. As I don't have any plans right now, I can show you. You don't want to be getting lost again now, do you?'

'No, no we don't. Thank you.' Sam said.

The old man squinted at the sun lowering in the sky and exhaled. 'Well, daylight's wastin' so we better get moving. Come on, follow me.'

The old man had looked so withered and crooked that Sophie expected him to shuffle off down the path at painfully slow speed, and was surprised when the opposite was true. He set off at a brisk tempo, arms still clasped behind his back. They followed the man as he walked a little way ahead of them.

'This has been a weird day,' Sophie said, still uneasy.

'Yeah, you're telling me. I don't get how we got so lost. The downside of exploring a new place I suppose.'

'Yeah, it all got a bit confusing.' There was more she wanted to ask of course and she was sure he was the same. There was the question of why the geography had changed. What had happened to the fence or the lake and the woman in the luminous joggers, but they decided not to address those particular elephants in the room as to think too much about them would only make them acknowledge that until they were back in familiar territory, the danger was still very real.

'I just can't wait to get home and watch some TV.' Sophie said, trying to steer the conversation to normal things so they didn't have to acknowledge the weirdness.

'Yeah, feet up and relaxing sounds good to me.'

'The old guy can move,' Sophie said, noting that he had opened a lead on them and was now around twenty feet down the path.

'Yeah, we better pick up the pace and catch up.'

They increased their speed, not wanting to get left too far behind. There was an incline ahead, and they reasoned it would slow the old man a little. 'Jesus that guy is fit for his age,' Sam said as the old man ascended the hill at the same pace, his feet still moving with the same monotonous rhythm, hands still clasped behind his back. Sophie said nothing, she knew something was wrong. They were walking faster than the old man now yet were getting no closer to him. If anything the gap was growing bigger.

They too started up the hill, the burn in their calves causing them to slow.

'Hey, can you wait for us?' Sophie shouted, hating the shrill desperation in her voice.

If the old man heard her, he didn't turn, nor did his pace slow. He was almost to the crest of the hill now and both Sophie and Sam sped up as they didn't want to fall behind. He disappeared over the top before they were halfway up it. Sophie stumbled over her own feet, twisting her ankle which exploded in pain. She winced but somehow carried on walking.

'You alright?' Sam said, holding on to her arm.

'I'm fine. Let's just catch up.' she said through gritted teeth, desperate to keep the old man in their sights.

They reached the top of the hill, both of them breathing heavily. The ground didn't level out, but dropped away again and curved off to the right before it was out of sight due to the tree cover on the right side of the field. They could see the old man but he was now impossibly far away from them. He was already at the bottom of the hill and making his way up the path, his pace still the same steady tempo, hands still clasped behind his back. The night was creeping up on them, the sun dipping behind the tops of the trees as the sky around it darkened.

'Can you run? We need to catch up.'

'I think so,' Sophie said. Her ankle was still tender and even walking was difficult. She was determined to try, though. They broke into a jog, and Sophie knew immediately it wasn't going to happen. She almost fell, wincing in pain as her ankle threatened to twist under her. Sam stopped and looked at her, but she could see he was agitated. Every few seconds he looked at the old man who still hadn't slowed.

'Go, just go catch up to him and tell him to wait. Don't go round the curve into the woods, though. Let's not lose sight of each other, please?'

'Okay, I promise, I'll wait for you at the bottom.'

There was nothing else to be said as he was already on his way, the decline aiding his momentum as he broke into a steady jog.

Sophie limped on after him, going as fast as she dared. The further away he moved the colder the fear in her gut became. The sky was now growing darker, and her shadow was no longer visible on the pavement. It was impossible, as they had only been out of the house for an hour, maybe less, and yet a full day seemed to have passed. Like everything else about the place, it troubled her greatly. Sam had halved the distance to the old man now and was definitely catching up. She focused on making her way down the hill. The last thing she wanted was to fall and further aggravate her ankle. The ground levelled out and with the trees on both sides of the path she was more aware of the coming dark. She could see the first signs of stars in the twilight, the constellations unfamiliar and somehow wrong. Ahead, the old man had gone around the curve and was lost from view because of the trees. Sam stopped and looked back, cupping his eyes over his brow. Sophie picked up her pace, relieved he was waiting for her. She waved to him, hobbling as fast as she could but he didn't return the gesture. He followed the old man into the woods.

'Sam, wait,' she shouted, but the words didn't project. They seemed to fall dead around her feet as she hobbled after him. The fear had crept into her now and she could feel her heart thundering. With the loss of the sun, the park had grown cold, the shadows thick and heavy between the trees on either side of the path.

'Sam,' she shouted again, but the words were lost again, this time by the wind which was starting to bluster and swirl dead leaves around her feet. As she rounded the curve in pursuit of Sam, she saw someone coming the other way. It was the woman jogger in the luminous pants.

'Excuse me, can I just ask...' Sophie let the words trail away. The woman didn't acknowledge her. Instead, she stared straight ahead with glassy eyes, face pallid in the gloom, arms pumping as she ran.

'Hello, wait, have you seen...'

She was already gone, heading towards the hill Sophie had just descended. Rational thought was hard now, as with every passing moment more fear crept into her. She knew if she let it fully consume her, she would be no good for anything and likely be stuck there forever. She glanced over her shoulder at the jogger in the pink pants and wondered how long she had been there in the park, trying to find the way out or get back to where she started. She turned her attention back to the path as it curved into the trees, expecting it to be empty, but to her surprise, she could see Sam just ahead of her. He had his back to her and was standing by the edge of the path looking into the trees. She hobbled towards him, angry at him leaving her.

'What the hell did you do that for? I asked you to wait for me.' She put a hand on his shoulder and turned him around, drawing breath as any hope of staying calm and rational evaporated.

It wasn't Sam. It was the old man. He smiled at her, dentured grin wide and far too perfect. The deep lines on his weathered skin had made his face a ghastly mask, and she stepped back. It was then she realised things had changed again. The trees were gone. She was now back by the pink rose bush at the top of the hill. His grin widened, a little too wide, and those dead dolls eyes looked her up and down.

'I understand you've lost your way? We get that a lot. It's a much bigger place than people think.'

Sophie couldn't do anything but stare. It was déjà vu in the worst possible sense. She had lived this before, experienced it already, only then she had Sam. Now she was alone. The old man inhaled, turning his face towards the rose bush.

'Please, I just want to get out of here.' She croaked, her voice brittle and close to cracking.

The old man exhaled and looked around. 'Well, the end is where you find it.'

Sophie took a step back, the pain in her ankle forgotten. Or maybe her body was just numb to what was happening. She heard someone coming and saw the woman in the pink lycra jogging towards them, eyes blank, black streaks on her cheeks where tears had dislodged her makeup. The old man watched her go and chuckled, clasping her hands behind his back.

'Please, where's Sam?' Sophie said.

The old man pointed a withered finger down the path towards the hill. 'Keep going that way. Stay on the path and you'll find your way back to where you were.'

Sophie shook her head. Everything was wrong and she could feel herself starting to slip towards the point of no return.

The old man chuckled again, the smile melting from his dead, featureless face. 'Not so confident. I get that. Easy to get yourself turned around in here. It's bigger than it looks.' He paused, flicking a shrivelled pink tongue tip against withered lips. 'Tell you what. As I don't have any plans right now, I can show you. You don't want to be getting lost again now, do you?'

'No.' she snapped, knowing it was too fast. Something told her that if she didn't play along with whatever was happening, things would get much worse for her.

The old man shrugged, glassy eyes locked on her. 'Don't want me to show you?' Better get on moving down the path. That fella of yours is on the hill last I saw.'

'He's not there I...' Only now when she looked, he *was* there. She could see him. Hands in pockets as he ascended. He wasn't alone, there was someone with him. A woman. One that looked just like her. 'This is impossible,' she whispered.

'Better get a move on, missy,' the old man said, turning back to his flowers. 'This place ain't too safe after dark.'

She didn't doubt it. Sophie started after Sam and the woman he was with, trying to ignore that his companion wore the same clothes as she did, that she had the same hairstyle from the back. She was even hobbling as if she had an injured foot. Sophie hurried after them, a passenger in her own body as night fully swallowed the park. The hill didn't seem as steep this time, and she closed the distance, halving it just before Sam and the woman crested the brow of the hill. She passed a bench she didn't recall seeing before to her right. The woman in the pink joggers was sitting on it, elbows on knees, head in hands, shoulders moving as she sobbed. Sophie knew she should be able to hear it, but the whole thing was silent as if muted. Beside her, the old man from the rose bush sat, one skinny arm draped over her shoulder as he consoled her, the too wide and white grin stretching across his face. Sophie looked away and focused on Sam. He was at the bottom of the hill now, but he was hard to pick out in the dark. She couldn't tell if the woman was still with him or not. She hurried, unable to tell if she was getting closer. She had heard about people disappearing all the time and wondered if some of them had wandered into places like this. Places which made no sense or had no real rhyme or reason to exist. It wouldn't be a surprise to her. She focused on the shadowy figure on the road ahead, still unsure if she was closer or further away or if it was even Sam at all. She couldn't think about that now. Sophie lowered her head and sped up, determined to find the end. The shadowy figure ahead rounded the curve into the trees and Sophie followed. Maybe this would be the end. Maybe this would be where she would find it. She was determined to do so, even if it took forever.

DON'T MAKE FUN OF THE HAUNTED HOUSE
Written by **Jeff Strand**

Harvey planned to make fun of the carnival's haunted house the entire time he was inside. No way would it actually be scary. His almost-girlfriend June would snuggle up against him in the car and he'd impress her by saying something funny every time there was a 'frightening' part. He hadn't worked out any of his material yet, but he was confident in his ability to come up with witty comments on the spot.

'This is gonna be so lame,' he said, as they stood in line.

'It'll be fun!' June insisted.

'Whatever.'

Harvey had to prove his bravery because he'd vomited after they rode the Ferris Wheel. He'd tried to blame the three deep-fried Twinkies he'd eaten earlier, which may indeed have contributed but not as much as his petrifying fear of heights. Though June had laughed it off, Harvey was now the kind of person who puked after a carnival ride, and girls didn't let guys feel their boobs after that sort of thing. Not that June had much in the way of boobs, but there was *something* under that sweater, and for his first grope, Harvey wasn't going to be choosy. He'd worry more about chest size in future girlfriends.

The line was moving quickly. The door to the ride, which was painted to look like a spooky iron gate, opened and a cart emerged. The rider was this old dude who looked almost thirty, and he'd only gone in about a minute ago, so it was a short-ass haunted house.

'What do you want to do after this?' asked Harvey.

'Roller coaster?'

Harvey hated that idea. 'Sure.' At least it wasn't one that went upside down.

They reached the front of the line. Harvey let out a tiny snort of laughter at the guy at the entrance, who was wearing a black cloak and had on stupid looking makeup like he thought he was the Grim Reaper or something.

'Where's your thing?' Harvey asked him.

'What thing?'

'Your sword thing. That thing you carry.' Harvey mimed swinging a bladed weapon.

'My scythe?'

'Is that what it's called?'

'I no longer carry a scythe. Too many innocent bystanders got their heads cut off.'

Harvey chuckled. But it wasn't an amused chuckle; it was a chuckle to show June how dumb he thought this Grim Reaper guy's joke was. He hadn't cut off anybody's head. If he *did* own a scythe, and he probably didn't, it was made of plastic or something lame like that.

He and June held up their arms to show him their 'ride all day' wristbands, then pushed through the turnstile and got into the empty cart.

'Phones in the spider web,' said the Grim Reaper, pointing to some netting in front of their knees. 'Lights make the ghosts angry.'

Harvey and June put their phones into the netting, then Harvey pulled down the metal lap bar. Like they would even need a lap bar on this ride. Ha.

June smiled. It looked like a genuine smile, as if she was excited for this haunted house. Maybe she scared easily. Harvey considered whether his approach should be to have fun on the ride instead of mock it, but decided that, no, she might think he was spooked if he didn't ridicule the horrors within.

The door opened, and the cart moved forward into darkness.

'Oooooh, darkness,' said Harvey in his most sarcastic voice.

'Am I supposed to be scared yet?'

June didn't answer his rhetorical question. A recording of piano music played that theme song to that boring movie with the guy in the white mask.

The cart moved forward for a few seconds then came to a stop. A skeleton lit up in front of them.

A skeleton? That was it? Even a three-year-old wasn't scared of a skeleton.

'Ooooooh, a skeleton,' said Harvey.

The cart turned right. Harvey wished he'd said something funnier about the skeleton, like 'I've got a bone to pick with you!' or 'That skeleton is so gay!' but it was too late now.

They rode in darkness for a couple of seconds, then a fake looking zombie lit up, making Harvey jump.

Had June noticed? He prayed June hadn't noticed.

She giggled and patted his knee. 'It's okay.'

He was humiliated..but then again, she'd touched his knee. She might not have done that if he hadn't jumped.

The cart turned left. The door opened and they emerged from the haunted house into daylight.

That was it? A skeleton and a zombie? Despite his flinch, this ride was even less scary than he could possibly have imagined. If he'd used actual tickets instead of the armband, Harvey would've been *pissed*.

The cart didn't stop. The door on the other side opened, and the cart returned to darkness.

'The Grim Reaper's incompetent,' said Harvey. 'I guess that's why he's running a carnival ride instead of collecting souls and stuff.' That was a good one. Harvey needed more jokes like that.

'Free ride!' said June. Harvey couldn't tell if her enthusiasm was real or not.

Technically, they could ride it as many times as they want. This just meant they didn't have to stand in line again. Harvey almost corrected her then decided against it.

They stopped at the non-scary skeleton, then they stopped at the non-scary zombie (Harvey didn't jump this time), and then the door opened and they emerged from the haunted house again. A woman and a little girl had just gotten into the cart in front of them. Their cart went inside. Harvey and June's cart didn't stop.

'Hey!' Harvey called out to the Grim Reaper as they rode back inside.

Harvey didn't think he could handle the boredom of going through this a third time. But, on the bright side, it gave him the opportunity to use the joke he'd missed before.

'I've got a bone to pick with you,' he said as they stopped in front of the skeleton.

June didn't laugh. That was extremely disappointing.

They stopped in front of the zombie again. Harvey wished he'd thought of a joke for that one. He should probably come up with one in case they went through a fourth time. And maybe a better one for the skeleton while he was at it.

'Hey!' Harvey called out again, after the door swung open. 'Don't forget to stop us this time.'

'You're not done yet,' said the Grim Reaper as they passed. The cart went back inside.

Harvey tried to pull up on the lap bar. It didn't budge. In fact, though it hadn't bothered him before, the bar was pressed against his lap pretty hard. He wanted to ask June to help him try to lift it, but didn't want her to think he wasn't strong enough.

'I guess I made him mad,' said Harvey as they stopped in front of the skeleton. 'He's just messing with us.'

'It's okay. I'll ask him next.'

They rode out of the haunted house yet again. 'I apologize for him,' said June with a laugh. 'We're ready to get off now.'

The Grim Reaper shook his head as the cart continued moving.

Harvey tried harder to pull up the bar. It absolutely would not move. June pulled as well, but working together made no difference. Harvey wasn't worried, of course, but this was becoming annoying.

'Stop the ride or we'll tell your boss,' Harvey said on their next round.

The Grim Reaper did not stop the ride.

Harvey wasn't *too* worried, but he was a *little* worried. What if the guy was mentally ill?

He decided to try a different tactic. The next time they passed the Grim Reaper he let out a big yawn to show how bored and not frightened he was.

The ride didn't stop.

The bar went all the way across the cart. Harvey tried to slide up, but, no, he couldn't move. Even June, who was smaller, was stuck.

'This isn't funny anymore,' said Harvey, as they stopped in front of the zombie. 'I'm going to make sure he gets fired. This is kidnapping.'

'We should call the police,' said June.

Harvey agreed. Unfortunately, they couldn't reach their cell phones.

Now he was starting to get scared.

'Scream for help when we come out,' he told June.

They emerged from the haunted house. 'Help!' June shouted at the six or seven people in line. 'We're trapped!'

The people at the front of the line laughed and waved like they thought June was kidding around. Surely they had to have noticed that they'd gone through several times already, right? Shouldn't they at least be angry that Harvey and June were getting all of these extra rides while they were waiting?

Skeleton. Zombie. Daylight.

June screamed for help again, flailing her arms this time. Now there were only three people left in line. Harvey could see that they'd closed off the line to newcomers, even though the carnival was open until nine and it was only about five-thirty.

'This isn't a joke!' Harvey shouted. 'We're prisoners!'

The people didn't seem to believe them. Harvey supposed he wouldn't have believed them either.

'Can you cry?' he asked June.

'Why?'

'If you're crying when we come out the next time, they'll believe us.'

Harvey almost thought he could come up with tears of his own if June couldn't deliver, but she was crying by the time they reached the zombie. Unfortunately, there was nobody left in line when they came out of the haunted house.

'Let us go!' Harvey shouted.

'You wanted to be scared, didn't you?' asked the Grim Reaper.

They went back into the house.

Skeleton. Zombie. Daylight.

Skeleton. Zombie. Daylight.

Skeleton. Zombie. Daylight.

'I'll kill you!' Harvey shouted.

The Grim Reaper didn't seem intimidated.

Skeleton. Zombie. Daylight.

'Help us!' Harvey screamed. 'Somebody! Anybody! We're trapped in the haunted house ride! He won't let us off! Somebody call the police!'

Nobody paid attention. Harvey didn't know if it was because they couldn't hear over the other loud carnival noises, or if it just sounded like something a teenager on a ride would shout to clown around.

Skeleton. Zombie. Daylight.

Again and again and again.

Finally they couldn't scream anymore. They sat in the cart, weeping quietly. Harvey no longer cared what June thought of him. He just wanted to get off this ride and go home.

The daylight gradually turned to darkness. Though there were still other colorful lights from the carnival, the haunted house itself had no outside illumination.

Skeleton. Zombie. Skeleton. Zombie. Skeleton. Zombie.

How many times had they gone through? Hundreds? Harvey didn't even know anymore.

Every once in a while he'd beg the Grim Reaper to stop. Sometimes the Grim Reaper would say no, and sometimes he'd silently shake his head, but the answer was always the same.

Harvey was sure that the background music was burned into his brain. He didn't think he'd ever *not* hear it again.

Oh, God, what if they starved to death on this ride? Well, they'd dehydrate first.

He didn't have to worry about that. You could live a couple of days without water. No way could they stay on this ride that long without the cops showing up. After the carnival closed and he didn't come home, his parents would get worried about him.

Skeleton. Zombie. Skeleton. Zombie. Skeleton. Zombie. Skeleton. Zombie.

Occasionally June would stop crying for a moment and giggle, which was worrisome.

He didn't want to die on this stupid ride, even if it didn't seem quite so stupid anymore.

The rest of the carnival lights went out, but the ride continued.

After several rounds of begging to be let off so he could go to the bathroom, Harvey wet his pants, which was so humiliating that he stopped caring if he *did* die.

He had no idea how long they'd been on the ride. It couldn't have been all night, since it was still dark out, but it felt like years.

'*Please*,' he said, his voice barely a whisper. He wasn't even sure if he was inside the haunted house or outside at this point. '*Let us off.*'

'Nope,' said the Grim Reaper, so they must've been outside. 'You wanted a scary ride, right? What could be scarier than being driven insane?'

Skeleton. Zombie.

Before the sun rose, the skeleton and zombie were laughing.

Harvey and June laughed along with them.

TRUST ISSUES
Written by Mark Cassell

The roar of music deadened as I closed the door behind us, though it still thumped beneath my boots. I followed the idiot, remaining close to his heels while inhaling the stink of cigarettes. We headed towards the mahogany desk where Deacon waited. Just as he had on our way through the nightclub, the man threw another pathetic glance over his shoulder. Yet again I glared down at him. My hand curled into a fist. I expected him to bolt at any moment.

Giving how I was feeling due to my own personal problems, I seriously wanted to hurt someone.

'Deacon,' I said and clamped the man's neck, 'this guy has some news for you.'

The boss removed his reading glasses and leaned back in the worn leather chair. It creaked. His lips whitened and he gave me a short nod. 'Thank you, Aaron.'

I tightened my grip and whispered, 'Tell him,' then released his neck.

He squirmed, coughed, and whimpered.

My jaw rippled as I bit down the urge to wrinkle my nose. His clothes reeked of more than cigarettes. Perhaps it was sewers, given the filth that caked his overcoat and jeans. I'd found him beside the truck, shivering. He'd looked even more pathetic than he did now, at the time jabbering about things in the fog.

God only knew where the rest of his boys were.

Deacon lowered his eyes to the paperwork littering the desk and began to shuffle them. 'So..'

The man began speaking. Rapid nonsense, something about the shipment, the guards opening fire, a glass cube, shadows and the fog, and—

'Shut up.' Deacon stood, both fists pushing into the desk. He leaned forward, eyes narrowing. 'Shut. The fuck. Up!'

The man's shoulders slumped and I shoved him. He grunted, and almost tripped over his unlaced shoe. I stepped away and manoeuvred round the desk to stand beside my boss. Again, I thought of earlier when found this man huddled beneath the truck, knees tucked under his chin.

'What's your name?' Deacon asked.

A lick of the lips, and a reply: 'Michael.'

'So, Michael, you're the little shit I trusted to undertake this job.' Deacon remained leaning into his desk, glaring at the other man. 'And what I get from the shit that just poured from your mouth, you've accomplished only half of it.'

'Technically, Boss,' I said, 'two thirds..'

Deacon shot me a look and raised an eyebrow.

I immediately regretted opening my mouth, and explained: 'We've recovered three containers as intended, yet one..'

'One what?'

I didn't know how to continue.

Again, the other man whimpered like a dog. We both looked back at him.

'One contains..' I said. 'Something else.'

Deacon stepped back. 'I have two containers of goods and *something* else. What's this about a glass cube?'

'A cube,' Michael said, 'a glass tank. But you don't under—'

'I understand enough to know that I have only two-thirds of what I wanted.'

'But the fog!'

'What about it?'

'Once we loaded the containers on the truck, we set off.' He raked bitten fingernails through his hair.

Through clenched teeth, Deacon asked, 'What?'

'We encountered the fog. Never seen anything like it.'

'What the fuck does the weather have to do with my

containers?'

'No light could cut through it. So thick. We waited for it to pass.'

Deacon sat down without taking his eyes off the man. He slid open a desk drawer and removed the .38 Police Special he kept there. A proper old-school weapon. The barrel glinted in the dim office lighting. Some things you never ask a man like Deacon, and one such question is whether it was true he'd used that gun to kill his own mother and brother. From what I'd learned of my boss over the past three years, he was more than capable.

'I need you to get to the point,' he said and placed the weapon atop the paperwork, barrel facing Michael.

The man dropped his gaze to it. 'While we waited, I inspected the containers and that's when I found that one of the boys had opened it.'

'The container? This glass cube?'

Michael's eyes darted around the office. He scratched at his cheek. 'It was insane.'

'Tell me what this thing is!'

'It's huge, like a cube-shaped aquarium tank with some kind of device fixed to the bottom section. The fog leaked from the top.'

'Now we're getting somewhere.' Deacon ran his finger over the gun's grip.

'There were things in the fog, shadows, phantoms, I don't know. They swept over the truck. The men... their screams were deafening. Gunfire and ghosts.. the men vanished. I mean that, they vanished. Yeah, it was like ghosts. I.. we.. I mean—'

'Shut up, Michael,' Deacon said, 'you're talking utter shit!'

The man stared at the gun.

'Aaron?' Deacon looked at me.

I nodded. 'All three containers are heading to the warehouse. Two filled with weapons, and the other with some kind of cube, just like he said. All are safe and secured.'

'What *is* this cube?'

'Don't know.' It was the truth, I'd never seen anything like it.

'You must have some idea.'

'Reminds me of a magician's tank. You know, the glass one's those crazy bastards lock themselves into while it fills with water, only to escape moments before they're gonna drown.'

'And the fog?'

'By the time I got to this guy's truck, there was no fog. Only inside the cube. It was fastened shut. Nothing leaked.'

Michael nodded. 'I secured it.'

'And,' I continued, 'I didn't see any ghosts.'

Deacon looked back at Michael. 'I have the weapons. No problem.'

Michael finally looked away from the handgun between them. 'No problem?' His eyes softened.

'Sure,' Deacon said, 'no problem.'

'Thank—'

Deacon snatched up the .38 and its roar filled the office. Michael staggered backwards, a round red hole in his forehead, the flesh around it blackened and smouldering.

The beat of the music through the floorboards drowned the gunshot's echo.

*

I thumbed the Merc's key and watched Deacon approach the five-storey building. The blip echoed into the night and hazard-lights flashed orange, reflecting in puddles. A peeling *To Let* sign shivered on the wind, crudely nailed into crumbled brickwork beside grime-smeared windows. I had no idea what this place once was, and I doubted I'd ever been to this part of London. Since the container haul, a month ago, he had remained more secretive than usual.

As I followed the Boss, I pulled out my phone and once more read the text Harriet sent earlier:

Its over

My stomach twisted, and I jammed the mobile back in my pocket. Those two words smacked my ribcage like a constant reminder. Bitch. She'd been seeing some guy for the last year. I was such an idiot to not even see it coming. Bitch. Since receiving that message, I'd resisted the urge to reply with precisely that word.

I concentrated on keeping up with Deacon. The man's shoes tapped out a rapid rhythm on the cracked tarmac as he headed for the glass-fronted entrance. A bunch of keys rattled as he brought his hand up to unlock the door. The darkness inside turned the windows into black mirrors, and so our shadowy faces stared back. Deacon's scowl was something he always wore and it made his eyes tiny, whereas mine, however, was something new. I was fucking certain Harriet had given me mine, especially those two short vertical lines between my eyebrows.

The lock clicked and Deacon pulled open the door. We stepped into the cold building and I watched him lock up and pocket the keys. Our slight movements echoed through a barren reception area that smelled of mould, concrete, and burnt plastic.

'First floor,' he said and headed for the stairwell. 'You'll be the first of the boys to see the Cube and what we've done with it.'

Rumours among the other boys were that a bunch of scientists under his employment had been active with the glass tank, and the peculiar device it contained. Deacon's use of words here confirmed it. I had to admit, I was excited and had no clue what to expect.

Once on the landing, Deacon shoved open the double-doors and led me into an open-plan area.

I squinted at the spot-lit section cordoned off by a metal barrier. The centre of which housed the Cube. The thing still looked like one of those magician tanks, with its scratched glass and rusted edges. Just as I'd seen it before after finding Michael huddled under the truck, instead of containing water, a fog swirled inside the glass panels. This time, however, the fog was as black as smoke. It stood on a pedestal amid tangled cables and pipes that fed from the base, trailing off to a bulky plastic box at the perimeter of the barrier. This was something that hadn't been in the container. A row of dials and nozzles jutted from the top.

On this side of the fence, a tall man dressed in a white smock hunched over a computer station. Its soft white glow reflected from his glasses as he looked up at us. He nodded, a sharp jolt of his head, then went back to whatever it was he was doing.

We walked towards him.

A dozen questions tumbled through my head. What was so special about this Cube? Why had Deacon kept quiet since its discovery? What had these brainiacs developed? Despite my frantic thoughts, I felt privileged that I was finally there.

Deacon glanced at me as he reached the table.

I'd stopped at the barrier to watch the churning fog, now only a few metres away from me. Mesmerising, it seemed agitated since we'd entered the room. I guessed the white-smocked man had done something, perhaps to impress Deacon. The man kept looking up, his gaze jumping from the Boss and then back to the monitor.

Because I was closer, I saw a cylinder similar to a diver's air tank had been fastened to one side of the Cube. Red lights blinked in a vertical row, up and down its length.

'What is this thing?' I curled fingers around the cold barrier.

'It's my new business venture.' The corners of Deacon's mouth curled. He gestured to the man beside him, who responded with a rapid tap at the keyboard.

The fog thinned, seeming to get sucked downwards. The blackness becoming grey, becoming white... and revealing—

'What the fuck?' I whispered, leaning forward.

Deacon unlatched a section of fence and it swung inwards. He stepped over several clear-plastic pipes and approached the Cube.

I followed. 'Is that—?'

Deacon laughed. 'Yes.'

An intricate harness had been fixed to the upper and lower corners. Michael hung, suspended in the straps that pinched the dead flesh of his wrists and ankles. Truthfully, the only way I recognised him was the bullet hole in his forehead. Now, however, he was nothing more than a naked, shrivelled mess of green-grey flesh. Mottled, covered in lesions. Few things sickened me these days – I'd seen plenty of shit during my time with Deacon – yet this turned my stomach.

I swallowed.

Michael's hands and feet were missing. Instead, several tubes were stuffed into each stump, crudely stitched with the ragged flesh. They snaked and coiled away to link with a metal device fixed to the floor directly under the body. Curls of fog drifted along it, teasing a metal grate. Something green flashed in the corner of my eye. I looked up to see the cylinder's lights lit up to the maximum level: now a steady green. I didn't know what this insane contraption actually did, but I guessed the cylinder now contained the fog.

'Deacon..' My tongue stuck to my teeth, so I started again. 'Deacon…' Although I didn't really know what to say.

He looked at me, his lips twitched.

My voice sounded miles away. 'Deacon?'

'The Ministry of Defence were experimenting with some weird shit, Aaron.'

'You're not kidding.'

'Portals and dimensions. Some kind of extraction.'

This was ridiculous. Horrific and crazy. 'You're extracting a portal?'

'Not quite.' He gestured to the unit directly under the dead man's body. 'That device attached to the floor, taps into a portal to extract an *essence*.'

'An essence of what?' I shook my head and stepped closer. Morbid curiosity seemed to guide my feet. 'How is this even possible?'

'The mechanics behind this fucking thing go way over my head,' he continued, 'but it will make me a lot of money.'

I stared at the shrivelled flesh of Michael's face. 'I remember he spoke about ghosts coming out of the fog.'

'They had no idea what they were opening. It wasn't ghosts they saw, but reflections of themselves as they died.' He gestured to the white-smocked man. 'He told me those men were absorbed into the fog to become a part of the essence itself.'

The closer I got to the Cube, the more I realised my eyes had widened. I tried to relax. 'This is a nightmare. Deacon, seriously, how does chopping off the hands and feet from a dead guy make you money?'

'That's just it, apparently I can make much more if this wasn't a dead guy.'

'What?'

'I need someone alive in there.'

Looking at the hole in Michael's forehead, I wondered if the bullet was still in there. The congealed blood around the hole was now black. 'Sorry, Boss, but this is mental.'

He said nothing.

'You need someone alive?' I sighed. What came next was all part of the job, I knew that. 'You need me to kidnap someone.'

He looked away from me and placed a hand flat against the glass. 'You've been preoccupied these past couple of months.'

That was something I could not deny.

'Everything okay?' he asked without looking at me. 'You want to talk about it?'

'Not really.'

'Oh?'

'Harriet left.'

'I know.'

'You do?'

'It's my job to know everything about who I employ.'

I shouldn't have been surprised.

'Figured as much.' He pulled his hand away to scratch his chin. 'You're a private man, I respect that. Always have. That's why I'm fond of you. That's why you're the first of the boys to see this.'

Standing beside a dead man in a glass cube, whose hands and feet had been lopped off, while my boss praised me, I did not imagine things could get any more insane.

'That's why,' Deacon continued, 'I'm going to do you a favour.'

'What?'

'She's been fucking someone else, right?' Finally, he looked at me again.

My jaw ached as I clenched my teeth.

'Thought so,' he said. 'In fact, I know so.'

Harriet had been fucking some guy called Brett, and perhaps I would've happily killed the bastard. But this? I again looked into the Cube. Could I submit the man to this kind of torture? Kicking the living shit out of him would be one thing, but I was not a killer. Under Deacon's employ, I occasionally witnessed that kind of thing, but I'd never actually killed anyone myself. Whatever the hell this contraption was, could I really be a part of this?

Yeah, I probably could.

This Brett guy had been having an affair with my girl for a year. Possibly longer, if I thought about it. So yeah, I'd be happy to cut off his hands and feet. And Harriet's, for that matter. Both of the two-timing fuckers. I imagined doing it with a hefty meat cleaver.

'Such a shame you've been distracted recently.' Deacon's words stole me from my thoughts. 'With this new venture, I can't be having any of my boys distracted.'

I began to turn, and—

A sharp pain flared in my neck. Heat… darkness swamped me.

*

I came to amid vibrations and a soft hum. I jerked, but my arms and legs were restrained. Darkness was still with me. My eyes stung, and an acrid stink burnt my nostrils. I tasted blood and chemicals. Something wedged my mouth open, clogging my throat, and my head was forced back to accommodate whatever it was. I tried to shout. Failed. I moved my neck. Pain.

What the fuck?

My heartbeat drummed, filling the dark, filling my head. My breath hissed through my nose, shallow.

Where was I?

Again, I twisted in my restraints. Still I could not move.

The Cube.

What had they done to me?

My hands. My feet. Dear God, but… I could still feel them. Couldn't I? I moved them – at least, it felt like I did. They were cold. Yet hot. Tingling, like pins and needles.

Didn't amputees feel their ghost limbs?

My lungs burned, my nostrils whistling, in, out, as loud as my heartbeat. I'd been mutilated. Jesus Christ, was this a time to start believing in God?

I wanted to scream, tried, and my throat convulsed. I shifted, desperate to rid myself of the tube stretching my windpipe. Agony lanced into my chest. I could still feel my limbs, they hadn't been chopped off. No. Had they? But—

Something clunked and a brightness poured over me. I squinted into the light, blinded. There were shapes in the white glare. In the corner of my eye, I saw the congealed mess of a bloodied stump, the raw flesh and gristle and bone trailing rubber tubes that snaked downwards into a rising fog. I strained my eyes in the other direction to see the same with my other arm. I wasn't surprised.

I writhed. Useless. More pain. My numb limbs, my ghost hands clenched into fists. I knew my feet were missing, even though I couldn't see that far down my harnessed body, such was the churning fog.

Shadowy movements beyond my glass prison stole my focus, and I peered through the scratched glass. Wherever I was, this was not the building where I learned what became of the Cube. How long had I been out? It felt like only moments ago I'd stood on the outside looking in, staring in disbelief at Michael's butchered corpse.

Now, I was inside my own glass hell, taken to a well-furnished room where sunlight blasted between red-draped windows. A chandelier overhead twinkled a thousand diamonds, raining light onto a crowd of people dressed in tuxedos and gowns.

The stink of chemicals rose with the fog, and my vision spun in a myriad of colours.

I blinked, my eye muscles aching as they strained to peer around the room. Coils of rubber hose covered the lush carpet like hundreds of snakes. Who were all these people? Why was I there? And why did everyone hold a hose, with the nozzle hovering in front of eager lips? Most faces I didn't recognise. However, was that the Chief of the London Metropolitan Police? Yes, it was. I recognised several high-ranking officers from the Met. In my line of work, I'd come to know too many important faces from high up. Again, I saw another familiar face, this time of a local MP.

There, strolling in front of the Cube, was Deacon. I'd never seen him so proud, wearing a smile sharper than his tux.

Again, I writhed.

Fog began to obscure my view and like a phantom, his silhouette approached me. His thumb twitched on the nozzle attached to the tube that trailed behind him. He leaned in close to the glass and spoke to me. His words were muffled, but clear enough.

'With one simple modification,' he said, 'will you look at the high demand for this Essence.'

In my mind, I screamed.

On the other side of me, was Harriet. Though I could've been mistaken such was the thickening fog. She looked stunning in a glittery red dress.

My eyes itched, my vision darkening.

Maybe Harriet smiled, maybe I didn't see her at all. My brain reeled, churning with the haze. Something buzzed, a hissing noise surrounding me, then dozens of far-away clicks sounded. Like so many insects click-click-clicking while the air hissed.

A warmth flowed over me.

Harriet raised the nozzle to her slightly-parted lips, and closed her eyes. Her chest rose as she inhaled.

The grey turned to black.

And then nothing.

THE SILENT INVADER
Written by Paul Flewitt

Yvonne was a favourite of mine. I've had a long old life; but Yvonne has definitely been one of my favourites. I loved to watch her from my corner in the room and watch as she busied herself in the mornings; getting breakfast ready for the kids and packing them off to school for their day, cleaning the house before settling down to work for herself. It would've been so boring if she'd worked too. I might've found myself a new home if she'd had to go out to work, but she worked from home and so we spent long afternoons with only each other for company. She would speak on the phone to her friends and I would listen to her laughing, such a melodious, sweet sound. It's a voyeur's life I lead, watching and learning; then making my influence plain; and it's always the watching and the becoming familiar that I enjoy the most. There is a rhythm to every house which is quite unique and beautiful; like the turning of the stars or the cycle of the seasons may be to you.

Over time, we become friends; Yvonne and I. She speaks to me in an absent-minded fashion and I babble back. I tell her stories, I bring her news from a near-forgotten outside world...okay, sometimes she stares right through me like I'm not even there; that's fine – it all fits in with the purpose. I am there purely for her entertainment, and I am glad to fill that post....for now.

I sit and watch the kids return from school and the chaos they bring in their wake; I watch Yvonne attempt to get those last few little chores done before the kids create a new disaster zone to deal with...she soon admits defeat. She asks me to entertain the boys, but I provide only limited distraction to them; they are not yet tuned into my frequency but I try. I perform clown acts and comedy acts, but the children are soon acting up again. I see

Yvonne become flustered as she disappears to the kitchen to prepare dinner. The boys are creating more chaos and Yvonne sends them to their rooms to play while she finishes up the food. She is truly a miracle...I have such admiration for her patience; almost as solid as my own.

Dinner is eaten and the boys head to bed after a long day at school. Yvonne has bathed the children and read them a story; now she sits with a glass of wine as she waits for her husband to return from work and we're alone again... for a little while. This is my time, when I have her undivided attention. She watches the place where I am and I give her the diversions she calls for, yet underneath it all I am whispering into her ear. I do it quietly, so quietly she barely registers that she is being spoken to at all; but there I am. There I have been for a little while by now. The time grows later and she stares in my direction with glassy eyes, not really concentrating on anything, just drifting. Perfect.

There is a sudden banging, shouts and giggles coming from upstairs – the boys are up and messing around again. She puts down her glass and leaves the room; I hear her admonishing the children, they should be in bed. She comes back to the room and she asks me to tell her a different story; and so I do. She sighs and picks up the glass to take a sip, but there is more banging from upstairs. Absently, she puts the glass down and leaves the room and I am left alone again. Her step is light so I don't hear her footstep on the stair as she goes up to control her animalistic offspring. I hear a creak as she steps on the loose floorboard on the landing that Yvonne's husband keeps on promising to fix, then sudden rushing footsteps as the boys rush to get to their beds. Suddenly there is panic, screams which suddenly become muted, begging for Mummy to 'stop, please stop!' And then there is quiet. No noise, no bumping footsteps, only quiet.

Yvonne comes back to the room and stares blankly at me, a silver sheen of sweat shining on her pretty brow and upper lip. She doesn't reach for the glass of wine or call on me to entertain her.

She doesn't move for hours, just sits and stares at me. She knows… I know.

When husband returns she runs to the door like a dutiful wife so that she is there by the door when he enters. He sees her there and smiles as she steps toward him, not noticing the glass that she has in her hand until it's too late. Yvonne smashes her glass into his neck, grinding the jagged edges into his flesh until blood gouts from the hole that she's made. The sight is pretty in its way, but I see no more… my work with Yvonne is done. I disappear down the wire from where I came, well satisfied with my work. Perhaps I will tell her story to my next friend sometime soon.

*

Aggie was my next friend; another one of my favourites. She never had children and her house is quiet. Her nephews and nieces rarely visit her so she is left with only me for company. I like Aggie, she talks back. I sit on a low table in her sparse living room, nicotine-stained walls which are bare of any ornament and just a battered old chair for Aggie to sit in; the seat so old and sunken that she might well sit on the floor. She sits opposite me and stares always directly into my eyes; she isn't aware of that…not yet. She likes entertainment that she can get angry at; the sort of things that appear on your news shows… the sort of stories that I especially like to tell. I think it was only a few hours before I told her all about Yvonne and the kids… how she raged, the beautiful, exquisite old bird. So, from early in the morning until late at night she sits and stares at me, berating me for my cruelty (more than once she has thrown her cane at me with such force that I've retreated into the wire in fear) yet always she is hungry for more… for worse. It is a simple thing to pass my message to one so isolated; not a chore to have this one hear my voice. It is a rare thing to find one so willing to hear; no need to paw and scratch at the psyche of ones such as these. Yes... I think Aggie was my very favourite.

Jean visits twice a day; Aggie's only friend and one that is paid to fill the position. She never stays long; her schedule doesn't leave time for niceties. Jean will change Aggie from day clothes to night dress and back again, prepare a meal and ensure that laundry is clean and folded. Jean can be a little rough with Aggie when dressing and undressing, sometimes she forgets to change her incontinence pad – her schedule affords little time for niceties.

Jean arrives and Aggie's day begins like any other as the carer performs Aggie's ablutions. The old lady sits in her chair and allows the younger lady to carry out her duties while staring at me. Jean slips a vest and blouse over Aggie's head, then bends to help with her knickers and tights. That is when things go wrong for Jean. Aggie waits until the carer's head is bowed to her task, her fingers tightening on her cane. One swollen and varicose-veined foot is slid into a leg hole of a pair of knickers and Aggie brings the cane down onto the lady's skull. Jean keels over and Aggie hits her again, the sound of cracking bone almost thunderous in the quiet house. Jean whimpers but Aggie carries on her assault, her cane moving up and down like a piston; arcs of red painting every surface with each upward motion, splashing my face... if I only had skin to feel it; the lips to taste it.

I do not see the coup de grace; I don't need to. I disappear back down the wire and on... on to my next new friend; a new ear to whisper my fables into. My work with Aggie is done, but I shall remember her well. Perhaps I shall tell her story to a new friend too... it deserves to be told.

*

I travel through the wire, speeding past views of homes and choosing which one I will occupy next. Finally I am here, in a room that I immediately like very much. I like the pictures that are on the wall and the colours that have been used to decorate the place. It looks like the home of people that could provide entertainment.

But what does all of this have to do with you? You're only sitting there in your living room, unwinding after a long day; why should you care about these heinous things that have happened because of my words?

Well, you see, this is how it works. There are rules that have to be adhered to; checks which have to be marked. I am telling you all of this because you have to understand what it is that you are consenting to. I know you hear me, although you think that you're watching a simple television programme. You believe that you are being entertained, lulled into sleep after your arduous toil, don't you? Look around; are you certain that your family is seeing me here? Are you sure? Have you switched off yet?

Do you feel that itch in your hands to do harm yet?

Do you already have the weapon in your hands?

No? Of course, this is only our first night together. There will be plenty more stories, plenty more horrors to warm your bed. Plenty of time for me to get under your skin. I shall just sit here on the wall and wait.

Are you getting up yet? No?

Goodnight. We'll talk more tomorrow.

THE CLAY MAN
Written by **Clare Riley Whitfield**

I opened my eyes to blackness. My lip was split and swollen. I reached out and hit a wall at twelve inches, but it was smooth, like painted wood. I was lying on what felt and smelled like mud. Around me, there were pieces of wood. I screamed and banged on the lid, I thought I had been buried alive.

'Shut up! You're going to make him come back.' It was a girl's voice.

'I think I've been kidnapped.'

'Be quiet,' she started to cry, 'I'm fucked. I'm so fucked now.'

'Why? I don't understand, what's going on?'

'Shhhh. He's coming back.'

Vibrations against my fingers increased with every footstep. Then light came through cracks in the lid. I heard a door open and the girl begging. They were moving past me, the shadows of their legs making dark flickers. The sound of metal clanking. Then my lid was unlocked and swung open and the first thing my eyes focused on was his angular face.

'What's your motivation? Towards or Away?' he said.

I shook my head, afraid to say the wrong thing.

'Get up.'

He dragged me over to where the girl was chained to the wall but I took in what I could. A concrete floor with two sunken holes and plywood doors for lids. A pink fluffy rug that jarred with everything else. Walls of exposed brick and a naked lightbulb. I saw a squat rack, bench, straps hung from the wall. Weights laid out in meticulous uniformity, shining silver. He secured me to the wall and I knelt down. The girl was a metre away also chained.

She stared at the concrete, ragged and gaunt, her mousy hair stuck to her head. She wore grey knickers and a black baggy bra. He walked up behind her, holding metal wire with wooden handles which he placed around her neck and twisted while he spoke.

'Most people answer towards. This simply isn't true. It means your goals motivate you: the mansion, the Lamborghini, the bikini body. But in reality, most people are away from types.'

The girl panicked, pulling at the wire as it cut into her skin but she couldn't get a finger behind it. Blood ran down like a necklace. He twisted and twisted. I pushed my face into the wall so I didn't have to watch and all the time he kept talking.

'For example, they get out of shape, swear they'll lose a few pounds but they are motivated by moving away from things, so as soon as they make progress they give up.'

Her struggle stopped and a warm trickle ran came from her against my knees. He let go and her body slumped forward, kneeling as in prayer, the wire still round her neck.

'So, what are you? A towards or away?' he asked.

'Towards?'

'Funny, that's what they all say. Now, you probably think I hate women, but I don't. I love them, I'm just very frustrated by their unwillingness to harness their potential.'

He pulled back the rug and opened another door. The stench of rotting meat exploded and he dragged the girl over and rolled her in. There was the dull slap of flesh against flesh, then he closed it and kicked the rug back into position. He sprayed air freshener above the rug, and above my head.

'I'm Elliot and we start our programme tomorrow. The first week or so will be rough, but remember, I'm here to help you become the best version of yourself. Oh, there is extra earth in there for you tonight. For your particular situation.'

I detoxed that first night. I thought centipedes were crawling into my ears, eating their way through my skin. I tried to claw my way out and lost three fingernails. My muscles spasmed until it felt like I'd been kicked all over. Then came the diarrhoea and vomiting. That's what he meant about the extra earth. Jonesing and twitching in my underground hole, he didn't know I still had a covered syringe hidden inside myself. I'd learnt this trick from older girls, the Police can stop and search, but they have to arrest you if they want to snap on the latex, plus I wasn't sharing needles with skanks.

*

I had been scrounging round the pub that night but my credit was bad. I had no leverage, I'd fucked and sucked everyone, I was just old meat begging for handouts. A man by the door in a red jacket grabbed me as I went to leave and said he could get a free sample for new business. He lent into my ear and he stank of strong mints. I thought he was brave poaching in that pub, but that was his problem.

He was tall and tight around the jaw, the sort who flips out if you spill anything in his car. He smelt of washing detergent and mints. I jumped into his car without a second thought. I only remember the second punch to the face.

*

The first day I had to scoop out the mess I had made in the hole into a bucket with my hands. He made me strip naked and he hosed me down with freezing water. All the while telling me how disgusting I was, my arse was gross, my boobs were droopy. He made me run up and down doing fucking bleep tests, laughing at me. I refused to keep going, so he made

me scoop handfuls of my own shit from the bucket and eat it. I couldn't swallow and threw up. I got a bowl of spinach and eggs once a day, then he made me crawl back in the hole again. Every day was like that. I waited for him to come home, still in his gym uniform with his shiny name tag. I had the syringe inside me but I was too scared to use it.

I tried talking to him, I thought if I made him like me he might be kinder but he told me to shut up and made me do squats that were too heavy, pulls up, deadlifts anything he knew was outside of my capability, so I would have to eat my own shit again. Once a week he would measure me and I was disappearing. I only had underwear, like the girl before me, my bra was gaping and my knickers wouldn't stay up so I had to tie knots in them. My hair stuck against my face, just like hers.

People always ask me what he was like but the truth is I don't really know. There is a familiarity you get with someone over time, but I never got much from him. He was a fat-free vessel of empty. My gut never developed an instinct, but then my gut just roared with hunger. Felt like acid. I was starving. But still he made me lift until I thought my arms would come apart and the tendons would snap. To me he was all obsessive sinew, twitching nerves and hollow muscle. Even his veins wriggled under his skin like they didn't want to be there. It was as if he was carved out of clay and then varnished over with fence paint. Even his hair was stiff; blonde, and quiffed up rigid. But his hands belonged to a young boy, his nails were round like buttons, and on the insides of his wrists you could see where the fake tan faded into pink. The only thing I would say, was that he hated women, like really hated them.

One time he told me, 'Poor girls are so predictable, especially pretty ones. They always pitch too low, undersell themselves, and they base their entire self-esteem on how fuckable they are, yet there's an endless supply of fresher, younger meat coming, it's a loser's game and you all play it.'

Another time he said, 'There's no such thing as a sisterhood, women want to be victims. You only have to make a girl come once, tell her she's beautiful and she'll follow you around like a fucking cunt no matter how much you kick at her.'

I think he must have been ignored, a lot, or mistreated. Now me and those rotting heaps of flesh under the rug were paying for it.

If he'd have raped me it would have been a transaction I would have understood.

*

One day I collapsed, I knew it meant eating dirt, but I didn't care anymore.

'Why are you doing this?' I asked.

'I'm trying to make you the best version of yourself?' he said, pushing a straggly hair behind my ear. 'Don't you want to be beautiful?' he asked.

I nodded.

'You don't want to end up under the rug, do you?'

I shook my head. 'I want to go home.'

'One more set.'

I fell apart, I begged to go back in the hole. I offered to eat shit instead and he started laughing. He said, 'You know what's hilarious? I can do anything to you, and ultimately, you'll blame yourself.'

I pulled at his trousers, but he peeled off my fingers and squatted down beside me.

'You see this girl?

He scrolled through his phone, showing me pictures of a prettier girl with red hair; glamourous, happy, photos taken without her knowledge.

'Is she the next one?' I asked.

'She is if you don't get up. One more set.'

I knew the minute that redhead came in here I was dead. That was the shot I needed. He was right, I was an away from, because I was not going to end up under that fucking rug. I swore if I had the chance I would run.

Then one day he came down those stairs in a thunderous mood, ripped open the lid to the hole and ordered me to kneel down in front of him. I felt sick, I looked about for the redhead but she wasn't there, I was sure he was going to kill me. Then he pulled his bottoms down and took out his cock.

'Make me hard,' he said. Staring at the wall above my head.

I was dumb struck. This was alien for him. It had never been sexual.

'Just do it.' he screamed.

'Ok, ok!'

Then I knew; he couldn't get it up. He could torture women all he liked, but we weren't the problem. He slapped me round the face because I took too long to touch him and it brought me to my senses. This was it.

'I'll make it work, trust me.' I smiled as sweet as I could.

He stared ahead, breathing stiffly, teeth grinding. I reached up inside and removed the syringe. I played with his soft and useless dick and with my other hand I uncovered the needle. Then I stretched out his foreskin tight and stabbed as hard as I could up through the

underside of his helmet, the needle almost came out the other side. The screams weren't human. He fell back against the wall, shaking and cradling his knob with the syringe still in it. I stamped on his knee, forcing it backwards and I heard a cracking noise that made him scream all over again and then I ran. Up the stairs, through the house, out the front door. I remember running through the house with its weird yellow softness and then I was in the street, running past horrified faces. I ran and ran, no way I was stopping. The police eventually cornered me like a dog on an industrial estate.

*

The way I was going, I would have ended up dead for sure and no one would have given a shit. But because of him I'm clean, a size zero and everyone loves me. I have fans. I get tear-stained letters from sexually abused teenagers and depressed housewives for fucks sake. I was told once, years ago when I was 14, that I had a face for porn. I suppose some people might have found that offensive, but I took it as a compliment. On the cover of my book there's a photo of me staring off into the distance, a soft unfocused gaze, just the way my publicist coached me. You see, I do have a face for porn; Pity Porn. I should figure out my next move my management tells me, so I think I'm going to write to him in prison, maybe a TV interview, when the book sales tail off.

ANIMUS
Written by Jim Goforth

It was ten year old Braden Holloway who first heard that something bad was coming. For a while he held that knowledge to himself, battling with it, and his conscience, wondering whether he should tell anybody. The likelihood of being believed seemed remote, just as always.

He was good at keeping secrets, always had been, but this one gnawed away at him, made him more apprehensive than he'd ever been before. The likely futility of anybody he told taking it seriously was ultimately outweighed by the growing, pressing need to reveal what he'd heard to somebody.

So he told his father.

It didn't pan out in any of the ways he'd envisioned it. It was instead, remarkably underwhelming. Either his father hadn't correctly heard what he'd said, or he didn't place much stock in it, confirming his initial fears about revealing anything.

Now, something bad was coming regardless, and he needn't have bothered even mentioning it, because nothing was going to stop it.

*

It wasn't unusual for single father, Jared Holloway to hear strange remarks coming from his son, nor was it unusual for the boy to converse and engage with imaginary friends. The death of his mother sent him into a terrible downward spiral, crushed him, and turned an ordinarily outgoing lad into a withdrawn introvert with an ever-expanding fantasy universe of make-believe characters.

Jared could hardly blame him, hell he'd wanted to sink into his own mire of depression and engage heavily with his not so imaginary friends, Jack Daniels and Johnny Walker. He didn't. Not to the extent it wrecked him, in any case, and he did that for Braden. All they had now was each other, and besides, Jared was hellbent on proving the death of his wife, Cindy, and Braden's mother, wasn't accidental.

A renowned chef, Cindy's untimely passing was ruled to be the result of a freak accident. One which saw the entire contents of a wooden knife block impaled in various parts of her body. It was widely assumed she'd happened to bump against the block in her place of employment's kitchen, in a rush, and tipped it over, upending it to the point where every knife spilled from it.

To Jared, this whole logic was so blatantly flawed, it was inconceivable to think it was so easily passed off as accidental. Considering she wound up with a carving knife through her throat, a paring knife lodged in an eye socket, a utility knife puncturing through the flesh of a cheek and the remainder of bladed implements adorning other parts of her lower body, she'd have had to have been storing the knives on some location ridiculously higher than an average kitchen bench, for them to be able to fall and skewer her in so many places, particularly the general cranial region.

That was just one of many inconsistencies, but all the same, even with so many flaws in the alleged tragic and terrible accident, Jared hit a brick wall trying to uncover or prove anything. He could find no proof of wrongdoing on the part of anybody else employed with Cindy, could find no witnesses, nothing to further his case. If the freakish death hadn't been some hideous accident, there didn't seem to be any avenue he could pursue to prove that; it was if he'd been blocked in every way from doing so.

The loss of Cindy was a raw wound for both remaining Holloways, but it impacted more visibly on Braden, hence the escalation in strange comments, withdrawn behaviour, and finally, more interaction with imaginary friends, as if filling the void with them.

Now, apparently, if his mumbled remarks were being deciphered correctly by Jared, the boy was at the point where he was talking to animals.

'There's something bad coming, Dad,' Braden said matter-of-factly, as Jared was getting ready for work. 'Something really bad coming.'

Jared glanced at him, raising a quizzical eyebrow. The boy hovered around just outside the bathroom door while Jared finished up shaving, his tone solemn and serious, his expression likewise. What tore Jared up just looking at the boy, not just now, but in general ever since Cindy's demise, was what else was visibly gone from him.

No longer was there the twinkle of life in his eyes, the spark of good-natured mischief that used to hover there, under the surface, ready to burst free in a fit of exuberance. Now those eyes were haunted all the time, dull and devoid of any sparkle. His voice, when he spoke at all, matched that.

'How do you know that, bud?' He tousled Braden's blonde hair, a gesture the kid really used to dig. Now, he merely tolerated it. 'You and I know better than anybody that something bad can happen at the drop of a hat, it can come out of nowhere.'

He stopped before he set off on a tirade, even as he felt it building inside him. Braden didn't need to hear about how it could change lives for the worse, rip families apart, wrench souls out, any of that. He already knew all about it. Instead, Jared changed tact, aiming to keep it light, some positive reinforcement.

'Anyway, good things can come along too, just as suddenly, and unexpected. You never know what's around the corner. Don't you reckon it's about time something good came our way? I'd say we're about due for it, wouldn't you?'

'It doesn't matter.' Braden's voice was flat, free of emotion. 'Something bad is coming.'

He sounded so certain that a slight chill trickled over Jared. He beat down any sense of dread. After all, considering the tragedy, it was hardly surprising Braden would react as though something bad was hiding in wait everywhere, skulking in the dark. It wasn't like the boy exhibited any prior tendencies towards premonitions, or knowledge of events yet to occur. If he'd any predisposition to anything like that, one might assume he'd have had an inkling his mother was going to end up skewered by a dozen of her own chef knives.

'Come on, bud, chin up. Nothing bad's coming for us again. What makes you think there is?'

Once, Braden was a confident speaker. He bordered on the verge of being too loud at times, boisterous and rambunctious, but now he had a propensity to mumble so badly his words were barely indecipherable. Sometimes, he even resorted to just whispers. His response to Jared now was a combination of that, and Jared was forced to try and pick key words out of the gibberish.

'Who told you? Animals? Did you say animals told you?' He was about to follow that up with a crack asking when the lad had actually started talking to any animals, but managed to stop himself. It stood to reason. Along the new imaginary friends he'd cultivated of late, why wouldn't he converse with whatever animals were around? The problem of course being that the Holloways had no pets. Perhaps he'd been carrying on conversations with the birds, local dogs or cats. Who knew?

Braden just stared at him, as if he'd resigned himself beforehand to his father not taking it seriously.

'Well, I guess the animals would know. Anything bad coming for them is usually man. After all, there's no other animal under the sun that inflicts the sort of...' Again Jared had to stop himself going off on a tangent. The boy didn't need a lesson on the grotesqueries and crimes humans perpetrated on one another. Let alone every other animal under the sun. 'Anyway, buddy, that doesn't mean something bad is coming for us.'

'It's coming for everybody,' Braden said, and this time his

voice was clear. 'It's coming.'

'Not sure those animals speak for everybody,' Jared said, wondering if he should pursue any specifics about which animal it was that seemed so adamant. Getting into it now probably wouldn't draw anything of substance out of Braden, and he didn't want to end up late for work by involving himself in one of the boy's phantasmagorical scenarios. Which by all accounts had taken a darker, bleaker turn for the worse.

'I didn't say *animals!* I said…'

The sound of the doorbell interrupted an impassioned outburst from Braden, and he let it die away, seeing his father's concentration broken.

'Okay, bud, we'll pick this up again a little later on, hey? That'll be Isabella, right on cue.'

'Okay.' Braden stared down at his feet, shuffling them.

At least he wasn't claiming he was too old for a babysitter, which he sure as hell wasn't. Besides, Isabella wasn't really a babysitter, more of a friend of Jared's who didn't mind keeping Braden company while his father was at work. Ideally, Jared wouldn't have left him with anybody, but it was hardly an ideal situation they were in now, and taking the boy to work with him wasn't ideal either.

Not when Jared worked at Augury Falls' central bar. The Night Owl. Rough as fuck on an ordinary day, let alone a hectic night when everybody in town descended on the drinking hole. No place for any kid.

At this point in time, with employment scarce around the town, Jared had to take what he could get, and he and Braden sure as fuck needed the money, with Cindy's income gone as swiftly as she herself was.

Right now, Braden needed him, as evidenced by his escalating bizarre behaviour, alongside his descent into fantasies, and further withdrawing into himself, but they needed to eat too. The boy was strong, and he genuinely liked Isabella, so it wasn't as though he was consigned to some kind of dreadful incarceration while Jared was absent.

Braden would come good, Jared knew. *Hoped.* He reacted positively to Isabella, even seemed to engage more with her than he did with Jared. Of course, Jared wasn't a strikingly beautiful woman who wrote thriller books. Dear old dad couldn't hope to compete with that.

In any case, if he kept at it, working hard for several months, maybe they'd have enough money to give them breathing space, and spend some quality time together. Things would start looking up; they'd conquer this together. Everything would be fine again.

*

If there was one common element that bound everybody in Augury Falls together, it was alcohol.

From the underage kids hanging out at the derelict skate park or other places of youthful congregation to engage in illicit drinking sessions, to the regular crowd propping up the bar in the Night Owl, from those with money to burn, to those in the large bracket of unemployed, alcohol was an omnipresent factor.

There were no particular sporting teams excelling there, nothing of note was exported or produced there. The only thing Augury Falls could legitimately lay claim to was the fact that it was a town indulging in drinking as a pastime.

The homeless denizens of the town weren't impervious to this, in fact they were habitual contributors to the escalating trend. Every coin obtained through the tried and true methods of beg, borrow, or steal went, as a general rule, not towards purchasing food to fill bellies as best as possible, but instead to alcohol. Granted, none of these folk were swilling Chivas Regal or Hennessy, but they were still swilling nonetheless.

Hal Robards couldn't care less about drinking the top-shelf booze. Once upon a time he'd had a taste for the good stuff, the finest quality there was, hell, then he could afford it, but life could change in the blink of an eye. And for him, it had. Drastically.

He couldn't even remember those days, or even how he came to be just another one of the wandering filthy transients of Augury Falls. All his memories were a constant swirling haze, a cornucopia of fragments and half-recalled happenings that he wasn't sure had actually occurred or whether he'd dredged them up out of alcohol-sodden dreamscapes.

These days it was a good day for him if he managed to scrounge up enough coins for a bottle of the cheapest, nastiest wine he could get his hands on.

Today had been one of those days. Loitering around outside the few cafes and office blocks had garnered him a few handfuls of half-smoked cigarettes and butts, swiftly snatched and pocketed before vigilant staff arrived to dump the ashtrays.

Now, he was taking up residence in one of his preferred drinking zones. Sitting on an old bench in a largely forgotten park bordered by thick woods. Infrequently it was encroached upon by dodgy local kids, looking to fuck, frolic, drink or take drugs, or whatever the hell it was the teenage delinquents around here did, and on those occasions, Hal gave it a wide berth, but for the most part it was just another overlooked part of town.

So much of Augury Falls had fallen into disarray and disuse, particularly on the outskirts. Anything that didn't comprise part of Main Street and its various businesses, and the scatter of residential areas that spiderwebbed out along streets extending off this principal concourse, was an afterthought, if even thought of at all.

That suited Hal just fine. Unless some pack of inebriated thugs came stumbling along into his domain any time soon, he was free to occupy his weed-entangled bench, drink himself into tranquil oblivion and smoke his swiped cigarette butts.

The cheap swill he had tasted truly heinous, but he wasn't drinking it with a connoisseur's palette. He was drinking for that pleasant hazy buzz, waiting for the fire of comfort to ignite in his stomach, and the shroud of intoxication to descend over him, whisking away reflections of anything else.

Hal hadn't been there too long, enjoying his solitude and his wine, when he felt a chill steal over him. Though the evening was quite warm, and he was dressed as usual in the long grime-encrusted overcoat with pockets laden with assorted meagre treasures, he still felt that unexpected glacial atmosphere arrive with an insidious stealth.

The moon was reasonably bright tonight, but the presence of towering trees all around cast long shadows over the boundaries of the park. That was part of the reason he so enjoyed being here on most evening's, able to remain undetected in darkness, but that sudden chill, seeming to lance right into him and gnaw relentlessly on his bones made him edgier than usual. Considering there wasn't any breeze in occurrence. No leaves rustled with whispering susurrations, no saplings or smaller trees swayed to and fro with any motion at all.

Hal knew he wasn't too drunk to have mistaken that, or to find it a little weird, and oddly disconcerting. He hadn't been here long enough to start feeling anything from the wine but tingles of warmth, slowly diffusing through his body. Now, the freakish cold snap was threatening to completely steal his buzz and leave him with horrifying sober paranoia.

He peered through the gloom. The icy wash of air around him morphed into an ice ball of fear growing inside him.

A piece of shadow down there among the stands of trees didn't belong. Hunched, misshapen, and just plain wrong, it wasn't a natural part of the woods. It moved with a deliberately slow pace, drifting out from the tree sanctuary, detaching itself from the rest of the darkness.

Having established already that he was nowhere near drunkenness at all, certainly not the level he wanted to be, Hal knew he couldn't pass it off as any boozy delusion. Nor could he pass it off as either a fellow lurking vagrant or any juvenile delinquent up to no good. It was something he'd never laid eyes on before, something grotesque and grim, something exuding an aura of utter malignance. He acknowledged, as the fear swelling inside him escalated to a point where he felt he might throw up, pass out, or a combination of both, that the arrival of this malformed oddity in conjunction with the polar freeze of the temperature drop was no coincidence.

He also dimly acknowledged that he'd pissed himself. The legs of his decrepit, dirt-caked trousers were temporarily warm as his bladder involuntarily released streams down each of them, but soon enough that went cold too, as if mere exposure to the swirl of chill encircling him was enough to leech any warmth away in an instant.

Then, almost as abruptly as it appeared, that dark menacing bulk was gone. Or at least, it was something else. A black swirl of haze, a miasma. A morass of eddying shapelessness, a perpetual drift of dusky vapour or smoke, or Hal didn't know what. It was hard to keep his eyes on anything or focus on the constant shifts. It looked like an unholy marriage between billowing black smoke and a dust devil, but as it appeared to disperse and spread thin black tendrils out in all directions, like impossibly long reaching fingers, it became even harder to concentrate on staring at any one fixed location.

He would have moved, tottering away on his piss-saturated legs, had he not been so transfixed rigid with terror, that he was rooted to the spot. The black miasma swirled throughout the entirety of the park; he felt it enveloping him and seeming to churn around his head. Even as he absently raised his wine bottle, he was sure he saw a sliver of black murk curl and vanish inside it. Nonetheless, he drank anyway, knocking back a good measure, hoping to jolt himself into some immediate state of inebriation.

The swirling black was gone now, completely dispersing and vanishing from his general vicinity, its vaporous tendrils being borne away to elsewhere, but he no longer cared or felt any fear.

Instead, as the alcohol coursed throughout him, so too did something else.

The paralysing fear that caused him to involuntarily piss his grime-caked trousers was gone, replaced by a new sensation. One never felt by the likes of Hal Robards before, either pre-vagrant drunk, or during. Malice. Malevolence. Deep, dark hatred and the urgent need to do harm.

It swamped him, engulfed him. Completely interred the drunken, shambolic persona that was Hal's beneath a barrage of utter darkness.

He tipped his head right back and downed the rest of the wine in one enormous quaff, then stood upright, shaking off his usual hunched gait to stand straight and unbowed. With a powerful swing, he smashed the wine bottle against the decrepit bench, sending busted glass showering over the weed-encrusted seat and the overgrown grass of the park grounds.

With a busted bottle neck clenched tight in his fist, he walked with purpose out of the darkness.

*

For the youth of Augury Falls, there wasn't a whole bunch to do in town in the way of recreation.

Once, back in the mists of time, there'd been a movie theatre, a pool hall, even a video games arcade. None of those things existed any more, making way for other businesses deemed more imperative to the townsfolk.

So now, with precious little else to do, the shiftless-and bored-teenagers followed in the footsteps of most of the other citizens. They drank copious amounts of alcohol.

For some, it was remarkably easy to obtain; for others, not so much. Even then though, they still managed. Cunning and ingenuity was cultivated early in life for the vast majority, and they learned plenty of methods to get themselves something to liven up the mundaneness of their existences.

Rich Ferrell, Steve Dawkins, Miriam Tate, and Tyla Greene were among those who had to rely on crafty wiles to get hold of liquor. All of them sixteen, and not having fake IDs, or any willing elder siblings prepared to buy booze for them, they had to resort to other methods.

Misfits at school, they hung around together, largely excluded by the cool crowd who never seemed to have any issues obtaining alcohol for their exclusive soirees.

Various failed attempts to come by anything to drink had the quartet scratching their heads with what they were going to do until evening delivery driver Wes Grant rolled up to the Night Owl, stupidly leaving his truck unlocked.

Up until then, the closest they'd had with any success was mustering up enough courage to approach a trio of older kids in leather jackets sitting outside the hardware store, smoking cigarettes and swigging on beers of their own. They were quite amenable to the idea of buying some booze for the underagers. On the proviso blonde Miriam was amenable to administering all three of them blowjobs as payment. Which she wasn't.

The foursome-or at least three of them-were at the point they were trying to coerce Miriam into changing her mind on that score when they happened past the Night Owl, and discovered Wes Grant's negligent blunder.

Now, they were assembled in one of their standard lurking spots, in the industrial part of town, where silent warehouses and currently closed factories stood watch.

'Looks like those guys will have to blow us to get some beers now,' Rich laughed as he distributed stolen beers to all the others.

'I can't believe you fuckers were trying to twist my arm to go back and do that,' Miriam chided them. Now they had booze aplenty for the evening, it was all a big joke, but at the time, she'd been pretty upset they'd consider using her as some tawdry bargaining chip.

'Fuck's sake, I've gotta piss,' Steve announced unnecessarily, scrambling to his feet, his beer left untouched on the concrete where he'd sat.

'Jesus Christ, *Dorkins*, breaking the seal already? Haven't even cracked your first cold one yet!'

'Fuck off, Ferret,' Steve fired back. 'I've been busting for hours, just been preoccupied trying to get the stuff. See, that's how considerate I am, holding on all this while, just to make sure all of you could get a nice happy buzz on.'

'Whatever. Go on then. Make sure you wash your hands!' Rich, pretty pleased with his wit, glanced around for approval at the girls, but both were more interested in getting their beers open.

'Funny man,' Steve muttered as he hastened away. Down here they were unlikely to get caught or spotted by anyone, bar a patrolling rent-a-cop security dude come to ensure all warehouses and whatnot were still locked up, and all that shit, so the quartet usually didn't go to any trouble to hide themselves.

One of the silent, dark hulks had milk crates and pallet stacks out front, so the friends normally sat there to drink. After they got a few in them and started feeling bold and adventurous, they gallivanted through the rest of the warehousing complex with gleeful, drunken abandon, coaxing and cajoling one another into increasingly ridiculous behaviour.

Steve was hoping that ridiculous behaviour went on a particular tangent tonight. One where the silly vandalism and crazy dares that usually comprised their inebriated tomfoolery were supplanted by more flesh-oriented pursuits. That hadn't ever happened before between any of them, but Steve was holding out hope that it would, preferably sooner rather than later. Maybe tonight was the night.

Once he was certain he was out of view, he ducked down a thin dark alley between two warehouses, trailing deeper into the gloomy shadows. He couldn't even hear the others anymore, so he assumed he was safe to unzip and get down to business, then head back for the more serious business of making inroads into those ill-begotten beers. No doubt, the other three wouldn't be wasting any time.

As he did just that, he felt the temperature drop all around him. It was as though a sudden cold snap descended out of nowhere, invading the pleasant warmth formerly comprising the evening.

Between the two buildings, he figured a gust of cold breeze sent the freeze down the narrow corridor, trapped in a wind tunnel, but he'd felt nothing to suggest the wind had kicked up at all. He hadn't heard anything, hadn't felt breeze rush against him, particularly those exposed parts of himself he'd elected to hang out.

The ground around the complex was generally littered with all manner of refuse, and Steve could see, even in the dark crowding this narrow space, that now was no exception. Candy wrappers, empty cigarette packets, crumpled newspaper, and other junk items were strewn everywhere, lining the bottom of the walls. None of which were moving, or even rustling minimally. Which, had there been any form of wind present, they should have been.

Steve wasn't kidding about needing to go, or having been holding on for some time, and now he was in a rush to finish and get back to the others. He was suddenly unnerved, filled with a growing trepidation that he found illogical, and yet impossible to force away. As he sprayed the wall, urging himself in a low, hasty mantra to finish up, something seemed to drift past the mouth of the alley, throwing a darker pall of shadow in the already gloomy recess.

He looked that way, and the escalating dread swelling inside him increased tenfold, though he could see nothing other than darkness. Then a big irregular sprawl of shadow stretched out over the plane of the wall before him, black and malformed on the grey surface. He didn't know what the hell it was, but nor did he stick around to find out. Rather than exit the way he'd come in, he bolted down the thin corridor between the buildings, backtracking to where his friends were, a completely different way.

Irrational or otherwise, he was gripped with a cold, cloying fear, one that swirled around him with the same atmospheric freeze as the bizarre temperature drop. Just getting back to his friends wouldn't do; the desire now was to get the hell out of here, as far away as possible.

He saw they were no longer still in their seated positions, atop pallets and milk crates. Instead, they were standing, a scatter of beer bottles on the concrete at their feet.

Rich held a beer bottle in his hand, though not in any traditional drinking sense. He held it by the neck, raised aloft. Miriam, blonde hair a tousled mess, wielded a piece of pallet board ripped from their former places of seating. Jagged and broken at the end she held, it had two long spiral shank pallet nails protruding from the other. And Tyla seemed to have somehow located an old rusty socket wrench, perhaps in the mess of debris left to accumulate around the pallets, or left outside by some negligent worker.

The fear swamping Steve grew even more, but there was a measure of relief in there too. So he wasn't being paranoid, wasn't being stricken by utter dread for no reason. There truly was someone-or *something* else-here, if the trio saw fit to scurry around seeking weaponry. As he ran, he tried to look back over his shoulder, fearing what he might see, wondering if whatever had so alarmed them was right on his tail.

Then he was almost amongst them, and as he switched his wide-open-eyed gaze back to them, he saw that black tendrils and curling slivers of darkness were eddying around them all, slithering in erratic undulations in the air.

Miriam swung her pallet board in a devastating arc, and the twin nails hammered right through the end of it punched into Steve's stomach. Agony sparked, simultaneous with the ragged breath being socked right out of him, then Rich was stepping up next to him. His beer bottle weapon clubbed the side of Steve's head with a force that shattered the glass and cracked skull too.

Blood spurted in a gory arc across the pale concrete.

Legs abruptly nerveless and jelly-like collapsed Steve's spasming body in a tangle on the concrete. Rich went down with him, thrusting, stabbing, and slicing with the jagged edge of the broken bottle neck. Shards of glass wreckage protruded from his own hand as he did, coursing rivulets of his own blood down to mingle with that pouring from Steve, but he paid it no mind, intent only on his urgent desire to cause maximum damage.

The girls converged, desperate not to let Rich monopolise the butchery. As Tyla sought to jam the socket wrench deep into Steve's head, via an ear canal, Miriam moved to his lower body and repeatedly hammered the pallet board against his buttocks and thighs, pummelling the nails in and out until blood flew off them each time she raised the weapon for another strike.

Heads swimming with a black haze of malice and supercharged violence they didn't cease their brutal attack until there was nothing left to assault, merely a ravaged hunk of bloody meat and shredded fabric, with a socket wrench thrust deep inside a ruined rectum and a pincushion of glass and bone fragments in the brain soufflé comprising Steve's head.

Briefly the blood-drenched trio eyed one another, contemplating unleashing the growing need to destroy and slaughter on each other, before all reaching the same conclusion at the same time. They turned away from the grisly mire, and ran with deadly intent back towards town.

*

The Night Owl wasn't a full house, but it was steady in there. It was still early, so the place would fill up later, as more patrons inevitably descended on Augury Falls' favourite drinking hole for most.

Right now the mix was comprised of groups of younger adults monopolising the pool tables, a knot of bikers watching their antics with a modicum of interest, a sprinkling of old-timers along the bar. A few couples occupied corner booths or private tables away from the more boisterous areas, while elsewhere, groups of office workers, still in suits and ties, or business skirts and blouses, assembled, winding down after work. Here and there, solitary customers drifted, or sat in seclusion eying proceedings with varying degrees of interest. Some were clearly lone wolves scoping the domain for any potentially available females, while others were habitual drinkers, there for no other reason but to get intoxicated and stumble home.

'Rowdy' Roddy McLain commandeered the jukebox, as per usual, which meant folks were either cursed with a steady diet of ZZ Top, AC/DC, KISS and others of that ilk, or dug the tunes he kept rolling. Occasionally he grudgingly allowed somebody else to step in and have a turn-usually so he could head off to the bar-replacing his rock numbers with whatever they saw fit to inflict upon the other patrons, but he always returned. His overbearing presence was almost always enough to ensure even the most stoic of souls didn't last too long around the jukebox.

It wasn't hectic, but it was constant. Enough to keep Jared busy, and yet relaxed enough so he could keep an eye on proceedings too, keep watch for potential trouble. He and his fellow bar staffers weren't run off their feet by any stretch of the imagination, but then again, it was still early. It seemed the later it got, the busier the Night Owl got.

Tonight, Jared wasn't looking forward to that. For one, that was usually when overly intoxicated fools started shit, with things often escalating from trivial to fairly serious in a heartbeat. Two, he just wanted to slog through a simple night's work, with no fuss, and get home to Braden.

Thinking back, he acknowledged he'd brushed the boy off earlier, once Isabella arrived. He knew Braden was serious about whatever it was he'd been trying to announce, even if it was something dredged out of his ever-increasing descents into fantasy

428

land, but it couldn't hurt to let the kid talk it out more, maybe probe him to go a little deeper, and get to the source.

Hell, Jared knew why Braden was acting how he was, but getting him to open up more, explore his feelings of grief and lay them bare would go a long way towards both of them healing.

As Jared finished serving a giggly blonde and her quiet redhead companion, half-watching with amusement as Rowdy chased off a couple looking to usurp his Hell's Bell's with slow love songs, he heard the bar telephone ring, even over the hubbub of patrons and the strains of AC/DC.

Tim and Lydia were down that end of the bar, much closer than he was to the phone. One of them could get it. Though he'd no customers currently clamouring for drinks, it didn't make sense for him to head all the way down there, when Lydia could basically turn around and grab it. She did that now, and Jared turned his attention back to the mostly mellow, albeit noisy, goings-on in the bar.

Until Lydia called out to him.

'Jared, phone's for you! Your girl.'

Swivelling around, Jared stared at her with confusion, before making his way down there.

'My girl? I don't have...oh!' The lightbulb clicked on in his head. Even if he wasn't yet about to admit it, or was still clinging to the notion that it was too soon after Cindy to even entertain a new relationship, most folks in town were already laying bets, making assumptions, and generally waiting for him and Isabella to become a bona fide item.

Despite the guilty pang that always hit him whenever he let his thoughts venture into domains where the gorgeous Isabella was more than a close friend and part-time babysitter for his troubled boy, a sheepish grin crept across his face.

'Yeah, that's right.' Lydia matched his grin with one of her own, a far cockier one. 'Don't get coy with me, Jared. Sooner or later...'

Hoping she'd covered the receiver up so Isabella wasn't listening to any of this, Jared snatched the phone from her.

'You'll keep,' he said, before the malevolent intro to Black Sabbath's N.I.B rang out from the jukebox, momentarily silencing a good portion of the crowd. In that transitory quiescence he spoke into the phone.

'Hey, Is, how are things going there? Everything sweet with Braden?'

'Well...' She sounded hesitant, tense. 'Actually, Jared, I don't think it is.'

'No?' He hadn't been expecting that. For a moment he was stumped, not even sure what to say. Words tripped over each other trying to be first on the tip of his tongue, and in the end he said nothing, waiting for Isabella to elaborate.

'Braden said he told you something bad is coming. Is that right?'

'It is. Yeah, he was telling me while I was getting ready for work, said something about the animals telling him something bad was coming. I tried to convince him to dial it back a little, that bad things can always happen, doesn't mean they're going to. I know his deal with imaginary friends and talking to people that aren't there is getting a little obsessive, especially now with the animals notion...'

'He didn't say animals told him, Jared. He said *Animus* told him.'

Jared felt an irrational spike of dread, stealing in to eradicate the good-natured, jovial feelings he'd been imbued with just a second ago. Animus. It wasn't even a word Braden should know. Certainly wasn't any kind of character name he'd picked up from cartoons or the like. Braden didn't watch cartoons.

'Animus,' he repeated. It wasn't a question, more of a reiteration of what she'd said. The word sounded even darker and more sinister than it had revolving around inside his head.

'Yes. Animus told him something bad is coming for all of us.

Everybody. He said he listens to Animus because he doesn't want to make him mad.'

'Oh, Jesus Christ.' Now it wasn't just trickles of illogical fear making themselves unpleasantly known to Jared, but there was coldness too, a glacial chill that was all around him.

For a moment Lydia had been nearby, covertly watching, probably eavesdropping as much as possible on his conversation, and in the short time he'd been on the phone, her face had run the gamut of expressions. Smugness was replaced by consternation and confusion, and now as he looked at her he saw that she too was reacting to the odd temperature.

Seeing that made Jared realise it wasn't just the strange and disturbing things Isabella was saying causing the cold chills to creep all over his body; the freeze was inside The Night Owl.

Isabella continued speaking, but it washed over Jared in a haze of indistinct words. He was staring at the wall behind the jukebox. Where a malformed shadow was spreading. A monstrous thing, it stretched up the wall in a grotesquely misshapen form that couldn't possibly be created by anybody, or anything, that was nearby.

Jared stared at it incredulously, bathed in a dark wash of fear he didn't understand. Isabella's words seemed to be coming from a very long way away. Black Sabbath sounded like they were right inside his skull, pounding the malevolent beast that was N.I.B against his brain.

'Is...is Braden there?' He finally managed. Still apparently a great distance away he heard a hushed address pass between Isabella and Braden, then his son spoke.

'Dad?'

'Braden, where did you hear about Animus from? What is Animus?'

'I told you something bad was coming.' Braden's voice was flat, dull, devoid of emotion. 'Animus wants the whole town to burn.'

As these words, delivered with no inflection whatsoever, seared into Jared's ears, the monstrous deformed shadow sprawled in hideous formation across the far wall fragmented, breaking away in black barbs, undulating tendrils, and wicked curves. Only they weren't mere pieces of shadow, splintering away across the wall, they were spreading out from there, infiltrating the whole room.

Rowdy, still monopolising the jukebox, nodding his head in time with Black Sabbath, tipped his latest bourbon up. A drink which should have been a warm amber colour, considering Rowdy drank his liquor neat. Instead, it looked ridiculously dark, black even. As if he'd suddenly decided to mix it with cola, or completely altered his tastes and ordered himself a fucking Guinness.

Maybe the jagged swirls of black Jared was gazing at with disbelieving eyes, peeling off the wall, and throwing black loops of vapour throughout the room were obscuring his vision. Fucking with it. He wondered if he'd had somebody slip something in his own drink, and couldn't recall when he'd last had one, water or otherwise.

Then Rowdy, normally one to slouch, stood bolt upright, gaining a few inches on his usual deceptive height. The empty glass flew from his hand as he hurled it, smashing it against the shadow-strewn wall in a shower of glass shards.

Big hairy hands, normally reserved for punching buttons on the jukebox and being habitually wrapped around a bourbon, flashed out with unexpected pace and closed around the nearest bystander, one half of the couple he'd been trying to chase away earlier.

Rowdy swung the man with such ferocity that the fellow was lifted clear off his feet, and was driven, in battering ram fashion, headfirst into the jukebox. The savage blow shattered glass, and did even more damage to the man being pummelled into the music player's unforgiving bulk.

The Night Owl's jukebox was neither a true vintage item with vinyl records, nor was it a modern entity that relied on MP3s. Instead, it was somewhere in the middle, still using the compact disc format. And as the brutalised man, his cranium cracked open and spilling blood in grisly streams, slumped in a limp pile of human wreckage on the floor, Rowdy turned his attention to delving into the jukebox for these compact discs.

Apparently completely disregarding the massive damage he was inflicting upon his own hands, Rowdy punched, hammered, and thrust with his hands inside the machine, tearing away glass and other materials to claw out discs. As others, approached, intent on pulling him away from the bizarre scene of his own creation, he dropped to his knees over the fallen man, and started trying to slice and cut with the items as if they were sawblades.

The lack of serrated edges didn't impede him much at all; the force he was applying and the speed with which he carried out his macabre ministrations yielded gruesome results. Several of the CDs actually sliced blade-like through skin and flesh. Several of them snapped and fragmented under the pressure, though that result was just as injurious to both Rowdy and his hapless victim.

'Jesus Christ! What the fuck?' Jared almost forgot he was on the phone with his boy, belatedly recalling now, as the violence exploded. 'Listen, Braden, hang on, there's some serious…'

'It's too late.' Braden's flat, emotionless voice intoned in a monotone. 'Animus is here.'

A dial tone sounded in Jared's ear. The connection was lost, Braden had terminated the call.

Even though Jared acknowledged this, it didn't stop him from shouting Braden's name a couple of times, followed by Isabella's, as if that was incentive for them to suddenly reconnect the call and answer him. Then bedlam erupted throughout the whole of the Night Owl.

The biker collective over by the pool tables pounded their drinks-beers infused with a swirling black haze-and stood, almost as one synchronised unit. One minute they'd been stationary, calmly draped over their assortment of chairs and reclining against walls, watching the college kids playing pool, albeit with a modicum of salaciousness, the next they were mobile. And bristling with weaponry.

Formerly concealed knives were now out in open carries, chains and batons were clenched in white-knuckle grips.

Jared didn't doubt some of these men possessed firearms, but a horrible burgeoning feeling inside told him none of them wanted to use anything as impersonal as a gun to do damage. They wanted to create maximum carnage and bloody brutality with implements that cut and carved, or bludgeoned and battered.

Any lecherous designs they had on the few women playing pool were obliterated by new cravings. Hideous hankerings to rend, maim, mutilate, and destroy.

It wasn't a one-sided affair however. The crew of pool players were downing just as much alcohol as the biker crew. Their drinks, also tinged with eddying black churns, seemed to instigate them to take up makeshift weapons too. Anything nearby that could, and would, be used as an instrument of dealing out bloody chaos, was grabbed, and wielded as the two groups collided in an orgy of bloodshed and supercharged violence.

'What the fuck? What the fuck?' Tim, originally prepared to jump the bar to rush in and aid in the Rowdy drama, now hesitated as everywhere within the Night Owl, patrons surrendered themselves to the malevolent depravity. 'What the fuck's going on?'

Despite not having a clue how to broach the subject, Jared knew with cold, hard clarity what the fuck was going on. He didn't know how, or why, or anything more than the hideous churn in the pit of his stomach, but he knew what this was. Animus.

Sheer hatred, animosity, enmity, all being demonstrated in gruesome displays of violence and destruction.

Something bad is coming. It's coming for everybody.

It's too late. Animus is here. Animus wants the whole town to burn.

'What do we do?' Lydia wailed.

That was a no-brainer for Tim. As a petite woman in business dress, one of the corporate set come in to unwind with drinks after work, launched an attack on those around her with her stiletto heels, he jabbed a thumb towards the exit.

'We call the cops, and we get the fuck outta here, that's what we do. We're not equipped in any way to deal with this!'

'Just leave the bar?' Lydia asked incredulously, as if it wasn't in her job description to abandon her post no matter how dire things were. However, right now, things were pretty fucking dire.

Alarmed by the hideous soundtrack now coursing throughout the whole of the Night Owl, one comprised of high-pitched screaming, unintelligible shouting, breaking glass and breaking bones, noises of flesh being abused in most horribly imaginative ways, and an array of other ugly cacophonies, Allan and Jasmine emerged from the kitchen. Expressions of confusion on their faces soon gave way to utter terror as they clapped eyes on the pandemonium unfolding in just about every corner of the bar.

The general reaction to such unanticipated carnage seemed to be a maddening litany of repeating *what the fuck* over and over, for both kitchen staffers did precisely this, gaping like landed fish.

Allan, on stunned autopilot snatched up a bottle of scotch.

Jared hadn't a clue whether he meant to take a slug of it as some coping mechanism or whether he intended for it to act as a weapon, but a strange and terrible realisation about the behaviour of the bar patrons hit him just now. He was pretty damn certain he knew the source of the hideous violence. Knew what medium Animus was using to unleash the desire to do harm.

Before Allan could get the bottle uncapped, Jared was lunging towards him, knocking it from his hands, dashing it against the bar.

'Don't drink! It's alcohol! That's how Animus is getting to people! What's the quickest way to reach people in Augury Falls, the common element in this goddamn town? It's fucking alcohol!'

Jared knew he wasn't making sense to any of them. He didn't care. All he knew for certain now was that getting out of there immediately, if not sooner, was what they had to do. Without drinking any liquor. Animus was that freakish, monstrous shadow on the wall. Animus was those elongated slivers of black swirling in malevolent twists around the bar. Animus was the darkening colours infiltrating drinks and infecting people's psyches and brains. Animus was violence personified. Animus was here.

Bemused eyes lanced into him. Expressions that danced between concerned and petrified skittered over the faces of them all, as they shot back and forth between him and the chaos populating The Night Owl.

Jared didn't care about sticking around here. Losing his job was the last thing on his mind. At this rate, there wasn't going to be a bar to come back to anyway. He cared that his co-workers would be smart enough and motivated enough to acknowledge they had to haul ass as soon as possible too, but ultimately, the care factor there was dwarfed by his only real desperately pressing concern. Getting out and getting to Braden.

The fleeting cogitation of the bar being reduced to rubble by these lunatics driven insane by the insidious influence of some entity he didn't understand, sparked a momentary flash of genius in the maelstrom of his thoughts.

Burn the Night Owl down.

Jared wasn't even aware he'd actually said it out loud, until the choruses of disbelief and shock started ringing in his ears. By then however, there was another concern.

One of the old-timers at the bar, one who'd probably been just about to find himself ejected from the premises was slumped forward, head reclining alongside his unfinished drink. Passed out or taking some alcohol induced-nap, he'd have been a heartbeat away from being woken and moved on, when the chaos unfolded.

Now, he sat up straight and suddenly, his palsied hand stretching for his schooner glass of oddly dark beer.

Since all the attention of his fellow bar-staff was temporarily on him, only Jared was facing that way. He lunged forward in a despairing dive to knock the glass free, but even three sheets to the winds and with his hand shaking like a leaf in a tornado, the old fellow got the glass to his lips. The liquid, infected, Jared knew with chilling certainty, by the violence-inducing contagion of Animus, sloshed into the old-timer's mouth.

And for a guy who'd looked like he'd fall ass over teakettle if he so much as tried to take a single step a mere second ago, the abruptly rejuvenated old-timer moved ridiculously fast. He smashed the empty glass against the edge of the bar, ignoring the shards and slivers that flew off and imbedded themselves in various parts of his own body. With the largest piece of the broken glass held aloft like some asinine dagger, he swiped over the bar, slashing with great scything arcs in the air.

For a brief moment, Jared was looking him in the eyes, and what he saw there terrified him. It was akin to gazing into a black infinite abyss, nothing but sheer darkness and malice existed there. Instead of looking into the rheumy, bloodshot eyes of an old drunk guy intoxicated beyond comprehension, he was staring into pure, unadulterated hatred. There was nothing of humanity left in there. There was only…Animus.

Then Allan had himself another bottle, a one litre Southern Comfort. There was no attempted drinking of this one; it was for an entirely different purpose.

He swung it like he was aiming for a home run, bashing it against the side of the old-timer's head. The blow knocked the cranium skew-wiff, and the Animus-plagued drinker turned would-be assailant took a graceless, sideways tumble from his barstool.

Jared wasn't about to wait around to see if he rose. Or to see if any other patrons, imbued with insidious black tendrils and vaporous trails of sheer animosity, were about to descend on those remaining behind the bar. The longer he stayed, the more chance some random drunk-of which there were plenty just wandering the streets of Augury Falls any given night-was being possessed by Animus spite and breaking into the home where Braden and

Isabella were.

'There's nothing here worth your lives,' was his parting shot to the rest of them. 'There's no point holding down the fort for a job you won't have. The demand for dead bartenders and kitchen staff is not great.'

Then he was vaulting over the bar, slipping and sliding in the tacky mire of myriad spilled drinks on the floor. He hadn't thought beyond getting to Braden, hadn't contemplated anything untoward occurring in between now and then. Even that masterstroke of an idea, blurted out unwittingly, to set the bar on fire, went back into the jumbled recesses of his mind.

Setting the bar alight, paying particular attention to the vast stocks of alcohol would cut off an enormous source of power for Animus, it would definitely lessen how wide the insidious influence could spread. If, as Jared suspected, it truly was that Augury Falls common factor of liquor enabling Animus to bleed hatred into the towns folk's minds, then limiting alcohol availability was a perfect counter.

Sadly, that would amount to jackshit for all those folk in here who'd already imbibed and been affected. Nor would it help the many dead and mutilated, stricken down by ultraviolence.

Nonetheless, all of that now was secondary to ensuring Braden was safe. Everything was secondary to that, and that included the welfare of his co-workers. If they chose to stay here in this drowning ship of deadly patrons intent only on doing massive harm to anybody and anything, out of some misguided sense of loyalty to the Night Owl's owner, or fear they'd lose their jobs if they abandoned ship, that was their choice. Being dead was a pretty fair indicator there wouldn't be many jobs available anyway, and the way things were going, there wouldn't be much of a bar left either, whether torched by the staff or smashed to smithereens by the hellbent customers.

He ran. He'd not given abundant thought to arming himself before doing so, but that thought struck him as another old-timer down the end of the bar, threw himself out in his path. Eyes as hate-ridden and soulless as the previous, hands gnarled knots wrapped around a barstool, this fellow came with the same blinding turn of pace. Jared, already at full pace, didn't slow, didn't dodge, didn't do anything to alter his trajectory.

He slammed into the malevolence-riddled drunk, and the impetus cleared the path remarkably well. Pain flared in Jared's shoulder, but he kept moving. He was pretty sure he'd collected part of the stool along with the spindly form of the would-be attacker, but he wasn't about to turn around and see. Partly because he just wanted his attention focused on where he was going, partly because he didn't want to see if hordes of the infected patrons were on his tail, or whether they'd started to converge on the remaining bar-staff.

He was a little surprised he even made it outside without more conflict than one old geezer trying to heft a stool at his face, but since the majority of patrons suffered their hideous afflictions well aware from the bar, he supposed it wasn't that astonishing.

Outside was going to be a whole different kettle of fish though. The Night Owl wasn't the only liquor serving establishment in town, nor did everybody in town who drank-and that was about eighty per cent of the population, including a large number of underagers-choose to do so at some licensed premise. Any night featured hordes of legal teenagers gathering to drink, as well as assorted adults. Underage kids elected to engage more covertly, in secret locations, away from prying eyes.

The town's homeless population spent every coin they managed to scrounge up on alcohol.

Plenty of people chose to drink at home.

Goddamn Augury Falls was fuelled on alcohol. The perfect location for Animus. And, Jared realised, he was one of those who'd been an enabler for Animus. Making it that much easier for whatever the fuck Animus was, to be able to spread black tendrils of terror everywhere with minimal effort.

Jared veered towards his car, and then swiftly changed his mind.

A trio of blood-drenched teenagers were jumping up and down all over his vehicle. Two girls and one boy, all of them so covered in blood they looked like they'd been spray-painted red from head to toe.

Jared assumed they were dressed, but he couldn't really tell. He knew by the distinctive hairstyle that the boy was Rich Ferrell, one of the misfit kids around town, which meant the duo of females were the same pair who usually hung around with him and another fellow, whose name eluded Jared at the present moment. Given that boy's absence, Jared could only fathom a guess what became of him. He could sure as hell tell what became of the three leather-clad older boys who'd been loitering around the hardware store earlier on in the evening.

They were dismembered hunks of meat sprawled over the sidewalk. Coagulating pools of blood spread out around them, trailing in thick rivulets down into the gutter, or tracing a path through cracks in the concrete.

One of the girls, bouncing with gleeful malevolent abandon atop the bonnet of Jared's car, was clutching a severed head by a long bloody ponytail, whirling it around her head, showering herself and her equally gory partners in blood rain.

Rich held a handsaw aloft, blood streaking its blade and streaming over his hand. Like those Jared had already suffered the misfortune of meeting the gaze of, there was nothing left of him inside, no humanity. There was nothing but Animus.

As they all caught sight of Jared, they bounded down off the vehicle, giving vent to an array of horrendous sound that turned his blood to ice water. Taking the car was out; he nixed that idea in a hurry.

Their feet pounded the pavement behind him as he ran; he could hear their monstrous gibbering gaining momentum as they followed, chasing like bestial bloodhounds.

Jared acknowledged painfully just how out of shape he'd let himself get of late. As a general rule he liked to keep himself fit and in top condition, but working so much to save for him and Braden meant he was so goddamn tired all the time. No time or inclination to workout, or even go for a jog around the block.

He was paying for it now, his breath punching out in ragged gasps, every muscle screaming a tortured protest.

Those bloodthirsty kids, powered by the unnatural desire to rip and maim, to tear flesh and slaughter, would run him down in no time. And if he still managed to somehow keep himself just ahead of them, he wouldn't escape. He'd be leading them right to Braden and Isabella.

As he made the split second decision to lead them elsewhere, and hopefully manage to shake them off his tail, something slammed into his spine, dropping him in a sprawling faceplant. He measured his length on the uneven plane of cracked pavement, and the hurled projectile that was the bloodied severed head rolled away in the gutter, spooling matted red locks of hair around it in a grisly nest.

Then the insane frenzied trio were almost upon him. A gunshot cracked. Another. Then another. Several more.

With each consecutive report, the oncoming threesome jerked, stopped dead and dropped. One after the other the bloodied kids were struck, their own blood puffing out in erratic spurts as bullets punched into them.

Jared, so breathless he was sure he was about to expire anyway, gory lunatic kids or otherwise, could do little more than raise his head to see his unexpected benefactor.

Chief of Police, Baxter Crane, stood, with sidearm still extended in a tight two-fisted grip, as if he was expecting the trio of gore-saturated kids to rise again like the undead. They didn't; they stayed still and they stayed dead, bloody sprawls of limbs mere feet from Jared.

'Jesus Christ, Holloway, what in tarnation is going on?'

'Animus,' Jared managed weakly. He hauled himself up to a seated position, then onto his haunches.

'What the fuck's that?' Crane looked perplexed. 'Some new drug? The whole damn town has gone stark raving mad. Two of my boys just shot a goddamn vagrant all messed up like those kids there, covered in blood like some goddamn Halloween costume, eating people's faces off and all kinds of crazy shit. And it's happening everywhere! I sure as shit didn't catch wind of no new-fangled batch of drugs hitting town, but goddamn…I've seen some crazy shit in my time, but never anything of this calibre.'

'It's not…drugs.' Jared was still struggling to suck air back into his lungs. 'It's…'

'Animus,' spoke another voice, and as Jared swivelled to look, he could see two more figures moving along the street back behind Crane. Not running, not charging in a blind, fearful panic. Sedately walking.

Isabella and Braden.

Crane jerked around like he'd been jabbed with a cattle prod, gun still aimed. Clearly he was expecting more apparently drug-addled crazies lurching in to gnaw faces off or sever heads with handsaws.

'Braden!' Jared made to move, relief and joy head-butting each other to take control of his emotions.

'Wait,' Braden said calmly, holding a hand up, stilling Jared's progress.

Confused, Jared froze in place. The boy walked hand in hand with Isabella, neither one of them seeming at all as concerned by much of anything, in direct opposition to that earlier phone call. Well, technically, Braden hadn't displayed any emotion then either, but now he just seemed wholly calm and unfazed. Certainly not panicked and raving about the terrible happenings coming for all of them.

Maybe, Jared thought disjointedly, because, just as the boy stated earlier, it was too late. The bad had already come. Animus was already here.

'Braden,' he tried again. 'What is Animus? *Who* is Animus? I'm pretty sure I've figured out how he-or whatever-inflicts his will on people and makes them do what they're doing...'

'Animus is in everybody,' Isabella spoke first, cutting him short. 'That capacity to hate, to do great harm, to inflict terrible violence and carnage upon one another, even just the darkest desire to do so, that's Animus. And it's in all of us. And the reason it has manifested now, the reason it is sucking this whole town down into the mire of hell where it deserves to be, is because that's the way *we* want it. The way it has to be.'

'This town killed my mother,' Braden spoke now, and rather than cracked, high-pitched or shaking, his voice was steady and resolute. It sounded like him, but the words coming from his mouth didn't. 'Well, technically she killed herself, but it was through being in this town. See, her death was an accident, after all, not what you tried to make it out to be, Dad. She died because she was drunk at work, playing with knives, taking stupid risks. She was drunk, just like everybody else in town, and so she died. So now, this town...this whole town...deserves to die too. Nobody cared enough to stop her drinking at work, nobody cared enough that she would drink at work. Nobody cared. Nobody cares now. And you, Dad, you go off night after night and just give all the idiots in town more reason to get drunk and do stupid things. And more people die. So now, everybody dies.'

'That's right.' Isabella nodded. 'That little knife incident was the catalyst for Animus. See, while Animus exists in all of us, most importantly, Braden *is* Animus. And he wants this whole town to burn. To disappear. To not exist in any capacity anymore.'

Jared stood, frozen in place. His mouth gaped soundlessly, as if all power of speech had just been whisked right away from him, leaving him an open-mouthed, slack-jawed mute. He felt like he'd been smacked with a cannonball. That feeling didn't alleviate any when he saw what was unfurling around Braden.

The grotesque, malformed shadow he'd first seen on the wall of the Night Owl spread like monstrous devil wings from the small figure of the boy, elongating and swelling into a stygian miasma all around him.

'Jesus H. Christ in a charnel house.' Baxter Crane blinked a handful of times in rapid succession, as if he were sure his eyes were playing some fucked up tricks on him. 'I need me a goddamn drink.'

Keeping one hand on his pistol, Crane reached into a pocket and withdrew a hip flask, uncapping it with his teeth.

'Good god, man! Fuck! No!' For what certainly wasn't the first time that night, Jared dove in a frantic lunge to prevent the police chief from drinking. His flailing fingers clipped the flask, knocked it flying. A spray of harsh alcohol burst forth.

Splashing into Jared's face. Stinging his eyes and splattering droplets against his skin. And raining tiny bites of fire down on his tongue, and down his throat.

For a brief second he cared.

Then he cared about nothing.

Except the burning, savage desire to see the town of Augury Falls and everybody in it burn and fall beneath the violence of those driven by pure Animus.

THE DEEP-SEA CONCH
Written by **Brian Lumley**

11 Tunstall Court,
West H. Pool,
Co. Durham
June 16th 1962

Maj. Harry Winslow,
The Oaks, Innsway,
Redcar, Yorks.

My dear Harry,

What an interesting tale that letter of yours tells. Hypnotic gastropods, by crikey! But there was no need for the apologies, honestly. Why! We all fancied you were ill or something, which you were as it happened, and so we didn't for an instant consider your actions as being 'inexcusable.' If only I'd known you were so, well, *susceptible* to shellfish; I would never have had oysters on the card! And for goodness sake, do put Alice's mind at rest and tell here that there's nothing to forgive. Give her my love, poor darling!

But that story of yours is really something. I showed your letter to a conchologist friend of mine from Harden. This fellow – John Beale's his name – spends all his summers down south, 'conching,' as he calls it, in the coves of Devon and Dorset; or at least he *used* to. Why! He was as keen a chap as your Corporal Jobling (poor fellow) seems to have been.

But it appears I must have a stronger stomach than you, Old Chap. Yes, indeed! I've just been down to The Lobster Pot on the seafront for a bite and a bottle, and I couldn't resist a fat crab straight out of the sea at Old Hartlepool. Yes, and that after both your story *and* this tale of Beale's. Truth is, I can't make up my mind which of the two stories is the more repulsive – but I might add that neither of them appears to have affected my appetite!

Still, I've just got to tell you this other story – just as Beale told it to me – so, taking a chance on further offending your sensibilities, here we go:

Now you'll probably remember how a few years ago a British oceanographical expedition charted the continental shelf all the way up from the Bay of Biscay along the North Atlantic Drift to the Shetland Isles. I say you'll probably remember, because of course the boat went down off the Faroes right at the end of its voyage, and it was in all the newspapers at the time. Luckily, lifeboats got the crew of *The Sunderland* off before she sank.

Well anyway, one of the crew was a friend of this Beale chap and he knew he was keen on shells and so on. He brought back with him a most peculiar specimen as a present for Beale. It was a deep-sea conch, dredged up from two thousand seven hundred fathoms beneath the Atlantic two hundred miles west of Brest.

Now this thing was quite a find, and Beale's friend would have found himself in plenty of hot water had the professors aboard ship found out how he'd taken it from the dredge. As it was he kept it hidden under his bunk until the boat went down, and even then he managed to smuggle it into a lifeboat with him. And so he brought it home. Of course, after a month out of the water – even had it survived the emergence from such a depth – the creature in the conch would be long dead.

You'd think so, wouldn't you, Harry?' .. As soon as Beale got hold of the conch he stuck it in a bowl of weak acid solution to clean up its surface and get rid of the remains of the animal inside. It was quite large, ten or eleven inches across and four inches deep, tightly coiled, and with a great bell of a mouth. Beale reckoned that once he'd got the odd oceanic incrustations off the thing it ought to be rather exotically patterned. Most deep-ocean dwellers are exotic, in their way, you know?

The next morning, Beale went to take the conch out of the acid – and as he did so he noticed that a great, thick, shiny-green operculum was showing deep down in the bell-shaped mouth. The acid hadn't even touched the incrustations on the shell, but it had obviously loosened up the dead snail (is that what you call them?) inside the tight coil. Which was where the fun started.

Beale took a knife and tried to force the blade down between the green lid and the interior of the hard shell, so that he could hook out the body of the snail, d'you see? But as soon as the knife touched the operculum – *damn it if the thing didn't withdraw*! Yes, it was still alive, that creature – even after being brought up from that tremendous depth, even after a month out of water and a night in that bowl of acid solution – still alive! Fantastic, eh, Harry?

Now, Beale knew he had a real curiosity here, and that he should take it at once to some zoologist or other. But how could he without dropping his friend right in it? Why! The deep-sea conch looked like being the best thing to come out of the whole abortive expedition....

Well, Beale thought about it, and a week later he finally decided to get a second opinion. He asked his oceangoing friend (a Hartlepool man, by the way, name of Chadwick) up to Harden where he brought him up to date before asking his advice. By then he'd bought an aquarium for the conch and was feeding it on bits of raw meat. Very unpleasant. He never saw it actually *take* the meat, you understand, but each morning the tank would be empty except for the great shell and its occupant.

Beale's chief hope in asking Chadwick for his advice was that the fellow'd tell him to hand the conch in. He hoped, you see, that Chadwick would be willing to face the music in the 'interests of science.' Not so. This Chadwick was simply an ordinary little Jack tar, and he feared the comeback of owning up to his bit of thievery. Why couldn't Beale (he wanted to know) simply keep the thing and stop worrying about it? Well, Beale explained that his hobby was conchology, not zoology, and that he didn't fancy having this aquarium-thing smelling up his flat forever, and so on. At which Chadwick argued why couldn't he just kill of that snail and keep the shell? And Beale had no answer to that.

He's not a bad chap, this Beale, you see, and he knew very well what he really ought to do – that is, he should hand the conch over and let Chadwick take his medicine – but damn it all, the fellow was his friend! In the end he agreed to kill the snail and keep the shell. That way he could get rid of the smelly aquarium (for the conch did have quite a bit of pong about it) and live in peace and quiet ever after.

But Chadwick had seen Beale's initial indecision over the conch's destiny, and he decided he'd better stick around and see to it that his pal really did kill the snail off – and that's where things started to get a bit complicated. That night, by the time Chadwick was ready to get off back to Hartlepool, they still hadn't managed to put the damn thing out of its misery. And believe me, Harry, they'd really tried!

First off Beale had taken the conch from the aquarium to place it in a powerful acid bath. Two hours later the deposits on the shell had vanished, allowing a disappointing pattern to show through. Also, the surface of the acid had scummed over somewhat – but the hard, shiny-green operculum was still there, tight as the doors on the vaults at the Bank of England! Now remember, our friends knew that the snail could get along fine for a least a month without food or water, and it looked as though the lid and the hard shell were capable of withstanding the strongest acid that Beale could get hold of without any great difficulty. So what next?

Even after his friend had gone off home Beale was still puzzling over the problem. It seemed an altogether damned weird thing this, and he was feeling sort of uneasy about it. It reminded him of something, this shell, something he'd seen before somewhere…at the local museum, for instance!

The next morning, as soon as his sailor friend turned up, they went off together down to the museum. In the 'Prehistoric Britain' section Beale found what he was looking for – a whole shelf of fossil shells of all sorts, shapes, and sizes. Of course, the fossils were all under glass so that our pair couldn't handle them, but they didn't really need to. 'There you go,' said Beale, excitedly pointing out one of the specimens, 'that's it – not so big, perhaps, but the same shape and with the same type of markings!' And Chadwick had to agree that the fossil looked very much similar to their conch.

Well, they read off the label describing the fossil, and here, (as best I can remember from what Beale told me, though I'm not absolutely sure about the thing's name,) is what it said:

Upper Cretaceous:
(—— ? —— SCAPHITES, a tightly coiled shell from Barrow-on-
Soar in Leicestershire.
Flourished in Cretaceous oceans 120 million years ago. Similar
specimens, with more
prominent ribs and nodes, occur frequently in the Leicestershire
Lias. Extinct
for over 60 million years...

... Which didn't tell them very much, you'll agree, Harry. But Beale jumped a bit at that 'extinct' notice – he had reckoned it might be so – and once again he asked Chadwick to turn the thing in. Why! It was starting to look as good as the coelacanth!

'No hope!' Chadwick answered, perfunctorily. 'Let's get round to your place and finish the thing off. For the last time, I'm not carrying the can for doing you a favor!' And so they went back to Beale's flat.

There waiting for them in the kitchen, was the conch – still in its bath of acid, and apparently completely unharmed. Well, they carefully drained off the acid and sprayed the conch down with water to facilitate its immediate handling. Chadwick had brought with him from Hartlepool a great knife with a hooked blade. He tried his best to get the point right down inside the bell of the shell, but always there was that incredibly hard operculum, all shiny green and tight as a cork in a bottle.

This was when Chadwick, having completely lost patience with it all, suggested smashing the conch. Suggested it? Why! He had the thing out on the concrete landing before Beale could get his thoughts in order. But the conchologist needn't have worried; I mean, how does one go about smashing something that's survived the pressure at two thousand seven hundred fathoms, eh?' Chadwick had actually flung the conch full swing against the concrete floor of the landing by the time Beale caught up with him, and the latter was just able to catch it on the bounce. It wasn't even dented! Peering into the bell-shaped mouth, Beale was just able to make out one edge of the green operculum pulling back out of sight around the curve of the coil.

Then Chadwick had his brain wave. One thing the conch had *not* been subjected to down there on the bed of the ocean was heat – it's a monstrous cold world at the bottom of the sea! And it just so happened that Beale had already made inquiries at a local hardware store about borrowing a blowtorch to lift the paint from a wardrobe he wanted to do up. Chadwick went off to borrow the blowtorch and left Beale sitting deep in thought, contemplating the conch.

Now, I've already mentioned how Beale had had this strange, uneasy feeling about the shell and its occupant. Yes; well by now the feeling had grown out of all proportion. There seemed to the sensitive collector to be a sort of, well, an *aura* about the thing, that feeling of untold ages one has when gazing upon ancient ruins – except that with the conch the sensation was far more powerful.

And then again, how had the conch come by its amazing powers of self-preservation? Was it possible? ... No, what Beale was thinking was plainly impossible – such survivals were out of the question – and yet the mad thought kept spinning around in Beale's brain that perhaps, perhaps…

How *long* had this creature, encased in the coils of its own construction (Beale's words), prowled the pressured deeps in ponderous stealth? 'Extinct for 60 million years…' Suddenly he dearly wished he had some means at his disposal of checking the conch's exact age. It was a crazy thought, he knew, but there was this insistent idea in the back of his head–

In his mind's eye he saw the world as it had been so long ago – great beasts trampling primitive plants in steaming swamps, and strange birds that were *not* birds flying in heavy, predawn skies. And then he looked beneath those prehistoric oceans – oceans more like vast *acid baths* than seas such as we know them today – at the multitude of forms that swam, spurted, and crawled in those deadly deeps.

Then Beale allowed (as he put it) an 'unwinding of time' in his mind, picturing the geologic changes, seeing continents emerge hissing from volcanic seas, and coralline islands slowly sinking into the hoary soups of their own genesis. He watches the gradual alteration in climates and environments, and the effects such changes had on their denizens. He saw the remote forbears of the conch altering internally to build a resistance to tremendous pressures of even deeper seas, and, as their numbers dwindled, developing fantastic life spans to ensure the continuation of the species.

Beale told me all this, you understand, Harry? And God only knows where his thoughts might have led him if Chadwick hadn't come back pretty soon with the blowtorch. But even after the sailor got the blowtorch going – while he played its terrible tip of invisible heat on the coils of the conch – Beale's fancy was still at work.

Once, as a boy, he had pulled a tiny hermit crab from its borrowed shell on the beach at Seaton-Carew, to watch it scurry in frantic terror in search of a new home over the sand at the bottom of a small pool. In the end, out of an intensely agonizing empathy for the completely vulnerable crab, he had dropped the empty whelk shell back into the water in the soft-bodied creature's way, so that it was able to leap with breathtaking rapidity and almost visible relief back into the safety of the shell's calcium coil. It's death for this type of creature to be forced from its protective shell, you see, Harry? That's what Beale was telling me, and once out such a creature has only two alternatives – get back in or find a new home...and quick, before the predators come on the scene! Small wonder the snail in the conch was giving them such a hard time!

And that was when Beale heard Chadwick's hiss of indrawn breath and his shouted, 'It's coming out!'

Beale had been turned away from what he rightly considered a criminal scene, but at Chadwick's cry he turned back – in time to see the sailor drop the blowtorch and fling himself almost convulsively away from the metal sink unit where he'd been working. Chadwick said nothing more, you understand, following that initial cry. He simply hurled himself away from the steaming conch.

Quick as thought, the flame from the fallen blowtorch caught at the kitchen tablecloth, and Beale's first impulse was to save his flat. Chadwick had burned himself, that was plain, but his burn couldn't be all that serious. So thinking, Beale leapt over to the sink to fill a jug with water. The torch was still flaring but it lay on the ceramic-tiled floor where it could to little harm. As he filled his jug Beale noticed how the overspill moved the conch, as though the shell were somehow lighter, but he had no time to ponder that.

Turning, he almost dropped the jug as he saw Chadwick's figure stretched full length half-in, half-out of the kitchen. Dodging the leaping flames and futilely flinging the jug's contents over them, he crossed to where his friend lay, turning him onto his back to see what was wrong. There were no signs of any burns, but, quickly checking, Beale was horrified at his inability to detect a pulse.

Shock! Chadwick must be suffering from shock! Beale pushed

his fingers into the sailor's mouth to loosen up his tongue, and then, seeing a slight movement of the man's throat, he threw himself face down beside him to get into the 'Kiss of Life' position.

He never administered that kiss, but leapt shrieking to flee from the burning flat, down the stairs and out of the building. He told me that apart from that mad dash he can remember nothing more of the nightmare – nothing, that is, other than the *cause* of his panic flight. Of course, there's no proving Beale's story one way or the other, the whole block of flats was burned right out and it was a miracle that Chadwick was the only casualty. I don't suppose I'd ever have got the story out of Beale if I hadn't met up with him one night and showed him that letter of yours. He was almighty drunk at the time, and I'm sure he's never told anyone else.

Fact or fiction? .. Damned if I know, but it's true that Beale doesn't go 'conching' any more, and just suppose it *did* happen the way he told it?

What a shock to a delicate nervous system, eh, Harry?

You can probably guess what happened, but just put yourself in Beale's place. Imagine the heart-stopping horror when, having seen Chadwick's throat move, *he looked into the sailor's mouth and saw that shiny-green operculum pull down quickly out of sight into the fellow's throat!*

And that's whole story, Harry. That's the story…

HELL'S LABYRINTH
(…the endless corridors of Horror)
An Afterword **by Chris Hall (DLS Reviews)**

My name is Legion, for we are many – Mark 5:9

Matt Shaw is a machine. The sheer volume of work and creative projects this man churns out goes beyond mind-boggling. In fact, I'm pretty sure in the rampant lunacy that is 'Shaw World', each day consists of considerably more than twenty-four hours. And here we have another example of the man's unrelenting productivity. An anthology bringing together some of the very finest names in contemporary horror fiction. Yeah, yeah, I know that's a line that's so often spouted out when a new anthology hits the proverbial shelves. More often than not the reality is you'll recognise two or three names at best; a handful of notable authors rubbing shoulders amongst a line-up of relative unknowns, desperate at the chance to get their names in an anthology with the aforementioned Top Dogs.

However, that's not the case here. When I say Shaw's brought together the absolute crème de la crème of writers in modern horror for his anthology, I wholeheartedly mean it. These truly are veritable Masters of Horror. Heavyweights in horror fiction, each standing as tall as the next in line. In here you had some true veterans of the genre, alongside some (perhaps equally) highly-revered new names in the field, pitched together with some true champions from the various niches in horror.

Shaw himself isn't exactly an unknown in our chosen field of fiction. Most notably within the extreme horror circuit - which is undoubtedly his forte (but certainly not his 'be all and end all') - Shaw is up there with the big hitters. For sheer volume of output alone this man is a force to be reckoned with. In fact, if you search for 'extreme horror novels' on the likes of Amazon or Goodreads, for the first ten or so pages of results, every page you'll be presented with will include at the very least one or two of his titles.

But the great thing about the horror genre is its inherent versatility. Horror is a huge umbrella for the vast array of fiction underneath its reach. It incorporates such a variety of settings and styles: from historical, to science-fiction, from supernatural to extreme, from wickedly dark comedy to gut-wrenching violence. In fact, this very collection illustrates the sheer diversity in horror fiction phenomenally well. Let's take a look at what we had...

Lumley kick-started the anthology off with a strangely eerie story involving a hypnotic sea-snail, told (via letter correspondence) with an incredibly creepy, almost Lovecraftian prose. Yes, it was a quiet horror – one that spent time building upon the time-set backdrop and characterisation - but because of the delicate whispering tone used, the horror was able to slither its way under your skin like a silent assassin. And from there, gradually its coldness infiltrated your senses, chilling your blood from the inside.

Then we had Ramsey Campbell's nightmarishly strange offering involving a withering old woman with a serious S&M fetish. How many of us had sleepless nights after reading that delightful tale? I know I did. Let's be honest, there's a damn good reason why Ramsey Campbell is regarded as Britain's most respected living horror writer – and that's because he's fucking awesome. Stories like this just go to prove the matter. Campbell knows how to mess with people's heads - and he's not once held back from doing so.

It's a tough gig to follow, but Sam West went next with her tale about a psychologically-disturbed writer with a chronic split-personality disorder. The story explored the furthest reaches of garnering inspiration for a short story, whilst delving into a difficult-to-swallow abyss of fucked-up-ness through the first-person-perspective of this deluded maniac. Witnessing all those brutal actions was clearly designed to make you feel uncomfortable in your own skin. As if you were in some way associated with the violence; partly responsible even. However after reading the tale, what might for some feel somewhat challenging (although it undoubtedly shouldn't) is that the author is a female. The writer's sex should obviously have absolutely no bearing on whether or not a tale is considered a success or not (indeed, only recently did West choose to reveal her true sex). However, we're possibly not quite there yet with complete equality between sexes (and race), even if it's just a subconscious judgement. Nevertheless, after reading an extreme horror novel where we see a young woman getting brutally assaulted, one which is written from behind the eyes of an incredibly disturbed male, knowing it's written by a female does still make you pause for thought. Whether that's right or wrong or completely irrelevant I have no idea. But it's what it is. And perhaps if anything it only goes to further show the talent of the author.

After this we had J.R. Park's strange, David Lynch-esque, creeping cosmic horror. The story threw us all over the shop with a disorientating domino-effect style perspective and snowballing narrative. Park's a writer who clearly loves to play around with the formula behind his tales; mixing things up with prose and roving perspectives. Once again that's exactly what we saw here. It's disorientating and intriguing, and through the use of such an ingenious structure, pulls you in with an addictive and effortless ease.

After this we saw Peter McKeirnon jump in next with his grim gut-punch of a story that started off like textbook torture porn, but gradually took on a very 'The Texas Chainsaw Massacre' style vibe. I'm sure you'll agree when I say the story's grim and bleak and more fucked-up than playing testicle-golf with a pick axe. But then wasn't it just so god damn entertaining for its fucked-up nature? Didn't you just lap up the bloody juices? Bathe in the malignant delight of it all? That's horror for you.

Following that we had Andrew Freudenberg's front seat view of one man's descent into madness, set during the stress and perils of a world war. Here we saw so much dirt and grime and soul-destroying vileness within a bastard-bleak exploration of slipping sanity that it felt almost suffocating. And of course we had our first (but not last) slice of cannibalism in the anthology.

Twisting horror into a completely different direction, Mason Sabre followed on with his kleptomaniac creep-fest; showing us the power of a well-executed twist-ending that was undoubtedly designed to scare the living shit out of us. It's one of those stories where we're once again sucked into the strange suspense which the author carefully nurtures to fruition. You know there's horror coming. You'll have possibly even guessed where the horror will manifest from. But were you expecting such an unleashing of eye-gouging grimness? Probably not. And by Lucifer's beard didn't it work well?

Then of course undisputed veteran to the genre, Shaun Hutson, came charging in next with a tale which sent us back to the glorious era of his blood-splattered rough and raw gritty thrillers. For the most part the tale delivered a dark thriller which gradually unravelled its mystery with each turn of the page. But as you saw, the final slice of the story was one drenched from head to toe in proper old school horror. Its twist and reveal ending was undoubtedly designed to leave you grinning with horror-adoring delight. Mission well and truly accomplished.

Of course, horror isn't all demons, deviancy, devilry and blood-drenched destruction. It can also be about dicks. Well, that's not exactly painting the whole picture here. Perversity and deranged lunacy can also play a big role within horror – as illustrated with magnificent effect within Anton Palmer's diabolically off-the-frigging-scales offering. A man turning into a giant phallus – come on, what's not to love? Bizarro meets horror in monolithic cum-dripping proportions. This story my friends, as I'm pretty sure you'll agree, was sheer unadulterated genius.

From a man transforming into a giant penis, to a fat guy desperately trying to get in shape before he's out fighting for survival in the savage post-apocalyptic streets of Las Vegas; you've got to hand it to Matt Shaw, this anthology really has it all. And with Wrath James White's offering, it seemed to pack in more fast-paced high-adrenaline shit than you know what to do with. For those who aren't already aware, outside of being a writer of pretty extreme and downright disturbing fiction, White is also a former World Class Heavyweight Kickboxer, distance runner, and a professional Kickboxing and Mixed Martial Arts trainer. Here we saw White playing to his strengths; shovelling in in-depth know-how of how to get your body bulked up and ready for action, whilst almost lazily slipping in that it's actually to survive a full-blown motherfucking zombie apocalypse! When the cats out of the proverbial bag, the urgency for the whole 'Beast Mode' workout hits you like a tonne of lead-coated bricks. And damn does it get you pumped-up and ready to face all those undead horrors outside. But it's the love interest that really surprises you in the end. The way it so naturally slips out from the side-lines and into the forefront of the story. Man I didn't see that ending coming either. What a ballbuster. How on earth did White get us to care so much so quickly? What an ending. What a frigging story!

Another way horror can manifest itself is behind the cotton white blanket of innocence. It's something Shane McKenzie knows damn well. And the bastard utilised this to its full effect here, with his story about six-year-old Dewey Davenport. Yeah, I'm pretty sure you all knew what really happened in that broken family home. But keeping that hidden wasn't the point of the story. Instead it's about how this horror is distorted and mutated through the eyes of an innocent. The wafer thin fabric of lies that barely hides the twisted truth. It's harsh, and grim and utterly gut-wrenching. This is horror that pulls at your heartstrings. And it's dark.

You'll find that sex, in some manner or other, will more often than not make its grubby way into most horror stories. After all, sleaze forms a wonderfully complementary side dish to the main meal of horror. Tonia Brown's black-as-coal undead comedy began with a splash of just this, giving us a touch of erotic asphyxiation that (as you'll no doubt recall) went a tad pear-shaped when our hapless protagonist accidentally snuffed out his girlfriend. But of course it didn't end there. With tongue-firmly-wedged-in-her-cheek, Brown forged the most unlikely of friendships, with the reanimation of Dan's dead girlfriend as the fucked-up catalyst behind it all. How much of that did you see wriggling its way out of the lunacy? The voodoo style ritual? The conflict between upbringings? The eventual companionship? I'd guess almost none of it.

Now then, if the jump between that story and Graeme Reynolds' ludicrously atmospheric wake-up-in-a-pit-full-of-corpses offering doesn't show you the sheer versatility in the horror genre, then I don't know what will. Here we had what can only be described as a homage to everything that is fucking awesome about horror, all of which is shovelled into one tightly packed pit of gruesomeness. Then you, dear reader, were shoved right into the dark heart of it all. After that, with our bearings all thrown to shit, didn't the gradual drip-feeding of our protagonist's sporadically returning memory just pull you in further? I don't know about you, but I was all but clawing at the pages to find out what the hell was going on. Furthermore, when Reynolds finally revealed his cards, the B-movie pulp-fanatic in me couldn't help but punch the darkening sky at the sheer fucking triumph of the story. Pack it in Graeme. Pack that horror in.

From here the absolute tour de force of blackened horror that is Adam Nevill took the anthology into strange and fantastically eerie new places. Adam Nevill is a master of nihilistic darkness. The atmosphere he manages to create through his words, the hopeless void that bears down upon the reader – personally I know of few authors who can achieve anything close. In his contribution we saw a clear reflection of this. It was a story that pulled us into a pit of all-encompassing despair. Okay, so there wasn't any immediate threat bearing down upon us. Everything had, in effect, already taken place. We witnessed the horror from a relatively safe place. Although that didn't dilute it down one iota. The horror was still just as present, as if the violent events that had taken place were still brutalising our senses. This shows the strength of this man's writing. The power of the imagery he can create. The atmosphere. The blood-chilling, unrelenting horror of it all.

From one horror heavyweight to the next. Following on from Nevill's quietly sinister offering we had Gary McMahon, stepping forward with a tale that further proves horror really can be born from so many vastly different places. Here we saw it rising from the darkest reaches of emotional scarring. As we've seen countless times before, McMahon is a man who knows how to reap horror from the fertile ground of the human psyche. A deeply troubled and emotionally crippled life can paint such a harrowing picture. When the mind is beaten down and irreparably broken, some of the most evocative horror can be born – and ultimately… hopefully… exorcised. With this story we saw just that (plus a greased-up midget without any arms or legs). I don't know about you, but I seriously contemplated permanently gluing shut our cat flap after reading that little delight!

And then we're dumped into the woods. What is it about woods that's so creepy? Is it because they're inherently wild? An area untouched by mankind's perpetual tampering? Or is it perhaps that the environment affords our imagination to run riot? To manifest movements and shadowy figures out of the trees around you? Whatever it is, horror authors have been utilising its effect on us for years. For his contribution, author Ryan Harding took this age old phobia, this ingrained fear, and brought alive a (similarly) ancient horror within it – the Wendigo (or Woodsman as he's more commonly referred to here). It's a story that capitalises on our childhood fears and brings back to life the nightmares. And it made it all real. If only for a little while, didn't that horror feel oh so shit-stainingly real?

Anthology compiler, extreme horror author and all-round grinning lunatic – Matt Shaw – charged in next with his disturbing letter from a serial killer. Undoubtedly based upon real life serial killer Albert Fish's letter to poor Grace Budd's grieving mother, Shaw's offering cuts like a cold-steel scalpel across trembling skin, more so because of the true to life horror lurking behind it. Like me, you might well have seen where Shaw was going with the letter. The twist, as they say, was well and truly in the wind. But did that lessen the impact as Shaw drove his foot into your gut at the letter's cripplingly cold end? Did potentially knowing that a needle-sharp blade was en route to your internal organs make you feel any less hollowed out when the twisted truth finally revealed itself? I doubt it. Because that's Shaw all over. When he goes in for the kill, the fucker's absolutely merciless.

Okay, so let's be honest, having our protagonist wake up in a darkened room, disorientated and having no fucking clue of how they got there is an opener that's kind of been done to death in horror. In fact it seems the whole 'waking up restrained and about to be tortured to absolute fuck' set-up has become somewhat of a recurring premise over recent years. However, that's never really been all that much of a drawback. After all, many horror stories use similar themes and ideas for the premise of their tales. However, it's where the author takes their story from that blurry-eyed waking moment that ultimately consolidates the tale's success (or not). Matt Hickman, as you saw, decided to take his story to complete-fucked-up-ville via a lengthy process of torture and agonising suffering. However, there was much more to it than that. We saw the tale evolve. Become far more than mere torture porn. More than a nightmare sequence that you just can't seem to wake from. It was a story split into two distinct halves. We saw a bigger idea at play. Something pulling it all together, enticing you to clamber around the abattoir floor searching for the linking body pieces. It has an idea. A message. And fuck me sideways if it doesn't come at you with a sledgehammer to deliver that blood-splattered telegram.

The backdrop as well as the period in time a story is set undoubtedly plays an integral part to a horror story. As such, when a tale adopts a less frequently utilised backdrop or place in history, then it will often breathe with a noticeably richer air of originality. Daniel Marc Chant's story took advantage of this. How many of us were instantly sucked into the dusty African setting as soon as the short tale began? But more than that, there was that distinct African vibe which the story continuously expelled, pulling us along in its strangely alluring draw. It was rich with atmosphere and a near-overwhelmingly oppressive gloom, whereupon the escalating and dominating horror was ultimately born. As you read Chant's offering, did you feel increasingly crushed by the seemingly irrepressible gloom of the piece? Did you struggle to break any sort of smile for a long time afterwards? Did it maybe even disrupt your mood for the rest of the day, evening or night? That my friends is the power of good horror writing. It can beat you down into the dust and dirt, just as easily as lift you up into the heavens above.

From the depths of Africa we were then flung into a completely different environment altogether - a British supermarket. Under the stark white lights of the checkout area, author Amy Cross slammed down a quick-fire tale told with a short, snappy, straight-to-the-point prose. The majority of the tale consists of colourful snippets from a young checkout girl's obsessive observations of a handsome hipster who happens to frequent the supermarket she works at. Almost diary-like in its delivery, the mystery and suspense that Cross managed to build up is, quite frankly, incredible. Did you predict where she was going to take the tale?

Did Cross' sneaky bluff fool you? Whether her ploy worked or not, one thing's for sure, I bet you were gripped like a horror junkie to the pages, desperate to find out what had happened to handsome John and his oh-so-slutty lover.

Right then guys and ghouls, what did you make of Kit Power's offering? Hard-hitting as a guerrilla's wanger wasn't it?! But, and be honest now, didn't the paedos getting their just deserts just feel so damn good? Comeuppance served on a platter of blood and guts. Yeah, it's simple but damn, damn effective. But the question Power poses to us now is: how much merciless vengeance do you, from behind closed doors, really find justifiable? In real life we're made to put a more sensible head on our shoulders. But in fiction we've got no such moral obligations to facilitate. We can hurdle our society's laws and social responsibilities. Due justice via a carefully regulated legal system can go fucking hang. Instead, in fiction, we can vent our anger at society's monsters in a much more immediate and easier to swallow manner. And so, ladies and gentlemen, in comes Kit Power. Let the bodies hit the floor.

Adam Millard is a veritable master of the wacky, weird and downright disgusting. He's a champion of Bizarro and an undeniable horror honcho to the perverse. His tales are nearly always laced from head to toe in a thick drool-like coating of tongue-in-cheek black comedy. But it's the weird and wacky imagination at the root of his stories where the real gold is found. Take the oddball offering in this collection as a prime example. Here we have a family who suffer from a hereditary condition whereby they will, at some point in their lives, melt away to nothing but a big old puddle of goo. It's all so weird and worryingly amusing. As you drank the madness in, I bet you sat there with a grin plastered across your ugly mug! It's just so entertaining, it's pretty much impossible not to. That's because we, my friends, can't help but love all that wonderfully disgusting oddball weirdness.

Okay, so Guy N Smith is not only a veteran of the horror genre, but he's also the undisputed godfather of pulp horror. Over four decades in the business and the Shropshire-based pipe-smoker can still spin a creepy, chilling, coldly-calculated yarn like the very best of 'em. Here we had ourselves another short, sharp, stab at spectral horror; drenched in gruesome history atop another signature rural backdrop. But it's invariably Smith's writing style, his infectious narrative and wondering storyline, that pulls you in so effortlessly. Yeah there was horror at the root of the tale. A grisly, tortured past reaching out through a long dead corpse. There was a definite chill factor to it all. But if you're anything like me, the real compelling strength to the story lay in the writing. It's the sort of stuff that's just such a pleasure to sit down and read. But then again, that's what Smith does. And he's an absolute master at it.

Knowing that the anthology you're submitting a story to is being compiled by Matt Shaw will invariably nudge you towards penning something quite hard-hitting. Even if you're not necessarily associated with extreme horror, having Shaw as the initial recipient is (more than likely) going to coax an extra lathering of extremity out of you. Jaime Johnesee did just that. And it was one hell of a gut-wrenching read. Did you feel sick after reading it? Was your sticky sweat-caked skin crying out for a shower immediately afterwards? Yeah it was short. A flash of white hot pain in a blood-stained pan. Like being cast into a vat of acid. The sheer brutality ripping your skin off, exposing your blistering nerve endings until everything's burnt off in a white heat of pain and suffering, leaving you as a cold, numb shell. I'm sure you'll agree, Johnesee's story was some fucking intense shit. Stunning, breathtaking and vile. That's extreme horror right there.

And then boys and girls the circus came to town. Well, sort of. In a miserable-as-a-sack-full-of-dead-kittens sort of fashion. That's the sort of dank, dark gloom that Craig Saunders paints his downtrodden masterworks with. It's a portrait of inner hurt. A lifetime of turmoil shoved into an anthology with mud-caked clown gloves on. Past meets present meets some disorientating middle ground where the reader gets to live and relive the worst, most painful parts of the whole messed-up ordeal. How was your mood after bathing in Sam Dunwich's stagnant filth? Did you feel wretched? Dismal? Contaminated by spoilt air? This is lived-in gloom. This is raw human sadness. You can leave your smile at the pub door.

After that we had Michael Bray's nightmarish short story. And when I say nightmarish, I'm sure you'll agree, that's pretty much exactly how this little treat read. The horror was far less visible than it had been in the preceding stories. But it was nevertheless equally as present. Bray played with our inner phobias like a demented puppet master. His story was akin to a nightmare sequence, where our terrors were allowed to mount and mount. The bastard toys with us. As you read his offering, did you feel trapped, lost, and increasingly nervous? The story takes a very different pathway, but the end result leads to the same playing field. Horror. Fear. It's a tale that really makes you squirm. And I bet that's exactly what you did.

Horror can come in many guises. What at first can look fairly mundane - a weakass attempt at trying to terrify its audience - can transform into something far more sinister by a carefully calculated tweak to its delivery. That's precisely what Jeff Strand did with his tongue-in-cheek carnival horror. Set in a cheesy-as-they-come haunted house, the story's strength lay in the witty delivery – told through the perspective of Harvey – a typical spotty teenager on a date and desperately trying to save face after vomiting on the rollercoaster. I'm sure you'll agree, the horror in the story takes a bit of a backseat. However, it's with all the amusing little details that Strand injects into the story's delivery - the inner-monologue style narrative and the dumbass jokes that the youngster keeps spouting out - which ultimately wins you over. And that ending. What an ending.

Now what better way to show the versatility in horror than to go

Hell's Labyrinth (Afterword) – Chris Hall

from that to Mark Cassell's chaotic sack full of thriller, crime and horror. More mad shit was flung around in that story than faeces at a G.G. Allin show. How much of that off-the-wall madness did you see coming? I'm guessing, like me, pretty much zip squat. There really was a bit of everything in there. Gangster crime, weird-ass science-fiction, horror, and that ever-present bitch that is human suffering.

One thing that short story anthologies allow authors to do is experiment. So often you'll see a writer trying out some strange new ideas and playing around with weird new perspectives. And that's pretty much what we saw with Paul Flewitt's 'possessed television-set' offering. It's a classic 'influence' style horror, whereby our corrupting antagonist works its way from 'new friend' to 'new friend' making them kill with no remorse. But the story's originality and captivating strength undeniably comes from the demonic presence's wickedly sinister internal monologue. That Manson-esque voice silently speaking out from those television sets gave the story a whole new edge. It gave it another layer. Putting it a step closer to the reader. To you. And in doing so, broke down some of the comfort zone between us and the nightmarish fiction we love to read. A silent invader indeed.

Then Clare Riley Whitfield had us waking up to blackness once again. Yeah, it was time for more abduction and torment at the hands of a seemingly deranged abductor. But, as you can probably recall, Whitfield had a different goal in sight. A twist or two up her sleeves to get you furiously ripping at the pages. You can never trust a horror writer's motives. You can never know for certain where the horror is coming from and where the suffering is ultimately going to take you. It's something we saw in abundance here. The pain, the hurt, the torment, it was all ultimately for something more. Something worthwhile. Or was it? One thing's for sure, it got you thinking.

After that we had Jim Goforth's monstrous tale of near-apocalyptic proportions. It was one of those stories that pulls you

467

in with a whole bundle of viciously-barbed hooks. Characters were introduced and subsequently disposed of without a second's thought. Yeah, the story is a proper 80's style action-rich energetic horror that takes you on a rollercoaster of a ride until the streets are literally caked in blood. Utterly entertaining. Utterly enjoyable. Utterly horrific.

Closing the anthology off we had Lumley's second slice of Lovecraftian-esque horror. A replying letter speaking of another deep-sea horror. Again, it was a noticeably quieter horror than many of the other offerings in the anthology, but it's one that nevertheless works its way right into the pit of your stomach as the final horror is unveiled. It's a brave man who throws back an ice-chilled oyster after reading that final offering.

And that my friends, was 'Masters Of Horror', from its deep-sea horror start, to its Eerie-Atlantic end (with more than a few fucked-up terrifying treats in between). How did you fair along the way? Did you feel like you were constantly being flung one way and then the other? At times shell-shocked by the extremity on show, at others curling your toes at the slowly slithering horror being unveiled? Now you're at the end, now that you're able to cast your eye back over the numerous dark ventures and nightmarish treats that awaited you, do you maybe see a larger web of horror than the sum of the book's pages would otherwise suggest? Perhaps a more complex tapestry that makes up the vast darkness that is the world of horror? If you do then Shaw has done well. His mission was to create the ultimate contemporary horror anthology. And through that, hopefully deliver a vision of the broadness and versatility in horror.

It's a genre that will keep stretching its claws outwards. Horror knows no bounds. It's hungry to explore new ground, to corrupt and mercilessly swallow other genres whole, no matter how well established they may be. Horror is truly a living breathing beast. Because it's in every one of us. It's our internal darkness. It's in our fears and our deepest, darkest desires. Horror knows us better than we know ourselves. And to feed the beast, is truly to feed one's own soul…

Chris Hall

www.dlsreview.com

Made in the USA
Monee, IL
03 April 2024